WILD WOODS

OTHER TITLES BY NATHAN EVERETT

City Limits

GEE EVARS WANDERED into Rosebud Falls on Independence Day just in time to rescue a toddler from the rushing torrent of the Rose River. And to lose his memory. In an attempt to make Rosebud Falls his home, Gee becomes a local hero and inadvertently leads a revolt that changes the balance of power in the town. But will he ever know who he really is?

The Gutenberg Rubric

TWO RARE-BOOK LIBRARIANS race across three continents to find and preserve a legendary book printed by Johannes Gutenberg. Behind them, a trail of bombed libraries draws Homeland Security to launch a worldwide search for biblio-terrorists. Keith and Maddie find love along the way, but will they survive to enjoy it?

For Money or Mayhem

COMPUTER FORENSICS DETECTIVE Dag Hamar is pulled from behind the safety of his computer and takes to the streets when he discovers a link between an online predator and real-life kidnappings around Seattle. His fledgling romance is threatened when his girlfriend's daughter is suddenly among the missing.

For Blood or Money

COMPUTER FORENSICS DETECTIVES Dag Hamar and Deb Riley discover secret files and hidden code can be as dangerous as dark alleys and flying bullets as they track a missing man and the billion-dollar fortune that went with him. Fourteen years after For Money or Mayhem.

Municipal Blondes

DEB RILEY CONTINUES the chase after Dag's untimely demise. She has a code to break, a mystery to solve, and an assassin to avoid. Disguise and deception are her only weapons.

The Volunteer

JOURNEY INSIDE THE head of a chronically homeless man. In a less politically correct time, he might have been called a hobo. But what keeps him wandering, hitching rides, and eating handouts? Piece together the story through his memories to find what made him volunteer.

Designed by Nathan Everett
Cover art licensed from Colourbox ID21746536
Printed in the United States of America

WILD WOODS

NATHAN EVERETT

ELDER ROAD BOOKS
BELLEVUE WA

A special thank you to my editors and advisers who stuck with me through this entire project. Your help was immeasurable.
Lyndsy Fernandes
Michele Palmer
Michelle Duncan
Margie Cantlon

CONTENTS

1

VOLUNTEERS

Identity Crisis

"IT COULD BE number one or four. The others are definitely out," Karen said. She sipped at the coffee in her hand. It wasn't Birdie's and tasted foul but she needed *something* to do with her hands. Her heart had been in her throat ever since they opened the curtain to show her the lineup of five men.

"O-kay," Detective Mead Oliver groaned. He pulled the curtain closed and dismissed the lineup. "Uh… Why do you say that?"

"It's confusing! It all happened so fast. I approached Rena, I was grabbed from behind, and before I could scream, he slapped that stinking cloth around my face and I passed out," she nearly shouted. "How am I supposed to identify the bastard? Those three are too short. That's all I know."

"He was tall?"

"Either that or he was on platforms taller than mine."

"You were wearing heels?"

"Wedges. An inch and a half. I liked those shoes. Did anyone ever find them?"

"I'm afraid we've found none of your clothes," Sheriff Brad Johnson said. "We've had some complications with the search. How do you know he was tall?"

"I don't… He grabbed me in a choke hold."

"How tall are you, Karen?" Mead asked.

"Five-ten."

"Plus a couple of inches in heels," he said. "I think I see. Brad, how tall are you?"

"Six-three."

"Give me a hand and get behind me." The sheriff stood behind the police detective. In a community their size, the two often worked together and since, at the time of the crime, the Wild Woods and quarry were technically outside the city limits, this required their cooperation to the fullest. The results of yesterday's election would put the area inside the limits. "Grab me around the neck. Karen, tell him if he's got it about right. I don't want to traumatize you by reliving everything, but this will help us in the search."

"I understand, Mead. That looks right."

"Okay, switch places with me, Brad." The sheriff moved to the front and Mead moved behind, placing his arm over Brad's shoulder.

"I think I'm too big for you to get that hold on me," Brad said.

"Exactly. I understand Karen's description now. The assailant had to be significantly taller than her in order to get that kind of upward pull. Otherwise she would have been pulled down."

"So, we're looking for someone over six-two," Brad nodded in agreement.

"Wow!" Karen said. "I didn't realize. Now that I've seen it, I can almost feel his face up next to mine and smell his breath before the cloth covered my face. I thought it was the stuff on the cloth. Strong peppermint smell."

"Sounds more like Tic Tac than chloroform."

"Any other impressions?"

"The arm under my chin was… smooth. It wasn't a rough fabric."

"Good."

"And I'd say older. I didn't realize that until I was listening to you two talk. Sheriff, your voice sounds younger than Mead's. The guy who grabbed me sounded older. And he was deadly calm like it didn't mean a thing that he was forcing me to eat poison nuts as he recited the names of the Families. I have impressions of a face, but it isn't even human. I was already hallucinating by then. I could hear the trees talking and prayed Gee would come to save me."

"You're doing fine, Karen," Brad said. "We're getting a lot more to go on now. I'm afraid the description the kids gave wasn't much help either. Oh. Gloves?"

"Yes. At first. Smooth. Leather. Like driving gloves. When he shoved the first nut in my mouth, I tried to bite him. He slapped me. After the first nut, I knew I was dead, so I just kept eating them."

"Thank you, Karen. Let's give it a rest. I know this is hard on you. If you think of anything else, please call. Anything at all. We want your attacker in jail."

"Thank you, Mead. You're a sweetheart. Sheriff, I promise not to walk into that kind of situation again without backup."

"Take care, Karen," Brad responded. "Give our best to Gee."

"Now what?" Mead asked as Karen disappeared down the hall.

"Now we let our number one suspect go free," Brad sighed. "Rev. Lance Beck is only five-five. He couldn't have gotten her in that hold without pulling her down."

"Sheriff?" Deputy Carlisle poked his head in the room where Mead and Brad were meeting.

"What is it, Jeff?"

"Not good, sir. We just got back from the church. It's clean. The dogs found no scent of drugs. If cleanliness is next to godliness, those people have one foot in heaven already. The place was spotless."

"That's great. Just great. Now we're worse off than we were before. Is there any chance they were tipped off?"

"It all looked normal. There was a work crew of church members who said it was their annual maintenance week. They were almost finished repainting the sanctuary and it looked like a couple of days work completed. They weren't happy about the dogs."

"Nothing like fresh paint to hide a scent. Damn it! Write up the report. I want impressions from everyone who was on the search team. I'm going to have to take it to Judge Warren and explain that our whole investigation is in the toilet." Brad waved his deputy out of the room and sank heavily into his chair.

"We need to search the Wild Woods," Mead said.

"For what? We already know there are nuts out there. The dogs would never pick up a drug scent. And the underbrush is so dense we were using machetes to get through to find Karen."

"Which means that whoever did this knows the woods a lot better than we do," Mead insisted. "Might even still be out there. Think about it. Two kids witness the attack and we get a 911 call. You're on the scene within fifteen minutes. From that point, there are firetrucks, ambulances, and police onsite for the next hour. That's when we get another 911 call from Gee. We start searching the woods. It's eight hours later that we finally find the cabin with Karen in it. During that time, we've got people closing in on the location from two directions. Foresters, EMTs, deputies, with firetrucks playing searchlights along the edge of the woods. This bastard has had time to drug and rape her, clean up all the evidence, including her clothes, and walk out without being detected."

"Right past us. Could have even been a forester helping with the search," Brad nodded.

"I don't think we need a warrant," Mead concluded. "Savage agreed to removing the fence. All we need is his permission to search the woods."

———— ⋖◆⋗ ————

AFTER LEAVING THE police station, Karen dragged herself into the office of *The Elmont Mirror*. She was immediately immersed in the excitement of getting the next day's paper ready. Election results had been reported and the paper put to bed last night long before two hundred kids and parents gathered to tear down the fence separating the Forest from the Wild Woods. Kelly Murray had been with Karen and managed some extremely good night photos. Lanterns and flashlights painted an eerie glow over the activities. Karen had hours of recorded interviews with parents and permissions to use their kids' names in her story. But the story still had to be written.

"What's the story on Preacher Beck's arrest?" Axel Hunter, the editor, demanded.

"What arrest?" Karen asked. She hadn't followed the police scanner while she was out at the fence.

"Beck was caught in Rena Lynd's hospital room last night and arrested. I thought that's where you were this morning."

"I don't know anything about an arrest. I was out at the fence all last night. You know I can't do any reporting on that story. I'm too closely involved."

"Any comments from the victim?" Axel sneered. Karen scowled at him.

"Yeah. This is a time of recovery for the victim and her family. We ask that you respect her need for privacy as she continues to heal from the trauma. No further comment is available at this time," she said while staring him in the eye.

Axel stormed away in his usual foul mood to call the police department. Karen set to work going through Kelly's photos and putting them together with her story.

Unwarranted Search

GEE DRAGGED HIMSELF into Jitterz for lunch after half a day at the Market. He got little sleep after the fence destruction the night before and hoped Karen would join him for lunch before he went home for a nap. His phone buzzed just before he reached the counter. "Don't wait. I'm tied up with the story. Deadline. Chaos," Karen's text read. Gee sighed.

"Coffee, Gee?" Elaine asked. Everywhere Gee looked, people appeared tired. Elaine and her cousins had been at the fence last night, too.

"I had a cup earlier. Just tea. And I guess an egg salad sandwich."

"Have a seat. I'll get it out to you," she said after he paid. An empty table by the window was inviting and he sank into the chair. Election results were the main topic of conversation around him. A hundred or maybe two hundred teens and parents had taken part in removing the fence between the Forest and the Wild Woods last night but it had been long after the paper was put to bed. Troy mentioned the fence in his morning broadcast but even he had focused on the election results and annexation of South Rosebud.

"Catalyst. That's the word I've been looking for," Birdie said as she set Gee's tea and sandwich in front of him. She dropped into the seat opposite him with her own cup of tea.

"What?"

"There were a lot of volatile elements floating in the primordial sea of Rosebud Falls six months ago but nothing was coming to life. Then you arrived. The atoms began to align on both sides of the fence. Now there is no fence. You are a catalyst."

"I didn't do anything."

"You didn't need to. You only needed to be present. Now, though, you'll have to take a more active role."

"I'm just…"

"No-no, Gee. You can't hide behind being a simple man with no memory. You're a leader. You're the Champion of Rosebud Falls. No one cares who or what you were before, any more than you care. But now that the elements are aligned, will we have fusion or fission?" Birdie said.

"I didn't know you were a scientist. What should I do? I just try to be a good person. Most of the time I don't know what the right thing is, I just hope it turns out okay. Do you know what Mead Oliver told me? I could be arrested for inciting civil disobedience last night. If they hadn't been so orderly, he'd have run me in for inciting a riot," Gee sighed. He just needed some sleep and he wouldn't feel so overwhelmed.

"You know Mead wouldn't do that—even if it was possible. You're a hero. You control the super-majority of stockholder votes at Savage Sand and Gravel. You're a role model. You're the Pied Piper of the library and the Forest. You're an equal with the Family heads, engaged to the Roth heiress. You cannot pretend to be stumbling along doing what comes naturally—even if that's true," Birdie lectured him.

Worry creased Gee's brow. "I have no idea what I'm supposed to do next, Birdie."

"I don't know nothin' 'bout birthin' babies, Miz Scarlett," Birdie mocked. "I don't think anybody is going to give you time to decide. You've got visitors."

Mead Oliver, for better or worse, always seemed to show up when Gee had done something—good or bad. Beside him, Sheriff Brad Johnson cut an imposing figure in his uniform. And following along in a utility kilt was the new Chairman and CEO of Savage Sand & Gravel, Pàl Savage.

"Can we join you, Gee? I mean, if you've finished your lunch?" Mead asked. Gee set his teacup on his empty plate and Birdie swept it away. The men pulled up chairs to the little table.

"To what do I owe the pleasure of this visit?" Gee asked. "Am I being arrested… again?"

"Never expected what a pain being City Champion would be, did you?" Mead laughed. "SSG has decided not to press charges for the vandalism of their fence."

"And we won't book you for inciting a riot," Brad added. All three men laughed at Gee's discomfiture. "Really, we've come for advice and to ask a favor."

"Of me?" Gee asked. "Sure. Whatever I can do."

"Pàl?" Mead said.

"The sheriff and police have asked for permission to search the Wild Woods," Pàl began. "On the surface it sounds like a good idea. We should know what's out there. I dug up the leases and discovered the Savage Family home was leased to a small group as an alternative to Flor del Día for fostering orphans and teaching. That was right after the war when my grandfather incorporated the company and took me to Scotland. There was no shortage of orphans and it seemed like a good thing. But ultimately, the shelter grew into the Calvary Tabernacle. When Mr. Beck was called as pastor a little over ten years ago, he was permitted use of the home as part of his compensation and the camp for troubled children was moved into the woods."

"We executed a search warrant early this morning on both the church and the house," Brad said. "It revealed no sign that children were in the residence nor had been for many years."

"I'm not fond of Pastor Beck," Gee said carefully. "Was there any other incriminating evidence?"

"No. We've eliminated Beck as a primary suspect in Ms. Weisman's kidnapping and the attempted murder of Rena Lynd," Brad continued. "He might still have been in collusion, but he didn't carry it out. And we've found no trace of drugs in either the church or the house."

"Still, we know the church has been bringing children into the area for deprogramming by Beck," Pàl added. "The two cabins found in the woods during Karen's rescue had been scrubbed clean. Are there more?

Are there children out there? Another processing plant to manufacture drugs? A storage facility? Sheriff Johnson wants to search the woods for evidence of wrongdoing."

"It sounds like a good idea," Gee said. "Why ask me?"

"SSG's rights to the Wild Woods are questionable. Mineral and resource leases can be interpreted in many ways. Anything found in the Wild Woods could incriminate SSG, not just the church. Our liability could bankrupt the company and possibly put present and former executives at risk," Pàl said. "You hold the proxies for over two-thirds of the stockholder votes. If we pursue this, those shares could end up worthless."

"And you want me to vote?"

"As CEO of the company, I would like to find a way to do this that minimizes our legal exposure. It could take a long time to do that and I don't yet know which people in the company I can actually trust. The control was securely in the hands of the church. Right down to the lowest levels of labor."

"In the meantime, there could be children being held or hiding in the Wild Woods," Gee said. "Drugs might still be manufactured there. Kidnappings might still be concealed." All three men facing him nodded as Gee contemplated the options.

Gee finally lifted his head to look them in the eyes. "Every person who gave me a proxy used the same or very similar words—almost as if they had a script," Gee said at last. "Each one asked me to vote my conscience to the benefit of the Forest, the City, the people, and the woods. To me, it was a clear commitment to ethical responsibility rather than profit. Since the sheriff is nicely requesting a search rather than simply presenting a warrant, I assume there might be some political or financial reasons for not just breaking down the doors, so to speak."

"Honestly, Gee, I have no idea what to request in a warrant or how to go about a search," Brad said. "It took us hours to hack our way to those cabins we found and we had GPS coordinates. I don't have the manpower to devote to an extended search for an unknown something."

"How about if we send the foresters in to do an assessment of the resources in the Wild Woods? We know they want access as soon as possible anyway. We could press some urgency to determine the value and dangers of our new annex. Of course, the sheriff and police department would be welcome to observe when they can and we'd want services on alert in case we... encounter an injury or other emergency. Would that resolve our difficulties?"

The three men looked at each other and silently nodded their assent.

"There's just one thing, Gee," Pàl said. "I'll authorize the foresters and volunteers to have access but someone has to convince them of the urgency to move now. That someone is you."

Gee sighed. He'd been hoping for a nap.

Enlistment

"I KNEW THAT action in the Forest last night would come back to bite us in the ass," David said. The head of the Lazorack Family was never one to mince words. "I have one job. It is to ensure the care and harvest of the Forest."

"But Harvest is over," Gee objected.

"The *nut* harvest is over," Jonathan jumped in ahead of his father. "Weather is getting colder each day and there will be snow soon. Before that happens, the foresters need to check every tree, make sure all the deadwood has been cleared, and supervise the gleaners who are still picking up late-falling nuts from the Forest floor. We can spare some people after snow starts in earnest."

"We can't wait," Gee stated.

"I agree," Jessie said. She and Jonathan had been married less than two months and, to many people, the couple represented the future of the Forest. "I understand we need to finish Forest maintenance but there could be children out there. David, I saw your determination when we went into the woods to find Karen. This is just as important. We have to dedicate people to surveying and assessing the Wild Woods."

David ran his fingers through his hair and looked at the map in front of them. The area depicting the Wild Woods was copied from maps that were over a hundred years old. They probably weren't accurate to start with. He looked at his friend and mentor.

"Gabe?" The old forester looked up from the map as if just becoming aware of the conversation. He'd worked alongside the other foresters during Harvest but spent most of his semi-retired time in the office. He glanced at the faces of the younger foresters.

"Yep. Gotta do it, David."

"Just stop our fall maintenance and send everyone into the Wild Woods?"

"No. But we could spare a few foresters. I'll supervise the assessment. We might not get all the way through the Wild Woods right away but we should get a good picture of what is out there," Gabe answered.

Gee breathed a sigh of relief, thankful for the old forester's support. "What about volunteers?" he asked.

"People are pretty burned out after Harvest," Jonathan said. "They've already spent ten days volunteering and ignoring school, work, and their families."

"Still, if you could get volunteers, we could use them," Gabe said. "Especially if they have an interest in becoming foresters."

"Like advance training? An internship? I might be able to get some of those enthused high schoolers out here on weekends," Gee said.

"We need to start tomorrow," Gabe answered. "Not enough time to organize anything formal. We'll just teach you as we go."

"Me?"

"You're our first volunteer."

"Seeking volunteers to help foresters assess the Wild Woods of South Rosebud," Karen read back to Gee. "Sounds like a classified ad. We've got the paper in layout already. Axel will throw a fit. Maybe we can squeeze in a sidebar to the story of the fence coming down. I'll have to do some rewriting."

"I'm sorry to cause problems for you, Karen. Thank you," Gee said to his fiancée. He'd never been inside her office at *The Elmont Mirror* before and felt like he was intruding on her private domain.

"Call Cameron and alert him to what you're doing. When Axel goes ballistic and calls his boss, I want him ready to support the delay in getting the paper to bed. Whom should volunteers contact?" she asked.

Gee finished giving Karen the details and then headed out to start recruiting.

———◁◆▷———

"Hey, Gee," Ryan said when Gee found him trimming lettuce in the vegetable display. The boy's tone and posture showed how exhausted he was. He'd had little more sleep than Gee after leading the youth tearing down the fence last night but still had to go to school and show up for his job.

"I don't think you should be working with a sharp knife today," Gee laughed.

"Done with this," Ryan said, carefully putting the trimming knife in its plastic sleeve. He pulled off his cutting glove. "I think you're right. Wow! That was sure something last night."

"It was. But now we have to live with the consequences."

"You mean like being so tired I can hardly stand up?"

"That's one," Gee said as Ryan pushed the trimming cart to the back of the store. "The other is that we have six hundred acres of new forestland to assess and protect. I'm going to work with the foresters for the next couple of weeks but we could sure use some volunteers to help us. We're spread pretty thin."

"I'd love to but… I mean, there's school. We can't exactly cut classes to go work in the woods."

"I wouldn't expect you to," Gee said. "But there might be time on weekends. If you're serious about learning forestry."

"That would be cool. I bet we could get some after school help once football season is over," Ryan said, warming to the idea.

"I'll be at the game Friday night. Why don't you let kids know I'd like to talk to anyone interested in volunteering?"

Ryan grinned at Gee. "We might need to reserve a section of the stands."

———◁◆▷———

"I don't know what else to say, Nathan. This is important. It was easy for people to ignore the Wild Woods when it wasn't part of the City. But it's our responsibility now and I guess I walked into it." Gee had gone directly from talking to Ryan to meeting with his boss and friend at the Market.

"Do you really think there could be people living out there?" Nathan asked.

"We found two cabins last month. The Wild Woods could hold a dozen of those and we'd never know. It's not just that there could be people…" Gee sighed and shook his head. "I have an uneasy feeling, Nathan. We could find anything."

"We'll miss you in the mornings. I guess we've survived without you before but I hope you get back to us soon. It's hard to get coverage for that shift," Nathan said.

"I'll keep an eye out for another employee. Hmm. Might even have an idea. Let me see what I can come up with."

———————⋯⧫⋯———————

"ARE YOU AS tired as I am?" Karen sighed as she sank onto the sofa next to Gee. It was a struggle for Gee to stay awake until ten when she got home.

"Exhausted," he said. "How'd it go at the office?"

"The expected big row about changing layout of the front page to accommodate your little sidebar but Cameron set Axel straight and the paper went to press. I think you might get flooded with volunteer inquiries at the foresters' office starting about noon tomorrow."

"Do you think that many will come out?"

"It's hard to say. The City loves its Forest. The Wild Woods is a source of mystery. I hope you don't want only men. There are likely to be more women available if you can accommodate school schedules."

"I never thought of that. I don't think there is any prejudice against women. Even I am overqualified for what we need to do," Gee mused.

"Well if *you* can do the job, certainly a woman can!" Karen laughed. Gee blushed.

"I sounded like an ass, didn't I?" he said. She kissed him.

"That doesn't often happen with you, sweetheart. I'm sure it's just the exhaustion."

"Say, how's your friend Timmy doing?"

"He was very concerned when I was in the hospital and brought me a flower. I think he's mostly worried that I won't take him back to the big city again. Why?"

"Nathan needs help stocking shelves and carting things at the market in the mornings. Do you think Timmy could handle it? It's hard to get a high school student for that shift."

"Hmm. It's possible. He's a very dedicated worker once he learns his job. He washes dishes at the Pub & Grub most evenings and does a good job there. If Nathan is patient in training him, he'd be able to do the work, I'm sure." Karen breathed a long sigh. "I'll have to talk to his mother."

"Raven?"

"That's their last name. Her first name is Lynda but with her black hair, everyone has called her by her last name as long as I can remember. I don't think she really likes me but I've been Timmy's friend for so long that she's accepted me. Without her support, Timmy wouldn't establish the routine he'd need to do the job." Karen kissed her fiancé again. "Can we just go to bed now? My head hurts."

"I think that's the best idea we've had today."

Recruitment

"IT'S GETTING CHILLY out here for football," Gee said as he and Karen moved into the stands.

"Only one more game next week and the season ends," Karen said. They took their customary seats next to Wayne in the stands. The teams were warming up on the field and their breath could be seen in the lights. Gee wrapped their blanket snugly around their legs.

"I'm getting a little worried about how cold it will be this winter," Wayne agreed. "Even Granda is thinking about going back to Florida."

"Really?"

"I think it's all talk. I see the look in his eyes when he's standing at his office window and can see the Wild Woods. He'll never leave. He's not too happy with his accommodations at my house, though," Wayne said. "I think he's considering moving up to the retirement home where Dee Warren and Celia Ransom live. Nothing brings life to his eyes like spending time with them, Heinz Nussbaum, and Coretta Sims. I don't think I'll ever really comprehend how close they were growing up."

"Wayne," Karen said suddenly, "do you have any idea where your Family tree is?"

"Uh… Granda has a chart with names on it. I assume it's packed in his things."

"Oh. That's not what I mean. Each Family has a rose hickory that is… I don't know… dedicated? It's the Family's connection to the

Forest," Karen said. "When I… had my ordeal, I promised the Forest I would visit all the Family trees. I know how that sounds, but it's a compulsion. Not that I'm rushing to finish the task but so far, I've visited Roth, Poltanys, and Nussbaum."

"I'll ask Granda if he knows. If I had to guess, I'd say it was on the property where Preacher Beck lives. That's the Savage ancestral home from what I understand."

"I didn't know that. Could be sticky getting in there."

"Not if Granda succeeds in evicting him. What about the other trees? There are seven, aren't there?"

"Cavanaugh, Lazorack, and Meagher."

"Meagher is still in touch with his tree," Gee said. "He ate a nut from it years ago."

"It scares me a little to visit him but I'll get to it soon."

"So, how was your first day in the Wild Woods?" Wayne asked, changing the subject away from Karen's discomfiture.

"Slow. We all want to just march through the woods in all directions but Gabe insists that we have to be systematic. I understand. As thick as the undergrowth in the woods is, we could miss entire sections if we don't take our time to do it right. You wouldn't think six hundred acres was so big. I could see getting lost out there and never finding my way out. I'm just worried there might *be* someone lost in there and we'll never find them," Gee said.

"Can the cabins be seen from the air?"

"Gabe ordered a helicopter flight for this weekend. They're going to photograph the whole region. In general, though, the canopy of the Wild Woods is almost as dense as the understory. And the two cabins we've found were camouflaged on the roof. If there is no heat source even infrared photography won't show anything."

"Gee's trying to get volunteers to help make the work go faster. He's working with ten foresters, but wants to get some high school kids involved."

"You'll do well with them," Wayne agreed.

⸻ ◁◆▷ ⸻

BY THE END of the game, snow flurries danced in the air—a potent reminder that winter was coming and time was short.

"Can we move to Jitterz or someplace warm?" Shannon asked. Ryan's girlfriend was shivering under the bleachers with over a dozen other teens who came to meet with Gee. It was obvious she had worn far too little for the weather.

"I'm good with that," Gee said. "Karen? Do you think they could find room for about fifteen people as a group?"

"I'll call. Is everyone walking or driving?" Karen asked. Ryan and Shannon gratefully climbed into the back of Karen's car for the short trip. Birdie was waiting for them and directed them to a section of the lounge she'd cleared. As soon as everyone had drinks or ice cream, they settled around Gee.

"You all did a great job Tuesday night when it came time to tear down the fence," Gee started. There were a few hand-slaps. "You're leaders. The former CEO of the company threatened retaliation for vandalism, but the current CEO quashed that and announced that he'd given permission. But we've got another problem."

"Is there more fence?" Barrett asked.

"No. It's the Wild Woods itself. It hasn't been tended for nearly a century or maybe more. The undergrowth is so thick we can hardly cut a path. But three weeks ago, we found two cabins out there that no one knew about. I think there are more. Call it a hunch if you like, but evidence says that Calvary Tabernacle used the woods for its child reprogramming camp."

"You mean there could be kids living out there?" Alyson asked. "Like abandoned? They could starve. Or freeze."

"Just my point, Alyson," Gee said. He noted the tall girl's hand rested comfortably in the hand of the varsity center, Viktor Nussbaum.

"It could be that. Or, a worst-case scenario would be someone trafficking children from a secret base. I've been investigating sex trafficking for fifteen years and there always seems to be a connection to this area. Just never a strong enough one to accuse anyone."

"Holy shit!" Barrett exclaimed.

"We also saw evidence that one of the cabins had been used for processing nuts, presumably into the drug Lustre," Gee added. "As Ryan put it Tuesday night, we need to put a stop to people using our nuts to make harmful drugs. We just don't have the people to devote to the task."

"What can we do?" James asked.

"We need volunteers who can help us search the Wild Woods," Gee said. "But before you get excited about running around out there, it is going to be a long tedious job. The blisters some of you got removing the fence are nothing to what it will be like hacking through the brush and mapping the trees. The foresters are adamant that it has to be done in an orderly manner or we'll risk getting lost ourselves and still missing what's out there."

"I'm in, but what about school?" Ryan asked.

"That's a problem. I know you guys have a lot going on in your lives but I'm hoping you could volunteer a day or two of your weekends—at least till the holidays. I'm going up to Flor del Día on Monday to see if I can work something out with the kids up there, too."

"We'll help," a young woman attached to Alyson's brother Barrett said. "Oh. I'm Jeanie Davis. I live at Flor. We often have days when the whole school volunteers in the Forest. Mostly in summer, but I'll bet some of us can get a release for volunteer work during the week."

"Before any of you volunteer, you need to decide if you are serious about the Forest," Gee said. "You know how organized and disciplined Harvest is. This search is going to be just as coordinated. We don't know what's out there. We nearly stumbled into a ravine filled with those nasty blackberry brambles a few weeks ago. We need to know where everything is. There are also hawthorn and firethorn out there. Safety gear will be mandatory."

"It sounds like hard work but I'm in," James said firmly. "What time do we report tomorrow morning?"

"I need to ask my parents," Shannon said. "And arrange time off from the store I work at." Several others needed to consult with parents, friends, and schedules but eight committed to showing up at the foresters' office Saturday morning.

Into the Woods

THIRTY KIDS AND adult volunteers arrived at eight in the morning Saturday. Most had appropriate outdoor wear, gloves, and boots. The six foresters on duty and Gee hadn't expected quite such a large turnout. It took nearly two hours to explain the process. Gee had not received such careful instructions when he started with the foresters.

Eventually, they split up into seven teams and each forester and Gee led a group into the Wild Woods. Gee's team included Alyson, Jeanie, and Shannon. It wasn't surprising since well over half the volunteers were girls and the foresters had intentionally split up couples.

"We're recording the location of every tree greater than twelve inches DBH as we proceed. That means we'll cut paths from tree to tree, not in a straight north/south or east/west direction," Gee explained as he showed the young women the GPS cache system.

"What's DBH?" Alyson asked.

"Diameter at Breast Height," Gee responded, having only recently learned the term himself. Looking at the three teen girls, he blushed. There was a significant difference between the breast height on Alyson and on petite Shannon. "Um… Well, the term has a history in the forestry industry. For our purposes, let's call it four-and-a-half feet." Gee stretched out a tape measure at the height and showed that it hit him in the chest. Each of the girls wanted to measure herself. "The idea is that we get a rough measurement for trees the foresters can use to estimate productivity, lumber footage, and yield. If the tree is growing on a slope, we measure on the high side. That's what the calipers are for. We'll divide up the work and you can choose your tasks. One of you gets the tape measure to mark the DBH, one gets the calipers to measure the diameter, and one spray paints the tree with its cache number. I'll record the findings in the geocache and hack a path to the next tree."

"You mean we're geocaching? I've heard of that." Shannon still had the tape measure extended and four-and-a-half feet was closer to her chin height.

"Essentially, yes. The foresters have used various methods for mapping the Forest over the years. The newest map in the office is based on the GPS coordinates. Geocaching software provides the interface for recording locations and data. We'll map other features besides the trees—like changes in elevation and manmade structures."

"You mean like the cabin you found?" Jeanie asked.

"Exactly. We located the first cabin based on where Karen's phone had been. Unfortunately, she'd been moved from that cabin by the time we got there."

"That bothers me," Jeanie continued. "Isn't this an awfully long process if our purpose is to search for drug labs and lost children?"

"Yeah. It frustrates me," Gee sighed. "I want to just plunge into the woods and look everywhere. Hopefully, we'll get into a rhythm that lets us mark and record a tree in just a few minutes and then move on. This is our first one," he said pointing to the tree they had hacked a path to. "Start measuring and I'll start cutting a path to the next one, over there."

———— ◁◇▷ ————

"You look beat, Love," Karen said when Gee dragged himself through the door. The sun had set long before he arrived home. They'd knocked off a bit after four to head back to the foresters' office. It was disheartening that after a day at work, his team had conquered an area only about the size of a football field. He'd spent time at the office putting Band-Aids on blisters and encouraging the kids as they dragged in from the woods.

"I don't know if the work drains me or if it's being responsible for my team," Gee sighed. "I had no idea teens could be so exhausting."

"Oh? You play basketball with some of those boys," Karen laughed.

"I guess I'm used to boys and what they talk about—mostly sports and cars. My crew was all girls."

"You aren't in trouble, are you?"

"No. Nothing like that. They just talk… about different things," Gee said. Karen started laughing. "They're lovely young women," Gee defended himself. "But I know more about boyfriends, teachers, other boys in school, parents, boys on TV or in rock bands, and teen anxiety over whether they will ever marry, have children, a career, or a home of their own than I'd ever imagined."

"Ten years makes such a difference," Karen sighed. "I remember high school and college and never had a doubt about my career choice. I don't remember feeling pressured in school to make life altering decisions. My family was rich. My great-grandmother wanted me to stay away from Rosebud Falls as long as possible and made sure my college was paid for and I had an allowance that I could survive on, even if I wasn't working. I was the very essence of privileged and didn't even realize it. Now, it's even worse. We don't occupy even a quarter of this house. I'm sure your crew are girls who are provided for but not rich. They don't see any of the possibilities that this privileged brat had."

"Jeanie's an orphan who lives at Flor del Día," Gee said. "Alyson's father owns a furniture company and her mother is a teacher. Shannon's great-grandfather started the Rexall drugstore in town."

"We should adopt them. Maybe we can adopt all of them."

"Really?"

"No. It just makes me sad. Especially the kids up at Flor."

"As much as I feel for them, these aren't the kids we need to help. I still believe there are children out there. Or at least there were."

"We'll find them, Love. And if they need to be adopted, we'll talk about that then. Right now, I want my fiancé to take me to bed and show me how much he loves me, even when he's been exhausted by teen girls. Go up and get showered. I'll have food ready by the time you get back to the kitchen and then we can go to bed."

Flight

"I'm saying you would be better off somewhere else. With that Scotsman giving the foresters access to the woods, nothing is safe."

"I helped clean the cabin. There's nothing there that can point back to me. Where is all my equipment?" Dr. Jones asked. He'd invested years in this town, subverting research at LaRue Labs into his private industry of distilling drugs from the nuts in the woods. Business was good and the side benefits had kept him happy for years.

"We have the equipment crated and ready to ship to you. There's a nice place in Georgia where we have contacts. A respected doctor like you should have no difficulty getting established. No one will think twice about you having a lab."

"If I'm that hot, what's to stop the Feds from tracking me down?"

"You know how closed this town is. They don't want any government interference in the operation of their little Forest. It will be bad enough with the safety investigators coming to town after Harvest this year. Local authorities won't alert the Feds to a missing laboratory scientist. Out of sight, out of mind."

"I hope you're right, Deacon. What about raw materials?"

"We have enough nuts in storage for you to process for the next year. And we'll start raising the price on the product. That will give us all a little cushion for retirement."

"I guess I don't have a choice. I'll go pack."

"Don't take too much. The more it looks like you were just called away, the better."

"My whole career. Just leave it all behind. You're a cruel man, Deacon."

"I'm helping you Dr. Jones. Don't make me regret it."

Dark Secret

"YOUR TEAM WAS as productive as any other," Jessie said when Gee complained about how slow the work had gone. It was seven-thirty Sunday morning and their crews were scheduled to arrive at eight. "Will they all be back today?"

"I think so. There were a few blisters but they were enthusiastic when they left. It was smart to split up known boyfriend/girlfriend pairs. I think we got more work done that way."

"Jonathan and I talked and have decided to increase your crew by one. I don't want to upset a good thing, but I've got a guy who just doesn't fit in with the other crews. I think he'll do better on yours."

"It might be nice to have another male. Is he capable?" Gee asked. "Please, not one of their boyfriends."

"Oh, no! We're going to keep that policy in place until we're at least confident everyone has been trained. The boy's name is Jason Dove. He's sixteen and from Flor del Día. He's… a little small for his age. I think the other guys intimidate him and he responds with a lot of bravado—pretty caustic. He'll get along better with the girls."

"Alyson can be pretty intimidating when she wants to be," Gee chuckled.

As soon as Jason was introduced to Gee's team, it looked like words might fly. Jeanie didn't look happy to see him. They stared at each other defiantly for almost a minute while Gee checked out equipment. Then Jeanie drew a deep breath and turned to the girls.

"Alyson and Shannon, Jason goes to Flor with me. He sometimes gets teased because he's sort of small. You guys won't do anything mean to him, will you?"

"Of course not," Alyson said. "Any friend of yours is welcome, Jeanie."

"We're not friends," Jason snapped. "I don't need to be protected, JD."

"Right, JD," Jeanie snapped back. "And I didn't say friend."

Gee looked at the crew uncertainly as they shouldered their packs and headed toward the Wild Woods.

Even with the rough start, the team gelled almost immediately. Gee showed Jason how to enter data into the GPS. That freed him to hack a path to the next tree instead of waiting for the entire crew to be finished before they moved on. He crosschecked the data on the first few trees Jason recorded and then simply started hacking through the underbrush. He had the fleeting thought that Jessie could have given him a football player to do the hard physical work instead of a computer operator.

"Gee?" There's something over here," JD called. Jason and Jeanie called each other JD but by lunch had settled that Jason would have the initials since Jeanie was already known to the girls. It was after three and the crew was winding down. Gee retraced his steps to find the four kids kneeling a few feet from the other side of the tree.

"What is it?"

"Um… the ground was soft here," Alyson said. "I was going to slip out of sight so I could tinkle and twisted my ankle a little when I stepped here. It looks like…"

"Somebody dug here," Shannon said. "You can see the shovel marks around the soft earth."

"I think something has been buried here," Alyson continued.

"Or someone," Jeanie said as she started to scrape away dirt with her hands.

"Stop!" Gee commanded. The kids looked up at him. "Step over on this side of the tree. We could be contaminating a crime scene. Police will want to investigate to see if they can find tracks nearby and the more we trample things down, the harder it will be for them."

"But there could be…"

"All the more reason to stay away. We have a procedure for this."

The sheriff's office couldn't monitor all the crews charting trees so had established a hotline for the foresters in case of emergency. Gee tapped his phone and reached Sheriff Johnson directly. He took the GPS from JD.

"Sheriff, we've found dirt that has been turned recently and is soft. It looks suspicious enough I thought I'd better call," Gee said. "Yes, sir. We have the GPS coordinates and there is a path cut.— I'd suggest shovels and maybe some light. We're losing daylight out here. We've moved away so we don't contaminate the area more than we already have. I'm afraid some was trampled down before the kids discovered it." Gee read off the coordinates and listened to the sheriff. "That's a good idea. I'll see you there."

"What are we going to do?"

"Head back to the office and call it quits for the day," Gee said. "This quadrant is now quarantined."

"But we should stay here to help."

"Guys, listen," Gee said. "You're doing a great job out here. We covered a lot more area today than yesterday. But there are people who know what to do in this kind of situation and we aren't them."

"What do you think it is?"

"Well, it's always possible that pirates came out and buried treasure. If that's the case, I'll see to it that you all get your share," Gee said, trying to lighten things up. He moved his crew back the way they'd come from the Forest.

"Yeah, right," JD sneered.

"Well, that's the best outcome I can think of," Gee responded. "There are all kinds of other, more sinister options."

"Like a body?"

"That would be bad. But look at some of the other alternatives, too. There are definitely people in the area who don't want us out here. What if they planted a boobytrap, figuring we'd start digging in to see what was there? You could all be injured."

"I never thought about that," Alyson said. "We should be more careful about where we're walking." She looked down at the path they'd cut.

"Good idea. But there are also more benign things it could be. Maybe someone just wants to delay us. We have to stop and investigate something like this every time. It could be nothing more than a pile of dirt turned over. Someone might have been hunting and buried offal. There are many things but we need to investigate all of them.

At the edge of the Forest, Gee sent the kids on ahead while he made another call.

"Sweetheart, I'm not going to get home right away," he said when Karen answered the phone. Neither had to work Monday morning, so both were looking forward to a long loving Sunday night.

"Oh. What's going on?"

"We found something and I need to wait for the sheriff and guide him out to the location."

"Another cabin?" Gee could hear shuffling and the rattle of Karen's keys. "I'm on my way. You can tell me about it when I get there." She ended the call abruptly before Gee could explain what they'd found. He continued to the foresters' office and found Sheriff Johnson and Detective Oliver arriving.

David and Jonathan geared up to join the group with shovels, lanterns, and an assortment of pruning gear and machetes. No one objected to her presence when Karen arrived and joined the group.

IT WAS FULLY dark beneath the dense overstory of the woods by the time they arrived at the tree. Sheriff Johnson stretched yellow tape across the path and held everyone else back while he and Mead Oliver went to investigate the turned dirt.

"David, we need lights but try to step carefully. We'll need to move dirt, so let's spread the tarp over here. Jonathan, Gee, and Karen, you need to stay back until we see what we're dealing with. It looks like there might be a broken trail that's been partially hidden. If we find something significant, we'll need to bring a search team out in the morning."

They watched the three older men as they carefully cleared a space around the turned dirt and photographed the area. The flash of Mead's camera created instant images, after-burned onto their retinas in the dark. Eventually, the two police officers waved David back behind the tape and began digging shallow scoops. Karen continued to snap photos on her cell phone.

"Might know it would be Gee's team that would be the first to find something," Jonathan laughed.

"I wish I could see the humor in that," his father snapped. "Gee, the trails you've been cutting with your team aren't clean. You need to cut closer to the ground and make them wide enough for an ATV."

"I'll try to do better."

"We can't just leave brush piled on top of the undergrowth beside the paths," David continued. "As it dries it will multiply the risk of fire. Jonathan, if we're going to work out here, we need crews devoted to removing and chipping the cuttings."

"Yes, Dad. We could use volunteer teams to do that without a for- ester to lead them." David turned away and watched the digging as it progressed. Jonathan whispered to Gee. "Don't mind Dad too much. The Wild Woods have pained him for years. He wants to see this area maintained like the Forest. We've been having some pretty intense dis- cussions about proper management of the new area over dinners in the evening."

"Finding something suspicious out here won't help," Karen agreed. "And knowing we'll have to report to the other Families."

"I'm going to leave that to you," David barked. "You're officially the Family reporter."

<hr />

IT TOOK ABOUT thirty minutes of carefully digging in the soft dirt before Johnson called a halt. Everyone was moving restlessly, trying to stay warm.

"Mead, bring that lantern down here closer," he said. The hole was about two feet deep. Johnson leaned over the edge and continued to pull dirt out with his hands.

"Ah, shit!" Mead said as he fell to his knees beside Johnson. "Better call Dr. Gaston. We'll need the coroner for the rest of this."

2

MOURNING AFTER

Breaking News

KAREN AND GEE stumbled into Jitterz at eight-thirty. They hadn't been home and weren't headed there yet. It had been a long night, dealing first with the discovery of the body, then the police, and finally, the Family heads.

"Oh, my. You two look wrung out. Double Birdie's Special coming right up. What would you like to eat?" Violet asked as they reached the counter. The contrast of her ginger hair with her caramel skin never ceased to intrigue Gee. He forgot to answer.

"Thank you, Violet. Two of the bacon and egg breakfast wraps, please," Karen answered. "Sorry we're so out of it this morning."

"I'll bet you aren't going to sleep now, either," Violet said.

"We have work to do," Gee answered.

"Go find a seat. I'll bring everything out to you."

The two sat at their accustomed table and simply looked into each other's eyes. Tears were not far from either after the exhausting night.

"In our woods," Gee said. They'd repeated the words in disbelief throughout the night.

"There's a darkness hanging over you," Violet said, approaching the table with their coffees. "And when there is darkness over you, there is darkness over Rosebud Falls."

"Are you following in your mother's steps as a psychic?" Gee said, trying to lighten the mood.

"Maybe. But some things are too obvious to miss. High school kids come in for coffee on their way to school most days. I listen. Whatever it is that happened last night, I'd guess it's all over the school by now."

"Rumors," Gee said. "We need to dispel rumors with news. There's no paper this morning."

"Is there anything you need from us?" Violet asked.

"Actually, there is," Karen said. "I need to talk to Collin Meagher. Can you tell me how to reach him?"

"You'll have to visit. He doesn't have a phone."

"I was afraid of that. I hate going down to that neighborhood."

"I'll go with you," Violet said. "I seem to be in his good graces. I'll fix breakfast for him."

"Thank you."

"How are things with you and Troy?" Gee asked. Over the past two weeks it seemed that Troy was with Violet whenever he saw her.

"Oh. He's like a sandbur. Gets stuck in your clothes and you can't get rid of it. You know, he's only trying to date me because Wayne Savage got to Jo Ransom first. Troy gravitates to opportunity. As the new Meagher Family heir, I'm opportunity with a capital O. You know how that goes, Karen. I saw you suffer through it."

"Try not to let my experience shadow yours," Karen sighed. "But be careful."

"I'm a big girl," Violet answered. A bell rang and she went to get their breakfast wraps.

"I think I should go to the high school and set the rumors straight," Gee said.

"I agree. Collin is the only Family head I haven't spoken to and he'll get the story in a little bit. It should be fine to talk to the kids. I'll get the story in tomorrow's paper but by then the rumor mill will have invented an entire graveyard," Karen said. Violet returned with their breakfast wraps.

"Violet, you should know…" Gee began.

"Don't say anything here," she interrupted him. "I'll find out when we talk to Uncle Collin. I'll go make his breakfast and be ready in fifteen minutes. I need to let Mother know we are going over. She'll probably meet us there."

"Is there anyone I should take with me to the high school?" Gee asked when Violet had returned to the kitchen.

"I'm sure they'd let you in with no difficulty," Karen said. "You are the City Champion. But just in case, why don't you see if Mead or Judge Warren would go with you?"

Gee had seen the judge just two hours ago at the foresters' office, so called him. While Karen and David debriefed the Family heads, Johnson and Mead had talked to the judge, coroner, and district attorney. The men had all been shocked silent.

Disbelief. "In our woods," was all they'd said, over and over. Pàl took it especially hard. His company should have been stewards of the Wild Woods.

Not just a body, but a child.

"ONE OF OUR worst fears," Gee told the twenty students who had been volunteers over the weekend. Judge Warren, Principal O'Reilly, and the school's counselor, Susan Parris, sat with them in a classroom. "You all worked this weekend in the Wild Woods. You know now why we're concerned. But we have more questions than answers right now. What we don't need is wild speculation. People will wonder what else the Wild Woods hides. I want to make sure you have the facts so you can reassure your classmates. Unfortunately, we don't have any suspects, we don't know who the victim was, we don't know what else we might find. We're depending on you to help control the rumors."

"There could be others," Ryan said softly. "There could be kids who aren't dead… yet. Mr. O'Reilly, can we get extended time in the woods for charting and searching? I'll… cut classes if I need to."

"Don't be too hasty, Ryan," the principal said. "That's what Gee is trying to warn us against."

"There's a delicate balance between moving quickly and potentially missing important clues. With more people, we are just as likely to destroy evidence as to find it. If Alyson hadn't stepped back into the soft dirt, we'd have missed the grave."

"Susan, don't you think this merits an assembly?" Principal O'Reilly said. The counselor nodded.

"It would be best if the students hear the story directly from you, Gee. That way they'll know that the source is as accurate as possible and that you're using these kids as your information channel to the rest of the student body," Susan said. Gee shrugged his shoulders.

"Okay."

"The end of third period bell will ring in ten minutes. I can preempt the class schedule with an announcement. We'll assemble in the gym." The principal and counselor left. Gee and Judge Warren followed the kids to the gym. The judge laid a hand on Gee's shoulder.

"I'm truly sorry, Gee. I gave you the role of City Champion thinking it was simply an honorary title that would give you an ID. But ever since, we've heaped more and more responsibility on you. I had no idea how important it would become to our citizens. And more than anyone, to our youth and children. I'll stand with you, but the hard work in this assembly is yours." Gee sighed heavily and entered the gym.

"Was it...? Was it my Renee?" Collin asked when Karen told him about the body they discovered.

"No, Mr. Meagher. The body was of a boy, not more than ten, according to Dr. Gaston. Preliminary analysis of the site indicated the grave was less than two months old." Karen said. Tears lurked behind her eyes, waiting for her to loosen control. Collin looked at her as if he were burning into her guilty soul. She dropped her eyes. "I've never stopped looking, Mr. Meagher. I never will. I won't lose hope that I'll find her."

Collin struggled up out of his wooden porch chair and laid a hand gently on Karen's shoulder. "It wasn't your fault. You were just a child yourself," he said softly. "I understand you want to visit the Family trees. Come with me." He led Karen, Violet, and Birdie around the old house and stopped before a very old hickory tree.

"You ate a nut from here?" Karen asked. Collin nodded.

"Back in the beginning, the Forest made a pact with the Families. You can say I'm anthropomorphizing plants, but there is a pact inherent in our position. The Forest gives us its bounty in exchange for our protection. We all assume we're supposed to protect the trees, but I'm sure there was more to it than that. We've forgotten more about our mission than we remember. Perhaps you will learn by talking to our Family tree. He's waiting for you." Collin led his nephew's wife and daughter away from the yard, leaving Karen alone.

"What am I supposed to do?" she pled, looking at the old tree. She felt like such a fool wandering around talking to trees as if they could answer her. Most hickory lost production at about a hundred years old but no one actually knew how long they would live if undisturbed. If Collin was right, this tree was over two hundred years old, started as a seedling from the Patriarch tree. It seemed impossible.

In the Forest, when a tree lost its production value, it was marked for harvest for lumber. The foresters made sure that old growth trees were only cut when it was determined that their natural lives were ending. But who knew?

Karen leaned against the old tree and closed her eyes. Even standing up, she drifted into sleep. It had been such a long night and she still had so much to do. The story and photos of the discovery needed to be ready by the three o'clock deadline. Axel had already sent half a dozen texts demanding to know how soon he would have something to read.

In her brief sleep, leaning against the tree, she dreamed of the Wild Woods. She had been in it only twice—once when she was kidnapped and poisoned, and again last night. The area beyond the reach of the lanterns was dense and mysterious. She was certain the Wild Woods could not be as primeval as she imagined it. In her mind, all manner of sinister twisted forms rose out of its shadows.

Karen jolted away from the Meagher tree as if she had been physically thrust from it, a solid image of a tree in her mind.

I need to talk to Gee!

It had taken Gee all morning at the high school and he joined the students at Flor del Día for lunch. He was invited to a podium in the multipurpose room.

"Students and teachers of Flor del Día," Gee said. "You live in the Forest. Well, the Forest borders three sides of the school. From conversations I've had with volunteers, I know you think of yourselves as part of the Forest. That relationship is so close that I've discovered over half of our foresters are former students from Flor. So, no doubt you've already heard that we found a grave in the Wild Woods last night. Maybe you didn't hear that word, but that is what it was. We uncovered the body of a child, dead about two months."

A few gasps, several sniffles, and a low buzz of angry whispers greeted the news. Gee continued once a minute had passed.

"I've met and worked with several students here, both in mapping the Wild Woods and during Harvest. I think you're a lot like me. I don't have any family other than those I've come to love in Rosebud Falls. Like you, I feel a deep connection to the Forest. We are hurt, not only by the loss of the child, but by the violation of our Forest. While the trees and nuts are of the same species, though, the Wild Woods are exactly that— wild. It is dense, untamed. And scary. I *fear* the secrets we'll discover there. And I'm filled with hope and trust that we'll be able, together, to rescue the Wild Woods and anyone who might be trapped there."

"Mr. Gee, can we all work in the woods?" Jason asked. The small boy had been with Gee's crew at the discovery of the grave.

"Yes, but probably not like you imagine. We have to be careful not to trample and destroy any clues. But there are tasks we need help with. They aren't easy tasks. They aren't glorious tasks. They're hard labor. We need to have people following behind the foresters and mapping volunteers to remove the underbrush that we've cut. I got bawled out last night for cutting a path too narrow and leaving too much stalk in the middle of it." There was a smattering of giggles before Gee continued.

"Seriously, we need to have the cut underbrush removed and fed into a chipper. Some of that cut brush includes berry vines, firethorn, hawthorn, and about anything else you can name that has a thorn on it. It's going to be nasty. But if you are willing to spend a couple of hours hauling that stuff off the paths we've cut, widening them to accommodate the ATVs with trailers, and chipping the cuttings, we could use you even for an hour after school. All I'm asking is that you *not* try to search the Wild Woods yourselves. Leave that to the foresters and sheriff. They know what they're doing."

Jeanie and Jason joined Gee at a table after the assembly, much as Viktor, Alyson, and Shannon had at Rosebud High earlier. They had a sign-up sheet and several students volunteered. Flor del Día was a residence as well as a school, and their proximity to the Forest was a benefit. Gee discovered several students already volunteered a few hours a week to help the foresters in getting the Forest ready for winter.

It was late afternoon before Gee left the orphanage school.

A Cabin in the Woods

AFTER THE MEETINGS at the schools, Gee made his way to the foresters' office to sit down with David Lazorack and Gabe Truman. Now that he had volunteers, they needed a strategy for using them. It was clear that Gee would be central in that strategy.

"We don't have another resource we can apply to this," David said. "I'm shuffling things around to get as much done as possible. Gabe and I have talked. He's going to switch from the Wild Woods to the Forest in hopes we can get the work done there before we're bogged down in snow. That's going to be a problem in the Wild Woods as well but it's the best we can do. You're going to be in charge of the Wild Woods but I'm moving Jessie and Jonathan over there full time as your support."

"The snow falls on the just and the unjust," Gabe chuckled from his chair in a corner of the office.

"It could be tricky in the Wild Woods," David continued. "I was out there today and I'm not sure how that thick canopy is going to affect things. Most of the trails we've cleared are just getting into the thick part of the woods. The canopy could keep snow off the ground but that means it could be a hazard when it breaks free of the branches and falls in frozen clumps instead."

"Is there additional safety gear we should be wearing?" Gee asked.

"Hard hats, goggles, and gloves are the best we can do. Just make sure everyone on your crew is wearing them," David said. "Jonathan and Jessie will take charge of the mapping and searching out there. You and I will use our volunteers to clear and widen the trails. Those cuttings need to be hauled out and chipped or we'll have a terrible time in the spring.

It's not likely that we'll catch up with the mapping as it is. I hope a few of our volunteers are eighteen because we'll need them to run the chippers. It's a big damned job."

"You know I'll do whatever you need me to," Gee sighed. "I need to call Nathan and tell him I won't be able to come back to the Market."

"I know I come off as harsh, Gee. I apologize in advance. You've proven you'll do whatever is needed," David said. "You'll probably be able to go back a couple of days a week after we get heavy snowfall. No matter how willing we are to work, if we go out to cut trails after that, we risk missing things. We just won't be able to see them." He looked at Gee hard for a second as if trying to see what the man was made of. "You should consider joining us as a full-time forester."

"Without training and schooling?" Gee asked.

"There are other ways to learn."

"Dad! Jonathan said as he and the other foresters working in the Wild Woods that day came in from their tasks. "We found another cabin!"

<hr>

THE FORESTERS ALL shed their coats in the warmth of the office and shook their heads when Gee, David, and Gabe started to reach for theirs.

"Too dark," one said. "And the sheriff has it blocked off."

"So, is this good news or bad news?" David asked. "Tell us."

"We think we found the place where that guy Reef was living. We cut a path from there out to the quarry and Sheriff Johnson is out there with a forensics team from Palmyra. They sent us away so we couldn't contaminate any evidence they found."

"Nobody in the cabin?" Gee asked.

"No, but this cabin hasn't been cleaned out like the two we found earlier. It's rustic but looks fairly comfortable," Jonathan said.

"Is this going to slow us down in getting the rest of the mapping done?" David asked.

"No. If anything, it's going to give us a path to follow. We found a camouflaged trail from the cabin but the light was going and the sheriff asked us not to follow it until morning. He'll send a deputy with a dog along with us. If we're right, the trail will connect to the other cabins. It definitely doesn't lead back to the quarry."

"That's good news. If there is still anyone living in a cabin, we should be able to find them," David said. "Well done, son. Crew."

"If it weren't for the risks of missing something completely, we'd have gone out tonight," Jessie said. "It gets dark out there a lot sooner than where it's clear. Not to mention it's extremely spooky. Since they found the grave, the sheriff wants to make sure we are alert to manmade dangers along the trail."

<hr />

BOTH GEE AND Karen were exhausted by the time they got home. It was nearly ten and they fell into each other's arms.

"How long has this day been?" Karen moaned. "Can we just go to bed now?"

"My estimate is somewhere around forty hours," Gee answered, kissing her forehead. "We both need a shower and some food. If you want to get started on a shower, I'll fix something to eat."

"Can't we do both together? I need you, Gee."

Special Delivery

"HELLO," LARRY SYRES said when his phone rang. He popped another beer. Work had been light lately and all he had to do was drink. Roxanne was getting tired of him hanging around and if he didn't get out of the house soon, he was going to smack her.

"We'll have the usual flatbed ready to go early Saturday morning. Pick it up and get out before dawn. The new management out here has been breathing down our necks," his contact at Savage Sand & Gravel said. *Stone to go*, Larry sighed.

"Where to?"

"The usual place southwest of Atlanta."

"I hate those mountain roads."

"You get paid to hate them. Drop the trailer at the loading ramp and deadhead home. We won't be using that one again."

"No return delivery? I could pick up a contract on the way back."

"You'll get a bonus as big as the fee if you're back in bed and asleep by eight o'clock Monday morning."

"Forty-eight hours to make sixteen hundred miles? Yeah. I can do it." It would be pushing regulations on how long he could drive without a rest but Larry had made the run enough times to know where to be careful.

"And Larry, try to keep your mouth shut about this. They've been poking into everything since that bar incident a couple of months ago."

"I'm still going to dig that bastard's grave."

"I'm sure you will, Larry. I'm sure you will."

Coming Up Empty

THE STORY OF the shallow grave ran in Tuesday morning's newspaper. Of course, Troy had broken the story on the radio Monday morning but had only sketchy details. His normal process was to read stories out of the newspaper and he didn't have a news staff to support his air time. He grumbled all morning, commenting that the town really needed a daily newspaper that didn't skip Sunday and Monday. He was none too subtle in his request that the publisher get with it.

"This is Troy. I've got one eye on Main," he said as he answered the blinking light of his phone.

"And I've got an eye on you. What's with taking digs at the paper? We've always worked together," Axel said.

"Nothing wrong with the paper that two more days of publication wouldn't cure," Troy growled back. "I've had phones ringing off the hook with nothing to put on the air."

"I'd send Karen over but she's a Family head now and I can't order her around. Cameron warned me already."

"Just give me a buzz if anything comes around before I get off the air." Troy hung up the phone.

———— ◁◆▷ ————

TUESDAY MORNING, WHEN the lines lit up, Troy had the newspaper in front of him, complete with photos of the grave. It turned his stomach.

"While there is no news on the identity of the body, police do not want to hold the case open longer than necessary. I've talked to Rev.

Reinhold Nussbaum at St. Luke's Lutheran Church and he says he
has been asked to conduct a funeral on Thursday this week. The body
will not be interred at that time, but will be stored 'in a peaceful setting' until such time that identification and contact of the nearest relatives can be made," Troy said, looking at the paper. "I'll try to get Rev.
Nussbaum in for an interview later this week to find out what his take
is on the whole affair. Reinhold, if you are listening, stop by sometime
for a chat."

Overall, the newspaper and radio coverage left more questions
unanswered than answered.

MOST OF THE trails that had been cut into the Wild Woods were not
wide enough to drive one of the forestry tractor and trailers down. Gee
and David's crews discovered the benefits of their long sleeves and gloves
quickly. There were now half a dozen access points into the Wild Woods
from the Forest and quarry. They led to an estimated mile and a half of
trails that had been cut from tree to tree.

"What's going to happen to all the trees that are too small to be
marked, Gee?" asked Trevor Graves, an eleventh-grade student at Flor.
He was too young to operate the chippers but was strong and capable
when it came to loading and hauling the brush wagon out of the woods.
The crew of eight students grabbed their water bottles to take a break
before Gee answered.

"I'm concerned about that, too, Trevor. The foresters have a standard
approach to thinning the trees and maximizing production. But part of
the agreement with SSG in giving over management to the foresters
was that no hickory would be cut unless it threatened the life of another.
And then, other alternatives have to be assessed first," Gee answered.

"Like what?" asked Rebecca, a twelfth-grader on an afternoon
release from Flor.

"Well, in the case of trees under five inches DBH, the first option is
to transplant. The problem will be finding a place to transplant to. There
is room for a few in the Forest as part of the continuing nursery plan but
space in the Wild Woods is at a premium."

"And if they're over five inches across?" asked Trevor.

"It's a risky proposition to attempt transplanting a tree that size. As I understand it—and remember, I'm not a forester—it's difficult to capture enough root ball on a tree that size to keep it healthy. If it is very close to larger trees, the root system of its neighbors could be compromised. The scenario most frequently proposed for a tree between five and twelve inches is that it will be harvested for lumber. But none of us want to do that."

"Why?"

"First, we committed to saving every tree in the Wild Woods that we can. We're discovering a unique ecosystem here—much different than the Forest. I'm not even in favor of removing all the understory like the foresters want to. There's something special about this. And second, there's a pragmatic reason that slows down even the foresters. If too many trees are cut, we could flood the market with Rose Hickory and reduce its value. Trees below eight inches don't produce that many board feet of usable lumber, so the most likely scenario would be to dry them and create briquettes out of them."

"You mean like charcoal?"

"Yes. Or straight wood for smoking and such."

"We need more land," Leslie, a freshman, said.

"What do you mean?"

"There's a lot of land around the quarry that's just empty—like sometime in the past it must have been cleared," she continued. "We should get that land from SSG and transplant the trees we can to it. Rosebud Falls doesn't need another housing development. It needs more trees. If the Families were serious about how important the trees are, they'd start acquiring more land bordering the edge of the Forest that's outside the city limits. I sometimes go running out along the roads east of town and there's plenty of land. All the Rose Hickory was cut from it a hundred or more years ago. We could extend the total acreage of the Forest by five hundred acres or more if the Families got off their fat asses and did something."

"Yeah. That whole parcel east of Silver Lake was cleared for a luxury housing development and only has a dozen houses. No one wants to live in a barren area. Surrounding it with more Forest would increase the property values of the homes that are there," said another of the kids.

Gee tried to remember the names of all his crew but would have eight new faces tomorrow.

"Hmm. Not a bad idea but I'm not one of the Families and I don't personally have the funds to buy a stamp, let alone an acre of tillable land," Gee said.

"But you are the City Champion. You could tell them."

"I'll definitely mention it."

<hr />

"WE THINK WE found what used to be the lab," Jessie said as the foresters gathered back at the office when it became too dark in the Wild Woods to continue work. "Each time we find a cabin, we have to vacate the area so the sheriff's deputies can perform forensics. This place had been stripped and cleaned, but apparently, whoever was operating out there didn't have time to take apart the workbenches or unbolt them from the floor. It definitely was not set up as a residence."

"And that's the only place the trail led?" David asked. Gee was glad David was asking the questions. He challenged every forester's assumption and was good at managing the investigation.

"There's a definite exit route from the lab out to a pickup point that showed recent use. It had been poorly camouflaged," Jonathan answered his father. "Tomorrow, we'll be able to take a crew from Reef's cabin to the lab and carefully look for side trails. What I'm wondering now is whether these trails were so carefully hidden to keep people out or to keep people in."

"That's a sobering thought," Gee said. "I hate to think there is anyone abandoned out there who can't find a way out."

"We're hampered by the short hours of daylight," Jonathan said. "We've got people who are anxious to find more trails but we just can't work in the dark."

"Pull anyone out of the mapping process you can use and focus on finding those cabins," David said.

"Assuming there are any others," Jessie said. The other foresters agreed. There were still too many unanswered questions about what lay in the Wild Woods. It was easy to walk past a clue in the dense undergrowth and several were speculating there was nothing else to find. It was a drug lair and nothing else.

Gee was hesitant to admit they might be right.

Forensics

THE FOLLOWING TWO days were tedious and disappointing to everyone.
Two more cabins were found on side trails farther south. Every cabin
had been emptied and scrubbed down.

"One thing we know from all this is that someone has been active
over the past few weeks," Sheriff Johnson said to the gathered Family
heads. "We've been lucky to have Forensics Detective Pete Remington
on loan from Palmyra to handle the evidence. Pete? Do you have anything to add?"

All seven Families were represented. Meagher had asked Gee to
represent him at the gathering and Karen represented the Roth Family
in the stead of Ben Roth.

"This is kind of unusual to expose investigations to non-police. Are
you sure this is okay, Brad?" Pete asked. He was younger than most of
those gathered in the room. He wore light blue scrubs and carried a
box of latex gloves under one arm. The meeting was held in the first
cabin discovered during the search for Karen nearly four weeks previous.
It had long-since been cleared as a scene of interest and the foresters
had established it as their field office in the Wild Woods. The late-night
gathering was shielded by the dark.

"It's the way we do things here in Rosebud Falls, Pete," Mead said.
"These people can shake loose whatever resources we need for the investigation. It's okay."

"All right," the forensics geek said. "I'll tell you this. Whoever
scrubbed these cabins is a hell of a housekeeper." The comment got a
light chuckle from the gathering but they were intent on what had been
uncovered. "The removal of all signs of human habitation is, in itself, a
sign of human habitation. I've even been able to identify the cleansing
agents that were used. To some extent, I can tell the order in which the
cabins were cleaned and how long ago. This cabin and the other one we
found four weeks ago had been cleaned out and sterilized over a year
ago. The layers of accumulated dust showed no sign of disturbance until

the activities of that night. Cabin three, the apparent residence of the man known as Reef, bore no sign of having been disturbed since that man's death. There were still dirty dishes, for example."

"How did these people live?" Heinz demanded. "There are no windows in this cabin. There's no heat. How did they stay warm? What did they eat? Where did they get water?"

"All good questions. If we use Reef's cabin as an indicator, propane gas was used for cooking and heating. There are connections in each of the cabins, but no tanks were found. There are also kerosene stains that indicate lighting, at least at one time, was kerosene lanterns. Reef's cabin had battery powered lanterns and a stock of new batteries. I'd guess waste disposal was done on a periodic basis. Reef had a composting toilet inside."

"Completely off the grid," Heinz mumbled.

"The most recently cleaned cabin may have been done this week, perhaps while foresters were working to find the place. The cabin identified as the lab was cleaned out within the past week, according to what I've been able to gather. Definitely since you opened the woods a week ago Tuesday," Pete concluded.

"And beyond that there's nothing?" Pàl asked. "Even after we took over the company, they were so confident they kept their operation going until we moved into the woods!"

"This all seems to indicate a big business," Loren Cavanaugh said. "I mean they even have housekeepers? How the hell can they keep an operation that size quiet?"

"Illegal immigrants," Mead suggested.

"This isn't Texas," David scoffed.

"And we're not talking about Latin Americans," Mead agreed. "Almost a quarter of our 'undocumented immigrants' are from Asia, Europe, Africa, and Canada. Sorry, Gee. That's all information I dug up when I was trying to find out who you are and where you're from."

"No problem."

"Here in the Northeastern part of the US, we're far more likely to draw from that twenty-five percent than from Latin America."

"So, a Chinese laundry worker comes in and scrubs down a bunch of cabins in the middle of the night and then disappears?" Heinz barked.

"Could be Canadian, Heinz," Brad said. "The likelihood, however is that they don't speak English, are not familiar with US laws or customs, have lived a life where silent servitude is the norm, and may be scared for their lives. If they don't actually see a dead body, they aren't likely to remember it as anything other than housecleaning."

"So, what is the minimum number of people it would take to run this operation?" Jan Poltanys asked. "Assuming a cabin like this could hold six kids and we've found four that could be residences, that's twenty-four kids. How big a staff would they need?"

"We're talking about Reef and at least one and probably as many as three working in the lab. Figure each house has a resident to watch over the captives. Make it eight on-site. Then someone is transporting drugs and maybe trafficking children, managing the operation, housekeeping, cracking the whip. Maybe a dozen or more who are probably residing somewhere in our jurisdiction," Brad said.

"We got a call from LaRue Chemical this afternoon," Mead said. "One of their star researchers hasn't shown up to work this week. Since the guy lives alone, we went over to investigate."

"What did you find?" Gee asked.

"It reminds me of Reef's cabin. The only thing that would make me believe he wasn't just at work was there were no clean clothes. At all."

"Lived like a slob?"

"Very few dirty clothes. It's more like he packed a suitcase with everything clean and left." The group sat in silence for a moment until Jan finally voiced a concern on all their minds.

"What was his area of research?"

"Distillation of RDH from Rose Hickory nuts."

WORK IN THE Forest and Wild Woods stopped on Thursday afternoon as the foresters and volunteers joined close to two hundred others at St. Luke's Lutheran Church for the memorial service. Nearly every relative, near or extended, of the seven Families filled the pews.

The other ministers of the town, including Pastor Beck, were also in attendance. Not knowing the faith or origin of the child, the Catholic priest and the Jewish rabbi also said a prayer over the closed casket.

"Gentle children of God," Reinhold began his homily. "We are gathered in memory of this child who passed without our notice. I know that sounds harsh. We're good people. We didn't want a child to die alone in the woods. We didn't know him or know that he was out there. It wasn't our fault. Yet a child died without our notice."

Gee and Karen were both unaccustomed to the formalities of church services but had managed to stand and sit as directed in the first part of the service. Gee supported Collin on his right, beyond whom sat Violet, Birdie, and Red Lanahan. Collin had tears in his eyes from the moment they entered the church and Gee heard him whisper to himself, "Renee. My precious little Renee." His grief extended far past the unknown child.

"This service is not really in memory of the child," Rev. Nussbaum continued. "We have no memory of him. This service is truly in memory of ourselves—the part of ourselves we have lost in the Wild Woods of our daily lives. It is in memory of the part of ourselves we have lost while paying bills, while cooking dinner, while arguing with a co-worker, or complaining about a manager. It's in memory of the part of ourselves we lose each day while doing more important things.

"What is this part? It is compassion and kindness for those outside our immediate sphere. Of course, we are compassionate. We are kind. But we reserve those emotions for our family, our friends. No doubt, any one of us would go to any length to help a friend or protect a family member. But few of us would extend an effort to help and protect a stranger. Fewer still would help or protect a foe. Each person we look at, we judge as to whether he is worthy of our help.

"But Jesus said, 'Let the children come to me, and don't try to stop them! People who are like these children belong to God's kingdom.' We pray that this child lying before us has found the Kingdom of God. But let us remember the next verse after this famous passage from the nineteenth chapter of the Gospel of Matthew: 'After Jesus had placed his hands on the children, he left.' Did Jesus leave because he was no longer concerned? Because he was finished with them? No! He left because he had deputized his followers, you and me, to care for them.

"It is that which we remember today. We, gathered here today, are people of different beliefs than Luther's ninety-five theses, or Matthew's

Gospel, or the Torah, or Koran, or even the Bhagavad Gita. We are a disparate and diverse population. But within each of our hearts is a light that illuminates our beliefs and our actions. I ask only that you let that light shine on the memory of this child and guide your action as our foresters search for any other children that might have been abandoned in the Wild Woods. Let us unite as a community to care for our children—all our children, whether of our blood, our spirit, our community, our nation, or our world."

Rev. Nussbaum left the pulpit to stand behind the tiny coffin. The other ministers, priests, and rabbis stood with him in a silent arc. The Nussbaum Quartet stood in the choir loft and began Céline Dion's haunting melody led by Elaine's incredible voice.

> *Every boy and girl*
> *Should dance on dreams*
> *Around this world.*
> *Aren't they all our children after all?*
> *Who will dry their tears*
> *And lift them up*
> *If they should fall?*
> *Aren't they all our children after all?*

The Last Cabin

"I THINK WE'VE found all the cabins there are," Jessie said. "We have the aerial photos Gabe took last week and have circled the areas where we found the six cabins. We overlaid the map of trails we've cut. You can see we've got pretty good coverage over the northern half of the woods. The spider trails in this area are paths between the cabins that we've located. As we get farther south, the old growth thins and there isn't as dense a canopy. We think any cabin that far south would have shown up in the pictures."

"How about this area on the far east side?" Gee asked, pointing at the section on the map that seemed not to have coverage. Jessie, Jonathan, Gee, David, and Gabe had established a routine of debriefing each afternoon. Everyone wanted to leave a little early on Friday so they could get to the last football game of the season.

"There's a remote chance of habitation in that area but the terrain is extremely rough," Jonathan said. "Here, you can see there are outcroppings of rock, for example. We need to continue mapping, but I don't have any hope of finding another cabin. We might not even be able to penetrate it fully before snow and cold block us."

"I have to agree," David said. "How about you, Gee? Any feeling we should be pursuing?"

"I don't know that my feelings count for anything," he laughed. His relationship with David had relaxed since working together with their brush hauling teams. Roughly half the trails cut during mapping had now been cleared.

"You keep going back to that spot, though," Gabe said as Gee continued to scan the area of the rock outcropping. "Something bothers you."

"I don't know if I'd call it bothered, but I can't help but think there is something important over there. It's not so much that I think there are cabins or graves there. I hope not. I just think it is important to continue exploring that direction."

"That's good enough for me. You have a crew tomorrow. Who else do we have?" David asked.

"Jessie and I both have crews," Jonathan said. "The other guys have put in seven straight days and need the weekend off."

"You've all put in seven straight days," David reminded them.

"Nine," Jessie corrected him. "I don't mind. I have a nice warm bed to go home to at night. If there are children out there…"

David sighed. "Three crews. Focus attention on getting into this section. It looks to be a bit over a hundred acres, give or take."

"We've only covered about three acres per day per crew," Gee said.

"We'll use the same strategy as we did in looking for the cabins," Jonathan said. "Instead of going from tree to the nearest tree, we'll move from one to the farthest one we can see. We'll spread out like fingers instead of a checkerboard.

"We need to recruit some more volunteers," Gee said. "If we put more focus on cutting the paths, we can stay ahead of those doing measurements."

"Good idea."

"GRANDA, HOW MUCH does stone weigh?" Wayne asked. He'd stopped by his grandfather's office at Savage Sand & Gravel to pick the old man up for dinner before the football game. While waiting, he stood at the window watching the shift workers leave.

"What kind of stone? Most of what we ship is construction grade limestone. It comes in at about a hundred fifty pounds a cubic foot. We don't quarry here any longer. The rose limestone is a thing of the past. We buy from quarries farther north or as far west as Indiana and it's shipped to us in blocks of two to five tons each. We cut and polish or do single roughs before shipping it to the customer. That's still only about ten percent of the business these days. It's almost all sand and gravel." Pàl continued to work on the notes in front of him as he talked to his grandson. He was only too happy the teacher was taking an interest in the family business.

"How much can come in or go out in a truckload?" Wayne persisted. Pàl looked up and saw him tapping on his phone's calculator.

"If an order exceeds twenty-two tons, it has to be split. We can do about forty tons on a tandem but don't. It's too much weight for drivers to pull safely. What are you working on?" Pàl stood to look out the window in the direction Wayne was facing.

"That flatbed out there. Assuming it's limestone under the tarp, it's a pile roughly four feet high, eight feet across, and twenty feet long. If I did the calculations right, that's forty-eight tons. What else do we ship?"

"Let's go take a look," Pàl suggested.

Friday Night Lights

"HEY, COUSIN. How you doing?" Karen asked Jo Ransom as she took a seat in the football stands.

"Cold," her cousin complained. "I spent my college life at Alabama. I completely forgot what it was like up here in the snowy North."

"You ain't seen nothing yet," Karen laughed. "We've only had three hard freezes since Halloween. Though I've heard the highest we'll see now until the end of February is forty-five. Our weather contact at the newspaper says it will be a heavy snowfall year. Each morning, I expect to wake up to a foot of snow."

"Please, not yet," Gee groaned. "We have so much left to do out there."

"How's it going?" Jo asked.

"I guess the stats will be published in tomorrow's newspaper," Gee said. "We've cut nearly two miles of trails and mapped over 400 trees. We've found six cabins. Only Reef's cabin showed recent signs of life. And one body."

"That's grim."

"I'm looking for more volunteers for tomorrow," Gee said. "I expected to see Wayne with you tonight."

"I did, too," Jo sighed. "He called a little bit ago and said he needed to stay over at SSG to help his grandfather for a while. Wouldn't say what, other than 'company business.' I know he'll volunteer, though. Put both of us down. I could use a little exercise."

"I suppose that means I'm in, too," Karen laughed. Gee took a firm hold of Karen's hand. "What have you been doing with your time, Jo?"

"Oh, job-hunting. I know, theoretically, I have an income from the investments I just inherited. But practically, I don't feel right without working. I mean, you're head of the Family and you still hold down a job. It isn't about money. I just want to feel useful," Jo said.

"I understand. I'm only the figurehead of the Family, not the head. But Ben is getting so frail that he wants Leah and me to handle all the Family business."

"How's Leah taking not being named heir?"

"Not badly. I've asked her to keep handling the investments and business side of things. Aside from sitting with the other Family heads, her responsibilities haven't changed. She said she had considered naming me her heir anyway since she doesn't have a son who is competent."

"She has a daughter-in-law who would like a chance," Gee surmised.

"Judith is a graspy little bitch," Karen exclaimed with unaccustomed vehemence. "She's at least fourteen or fifteen years younger than Joseph and controls him like a sock puppet. I doubt the marriage will last past her twentieth birthday. Sorry. Too much dirty laundry. I guess I'd have to say Joseph got exactly what he deserved."

THE GAME WAS a close loss for the Fireflies, ending their season at six and four. It was understood county-wide that Rosebud High School and Flor del Día would forfeit one game a year when Harvest came around, so neither would ever have a perfect season. It was a good evening for Gee, however, as he recruited two more volunteers from those he'd worked with before who would come to help Saturday morning. Gee, Karen, and Jo were near the gate when Troy Cavanaugh caught up with them.

"What's up, Gee?" he said casually.

"Hey, Troy. Just recruiting some volunteers to help in the Wild Woods tomorrow. Do you have plans?"

"Well… I usually sleep in on Saturdays. I guess I could put in a few hours," Troy stammered. "Oh, hi, Jo. Where's the Savage?"

"Got tied up with his grandfather at SSG tonight," Jo said. "Where's Violet?"

"Oh, you know. Preparing for the after-game crowd at Jitterz," Troy said. "Hey! We're all young and single. Why don't we go over the Pizza Palace and get warmed up?"

"Saturday is usually my day to sleep in, too," Karen said. "But I promised this slave driver I'd go traipsing about in the woods at dawn. I think I'll go home and hit the sack."

"Sunrise is too early, even with the end of Daylight Saving Time," Jo said. "I'm heading home, too."

"I skipped dinner before the game," Gee said. "I could use a pizza. We haven't had much chance to catch up since it got too cold out for basketball. Why don't the two of us head over to the Pizza Palace?"

"Oh. Uh… Okay," Troy said. "Sure you ladies won't join us?" It was clear where his interest lay.

"Have fun you two," Karen said quickly. She gave Gee a kiss on the cheek. "Don't wake me up, okay? Need a lift, Jo?"

"Thanks, Karen. See you guys tomorrow."

Gee and Troy headed to the Pizza Palace without female company.

Cargo

"I'd RATHER NOT wait until morning, Pàl. If there is contraband in there, I'll want to follow the truck to its destination and see who receives the shipment. It's your call. I can have a warrant in half an hour," Sheriff Johnson said.

"Can you do that? The manifest gives a destination in Florida," Pàl said.

"It depends on what we find. If all we have is a suspicion, I'll have to call the feds."

"I've been scrutinizing the employee rosters pretty carefully. This was loaded and prepared by the second shift crew. Let me call the first shift supervisor and get him out here to help. He'll know who's dependable and can get us some muscle. According to the scales, the load is certified at nineteen tons. By measured volume, it should be more than twice that."

"With luck, it won't take long to find a hollow container under one or two layers of rock," Wayne said. "Let's do this."

———— ⬥ ————

LOADING AND UNLOADING palettes of rock is neither a pleasant nor fast job. By midnight, Pàl resolved to make sure the three-man crew received a healthy bonus for this unexpected overtime. Binding straps that held the cargo in place were cut and Doug O'Neil recorded the seal numbers so he could reproduce them when it was time to get the cargo ready to roll before morning.

"That, to my untrained eye, is lab equipment," Johnson said when they opened the first container they uncovered.

"And those are Rose Hickory nuts. Probably enough to keep the lab running for a year or more," Pàl added.

"I don't think we have enough labor to empty the crate and get everything sealed up again. There's room for another container ahead of this one and we should be ready to follow the shipment when it leaves in the morning."

"The bill of lading says Kissimmee, Florida. We could be down there waiting for it," Pàl confirmed.

"My instinct tells me this isn't going where the bill of lading says," Johnson said. "Let's seal it back up and confirm what's up front."

They sealed the container as two of the laborers kept working on the front portion of the trailer. As soon as the container was sealed, Wayne and the third man started covering the back container with even rows of rock once more. It took another two hours of heavy labor to uncover the front container. Once enough rock had been shifted, they released the lid of the second container.

"Jesus Christ!" Wayne breathed as he lowered himself into the container.

"Janice," barked Johnson into his cell phone. "I need an ambulance at SSG immediately. Use your cell phone to dispatch. Do not—I repeat—DO NOT use the open channel dispatch radio. Do you understand?"

"What's going on, Sherriff?"

"You have all the information I am free to give and that you need. Get on it, now!" he yelled at the dispatcher.

"Yes, sir."

Johnson had no more than disconnected when he thumbed another number on his phone.

"Poltanys."

"Doctor, I have an ambulance incoming. Patients need the utmost of care and security. Mead Oliver will be present when they get there. Do not put them through admissions. No one is to know."

"Them?"

Johnson looked into the container where Wayne held a mass of wool blankets in his arms.

"Yes. Three children."

3
CHILDREN

Sàmhach

AS CLOSE A RELATIONSHIP as the police, sheriff's department, and Families had in Rosebud Falls, it still wasn't prudent to have many people knowing what they discovered. It would be hard enough to contain the story while Johnson investigated. He wasn't as suspicious of the Savage Family per se as of their company. The evidence was that drugs and child trafficking had been going on here long before Wayne or Pàl showed up. The sheriff still had one trump card to keep the investigation under wraps. He needed to play it now while everyone was still in shock at discovering the children.

"Pàl and Wayne, you're here with us, so there's no way I can prevent you from knowing what we just discovered. I can't have you investigating on your own while we're following this shipment."

"Just say what you want, Sheriff. You'll find us cooperative."

"There is a longstanding code among the Families that binds them to secrecy and allows law enforcement to withhold information from them. We haven't invoked the code in several years but it is paramount that we keep this under *sàmhach* for forty-eight hours. Silence. Do not speak to other Family heads or anyone else."

Pàl smiled sadly. "You know, that is one of the possible translations of our name. We understand."

"I'll take care of the workers and the EMTs," Johnson said.

"NOT TO ANYONE, Wayne. Even Gee and Karen," Pàl said as they watched the ambulance pull away. By this time the workers had nearly replaced the entire top layer of rock in the shipment and were already strapping down portions before covering the load with the tarp. After a short session with the sheriff, they nodded their heads and went home.

"Don't the other Families have a right to know what we found?" Wayne asked.

"The Families seem to be all-powerful to you, don't they?" Pàl asked his grandson. "In a way it's true. What we say is *almost* law. But we hold that power in trust. It's always a delicate balance. If the Families betray the trust of the people, they will fall. The police department, sheriff's department, City Council, Family heads… When part of our infrastructure invokes *sàmhach*, we need to respond with silence."

"As long as it isn't used to circumvent justice, I guess I'm okay with it."

"With eleven people already knowing, the chance that we can keep our silence for forty-eight hours is slim," Johnson said as he rejoined them. I have two deputies in unmarked cars waiting near the exit roads to follow the truck when it pulls out. They will follow wherever it leads. If what we know is discovered before the truck arrives at its destination, a phone call could abort the delivery. We need to know where those kids were going and who sent them."

"You have our word, Sheriff," Wayne said.

"I know. You're Family."

"HOW ARE THEY?" Johnson asked Mead at the hospital. It was nearly four in the morning and both men arrived in unmarked cars. Johnson had stopped long enough on his way from SSG to change into street clothes. From a distance they looked like any other late-night visitors to ER.

"Completely silent," Mead said. "Adam and Julia are taking care of them but the children haven't said a word. EMTs said they didn't say anything all the way here. Usually, kids show excitement or fear when they are loaded into an ambulance. Nothing."

"Then the EMTs don't have anything they can tell. We didn't tell them where we found the kids, so as far as they know they could have wandered in from the Wild Woods."

"Unless Adam has gotten through to them in the past ten minutes, none of the kids have done anything but stare into space. We're going to need help for them, Brad. The hospital's chief physician and his nurse sister can't disappear into isolation without raising a lot of suspicions." They stepped off the elevator and Mead led the way to a hall with a closed door that said 'Long-Term Care.' Dr. Poltanys looked up when they reached the children's room.

"I'm not sure why they aren't completely comatose," he said to the two officers. "Though this... waking coma isn't much better."

"Any analysis?"

"We drew blood as soon as they got here and sent it down to the lab with a rush on it. Then we got them into the bathtub. I just hung up with the tech. The tests all came back with sufficient RDH in the blood to render them as unconscious as Rena Lynd."

"The first time we brought her in, she had taken a super dose but was still conscious," Mead said.

"That's true," Poltanys said. "And she woke up coherent, even though disoriented. It took a month for the hallucinations to finally be purged. It surprised me that she took more so soon after her recovery."

"She didn't take it willingly. Karen said she kept repeating that he didn't have to give her the drug. She would have done anything he asked. I just wish we knew who *he* was," Mead said.

"So, in the past few months, we've had five cases plus these three with a super dose of RDH. Reef is dead. Rena twice and is now in a coma. Gee and Karen were both out for a while and reported continuing hallucinations and fantasies," Adam said.

"I hear what you're saying. What fantasy is playing out behind their eyes, Doctor?" Johnson asked.

The children moved. Their eyes snapped to Adam before he could answer. As one, the children rolled to their knees and pulled down their pajama bottoms.

"What the hell is going on?" Mead exclaimed.

"Damned if I know. Julia, help get them dressed. I don't want to sedate them in their condition. Let's see if we can settle them for sleep." The policemen stepped back by the door as Adam and Julia did their best to comfort the boy and two girls. Mead estimated their ages between five and eight.

"Go to sleep now," Julia whispered as she tucked them in, motioning Adam away from them. The eyes of all three children closed at once.

"A trigger," Adam said. "No one else has used my title since they arrived. I think we can safely say these kids were conditioned to respond to a d-o-c-t-o-r. And he was not a nice man."

"Adam, someone needs to stay here with them. I'll call for a cot and sleep here. I think we need to bring in Mother or Ellie," Julia said.

"Not your mother," Sheriff Johnson said immediately. "I'm sorry but this is strictly under *sàmhach*. We need forty-eight hours."

"Understood, Sheriff. We can trust Ellie."

Trailblazing

"JONATHAN, IS IT normal to have such dense undergrowth when the canopy is so complete?" Gee asked as the three teams gathered together for lunch. Drake Oliver, Mead's son, had joined Gee's crew and was a great help in handling the pruning shears to cut through the thicket. Karen was on Gee's team but Jo had joined Jessie. Surprising no one, Troy had not shown up.

"Not really," Jonathan said. "This underbrush isn't even common in our part of the country. It's all hardy plants that thrive in shade—almost as if someone seeded the area."

"How recently would that have been?" Karen asked. "Could they have put this in as a way to conceal what they were doing out here?"

"Offhand, I'd say no," Jonathan said. "This is too dense and mature to be less than ten years old. I'd say it's more likely to be fifty years. It could be longer. Dad says there has always been a division between the Forest and the Wild Woods, even before the fence was put up."

"Well, that shoots down that theory then," Karen said. "It just seems too convenient for nefarious purposes."

"Doesn't mean people aren't using it to hide things," Jessie said.

"It seems to be getting thicker," Gee acknowledged. "We'd better get started. I think we'll need more teams to handle the cut brush this week. And we really haven't advanced far." They'd started at the cabin closest to the uncharted area and moved in three directions but none of the teams had managed more than a hundred yards during the morning.

They put away their lunch remains and the teams went back to work. While Karen, Jason, Alyson, Jeanie, and Shannon were not as strong as Drake and Gee, they were still able to help with the trimming and piling of the brush between the trees they targeted for mapping. As clouds closed in during the morning, it got colder, but their work kept them warm.

By the end of the day, each team had cut another hundred yards into the Wild Woods. Jonathan blew his whistle and all three teams met back at the cabin to head out of the woods.

"I wonder if we could put a propane heater in this cabin like you have in the field office?" Gee said. "As weather gets colder, we might need to take breaks to warm up. Especially for meals and such."

"Not a bad idea," Jonathan agreed. "All the connections are here. I'll talk to Dad."

"We can probably get a bunch of kids out tomorrow to move the brush piles to the chipper," Jeanie said. "Is it okay for them to do that without a forester to supervise?"

"They won't be able to operate the chipper," Jessie said. "But just getting the brush out of our cleared paths would be a great help."

"I bet we can get more kids from school out," Drake suggested. "Alyson and Shannon, do you think you could call the girls?"

"Drake, are you still too shy to call a girl yourself?" Shannon teased.

"No... uh... I... uh... just thought we could split it up and I'll call the guys. You know."

"Yeah. We know, you goof," Alyson laughed. "You know, one of these days we're going to get you a girl who lasts more than one date."

"You guys are mean," he said. Then he laughed. "But if you find her, let me know, okay?"

———◅◆▻———

"Hear anything from Wayne?" Karen asked Jo.

"Yeah. He called and begged off tonight, too. Said he'd try to be available tomorrow afternoon for a while but his grandfather needed help at the office. Something to do with funny bookkeeping," Jo said. "I hope he's okay. You know, his grandfather wants him to quit teaching at the end of the school year and get more involved in the company. I think Wayne would really miss teaching, though."

"I thought sure someone would be out to check the progress today. Loren has been really interested," Gee said. "I didn't even see David at the office. It's like a silence has descended over the whole town."

"Let's break it and call Leah and Don up for dinner. Jo, think you could get your grandmother to join us at our house?"

"Are you sure that's not too much work, Karen?"

"It gets dark so early, we've got plenty of time. Let's make it dinner at our place at seven."

"Thanks, cousin. See you then."

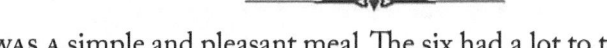

IT WAS A simple and pleasant meal. The six had a lot to talk about, much focusing on Ben's poor health. Once he'd declared Karen as his heir, the old man seemed to fade.

"When will you move over to the estate?" Leah asked.

"I don't really want to think about it," Karen said. "We're so comfortable and I hardly know the place over there. This is our first home together." She smiled at Gee and took his hand. "Maybe Jo should occupy it."

"Um… no," Jo said. "I'm still adjusting to having an apartment that's bigger than a bedroom. Why does someone need to live there? You could sell it for a fortune." Leah looked at her in horror and even Celia shook her head. Karen sighed.

"It's the tree," she finally said. "Our family, even if it doesn't bear the ancestral name, needs to keep the tree."

"Rather mystical," Don said. He and Leah once thought they would eventually move into the mansion. He just assumed that when Karen took the mantle of the Family, she'd move there.

"It needs to be owned by the Family but I suppose you don't *have* to live there," Leah said.

They let the conversation hang, no one really willing to contemplate the day when Ben Roth would no longer be there. He was ninety-two years old and no one lives forever.

"Here's something to run past you, Leah and Don," Gee said, changing the subject. "One of my crew this week suggested that we need to expand the Forest."

"We just did with the Wild Woods," Leah said.

"Oh. Yes. Well, what she was talking about is that there are a lot of trees needing to be relocated. They are too close together and some are going to suffer."

"Don't they cut them?" Don asked.

"One of the conditions for taking over the Wild Woods was that no tree would be cut unless it was dying or in imminent danger. Collin made me put that into the contract with SSG and the foresters. We're talking about moving some into open area adjacent to the woods. You bought some property out that way, didn't you? Would you entertain the idea of expanding the Forest onto it?"

"You have enough votes now that you could change the agreement," Leah said. "I respect Collin's position, but his mental faculties aren't all there."

"I made an agreement with him," Gee said. "How could I justify breaking it? Who would ever make an agreement with me again? The whole coalition would fall apart."

Leah sighed and Don scratched his head.

"We seldom find people who are as good as their word," Don said. "That's why bank lending agreements are so many pages of legalese. You give us all a lot to think about. We'll consider it when you get a plan together."

"We aren't talking next week," Gee laughed. "It will take close to a year before we've fully assessed the land and the needs of the Wild Woods."

Tails

"THIS IS JOHNSON. Talk to me," the sheriff barked into his phone. It was seven o'clock Saturday evening and seemed like he hadn't slept since Election Day. Pàl and Wayne had brought in a box of shipping documents. They'd tracked thirty orders over the past ten years to the same address in Florida.

"Sheriff Reynolds down in Kissimmee," the caller said. "I sent a man out to the address you gave us. You sure chose a good one. This area around Kissimmee has been filled in and developed over the past forty years but it was mostly swampland to start with. You're shipping tons of rock to one of the few swamps left down here. There's no warehouse and no business out there."

"Thank you, Sheriff Reynolds. We were suspicious that it was a fake bill of lading. This will help our investigation immensely."

"You're always welcome to come and check the location personally, Sheriff. Disney World is just six miles from our office. Bring the wife and kids for a break."

"Thank you for the invitation. I'll consider it. It gets cold up here in January." Johnson disconnected and turned to his companions. "Pàl, where did you live in Florida. That's where you were before you moved up here, right?"

"Port St. Lucie," Pàl responded. "It's about a hundred miles southeast of Kissimmee. I moved there soon after Wayne was born and Scotland started to make my bones ache. Not much there. Seemed like a nice quiet place to watch over my son and his family. Sorry to say, my son passed away nearly ten years ago."

Johnson didn't probe as to the cause of Pàl's son's death. "That's where you've lived all your life, Wayne?"

"Close. I went to USF in Tampa for college and taught elementary school in Fort Pierce nine years. I moved up here in August."

"And never had anything to do with the company in all that time?"

"I kept track of the business financials as a stockholder, but didn't want to make a move until I had a hope that we could rally a takeover," Pàl said.

"We have a truck leaving Rosebud Falls about three times a year for ten years with a bill of lading designating a non-existent address in Florida. Where does it go? My deputies tailing the load say it's definitely headed south and doing a pretty good clip. By the time they reached Virginia they were beginning to think the guy had no bladder. He isn't speeding enough to draw attention and makes the Port of Entry and weigh station stops. According to the deputies, that tractor of his must have a pretty powerful engine the way he's walking up the hills."

"Any guesses where he's going yet?"

"Last check-in was Charleston, still headed south."

Johnson's phone rang again. He checked the caller ID and answered.

"Johnson. What do you have, Doctor?"

"Not much, I'm afraid. I gave Mead a report an hour ago but he wanted me to talk to you directly," Adam said. "The children... We need someone in here who can develop a rapport with children. Julia doesn't have children and Ellie's are grown. My ex took my son and moved west when he was three, which tells you something about my parenting skills. We're okay but don't understand what's going on. The children don't do anything without direction."

"You mean they ask permission for things?"

"No. It's taken us a while to figure it out. They simply wait until told what to do. We set food trays in front of them and they did nothing. Told them they could eat now and still nothing. It wasn't until Ellie got frustrated and just said, 'Eat!' that all the children immediately started eating. None of them has asked to use the toilet. Julia takes them in one at a time and tells them to go to the bathroom. They have no will. It's like their minds are blank."

"How about triggers? Have you found any other words they respond to like 'doctor'?"

"No. We're being careful with what we say. We don't want to trip any responses without knowing what we're doing."

"And they won't answer any questions?"

"None of them talk. Or they won't talk. When they're asked a question, they look conflicted and frightened but won't say anything."

"Anything else?"

"Just one thing. Apparently, rules change when the lights go out. Ellie got them all fed and to bed this evening. When she turned out the light, the two older ones got out of bed and crawled in with the little one. They're huddled together asleep now."

"This has to stop!" Johnson said in frustration. "How can anyone do this to a bunch of children?"

"We need help, Sheriff. We aren't trained to handle this kind of thing."

"As soon as I call in anyone else, we'll have state and probably feds crawling all over. I need more time before anyone knows we have them."

"I have an idea."

Sheriff Johnson listened and saw the sense in the situation. He finally agreed to consider Adam's request, though he doubted it would help.

———◁◆▷———

MEAD CAREFULLY PUT together an evidence packet that would not tip his hand. Under the temporary assumption of rendering emergency aid, police had opened the apartment of the missing Dr. Jones. After verifying the doctor was not in the apartment and appeared to have packed a bag to leave, they relocked the door and left. They were not authorized to search for anything else and nothing they discovered during this incursion was usable as evidence.

"And why do you think you need a search warrant, Mead?" Judge Warren said. "Your officers found no sign of foul play, right?"

"Judge, the disappearance of Dr. Jones coincides with the discovery of Cabin Four in the Wild Woods, the cabin labeled as having been the lab. Everything was cleaned out of the cabin. Reese Ecklund at LaRue Labs has investigated Dr. Jones' work area and determined there is reason to believe some of his research is also missing. Of course, it is their right to search any company property but Dr. Jones's apartment is not company property. Since the doctor's work at LaRue was tied to the distillation of the chemical components of Rose Hickory nuts, we believe there could be a connection between him and the unauthorized laboratory in the woods. We wish to investigate this connection and search for any notes and materials that could be considered property of LaRue Labs."

"Well done, Mead. I've had a bad feeling about this from the time we found he was missing. You put together an adequate evidence packet for a warrant." The judge signed the search warrant. "Are you planning to execute this tonight?"

"No, sir. As much as I hate calling an officer to assist on Sunday morning, I think it's preferable to late Saturday night. You know how Saturdays are, even here in Rosebud Falls."

"Mead, is there something else I should be aware of?"

"Nothing I can tell the court, your honor."

"What?"

"Sàmhach."

"That word hasn't been used in Rosebud Falls in ten or twelve years."

"Not since the investigation of the kidnapping of Collin Meagher's great-niece."

Judge Warren stared at Mead as if willing him to give details. Mead knew, however, that having invoked the silence, he could not be pressured by any Family member to reveal the subject. Even though the judge had a level of civil authority, he was still Family. Finally, Warren handed the warrant to Mead.

"Thank you, Your Honor."

<hr />

"Sheriff, we lost him."

"Oh, Christ," Johnson moaned into the phone. "You're sure?"

"I don't see how he can keep driving like this. He must be downing energy drinks one after another. God knows, I've had a few. He surprised us in Atlanta when he switched from the direct route south on I-75 to I-85 southwest. We've been rotating tail and lead for twenty-four hours. Bruce headed down to LaGrange to get some sleep while I dragged behind. He passed the truck about twenty-five miles southwest of the metroplex. When I pulled off at LaGrange, Bruce was still waiting for him to show up. He had to have turned off in that region."

"Well, that ends that," the Sheriff sighed. "Get some sleep and head home. We're going to end up with feds whether we want them or not. You guys did the best you could. At least we know now the shipment wasn't headed to Florida."

Call for a Champion

"Gee, this is Sheriff Johnson. I hope this isn't too early."

"Not at all, Sheriff. We're almost ready to leave for the woods. I have a weekend crew."

"About that," Johnson said. "I need your help. Urgently." Gee came instantly alert, setting down his coffee cup.

"How can I help?"

"We have rescued three children. They are unstable and we can't get through to them."

"And you think I can?"

"These kids are part of your mission, Gee. They're why you said you wanted to open the woods."

"I need to cancel my crew. I'll tell Karen and call Jonathan and Jessie. If there are children from the woods, that's my highest priority."

"Listen, Gee. Before you start calling people, you need to understand; no one knows about this. Tell Karen you have been summoned by the police on a matter of *sàmhach*. It is critical that you do not tell *anyone* about the children or precisely where you are going. A deputy will be by in thirty minutes to pick you up."

"But I have to tell Karen. She's my…"

"No, Gee. She's Family. If she's unfamiliar with the term, have her call Mead Oliver."

"Uh… how do you spell that?"

<hr />

"I KNOW I'VE seen the word. It's in my great-grandmother's notes. Or perhaps her father's," Karen said as she searched through her desk. "It had to do with an attempted murder back in the forties. There is so much history in this room. Here it is." She pulled out a journal and began to thumb through its pages. "Sometime just before the seven heroes went to war." Gee stood by. Karen hadn't challenged him about not telling her where he'd been called to. She wanted to know the meaning of the word and would prefer not to call Mead for a definition of something a Family head should know.

"He didn't give me a definition. Just said you'd know."

"Here it is. 'Police did not inform the Family heads that they were investigating a murder attempt on the youngest Cavanaugh son. When Leo Cavanaugh wanted to call a meeting of the Families, Police Chief Arlan Graves simply invoked *sàmhach*. We hadn't used that word since the early twenties. *Sàmhach* means 'silence.' Our forefathers realized there would be times when a Family fell under investigation. In fairness to the community, Families had to be kept silent and out of communication with others and even within the Family itself. *Sàmhach* means complete silence. To preserve our heritage and position, it must be honored.' I see," she said.

"I'm sorry…" Gee started.

"Look at the time!" Karen interrupted. "I'd better get to the woods so we can get organized. I love you, Darling." She kissed him intently and looked into his eyes. "What you have to do, do well." She stomped into her boots and left. Five minutes later a deputy was at Gee's door.

"I NEED BOOKS," Gee said after unsuccessfully encouraging the children to talk. "Is there anything in the hospital?"

"We have a small library and there is a children's section. I'll go get a few."

"Thank you, Ellie. I don't know what else to do."

"They completely ignore Julia and me but their eyes track you no matter where you move. It's the same with Adam or Mead. They track a male. But they don't seem frightened of you. They try not to show it but I can see the fear in their eyes when Adam is around."

"LOOK AT THE bunny, Littlest," Gee said as he read to the children. They sat where he'd placed them on the floor next to him. Ellie had brought a beanbag chair from the children's wing and Gee was comfortable as he read book after book. Unlike his times in the library, instead of starting with picture books for the youngest and progressing to older children, he found himself working down to more and more basic books as Ellie brought them to him, searching for the level the children could understand. "Do you want to touch the bunny's soft fur? Pat the bunny, Littlest."

The smallest of the children snapped her eyes to Gee and he nodded. She reached out her hand and touched the bit of fur pasted in the book.

"Brother? Wouldn't you like to pat the bunny? Go ahead. Pat the bunny."

Looking toward Gee for confirmation, the little boy—about six, Gee guessed—reached out a tentative hand to touch the fur. He looked at the tiniest of the children. Gee guessed she might be five. They had a hint of a smile. In the absence of other names, Gee called the children Littlest, Brother, and Sister. He had no idea if they were related. He turned to Sister—maybe eight. She reminded him of Sally Ann Metzger.

"Sister, isn't it nice how Brother and Littlest are patting the bunny? Can you pat the bunny?" The girl did not respond to the question. She simply looked at Gee. "Go ahead. Pat the bunny, Sister." Immediately the girl reached out her hand to touch the bunny. He watched as her fingers intertwined with the other children on the tiny bit of fur.

"It's nap time, Gee," Ellie whispered. "You need a break."

"Okay, children," Gee said. "Our friend Ellie says it's nap time. Everyone up and go use the toilet. Sister, help Littlest up on the seat." The children finished taking turns on the toilet and after being prompted, washed their hands.

"Time to hop in bed now," Gee said. The children looked quickly at each other and the boy climbed onto a bed. Sister lifted Littlest up to the same bed and climbed in next to her.

"They all got in the same bed," Ellie whispered. "They each have their own."

"Let them," Gee said. "Let them rest where they are comfortable." He turned to the children and touched each of their heads softly. "Sleep now and I'll come back to read some more in a little bit." Gee knew they had to be pretending sleep as they all closed their eyes at once, but perhaps they would fall asleep before long. Ellie pulled the shades and turned out the light. She stepped outside the room with Gee.

"That was amazing," she said. "You've been reading to them for three hours."

"They're babies," Gee whispered. "Just babies."

"But they smiled," Ellie said, softly laying her hand on Gee's shoulder. "For you. When they touched the fur, they smiled."

"Who could have done this to them? Who could do this?" Gee sagged against a wall.

"I'm sure we'll find out," Ellie encouraged him, kneading the shoulder she still grasped. "Go get a cup of coffee. Adam is in the cafeteria. He'll talk to you."

———————◁◆▷———————

"THEY'VE ALL THREE been abused," Adam reported to the two police-men and Gee in the cafeteria. "In ways that would put a man in prison for life."

"Life?" Gee asked.

"Pedophiles don't live long in prison," Johnson answered. "Continue, Adam."

"They are malnourished and drugged. They are afraid of doctors but are immediately obedient to any command. God knows what other responses have been programmed into them under the influence of that fantasy drug."

"If we can find Dr. Jones, we might get an answer. We've issued an APB," Mead said.

"You got the Lab's research?" Johnson asked.

"No. But when we opened his medicine cabinet, there were sev-eral pill bottles with prescription tags on them. That wouldn't raise an alarm if the person still occupied the apartment. But no one leaves for an extended period without their prescriptions. Upon opening, we discovered that all the bottles were filled with the same pills. We have them out for full spectrum testing, but we believe they are Lustre," Mead said. "We issued a warrant for his arrest on charges of drug trafficking"

"What have you found after a morning with the children, Gee?" Johnson asked.

"I don't believe the children have been programmed with a lot of trigger words like they respond to 'doctor'. They follow direct orders which leads me to believe they have been conditioned to absolute obedi-ence and lack of initiative," Gee said. "I guess I can relate to them because they don't have a memory. Worse than my problem by far. They know basic care and respond to language. Aside from that, they're babies."

"How do you figure that, Gee?" Mead asked.

"They listened blankly to the books I read them this morning with-out curiosity or comprehension. Until I got down to baby books. They responded to *Good Dog Carl* and *Pat the Bunny*. But even then, only when I give them explicit instructions."

"Blank slates ready to be written on," Adam said.

"By whoever owns them," Johnson agreed.

"I can't do this alone," Gee said. "I'm not even the right person to be interacting with them. They need a counselor. And a mother."

"Ellie and Julia say they don't respond to women. And you're the only man they seem not to be afraid of. I'm not sure they have a concept of 'mother'," Adam said.

"Still, I can't be with them all the time. And what am I going to tell Karen when I get home? I just can't do it."

"I understand. If it weren't for Julia at home, I'd be in the same boat," Adam said. "I think Karen should be told." He looked at Mead and Johnson. Eventually, they nodded.

"We'll tell her. She'll have to break the story in the Tuesday newspaper anyway. We just need to keep quiet until the deputies get back from their wild goose chase to Georgia," Mead said.

"We have two live leads," Johnson said. "Dr. Jones on the drugs and Larry Syre, the truck driver hauling the children and drugs. We'll be watching the roads into town and Larry's house for the next twenty-four hours. We'll get one of them. If you pull out the right block from the Jenga stack, they all fall down."

Alliances

"MAY I GO see them?" Karen rasped that evening after Mead Oliver and Brad Johnson talked to her. When she saw the two policemen at the door, her first instinct had told her something happened to Gee. She'd collapsed before they got the first word out. Mead had finally gotten through to her that they weren't there about Gee.

"We hope you will," Johnson said. "We understand that both you and Gee have jobs to do but we want to keep this as quiet as possible until the newspaper is out Tuesday morning. We need to catch the criminals and if people know we've found children, the ones responsible will go to ground. They may have already."

"We wanted to let you know where Gee has been all day so you wouldn't worry," Mead said. "And to enlist your help. I'm sorry we scared you when we showed up."

"With as many times as Gee has been injured or mistakenly arrested, I'm asking anyone who wants to talk to me to start out with the words, 'Gee is okay!' Then we can talk," Karen said.

"He's been with the children all day at our request and is making some progress," Johnson said. "He'd probably appreciate a lift home."

"I'm on my way," Karen said. She slipped on her coat and shoes and headed for the car.

SHE DROVE HOME after meeting the children, not really seeing or hearing anything. She'd watched Gee hug each child and kiss his or her head as he tucked the three into the same bed. Julia turned down the lights and prepared to take her shift on the other bed for the night.

Gee's eyes were as moist as hers when they opened the door and finally indulged themselves in the comfort of each other's arms. She sobbed against his chest.

"How could they? How could they be so cruel? Gee, what can we do? What can we do?"

"All we can do is love them and take care of them," he whispered as he breathed in the scent of her hair.

"Hold me. Take me to bed and hold me," Karen said leading him to the stairs. She'd had nothing to eat and wasn't sure she could stomach anything more than a bit of wine. Gee had eaten with the children. Karen had opened a bottle and set it by the bed before the police arrived. She poured two glasses.

"I'm so tired," Gee said with a huge yawn. "You never told me having children would be so exhausting." She gave a soft snort as she handed him his glass.

"I never intended to have triplets. But I know now, you are the right father. You're a good man, Gee. So much better than I deserve." They leaned against each other as they sat in bed. Gee took a sip of the chardonnay and sighed.

"What if I'm not?" he whispered.

"What do you mean?"

"What if I'm not a good person. Perhaps the loss of my memory was a way to escape what I've done somewhere in the past. Could I have hurt children? Could I have given children drugs or starved them like that? Karen, what if I am truly an evil person? I need to make amends. I need to find anyone I've hurt and apologize. I need…"

"Shh. Gee, it isn't like you to get upset like this. Of course you are a good man. We see evidence of it every day. The man you are up here… who doesn't remember?" she said tapping his head. "He could never overwhelm the man you are here." She moved her hand to his heart. "This man, the one I love, could never be evil. You spent an entire day reading to three little angels and trying to draw them out of their shell. I talked to Ellie when I got there and Julia was going into the room. They're as tired as you. All they could talk about was how caring and careful you were with the children."

"I don't even know why they called me," he said. "I'm just a stranger."

"The children love you. From your reading at the library on Wednesdays to your Harvest crew to your high school crews in the Wild Woods. They'd do anything if you led them. That is something extraordinary. *You* might not know why you are in Rosebud Falls, Gee, but I do. You are here to save the children."

"I don't feel like a savior," he answered his fiancée. "Wayne would be much better at this. He teaches first graders. They love him. I bet he would know what to do in this situation. Much better than I do."

"If you feel that way, call him. He's on the list the Sheriff gave us of people who know. And he's your friend. Call him."

"It's late and I'm too tired to move right now," Gee said. He kissed Karen lightly and laid his head on her shoulder. "I'll call in the morning when I've had some sleep."

Karen put her nearly untouched wine on the bedside table and turned out the light as they snuggled into the comforter and each other. In moments, they were asleep.

Arrest

"Detective, we have movement," Officer McCarran said into the phone. He'd had the overnight shift watching the Syre home. It was seven o'clock Monday morning and he'd dialed Mead's cellphone.

"What do you have."

"Syre's tractor just turned up the street toward his home."

"Let's move," Mead said. "I'm three minutes away. Get between him and the door of the house. It will be easier to take him outside than if we let him get inside the house." Mead pressed Sheriff Johnson's number as he flipped on his lights and headed toward the row of houses where the Syres lived. He could hear the sheriff's siren coming from a distance. When Mead pulled into the drive behind the truck, Larry Syre had yet to emerge from the idling rig. Mead gave a blast from his siren.

"Larry Syre!" Mead called over his loud speaker with his sidearm drawn. McCarran, following his boss's lead, moved behind the porch rail and drew his own weapon. It was an uncomfortable feeling to Mead. He seldom had his gun drawn except on the practice range. "Step out of the cab and keep your hands where we can see them!"

"What the fuck?" Larry yelled as he pushed the door open. "I haven't had anything to drink. I've been working all night." He stepped out of the cab with his hands held out as the sheriff swung in behind Mead and flung his door open to offer backup.

"You are under arrest for transporting stolen property, including a cargo of stone, across state lines," Mead called.

"That's bullshit! I took a load to Georgia and delivered it."

"The shipping order was for Florida," Mead said.

"The hell it was. I've got the bill of lading right here." Larry turned back toward his cab.

"Don't move!" Mead shouted. "You are further arrested for attempted child trafficking and transporting a controlled substance. Get down on the ground."

"Well, fuck you!" Larry yelled. He dove for the cab and spun with a shotgun in his hand. A shot rang out and Larry Syre pitched forward, the gun spinning from his hand. McCarran stood to level his gun just as the door of the house flew open and hit him in the arm. His shot rang out but the gun was jolted into the air as Roxanne Syre burst from the house.

"What's all the noise? Larry!" she screamed as she ran toward her husband. The three officers rushed forward. McCarran pushed the woman down beside her husband as Mead kicked the shotgun into the lawn. "Larry!" she cried out again. McCarran pulled the woman's hands behind her and slapped cuffs on her as Mead checked the condition of the fallen driver.

"We need an ambulance," he yelled.

"On the way!" Johnson responded as he clicked off his shoulder mike and kept his gun trained on the scene.

"What a fucking mess," Mead muttered. He rolled Larry over and pressed his hand against the wound with a wad of the driver's shirt.

Sirens screamed in the quiet of the morning as an ambulance made its way through Rosebud Falls to the community on the north side of town.

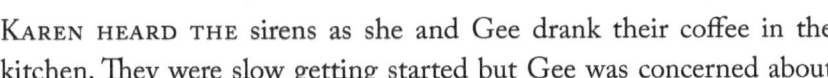

KAREN HEARD THE sirens as she and Gee drank their coffee in the kitchen. They were slow getting started but Gee was concerned about getting to the children.

"I wanted to be there when they woke up," he mumbled.

"You needed the sleep," Karen said. "So did I. Two days of labor in the woods is more physical exertion than I've had in a long time. As soon as we've eaten, I'll drive you to the hospital. Ellie or Julia will call if there is any difficulty this morning."

"I know. I just worry. We need a mother. You, Ellie, and Julia are great but…"

"I know. We aren't mothers. The silence is sure to be lifted soon and we can call for reinforcements. Even another nurse would help. The three of you can't continue working around the clock."

"I'm going to call Wayne to see if he can call in sick," Gee said. As he scrolled through his contacts, Karen's phone rang.

"Hello."

"Karen, it's Mead Oliver. *Sàmhach* has been lifted. See how soon you can get the Family heads to the hospital for a briefing. Let me know when."

Families

"WHAT'S HIS CONDITION?" Heinz Nussbaum asked after Mead told them of the arrest and shooting.

"He'll recover," Adam said. "Dr. Gaston is with him now and has re-sectioned the perforated bowel. It was a clean shot."

"And his wife?" asked Karen.

"Treated and released. We don't believe she intended to interfere in the arrest. She just heard the commotion and burst out the door," Mead said. "She's waiting in the cafeteria for word on her husband."

"Who gives a goddamn about the bastard?" David demanded. "You said he was trying to transport children. Where are they? Are they healthy? Are there more? I'm calling all foresters into the Woods for a complete search."

"Healthy?" Adam scoffed. "They're malnourished, drugged, mute, and frightened. If you ever saw pictures of the Chinese refugees who came into Seattle in shipping containers a few years ago, you'll have a pretty good picture of what we have."

"Based on conditions inside the container," Sheriff Johnson said, "we estimate they'd been concealed in it for at least three days before we found them. That would take it back to right after the foresters found the Lab Cabin. They'd already been evacuated. I doubt there are any others."

"Wayne and I spent the weekend auditing shipping records," Pàl said. "We can't identify anything else in the past month that could have held human cargo. There were two other shipments to the same location earlier in the year—one in June and one in September."

"This is sick!" David said. "That church is at the bottom of it. They're the ones with the child reclamation camp. You should roll up everyone who has anything to do with it." There were nods around the table as most considered David's option a good one.

"We can't do that," Judge Warren sighed. "You know that. Even if the church is involved, there's no evidence the members know what's going on. If Larry Syre identifies his boss, we might have a clue that lets me sign more warrants. I have to say the rest of our hope is based on finding Dr. Jones. It's looking like he's the one behind it and might even be who the cargo was destined for."

"Where's Gee?" Collin asked softly. He'd sat quietly with Violet there to support him for over an hour. It was the first meeting of Family heads he had attended in fifteen years and his voice startled the others.

"He's with the children," Karen answered. "So far, he's the only one they respond positively to."

"Now that the silence is lifted, we rushed a child psychologist up from Palmyra," Adama said. "She's observing the interactions."

"I want to see," Collin said.

"I agree," Loren said. "I want to know what our community has come to. I'd kill myself and leave the Family to my niece, Jessie, but I just can't do that to someone so young. It's our mess and we need to clean it up. Violet, I'm sorry you have to witness the Families at their lowest. Maybe we've all outlived our usefulness. I feel very, very old."

"RENEE," COLLIN WHINED as he looked through the window into the playroom where Gee was reading to the children.

"No, Collin. It isn't Renee," Karen comforted the old man. "We'll find her. I swear we will. But she disappeared fifteen years ago. This little girl isn't more than five."

"Is that what they did to my little girl?" Collin asked. "Did they destroy her mind and take away her childhood? Did they use and abuse her? Hang every one of them from the highest hickory! This evil must be purged from our Forest and Wild Woods!"

There was uncommon strength in Collin's voice and Karen wondered where it had come from. For a moment she saw a flicker of some otherworldly light in his eyes but it faded rapidly as he sagged against Violet. She led him away to take him home.

I Littlest.
Brother. Sister. Gee.
Gee let me pat the soft bunny.
Not like doctor. Doctor hurt.
Gee put me to bed with Brother and Sister.
They hold me.
I don't cry. Be quiet. Doctor will hurt.
I do what Gee say.

Observation

"THERE!" DR. SALINGER said. She was a soft woman in her early fifties and one could imagine children treating her like a grandmother. She had carefully cultivated that image over years of dealing with children's psychiatric issues. She'd seen all too many abused children in her practice. "I don't know what just happened, but the one you call Littlest just relaxed."

"She looks the same as she did before," Julia said. "Same glassy stare. Same quiet acceptance."

"Look at her hands. They were rigid. Now they're relaxed. The older two haven't made that transition yet. They respond only when directed. Now look at her face. Littlest is smiling."

"She is?"

"The muscles in her face relaxed and that indicates a smile," Dr. Salinger confirmed. "It might not be obvious but it is progress. I want to consult with the reader while the children eat their meal. Who is this again?"

"His name is Gee Evars" Julia said. "He shares a similar problem with them as he lost a huge chunk of his memory. He's spends one night a week reading to children at the library. His Harvest teams were all second and third graders who adored him. He leads high school work parties in the Wild Woods—something we've taken him away from so he could help the children. Children respond to his gentleness and caring ways. He's become a champion for them—for the whole city."

"And nothing inappropriate?"

"Not remotely. He is a fierce protector of children. And everyone else."

"The children's recovery should be guided by a trained therapist," Salinger mused. "At the same time, it would take me days—maybe weeks—to develop the rapport he has with them. I'll continue to observe and offer suggestions for now. Whatever else you do, don't call CPS. They only know one way to deal with children who have been in abusive homes and that is to split them up into foster care. That would send these children back to being vegetables."

"THEY HAVE A limited frame of reference," Gee said. "The picture books are best but I'm not even sure they know what the pictures are of."

"Very good observation," Salinger said as they ate soup in the hospital cafeteria. "I believe you need to give them more time to learn about the things you are telling them. You got good response with *Pat the Bunny*. Let's see if you can include more tactile experiences. I'll suggest some stuffed animals. Tell stories about the animals instead of trying to get them to read the stories with you. They need to learn what the animals are. You are doing a very good job, Mr. Evars."

"Please, just Gee. Everyone calls me that," he sighed. She looked at him and read his burdened posture.

"How about you, Gee?" she said softly. "How are you holding up under this burden?"

"Children are no burden," he said immediately. "Oh, I'm tired. It does require all my focus when I'm with them. But work in the Wild Woods is slowing down because I'm here. The children are just more important than the trees."

"That's a good attitude. But what about *you*, Gee. Is this bringing back any of your memories? Are you experiencing discomfort because you can't access them?" Her gentle voice was easy to trust and she saw his shoulders relax a little.

"I worry sometimes that I wasn't a good person and that is why I lost my memory. But if I can be a good person in the present, I guess that's a step in the right direction. I wonder who I was but, with Karen's help, I've seen that who I *am* is more important. I only hope that who I was never harmed anyone like these children have been harmed," Gee said.

"I know you want to get back to the children," Salinger said. "I'll continue to observe and offer pointers to you when I can, but you're doing a good job with them. Just remember, you can talk to me about your personal concerns as well as about the children. Perhaps as you help them, you will also help yourself."

Assignment

"WE HAVE A problem."

"Since when did any problem of yours become a problem of mine?" Troy snarled into his cellphone. He looked around to be sure no one was near.

"The night you decided to rape and impregnate a fourteen-year-old three years ago."

"No one could ever pin that on me."

"Just because we encouraged her to deny knowing anything and to refuse a DNA paternity test doesn't mean she won't have a change of heart. You know what that would have shown."

"I thought you took care of that permanently. What did I pay you for?"

"She's secure."

"How long are you going to hold this over me?"

"As long as it's useful. Which brings me to our problem."

"Which is?"

"The doctor who assisted us has become a liability to us all. He knows what lurks in your past and what was done to be sure it doesn't rise in the future. He's officially a missing person and if the police get hold of him, it could be disastrous."

"You can't ask me to murder someone."

"Of course not. Just eliminate the risk, Troy. If you think spending the rest of your fortune on him will keep his silence, by all means do so."

"You know that won't work," Troy sighed. If it would, he wouldn't be a problem now.

"Dr. Jones handles dangerous chemicals on a daily basis. Accidents happen and no one would miss someone of such a perverted character."

"What's in it for me?"

"Always wanting something for you," the voice on the phone sighed. "You need a wife, Troy. A young pretty one. A single mother would make her perfect in establishing you as a kind of hero. The woman I have in mind would be very compliant with your wishes and would welcome your attention. She'd worship you and attend to your every need. She's even capable of intelligent conversation if you need that on occasion. She's our greatest success. Just take care of the risk."

"Where do I find him?"

4

PATRIARCH

Farmhouse

"HRRM," MEAD CLEARED HIS THROAT as he clicked on the tape recorder. "Present at this time are Rosebud Falls Police Detective Mead Oliver, suspect Larry Syre, and attorney for the suspect, Matt Hogue. I have some questions regarding your activity this weekend and it will be much to your benefit if we can get quick answers." Larry glared at the detective.

"Where's the bad cop who shot me?"

"Larry, I've known you for a long time. Being a smartass won't help you," Mead said.

"I have instructed my client to answer and assist in your investigation as much as possible without incriminating himself," Matt said. "I may, at any time, interrupt if I deem the questioning is inappropriate." Mead nodded at the attorney.

"Mr. Syre, did you pick up a loaded flatbed at Savage Sand and Gravel on Saturday morning, November 17?"

"Yes."

"Was that trailer destined for Kissimmee, Florida?"

"No."

"Where did it go?"

"To the address on the bill of lading, idiot. Newnan, Georgia." Mead had dealt with Larry Syre, usually intoxicated, enough times over the years to ignore the insult and continue.

"What was your cargo?"

"That's on the bill of lading, too. Twenty tons of cut limestone."

"Do you know the rough shape and size of a load like that?"

"It's a big rectangle that sits on the bed of the truck. Why would I pay attention to anything but whether the load is secure and the scales tip correctly?"

"When did you receive word that you had a load waiting?"

"Friday, a little after noon."

"Is it typical for you to get a load at such short notice?"

"Yeah. They aren't that organized over there. Especially since that fairy in a skirt took over," Larry snorted. Matt shook his head and moaned but didn't interrupt.

"Who called to give you the job specs?"

"Simon Alexander. He's the second shift crew foreman. Mostly they load gravel trucks that local drivers deliver the next day."

"Is it unusual for a second shift foreman to call you at noon on a day he isn't working?"

"Nah. He knows I sleep late. And it was a quick call. Pick up and deliver. Be back by Monday morning and get a bonus."

"That's a long drive. Why didn't you leave immediately?"

"I… uh…" For the first time Larry seemed unsure of himself. "I was still hungover," he finally said. "Yeah. Never drink and drive. I hit the road as soon as I was able."

"That's all for now. Let me remind you that you are under arrest, even though you are in a hospital. You will remain cuffed to the bed and an officer is on guard outside your door. You have access to your attorney and your wife may wish to visit. Pending further investigation, we are holding you on suspicion of transporting stolen property, possession of controlled substances and paraphernalia, child trafficking, resisting arrest, and threatening an officer with a firearm. I suggest you and your attorney discuss ways in which you can cooperate with this investigation to clear your name. You will be transferred to the county jail in two hours, pending doctor's release orders." Mead turned on his heel and left the room.

"Well, fuck you very much," Larry sneered at the closed door. Matt finally broke his silence and leaned toward him.

"Larry, stick to your story. You could have been out of here and asleep at home if you hadn't pulled that stupid stunt when they arrested you. You'll have to pay for that but everything else… you're just a dupe."

"Hey."

"Sorry to say it, but you don't know anything about anything."

"I hated to throw Si under the bus."

"Makes no difference. I doubt he knows any more than you do. Or me. Just stick to what you know and don't say anything else. It's the same as when you get drunk and disorderly."

Matt left the hospital room with a tight smile on his face.

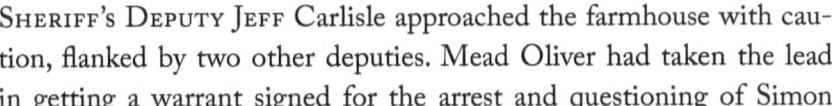

SHERIFF'S DEPUTY JEFF Carlisle approached the farmhouse with caution, flanked by two other deputies. Mead Oliver had taken the lead in getting a warrant signed for the arrest and questioning of Simon Alexander but the farmhouse was outside the city limits so the sheriff's office had to execute it.

Jeff pounded on the door and listened. The other deputies took positions at the corners of the house with their hands on their guns. No one responded.

"Anything?" Jeff asked his partners.

"All clear," both responded.

"Sheriff's Department. Open up!" Jeff shouted as he pounded on the door again. Again, there was no response. "Okay, guys. We'll have to go in. Be ready for anything." They drew their weapons. One deputy backed up Jeff while the other circled the house. The deputy with Jeff prepared to crash the door but Jeff turned the doorknob and it swung open.

The sight that met them explained the silence when they knocked. Like most farmhouses, the door opened to a combination living room-dining room. Simon Alexander sat at the table with his wife. Both were slumped over their food, a plate of cold spaghetti and meatballs. Jeff rushed to the table and checked for a pulse on the cold bodies.

"Call the coroner," he said softly.

Breaking News

CAMERON LACOE STORMED into the office of *The Elmont Mirror* in a wave of fury.

"Kelly! Get to Simon Alexander's farmhouse and find some way to get pictures! Ken, go with her and get the story. Karen? What's the status on the children story?"

"What's going on?" Axel demanded as he came out of his office.

"What's going on? We have three of the biggest stories in Rosebud Falls breaking right now and your staff is sitting on its ass. That's what's going on," Cameron shouted. Most of the staff didn't know Cameron owned the *Mirror* through his trust.

"Cam," Karen said softly. "Everyone is on task. We just intercepted the news of the raid at the Alexanders'. We didn't get advance notice like we usually do, so it must have come through the *sàmhach*. Kelly's on her way. I was going to go with her, but Ken's a good choice. We're not just sitting on our asses here."

"I want to know who ordered *sàmhach* and kept us in the dark," Cameron continued, only slightly abated. "Who cut the news outlets out of a discovery like this?"

"The Family heads know. You should talk to your grandfather. The Nussbaum," Karen rebuked him. Axel looked at the disturbed people in the office and waved to Ken and Kelly to get out the door.

"Would you at least come into the office so we don't disrupt getting this newspaper out?" he said. Cameron followed Axel and turned toward Karen when she didn't follow. She held up her hands and shook her head.

"You two are the bosses. I have to finish editing the Larry Syre arrest story and get the released details out on the children." She turned her back on the men and went to her desk. Cameron started to say something but Axel dragged him into the office and closed the door.

"What the hell gives you the right to charge into *my* office and start ordering *my* people around?" he shouted at Cameron.

"I'm the owner and publisher. This being the last to know has got to stop."

"We're never the last to know," Axel responded. "The people are the last to know because some punk asshole charges in and disrupts us getting the news out."

"Watch yourself, Axel. This punk asshole can throw your ass out of here."

"Go ahead. What will you accomplish? Are you going to sit behind this desk and edit every story, lay out the paper, and get on the press by ten? Maybe you should fire everyone and write all the stories, too. That should do a lot for people's confidence in what we report."

"We need to move to daily operation and put a person firmly on the police beat," Cameron insisted. "Things are moving too fast in Rosebud Falls for our sleepy little newspaper."

"We publish the news Tuesday through Saturday. Nothing happened over the weekend that we could have reported on Monday. We had no information about what was going on. And for good reason," Axel insisted. He was over twice Cameron's age and had been in the newspaper business his whole life. He'd never had an interfering publisher before and was just this close to quitting.

"I want to go to six days instead of five. I'd go seven if I thought we had the advertising. Those kids have been in the hospital for three days and no one knew. Gee has been there. Why didn't Karen get the news in here before the Family meeting this morning?" Cameron was settling down, though still obviously upset.

"Fine. We'll go to six days. I already have a budget. It will cost you a third of what the paper costs now to increase one day. That means we need to raise revenue by thirty-five percent. Do you want me to raise the advertising price or send someone to Palmyra to try to get the city businesses to advertise? We've already maxed out the business advertising in town," Axel said. He'd always wanted a daily paper but the numbers just wouldn't support it. "And what difference would it make? You aren't thinking of breaking the tradition of silence when it's imposed, are you? We won't get any news at all. From the story Karen got, keeping the silence may have been the only way they managed to capture the driver."

"Yeah, we'll keep the silence. But the people have a right to know what's going on in our town. We print Friday's news on Saturday and don't give another word until Tuesday. By then, it's all old news."

"There's never been more news than that," Axel insisted.

"There is now. No matter how much we try to keep a lid on it, we aren't local any longer. State police were called to investigate the Sheriff for shooting a suspect. We're all lucky it wasn't fatal. By the end of the week there will be feds here to investigate the children. And the transport of Syre's cargo—which we still don't know the contents of—is an interstate felony. Now we have dead people in a farmhouse and a missing researcher from LaRue Labs. I want to know what is happening in this town."

"That's really the issue, isn't it, Cameron. You don't know what's going on. It isn't about getting the news out to the people. Troy broadcast about the children from Karen's notes before noon today. It's all about you not knowing. You should get out of this business. It isn't your private gossip channel. You have your cousins for that."

"Troy ended his broadcast today by claiming he's been sick over the weekend and is going to Palmyra for tests. What the hell is wrong with him that can't be checked out at our hospital?"

"Nosy Families, that's what. Doesn't make a difference to the people of Rosebud Falls. You still aren't the Kardashians," Axel said. Cameron scowled at him, the wind taken out of his sails.

"Get me a daily newspaper by the end of the month, Axel. Six days a week. If you need help, hire it. If you can't do it, I'll get someone who can." He left the office as abruptly as he arrived with only a passing glare at Karen.

Here/Now

IT WAS ALREADY dark when Gee left the hospital. He looked up into the cold night sky and could see the stars through his own breath. He'd eaten with the children and then played with them after dinner until they got sleepy and he tucked them in bed.

"We've given them a light sedative with their meal," Ellie said as she led Gee away from the children's room. "Adam needs to have blood drawn and we're afraid the process might traumatize them. As soon as we know they are fully asleep, we'll draw the blood and they won't remember it at all."

"Isn't that what we're dealing with? They don't remember at all," Gee sighed. He'd kissed each child goodnight on the forehead and thought he caught a hint of a smile on Littlest's face.

Why do I care?

His thoughts raced as he contemplated the sky and slowly walked home in the darkness. Of course, everyone cared. He was no exception. He felt compelled to do more than nod his head as the doctors discussed the children's condition. He needed more than to wish for them to find a cure—whatever that might be. The first time he'd seen the children he knew he couldn't leave them to face whatever the future held by themselves. Healing? Hope? Heartache? Whatever, he would be there with them.

I have something none of the others have. I have no memory.

It seemed odd to consider the absence of something in his life to be a thing he could use to help them. He was sure they held more in their heads than had been discovered in these three intense days. When he lost his memory... Gee tried to think back but still remembered no specific events prior to entering Rosebud Falls. When he lost his *identity*, he still held fundamental knowledge he had accumulated through his life. He could read, write, do math, talk, and carry on with the habits of life. He'd even fallen in love. He was sure the children still held that spark of knowledge within them, too, even if the horrors of the life they had lived were better left buried.

"GEE? ARE YOU here, Love?" Karen called as she came up the stairs.

"In bed waiting for you" he called back. The walk in the cold and the long hot shower he'd taken did little to soothe him. But Karen...

"Oh, how I like hearing that," she laughed as she entered the room. For the first time in her life she felt like she had a reason to be home at night and was becoming resentful of the evening hours spent at the newspaper. She crossed quickly to the bed and kissed him. "I'll join you as soon as I can get ready." She headed toward the bathroom, removing her work clothing as she went.

"How were things at work?" Gee asked through the open door.

"Oh, crazy, of course. We have three competing headlines for tomorrow with the discovery of the children, the arrest of Larry Syre, and the two dead people found at the farm," she said.

"What? When did all this happen? I mean, I knew silence had been lifted and you'd be writing about the children. What else?" Gee asked.

"Oh, dear," Karen said, coming to the door with her toothbrush in hand. "You've been so focused on them you didn't even hear about the other things going on. Mead and Brad arrested Larry Syre when he rolled into his driveway this morning. There were shots fired but Syre is recovering in jail. He drove the truck that was supposed to deliver the children to some place in Georgia. Sheriff's deputies went to the house of the man who gave Larry the driving job and found him and his wife dead at the dining room table." Karen stuck the toothbrush back in her mouth and returned to the bathroom as Gee looked after her.

"So much happened!" Gee said. He waited patiently for Karen to finish in the bathroom and come to bed. "Anything else?" he asked as she cuddled next to him.

"Well, that was the news. But just after we heard about the Alexanders—the dead people—Cameron stormed into the office. I don't think most of the staff even know he owns the paper. Owners have always kept a low profile. He started shouting orders to people and hauled Axel into his office where there were more raised voices that we all tried to ignore while we did our work. When Cameron left, he yelled, 'Do it or I'll find someone who can.' Axel looked shell-shocked."

"What did Cameron want him to do?"

"Axel wouldn't say. I'm pretty sure I smelled a healthy dose of alcohol on his breath when I left the office tonight."

"Gee wrapped Karen in his arms and gave her a sip of wine. She took it gratefully.

"How are the children?" she asked.

"A child psychologist showed up today."

"Adam told us this morning in our briefing that they had an expert coming up from Palmyra. Are you being relieved?"

"No. I'm getting some good tips as to what to do when I'm with them. She's observing from outside."

"We watched you for a bit from outside after the meeting. Poor Collin. He's heartbroken. Are the tips helping?"

"I think so. Littlest smiled today."

"Oh, that's wonderful!"

"I just wish I knew what I was doing. I feel like I'm wandering around in their minds and could do so much damage if I'm not careful."

"Have you planned what you'll do tomorrow?"

"Not so much. I've been wallowing in 'why me?' I don't mean that to sound like I don't want to be doing this, but why me? Why am I… able?… at least a little… to connect to these children."

"Are you helping them remember?"

"No. I'm going to talk to the psychologist tomorrow. I'm not sure I want them to remember."

"Why not, Gee? It seems so important."

"What do they have to remember? They've been held in isolation somewhere for long enough that they could have their minds wiped with drugs and learn they had to be blindly obedient to anything they were told to do. How long was that? Certainly, no less than three months. With the age range of the children, the process could take a year or more. The most recent part of their lives was filled with discipline and abuse under the influence of drugs. Is that what we want them to remember?" Gee pleaded. The tears in his eyes broke and trickled down his face.

"Are you afraid to face your memories from before you arrived here in Rosebud Falls?" she asked as she kissed his cheek.

"No. Maybe. I don't know. It's just never seemed important to me. I found my life here. I found my love." He returned her kiss. "Being now is all I can remember as important."

"Maybe that is what you should teach the children," Karen whispered. "Teach them to be here and now like you are. If there is a purpose to things, maybe that is why you are with them. Show the children how to be here and now."

Investigation

"JUDGE WARREN AND District Attorney Mazzenga, we've completed our investigation of the discharge of weapons by Sheriff Johnson and Officer McCarran on Monday, November nineteenth," the state trooper said.

"That was fast," Warren commented. It was only Tuesday afternoon the twentieth. "Please proceed."

"In short, we find that everything was conducted according to proper procedures. Detective Oliver approached the driver with his weapon secured, per protocol. He was backed up by Sheriff Johnson and Officer McCarran, who had their weapons trained on the suspect. The suspect was warned not to move when he suddenly spun to the cab of his truck and brought a shotgun to bear on the detective. Responding to the clear danger to his fellow officer, Sheriff Johnson fired on the suspect, hitting him in the lower right abdomen. The suspect pitched forward, losing his grip on the shotgun. This has been confirmed with footage from Detective Mead's dashcam."

"What about McCarran?" District attorney Kendra Mazzenga asked.

"We have determined that McCarran did not have a clear shot on the suspect, who was partially hidden by the open door of the cab. His weapon was accidentally discharged when Mrs. Syre struck him with the storm door as she rushed out of the house. The spent bullet was recovered from a pillar on the porch. Officer McCarran is still relatively new on the force and should be given additional training in suspect apprehension and assessment of environmental threats as well as personnel threats."

"Any further recommendations?" Judge Warren asked.

"There is no reason both men cannot return to active duty unless they request time off for counseling. In that case, we recommend they receive the time off with pay. Discharging a firearm in the line of duty always has an emotional effect on the officer but both of these men seem at peace with their actions."

"Very well. Thank you, Trooper Smith."

"WHAT'S OUR CASE status?" Sheriff Johnson asked as he strode into his office Wednesday morning.

"Sheriff. Good to have you back," Jeff Carlisle said as he stood. "This chair doesn't fit me."

"I hear you filled it well. Now, where are we?"

"I have Deputy Elliott standing watch at the farmhouse as that forensics expert from Palmyra goes over the scene. Every effort was made not to contaminate the crime scene. We even spread plastic before the bodies were removed by the coroner. The preliminary report from Dr. Gaston indicates the couple was poisoned. The exact substance is not yet known. However, it must have been very fast acting as both appear to have died within moments of ingesting it. We don't have anything from forensics yet, but you've worked with Pete Remington before. He'll probably be able to tell us the vintage wine they were drinking."

"Did the coroner give a time of death?"

"Yes. He estimates they died at dinner Friday night, about seven o'clock."

"Hmm. Detective Oliver says Syre was slow getting out of the truck because he was texting Alexander to tell him the delivery was complete."

"Alexander was already dead."

"Mmmhmm. So who texted back 'Good'? Who has Alexander's cellphone?"

"I'll call Deputy Elliott and have him check the premises. There was no cellphone listed in the effects of the deceased."

THE ALEXANDER FARMHOUSE was outside Mead's jurisdiction but he and Brad Johnson had worked so closely coordinating city and county operations that it was only natural for him to accompany the sheriff out to the farm.

"What do you think of all this, Mead?" Johnson asked.

"The investigation? I think someone is working overtime to throw us off."

"Syre?"

"No. He's brawn, not brain. He's well-known in the jail from previous arrests, mostly on drunkenness and domestic violence. He'll get six months for resisting arrest. That's about the best we can hope for him. I don't think he had any idea what he was transporting," Mead said. "His attorney, Matt Hogue makes me uncomfortable."

"Something shady?"

"Just reputation. He used to be General Counsel for Savage Sand & Gravel before the takeover. Now he's set up an independent practice in town and was right on the spot to represent Syre. He could be covered in mud or just slippery as hell. Either way, I don't trust him."

"Well, here we are," Johnson said, pulling into the long driveway of the Alexander farmhouse. "Let's take a look inside."

"This place is sure isolated," Mead said when he stepped out of the car and looked around. "It's easy to forget how much open country there is around our little city."

"Yes. The new annexation gets it a little closer, but once you hit the county roads, the population density drops drastically."

"That would be the border of the Wild Woods back there, wouldn't it?" Mead asked, pointing at a line of trees visible from the house. Johnson nodded. "I wonder if there is an access point from here."

"It wasn't suicide," Pete Remington said. "They didn't poison themselves. There was nothing in the food. Of course, we'll have to wait for the coroner's report before we know what toxin we're looking for. But there is other evidence."

"Like?" Johnson and Mead were being led through the house on a plastic mat that had been laid down from the front door to the kitchen.

"Mrs. Alexander was a meticulous housekeeper. Notice how the carpet stands in the living room with the vacuum marks still in place? You can see on the other side of the mat that the same marks continue through the dining room and under the table. Notice how they are flattened and trampled around this end of the table?"

"That's where they were found, right?"

"Right. But look there, under the table. The area under that third chair is just as matted and flattened as the area under the chairs where the bodies were found. This leads me to believe a third person was at dinner with them."

"Where's the third person's food?" Mead asked.

"Exactly," Remington continued. "Remnants of it are in the garbage disposal." They continued into the kitchen. A white sheet on the floor in front of the sink displayed a disassembled garbage disposal. Remington opened a cabinet and pointed at wine glasses. "Notice anything strange about this display?"

The two policemen looked. Mead's left eye squinted and the corner of his mouth pulled back.

"The glasses in the front row are right side up while the rest are upside down," he said.

"Someone who didn't know Mrs. Alexander's methods replaced the wine glasses the wrong way," Remington acknowledged.

"Mightn't she just keep glasses in front that were often used?" Johnson asked.

"Certainly. But that would only account for two glasses, not three. And, while I haven't dusted them, you can clearly see that these three glasses have no fingerprints. They've been washed, polished, and put away without so much as a partial print on them."

"Gloves?"

"Undoubtedly. But you can see from here that all the other glassware in the cabinet has at least a partial print." Remington shined an ultraviolet light on the glassware and the difference was obvious. "And there are no gloves under the sink or in the trash."

"Let's reconstruct this," Johnson said. "The Alexanders had a guest, someone they knew, for dinner. That person poured poisoned wine that the Alexanders consumed but he didn't. When they collapsed at their places, the perpetrator collected the glasses and wine bottle, dumped his own plate of food in the garbage disposal, washed the dishes while wearing gloves, put the glasses away wrong, and finally took the gloves and wine bottle with him. Probably with Simon Alexander's cellphone. That's a lot of speculation based on only a few clues, Pete."

"I can only give you the evidence and summarize what I think it points to," he answered. "Some of it probably doesn't mean a thing. Like Mrs. Alexander using the exact same cleaning products that were used to scrub down the cabins in the woods."

Big Plans

"TOMORROW IS THANKSGIVING Day. Do you have special plans for the children?" Dr. Salinger asked Gee as they sat together in the cafeteria. Gee had begun to evolve a routine in which he left the children alone for a while and then returned. Of course, Ellie or Julia remained nearby but interactions with the nurses were still reserved. When Gee left the room, the children tended to sit quietly.

"I scarcely have a plan when I walk into the room, let alone a day ahead," Gee chuckled. "Any suggestions?"

"Don't subject them to a big family gathering with a lot of new people. You didn't intend that, did you?"

"No, I wouldn't think of it. But I should check with my fiancée to see if she has a traditional family meal. I haven't had time to ask," Gee said.

"Perhaps she would join you here to eat a nice celebratory meal with the children. Not elaborate, but enough to mark it as an occasion," Salinger suggested.

"That sounds wonderful. I'll talk to Ellie about getting a special meal sent up. I'm sure Karen would love an intimate family celebration."

"You're already considering these children part of your family, aren't you?" she asked softly. "I can see it in your eyes. I'd caution you against it, but experience tells me that would be a wasted effort."

"I just want to help them."

"I've been a child psychologist for thirty years, Gee. I've met many children I wanted to adopt."

"I'd like that but Karen and I aren't even married yet. They need a mother. But Karen has a career and I've been asked to become a full-time forester."

"And you are on call as City Champion," Salinger added. "I'm not saying you couldn't adjust your lives to make an adoption successful but adding three special needs children to a new relationship is more stress than any couple needs. And, Gee, what happens the next time an orphan comes to town or the next time you rescue one from the woods? Do you think you could adopt them all?"

Gee shook his head sadly and went back to play with the children.

<hr />

"Of course I want to have Thanksgiving dinner with the children!" Karen said when they were home in the evening. "How shall we arrange it? I need to go shopping."

"Ellie is arranging the meal with the cafeteria. They do something special for patients. We've adjusted the height of a table for their room and it's almost comfortable for both the children and adults."

"As to other Family celebrations," Karen sighed, "we haven't had a moment free to talk about such mundane things."

"Your family is scarcely mundane," Gee laughed.

"Well, all the drama aside, Ben can't take another big family gathering. As a dutiful heir, however, I should… *we* should stop in to see him and pay our respects. Leah, of course, has invited us to dinner with her family. I understand Levi has consented to return for the holiday since the matter of an heir has been settled. He made it clear before he left for college that he had no interest in anything Family-related."

"I do like Jude and Laura," Gee said.

"You like the strangest," Karen laughed. "The poet and the grave keeper. They were made for each other." She spent a moment kissing her fiancé as they relaxed before bed, getting lost in the warmth of his embrace. "All the other Families have issued an invitation for us to join them at some point during the day. You don't want to accept all those, do you?"

"No one will be offended if we don't, will they? I'd rather not spend the day doing politics. I need some time to walk in the Forest and the Wild Woods. Not for work, but…"

"She has her fingers tangled in your hair," Karen said softly as she ran her own fingers over Gee's short hair. "The Forest is like a mistress and you miss her. I understand. When I was working out there this weekend I felt truly at peace. I kept thinking I need to spend more time out there with the trees."

"They inspire loyalty," Gee mused. "Even the kids who volunteer feel it and give up time they could spend doing teen things to spend time there. The students at Flor del Día practically live in the Forest and over half the foresters were once residents there."

"It must be something in the air."

"I sound like a mystic when I say I can feel them. But this week I've felt increasingly that I need the trees' advice on dealing with the children," Gee said.

"I saw a tree a few days ago. I was at Collin's house and I know I was hallucinating while leaning against his Family tree," Karen said. "I was going to tell you about it and in the rush of things, it slipped my mind. Now I can't grasp the image fully. I just know it was a tree and it was important."

"Let's plan on an early lunch with the children before we visit Ben and go to dinner at Leah's. I'll stop and see the children again so they get used to me coming and going and not being abandoned. Then I'm going for a walk in the Wild Woods."

"You are such a good father to them, Gee. To all the children of Rosebud Falls."

Thanksgiving

"Look!" Ellie exclaimed softly when Gee and Karen entered the children's room. She pointed toward the bathroom. The three children were washing their hands.

"They went to the bathroom?" Karen asked. "Is that unusual?"

"They went without being told," Ellie whispered. "They were sitting quietly in their… um… waiting mode, I guess. Then Littlest tugged at Sister's hand and pointed to the bathroom. I'd been reading and didn't glance up when they looked over at me. I was about to suggest they go to the bathroom when all three got up and walked in, did their business, and washed their hands."

"That's wonderful!" Gee said. "It's the first sign of independent action we've seen since they crawled into bed together. Thank you for giving them room to act."

The children turned from the bathroom and spotted Gee. For a moment they looked frightened and hurried to stand in a line in front of him. Gee dropped to his knees and hugged each of the children to him.

"I'm so proud of you," he said. The children tentatively hugged him back but Littlest gripped him with as strong a hug as she could manage. "Look! I've brought Karen with me. She's going to have lunch with us." Gee pulled Karen down next to him and gave her a hug. She turned to the children who looked at Gee. Then Littlest hugged Karen. Sensing Gee's approval, the other two followed.

The meal, when it arrived, was simple but included typical Thanksgiving fare. Karen and Gee kept conversation going all through the meal, including the children as if they were responding. Karen reached across the table and wiped a drip of gravy from Brother's chin. He was startled for a moment but when she laughed, he smiled at her.

"We are so thankful we found you," Gee said, smiling at the children.

"We're glad you are safe and we can be with you," Karen added.

"Who wants pumpkin pie for dessert?" Gee asked. The children had eaten everything set before them. Gee wondered if they were still hungry or if they were overfull.

"Oh, me! I do!" Karen laughed, bouncing up and down. The children looked at her and then all mimicked her, holding up a hand and bouncing on their seats. Eyes popped open when they took their first bites. It was a new taste for all of them. For the first time, the children finished eating before the adults.

Gee moved over to their reading spot and Karen settled on the floor to lean against him. The children watched, uncertain what was expected of them but not receiving any direct instructions. Finally, Littlest ran across the room and crawled into Gee's lap. He wrapped his arms around her and held her. The older children looked uncertain until Karen held out her arms and beckoned them. Brother entered her outstretched arms and she took his light weight onto her lap. Sister cuddled under Gee's arm and held Littlest's hand.

"Sister, please give me Felix the cat," Gee said. Sister immediately scrambled in the toys to find the stuffed toy. "and can you give me Rover the dog?" She looked at him and he nodded. She returned with the stuffed dog. Once he had the two stuffed animals, Gee began storytelling—a dialog between Felix and Rover about what they had to eat. Gee used the toys to investigate each of the children to see if they'd left any crumb around. They were delighted when Gee had Rover lick Karen's chin to get pumpkin off it. Brother looked up and pointed to his chin as well.

As usual after a meal, the children began to get sleepy. Gee wondered if it was something they'd been conditioned to. He and Karen carried the sleepy children to bed and tucked them in.

"I'll be back later," Gee said as he kissed each head. "Tell Ellie or Julia if you need anything. Have happy dreams."

They met Julia outside the door.

"Aren't you having Thanksgiving Dinner with your family?" Gee asked.

"Later. I wanted to give Ellie a break so she could enjoy the day. You know, she hasn't said anything specific but I think she has a boyfriend."

"You two are spending so much time here!" Karen said. "We need to get you some relief."

"Oh, now that the secret is out, we have support from the rest of the nursing staff for this ward. Ellie and I take turns during our day on the normal shift and usually leave when Gee is with the children. We have a night nurse who sits in the rocking chair while the children are asleep. They need a nanny."

"Or a mother. I don't think the investigation is revealing any relatives," Gee said. "I'm glad you're getting some time off. Being on duty every day can be draining."

"Says the man who has been on duty every day," Julia laughed. "Don't worry, Gee. We're going to do everything we can to get these children healthy."

THE EARLY MEAL with the children gave Karen and Gee plenty of time to visit Ben Roth before they joined Leah and her family. Karen had made weekly visits to the old man since being named his heir and reported on the happenings of the week as he sat in stoic silence. Today, he sat in his accustomed chair, back straight and both hands on the head of his cane. His tired eyes, however, spoke of a life nearing its end.

"There's been a lot happening this week," Karen said. "When the silence was lifted, the…"

"Yes," the old man interrupted. "I've read the newspaper. You're doing a good job with these children?" he asked Gee.

"I'm doing my best. I believe we're making progress. They smile more."

"Good. I'm glad you're here for them. Karen?" he barked.

"Yes, sir." The habit of snapping to attention before the old man seemed ingrained in her.

"Do you regret being made the Roth heir?"

"I don't think so. It is a heavy responsibility but with Gee's and Leah's help, I'm adjusting. I might need to cut back at the newspaper, though. There's too much else to do." Gee looked at her in surprise. It was the first he'd heard she was thinking of cutting back.

"Gee is your spiritual partner. Leah will handle the business. Leah is a good woman and will support you well, as she has me. I believe you'll lead the Family wisely… better than I did. But I don't think you have the business savvy that's needed."

"I agree, Ben. I want to keep Leah handling the business as long as possible."

"But she's aging just like the rest of us," Ben declared. "She has years ahead of her unless she gets tired of it, but you need to train someone to take over that aspect."

"Someone?"

"Jo Ransom. The girl is quick and intelligent. If you have Leah train her, you will always have a good counselor at your side. Do that."

"I'll do what you want," Karen answered. "Will Leah take her on?"

"She knows her sons are a waste of air as far as the Family business goes. Not her fault. That goy she married. When you see them this afternoon, though, please ask Levi to stop by before he leaves town again. I want him to know he has my blessing. He will be a fine doctor."

"I'll do that. Speaking of which, we'd better go. Leah's expecting us soon."

"Is there anything you need, Mr. Roth?" Gee asked. "I'm happy to help you if you want to move someplace or if you need anything."

"You're a good boy, Gee. My keeper, Irma, will be at my side before the door has closed behind you. She handles me quite well. I suspect I will spend some time sitting on the veranda overlooking the river. When you move here, you'll come to love it as much as I do."

"Do you really think we should move over here?" Karen asked. "Jo could inherit the mansion."

"Show some sense, girl. Give Jo your house if you must. Then fill this one with children. There have not been children here in too many decades."

Gee and Karen left.

"I NEVER THOUGHT I'd see the day when a Weisman sat down to a meal with the Roth-Augellos," Levi said when he greeted Karen and Gee. "I welcome the new head of Family Roth."

"Oh, the lions and lambs have been sleeping together," Karen laughed. "How are you cousin? I haven't seen you in years."

"Oh, you know. Happy to be out of Rosebud Falls. And happier still that the inheritance is set."

"And med school?"

"Kicking my ass from county to county," Levi answered. "But I love it. It might put me someplace where I can eventually do some good with my life."

"Good attitude. Levi, this is my fiancé, Gee Evars. Gee, my cousin, Levi." Gee extended his hand and Levi grasped it firmly.

"I've heard a lot about you," Levi said. "You're famous even in Syracuse."

"That's a long way for my name to have traveled."

"Oh, there's quite a Rosebud Falls fan club up there. For some reason, Syracuse University attracts a lot of the local kids who are university-bound. Especially those from Flor del Día. I think there is some kind of arrangement between the two schools."

"Is that where you went, Karen?"

"No. I went the other direction to CUNY to study journalism. Cameron LaCoe went to Syracuse with his cousin Krystal, though. Then he breezed through their law school."

"And there's a med school there, too?" Gee asked.

"Not as part of the University, but nearby at Upstate Medical University. That's who owns my life at the moment," Levi laughed. "Mother is going to be displeased if I detain you any longer instead of ushering you straight into the *chavurah*." Levi led them into the house where his brothers and their partners had gathered with Don. Leah came from the kitchen to greet the couple. In a few minutes, Gee had been given a yarmulke and they stood around the table as Jude, the most traditional of the brothers, gave the blessing.

The gathering was sociable. Laura, Jude's fiancée, was quiet as always but opened up when Leah started asking questions about their upcoming wedding.

"Rabbi Schlesinger has agreed to perform the ceremony on New Year's Day. I'm meeting with him once a week to get indoctrinated," Laura said. They laughed and Gee saw some of the lightheartedness that was hidden deep inside Laura. He wondered if she would continue to be the groundskeeper at the cemetery on the hill after she was married.

"Don't you have a priest or minister or something that wants to be involved?" Levi asked. Laura smiled at her future brother-in-law.

"The Lazoracks have a mixed heritage that has seen nearly every brand of religion in the world at one time or another," she said. "So, this time it's Jewish. Jessie and Jonathan were married under the wedding tree at Harvest with our resident flyer here," she nodded toward Gee. His plunge from the tree during the wedding was almost legendary by now. "We thought a nice private wedding would be a relief after that."

"Speaking of which," Don said, "when is the resident flyer taking our heiress to wed?" Joseph's wife, the teenaged Judith, openly scowled at Karen. She'd married the much older brother expecting he would inherit the Family leadership and wealth.

"We don't want to detract from Laura and Jude's wedding," Gee said. "Karen is expected to have the other Family heads present at her wedding. We thought we would wait until spring so we can be married out of doors."

"In the Forest," Karen clarified. "We might not wait until Harvest but we want our nuptials to be in the Forest. Gee practically lives there already."

"I understand these children they found are putting demands on your time," Leah said. "How are the poor things?"

"Traumatized. Reclusive. Silent. We're making progress but it's slow. I'm going to try increasing their socialization next week by inviting some other children to play. At the moment, 'play' is a new concept to them," Gee said.

"I'd love to meet them," Leah said, "but I suspect it is too early to have a Looky Lou come in. I wouldn't know what to say to a child who didn't speak or respond. Just know that if there's anything we can do to help, we're here."

"That means a lot, Leah," Gee said. "We're learning about how parents relate to autistic children. We simply behave as if they were completely normal and let them find their own way to respond. We got smiles from all three children this morning."

"Smiles," Karen said fondly. "And after a week, that seems like such a huge step."

"Are you going to adopt them?" Jude asked. Karen and Gee sighed in unison.

"It would require a huge shift in our lives to accommodate three children with special needs when we aren't even married yet," Gee said. "I just hope they'll be given a home where we are still welcome to participate in their lives."

A glance passed between Jude and Laura, but Gee found the expressions of the philosopher/poet and the grave keeper hard to read.

A Walk in the Woods

AFTER STOPPING BACK at the hospital to read to the children for a bit, Gee excused himself to go for a walk. The children had been introduced to the television and were watching Winnie the Pooh movies. Gee hated to think the television could become their babysitter but it expanded their exposure to the world from what he could provide himself. Dr. Salinger recommended the playlist.

He stopped at home to pick up his walking stick. Since there was a Friday morning newspaper, Karen had to go in to the office but didn't expect to be late. Even in a small city like Rosebud Falls, the Black Friday advertising had to go out. He headed across the bridge and out of town into the Forest with no specific direction in mind. A few kids were playing a game of touch football at Flor del Día and Gee paused to watch their carefree activity. He wondered what they'd had for their holiday meal. Or perhaps Thanksgiving dinner was served there in the evening. *Is Flor del Día an option for the rescued children?* Over 200 children were resident at the orphanage school and Gee had worked with many of them in the woods. They seemed generally happy and as well-adjusted as kids without parents could be. *Why did he never hear of an adoption of one of the orphans?*

Gee walked down the newly cut paths through the Wild Woods to the quarry. The chain-link fence surrounding the open pit was rusted and broken down in many places, including where Karen had been kidnapped and Rena Lynd pushed into it. Some million cubic yards of rose limestone had been taken from the quarry in the centuries since Rosebud

Falls was settled. The pit was now filled with water up to about twenty feet from the top edge and had not been mined for over fifty years.

Gee returned to the rough paths, knowing there was far more mystery in the area than he would ever comprehend. And perhaps he should not try. Like himself, what was important for Rosebud Falls was what the Wild Woods was now, not what had been fifty years ago.

The trail tapered off at a stand of young trees growing close together. The understory was less dense, consisting mostly of saplings and shrubs. Gee recognized the distinctive red berries of stunted holly trees and other shrubbery. What was lacking were the thorny berry bushes and twisting vines they encountered elsewhere. This made pushing his way through the undergrowth easier.

Before he realized he was off the path, Gee was deep in the fallen leaves of the larger hickory trees, stepping around the denser shrubs and between the straight trunks of the younger trees waiting for an opportunity to extend into the canopy. It was warmer in this area of the woods than in the Forest or outer woods. The tangle of branches and limbs overhead would be impenetrable in the summer but now with the leaves fallen, the sun cast latticework shadows on the forest floor. Gee paused to drink from his water bottle and looked around, realizing he could no longer see the cleared path behind him nor identify the route he had used to reach this point. The sudden awareness of his environment sent a prickle of fear down his spine. It was late in the afternoon and only a couple of hours of daylight remained.

Gee pushed on, searching for the path he had followed but not finding it. The understory and trees were thinning, though, and even if he had gone the wrong direction, Gee was certain he would come out of the woods eventually. He could hike around it to get back to town. After all, the Wild Woods was not infinite.

THE TREE WAS in front of him before he realized the saplings had given way to ferns and mulch. The Tree was massive—not that he could tell if it was any taller than the others but the bole seemed to be a twisted mass of trunks that had grown together into a single stem close to five feet across. It had the look of great age about it.

Gee walked around the tree, ducking beneath one of its lower branches that nearly dragged on the ground. Careful pruning over more than a hundred years had eliminated low-hanging limbs from the trees in the Forest. Here in the Wild Woods, however, they were not uncommon. A twisted multiple trunk like this tree's would have been removed many years ago. It would not even make good lumber. It would be turned into chips and charcoal. But here was a tree which had grown wild and free for a hundred years. Perhaps hundreds of years. Its rough surface told the story of a time before settlers had arrived in Rosebud Falls.

Gee simply stared at The Tree, unable to collect his own thoughts in the presence of such age and power. This was what had drawn him to the heart of the Wild Woods. It was what drove the effort to chart paths into this last unplumbed section. He was in the presence of the Patriarch of the Forest and the Wild Woods. This was where it had started.

Finally, he moved forward and reverently placed his hands on The Tree, leaning his staff against it. He wasn't sure what he expected. The grandfather tree of the Forest that gave him a nut had spoken to him… or he dreamed it had. He carried a piece of it as his walking stick. It had brought Karen back to consciousness and she, too, had heard it speak. Hallucinations, according to Dr. Poltanys. They had heard so many stories of the Forest and had such reverence for it that hallucinations would naturally bring it to life. The experience was mystical but intensely personal. The Forest had not given them any new or useful information.

If the Patriarch spoke to Gee now, it was in a language so ancient and obscure that he could not sense it. He breathed deeply of the scent of the tree and the decaying mulch that surrounded it. At the edge of its canopy grew the younger, straighter trees amidst the short and bushy holly and dogwood. He sighed and sat beneath the tree, drinking again from his water bottle.

A nut fell from the tree into his lap. He looked up and could see no other nuts on its branches, nor could he see windfall on the ground. The thin shell cracked between his finger and thumb. Gee picked the meat out and ate it, washing it down with the remaining water. He sat waiting. Listening for the voice of The Tree in his mind. Watching for the hallucinations to begin or the poison to claim him.

Eventually, he slept.

WHEN GEE WOKE, it was dark. His phone said it was only six o'clock. If all went well at the office, Karen would be home soon. He was confident now that he could find his way out of the Wild Woods in the dark. Where this confidence came from was irrelevant to him.

He grasped his staff and turned to face The Tree. He bowed to it and in that moment a voice burst within his head. There had been no mystic revelations he could associate with the nut until the overwhelming presence of The Tree broke through his consciousness.

I will call my children home.

5

LEVAYAH

Recruiting Mommy

"PANZA RESIDENCE, this is Marian," the bright voice on the phone said. "Marian, this is Gee. How are you?"

"Oh, Gee! How nice to hear from you. I hope you had a good Thanksgiving. Things here are bright. We just announced to the family that we're expecting another child. I planned to call you today," she answered. Marian and Nathan Panza had been the first friends Gee made in Rosebud Falls when he saved their son, Devon, from the Rose River. They had given him a home and a job, and through no real fault of their own had also told him he had to leave. Nonetheless, their friendship had survived and Gee saw Devon each Wednesday evening at the library reading time.

"That's wonderful Marian! I'm so happy for you."

They celebrated on the phone, Karen adding her congratulations as well.

"Did you want to talk to Nathan?" Marian asked.

"Not just at the moment," Gee answered. "Actually, I need some advice and perhaps some help."

"Of course! Whatever we can do."

"Did you read about the children recovered in the woods?"

"Yes. How awful. I'm so glad they were found. Have you met…" Marian broke off suddenly. "Oh! Did *you* find them, Gee? The story was a little short on details. Are you okay?"

"I'm fine, though a little tired," Gee said. "I wasn't the one who discovered them but I've been helping them. I spend a lot of time each day reading and trying to understand them. Marian," Gee struggled to keep his voice calm even though tears welled in his eyes whenever he spoke of the children, "they are five to eight years old physically. Mentally, they're babies. They've never known a mother. I hate to ask so much of you, but would it be possible for you and Devon to have a play date with them? I'm not sure they've ever known another child."

"At the hospital, Gee? I'll be there at ten."

"A BOLD MOVE, Gee," Dr. Salinger said as they watched Marian and the children through the observation window. I wholly agree with bringing in the mother but I wouldn't have thought of bringing her son with her. It might have been risky to introduce the children to another child."

"Devon is a pretty capable three-year-old," Gee said. "Here's what I was thinking: As far as we know, the children have never known or don't remember knowing a mother. So how would they distinguish Marian from just another nurse or woman who brings food? By having Devon with her, they get the concept of mother and an example of how a child acts with a mother."

"I can't argue with that. And Devon seems relaxed with them even though they aren't speaking."

"He has a joy in life that is hard to match."

"I understand he was your introduction to Rosebud Falls."

"I guess you could say that."

"Does it anger you that he caused the loss of your memory?" Dr. Salinger often asked Gee questions about his own life and seemed devoted to helping him come to terms with his role in the lives of the children. But Gee was puzzled by this question.

"He what?"

"You dove into a river to save him and came out with a little boy and no memory. Doesn't that bother you?" she asked.

"Oh, I see. No, not particularly," Gee answered. He had learned to respond to the psychologist's questions as honestly as possible. He'd struggled with feelings of doubt in the past weeks. She helped him see what kind of man he was. "I don't know if I had any memory before that. I do remember back as far as walking into town that day. Perhaps it was crossing the city limits that erased my memory and if I just left town it would return. Dr. Poltanys says there was no physical trauma that would cause my memory loss. It's just another of life's mysteries."

"You are so calm about having a piece of your life missing."

"Karen has commented about what she sees as a lack of concern for my past. I *do* question it sometimes. First, whether I am suffering from this loss as a way of coping with some terrible thing I did in my past."

"Fundamentally, a loss of memory would not change the kind of person you are," Dr. Salinger assured him.

"I guess the only other thing I'm concerned with is whether I have hurt someone by disappearing from their life. The book I carried into town was inscribed, 'Love, Rae'. I'm sad that someone out there cared for me and I can't let her or him know I'm okay."

They watched Devon take Sister's hand and guide it to the stuffed bear Marian held. Sister smiled at Devon and brought Littlest to the bear.

"Look at him," Gee said. "Even if foolishly diving into an unknown river to rescue him caused my memory loss, wouldn't you give up *your* life to save him?"

Forest Management

THE LONG-AWAITED SNOWSTORM struck late Friday night and snow continued to fall in fat wet blobs Saturday morning. It was more like having snowballs thrown at the windshield than flakes. Karen calmly held her Lincoln firm on the narrow road to the foresters' office. They had stopped briefly at the hospital to tell the children Gee would be back to have dinner with them. Before they settled into their quiet wait-ing mode, as Julia called it, Marian and Devon had arrived with a new batch of books and toys.

"Do you think anyone will show up to volunteer this morning?" Karen asked.

"We are," Gee chuckled. "I just want to see what the forest looks like in the snow. I'm sure someone will want to go for a walk with us.

If not, we'll go. I've something amazing to show you that I discovered Thursday."

Three other vehicles were parked at the office. Karen and Gee stomped the snow off their boots in the entry. Jessie and Jonathan were in the office along with much of Gee's normal crew. Drake Oliver talked to Alyson and Shannon. JD and Jeanie were glaring at each other from opposite sides of the room. In a corner of the office, Gabe leaned his chair back against the wall as he sipped coffee and watched the kids' interactions.

"I don't think we're going to get much cutting done today," Jonathan said as Gee and Karen shook off the snow. "Your crew here has more enthusiasm than sense."

"I'm proud of my crew," Gee said, smiling at the kids. "I've never been in the Forest during snowfall. I'd like to see how the canopy affects the ground coverage. If you and Jessie are willing to teach us today, we'll try not to throw snowballs at you." The teens let out a disappointed groan.

"Snowballs are half the fun," Jeanie said.

"Just remember who's carrying the GPS and can get you out of the Wild Woods," Jessie joked at her. "I think Gee's got a great idea but you all need to gear up with essentials. Let's get your equipment and check to make sure everyone is ready for wet and cold."

As the kids got ready, Gee talked quietly to Gabe.

"I found something out there Thursday," he said. "It's so incredible to me, I'm still having trouble believing it was real." Gabe brought all four feet of his chair to the floor and looked at Gee. His silence was all the encouragement Gee needed to continue. "Off in the southeast section where we've been pushing with small paths, there's a stand of straight young hickory that grow four to seven feet apart. You can walk between them but you can't see past the next tree. They open up on a clearing—a single tree with a canopy so dense that even without leaves, the sunlight barely makes it through. One Tree. It's huge." Gee's eyes unfocused as he saw the old tree in his mind's eye. Gabe stood and went to the map table.

"Where?" he demanded. Gee checked the coordinates he'd entered on his phone's GPS and pointed at the map.

"We've been cutting paths all around it but never getting to it," he said.

"I think I'll take a walk in the snow with you all this morning," Gabe said as he reached for his coat.

———————⋖◆⋗———————

WITHOUT COMMENTING ON where they were headed, Gabe gently guided the nature walk into the Wild Woods. Jessie and Jonathan explained a bit about how the terrain affected the growth patterns of the trees and could also be used to estimate productivity of a region under cultivation. Gabe occasionally pointed at an invasive plant and had one of the kids cut it back. By noon, the snow had stopped falling and the sky was clearing. Sunlight on the snow was blinding, but the farther into the Wild Woods they went, the less snow was on the ground.

"Gosh. It didn't snow as much back here," Drake said. Jessie laughed.

"I think just as much snow fell here as in the Forest," she said.

"Did it melt faster?"

"No, but if it's not on the ground, where would it be?" Jonathan asked. Drake looked up into the branches just in time to catch a face full of snow sliding off the upper limbs.

"One of the dangers we have out here is the canopy is so dense that snow and ice will stay on top. This is the first storm of the winter, so the amount of snow caught on the branches weighs considerably less than leaves and nuts would in the summer," Gabe instructed. "Let's stop at this cabin to warm up and have our lunch." The foresters had hauled propane tanks and heaters to each of the cabins, preparing for continued work in cold weather. They no longer had any intention of stopping the exploration and mapping of the Wild Woods because of cold weather.

"I suppose that face full of snow I caught was just a warning," Drake said. "If we get a lot of snow and if it freezes, that could have hurt."

"One of the reasons we always wear hard hats when we're working out here," Jonathan said.

"Snow and ice are dangerous not only because it falls, but branches will break under the weight" Jessie added. "Even if they don't make it to the ground during the winter, they create a hazard in the summer when a good wind could knock them out of the trees. That's one of the reasons we patrol the Forest all winter, watching for danger signs."

"Our purpose in the Forest is not only to guarantee the health and productivity of the trees but to assure a safe working environment for the volunteers. If we hadn't felt such urgency to find the cabins and rescue any remaining children, we would not have risked so many volunteers in the Wild Woods," Jonathan said.

"Do you think there are still people... children living out here, Gee?" Alyson asked. Gee shook his head.

"Why are we pushing so hard to investigate and cut paths?" Drake asked.

"Gee had a feeling it was important," Gabe interrupted before Gee could respond. "In the Forest, we trust feelings." They turned off the heater and packed their garbage. "Lead on, Gee," Gabe said. Gee found the path he had followed two days before and set off. Soon it ended and Gee searched for signs of where he had worked his way between the saplings. The Tree was like a magnet to him. He heard the others gasp as he broke into the clearing under its canopy. Even Jonathan and Jessie clung to each other. Gee saw tears in Gabe's eyes.

"I dreamed of this," Karen whispered. "I thought it was a dream. I tried to tell you about it but we were working crazy hours and then we found the children. The vision started to fade and I couldn't remember what I needed to tell you."

"It's the Patriarch," Gabe whispered. "We all assumed it had been cut or died more than a century ago. Instead, it was hidden."

"What's a patriarch?" Shannon asked.

"The origin tree," Gabe said. "It's where the Rose Hickory started."

"You mean the whole Forest started here?" JD asked. "Cool!"

AFTER THE INITIAL awe passed, the kids wanted to explore and put what they'd learned to use. They hadn't brought calipers and the equipment wouldn't have been large enough to measure the DBH of the massive tree. Alyson and Drake stood on opposite sides of the trunk with arms outstretched. Jeanie and Shannon measured the distance between them. JD entered the measurement on the geocaching software. Five feet, seven inches. He captured the coordinates more precisely than Gee had been able to on his cellphone.

"We need to cut about two-thirds of these surrounding trees," Jonathan said. "They'll make great lumber as straight as they are but they're too close together to ever bear nuts in any quantity."

"No," Gee said flatly. "None of them get cut."

"Gee, good forest management requires that we not leave these so densely packed together. We'll preserve as much as possible and harvest the rest," Jessie said. Gabe was shaking his head but it was Gee who responded.

"No," he repeated firmly. "This is not the Forest, managed for maximum output. This…" he touched one of the straight trees surrounding the Patriarch. It had no limbs less than ten feet from the ground. "… These trees are not Forest plantings. They are the direct children of the Patriarch. They are older than they look because to some extent their growth has been stunted. But they are not fourth or fifth generation trees. These are first generation."

"Transplanting," Gabe said. "I agree with Gee. These trees are far more valuable than the board feet of lumber they represent. I agree the area needs to be thinned, though probably not to the extent you estimate, Jonathan. But we can't lose these trees. They could completely revitalize the Forest."

"And expand it," Alyson agreed. "We've been talking at school about how to expand the Forest. We even have a group that spends study hall with plat maps of the entire county to see where we can plant more trees."

"Attempting to remove these trees could significantly damage the roots of others nearby," Jonathan said. It was clear he was unconvinced. Usually the roots of cut trees were left in the ground to compost without disturbing the soil. With large trees cut in the Forest, they often hollowed out the stump and planted a seedling right in the same root ball.

"Air compressor," Gabe said. "I read an article not long ago about a tree doctor in Minnesota who was concerned about damaging roots when attempting to vaccinate trees against invasive pests. The treatment had to be delivered deep in the root system but digging with shovels was prone to leave nicks in the epidermis and make the tree even more vulnerable to infection. He developed an air blade using a compressor. He moves the dirt with forced air. It has some problems to be worked out, but we could feasibly dig deep enough around a tree's root ball to lift it out of the ground with little or no damage to surrounding trees."

"It sounds like it's going to take some time," Karen said.

"Years," Gabe responded.

———————⊰◆⊱———————

"WEDDING," KAREN SAID as she lay next to Gee in the aftermath of their loving late that night.

"I'm all for it," Gee laughed. "Do you want to set the date?"

"We can work that out with the foresters and weathermen," she said. "I want to set the location."

"I suppose we need to reserve a space if the wedding has to accommodate all the Families, foresters, crews, and friends. Where is big enough? Do we have to get married in the football stadium?"

"Silly man," Karen said, poking at his ribs. "I want to be married under the Patriarch's canopy."

Gee held her close and kissed her.

Dead End

"SHERIFF, WE FOUND that boy y'all was a-huntin'," drawled the deputy from Georgia over the phone. "Ain't much left of him."

"What's the story?" Sheriff Johnson asked. Finding Dr. Jones had been their hope of untangling the drug and child trafficking cases.

"Once we found that flatbed full of stone you put us onto, we started canvasing outward from there. I know this took a while but we gotta be careful when we're searching the hills out near the state line. 'Bama moonshiners get tetchy. Well, we heard 'bout a Yankee buying up a bunch of supplies in Centralhatchee and got on his trail. He was hid out in a shack up in the hills near Yellowdirt."

"You were able to apprehend him?"

"Oh, no, sir. He was already apprehended. Dead for a few days according to Doc Wilson. Sittin' in a chair with his computer open and his pants down with a plastic bag over his head. I heard of that stuff before. Googled it. Sexual asphyxiation. 'Fraid the weather down here's been hotter'n hell this fall. Don't remember anything like it. Oh. Anyways, Doc says decomposition is pretty bad. Wants to know what you want done with the body."

"Thank you, Deputy. I hope I can do something for you one day. How about we send a couple guys down with a box to put him in and haul his ass back up here so you don't have to deal with it? I can get a guy down there by tomorrow night." Johnson relaxed into a friendly tone with the deputy, drawing on his own country upbringing. Inside he was seething. Jones was their only lead. "We've got a list of stolen property that the owners want back real bad. Mind if our guy goes through the shack to collect it? We've determined there are no other relatives."

"Sure 'nough. If you can empty the place, our volunteer fire department could burn it for practice. We don't need no feds getting' involved. Maybe you can load it all on that stone truck and haul it back."

"I'll send a tractor. You a coffee drinker, Deputy?"

"When I can't get whiskey. Course, that's whenever I'm on duty, Sheriff."

"I'm gonna send along a few pounds of the best coffee you'll ever taste. Just a little thank you."

"Much obliged, Sheriff."

Johnson stared at the phone in disgust. If Larry Syres wasn't forbidden to leave the state while he was out on bail, he'd send the guy down to haul the load back. Just maybe there would be a clue in the containers or in the shack.

"Deputy Carlisle!"

"Yes, Sheriff."

"I've got an assignment for you."

Nanny

"MARIAN, I JUST want to thank you again for spending time with the children," Gee said when she and Devon showed up on Thursday. "I've felt better about spending some time working in the woods and leaving them here. They've been playing with some of the toys after you and Devon leave instead of going into their waiting mode. It means a lot to all of us."

"I wish we could spend more time here. I just… with a son and husband and one on the way… Well, I just wish," his friend said.

"The time you spend is precious to all of us. I wanted to tell you we've run an ad here and in Palmyra searching for a nanny. None of us can spend all our time up here and we don't have an option for where they can live and get the attention they need."

"I wish I could apply," Marian said. Devon bolted and went into the room to greet his playmates.

"I thought that I'd let you know that we're searching in case you think of someone. It won't lessen the need for volunteers but it will give the kids some stability if someone is here regularly, at least overnight. The nurses have been great but they have other patients on this floor."

"I saw that poor girl, Rena, is just down the hall. We don't have a separate long-term care facility here. It bothers me that most of the others on this floor are just waiting to die," Marian said. "I'd better get in there before Devon teaches them about the call button. It's his new favorite thing. He wants one in his room at home."

"I won't delay you any longer. I just… Thank you, again, Marian."

"Gee!"

"Oh, hi, Laura. I don't often see you about. How are you and Jude doing?" Gee tried to sit in Jitterz early at least one morning a week just to greet the high school kids who stopped on their way to school. It was the first time he'd seen Laura Lazorack in the morning.

"Great, thank you. Lots to do, getting ready for the wedding. It's not like we're heirs, but Family weddings tend to draw a crowd. I trust you plan to join us New Year's Day."

"Wouldn't miss it. I'm very happy for you."

"How are the children?" she asked.

"They're doing better, I think," he answered. He motioned Laura to a seat at his favorite table at Jitterz. "Bringing Marian and Devon in on a regular basis has helped with their socialization. They're beginning to learn how a mother and child interact. We've advertised for a nanny or two. Interested?" he laughed.

"That's actually why I'm here," she said. "I hoped I'd catch you. "I have some experience with children. Not lately, but before I took over caring for the cemetery."

"Isn't that a full-time job?"

"Hardly anything to do in winter except plow the road unless someone dies. Someone who isn't Jewish," she amended. "I wondered if you would object to me applying for the job."

"Laura, if you can do the job without disrupting your plans and time with Jude, I think you'd be great for it," Gee said. "This might sound a little weird but spending time with them has been strangely peaceful for me and for Karen when she can join me. I sometimes wish I could just take them home."

"I'm looking forward to that. I think I've spent too much time among the dead for the past few years. Children might be just what I need."

Too Tidy

"Your Honor. District Attorney Mazzenga. This appears to wrap up the case," Mead said. Sheriff Johnson sat next to him, facing the judge and DA Wednesday morning. He shook his head.

"Appears?" Judge Warren asked. "Brad? What's your assessment?"

"It appears," Johnson said. "I don't like it but we don't have any reason to keep the kidnapping or drug cases open other than continuing our search for parents. It's as hard a task as searching for Gee's identity and just as fruitless."

"But...?" Mazzenga asked.

"I hate it when everything is wrapped up with all the suspects dead."

"It saves the state time." She looked over the packet presented by the policemen. "Did we have anyone in Georgia when Jones was found and examined?"

"Deputy Carlisle and Dr. Gaston went down to collect the body and empty the shack. Gaston completed an autopsy Monday night. Everything checks out with the coroner's report from Georgia. We recovered the research notes for LaRue Labs, including nearly twenty years' worth of personal notes on drug distillation from Rose Hickory nuts on his computer. Apparently, Lustre wasn't his first try at creating a drug. We also found a bottle of the poison used to kill the Alexanders. We've recovered the flatbed of stone, in which the lab equipment and children were being shipped. Everything points to Jones."

"Jones masterminded the whole project?" Warren said.

"Yes. It even seems likely that he was the assailant who kidnapped and attempted to poison Karen Weisman. He was six-two and we brought back a coat that matches the description Ms. Weisman and the kids gave," Mead said. "Not a chance they could identify the body, though."

"All tied up in a neat little package with a bow on top," Johnson sighed. "That's what has me upset. We've got the kids and drug paraphernalia shipped to him. We've got drugs in his apartment here. We've got research notes on his computer. We've got a poison match with the Alexanders. If we get a DNA match with specimens taken form the buried child, we'll have tied that murder to him as well. It's all so neat and tidy. That's what I don't like. Nothing gets wrapped up that neatly. We have everything except a clue about where children were sent after they were drugged and conditioned."

"I don't see a choice other than to close the open files and keep an ear out for anything that could lead to reopening it," Judge Warren said. "Especially regarding the trafficking."

"Officially, I agree," Mazzenga said. "Unofficially, I think we have too many conveniently closed or uninvestigated oddities in this town lately. I know you don't want to hear this, but that includes the mysterious George Evars. It takes serious money and influence to make a person disappear from all public records. Something on the level of a witness protection program. Since he arrived in town, we've had four unexplained deaths. The man known only as Reef, who also appears to have no known identity. The Alexanders. Dr. Jones. We have a woman still in a coma from an attack during the alleged kidnapping of Karen Weisman. Add to that, three unidentified children in the hospital. I like cases with concrete evidence that we can take to trial. Even Larry Syre is likely to plea bargain down to resisting arrest and his lawyer is arguing that was the fault of the arresting officers who had no evidence against him in the first place. I doubt the case will ever make it before Judge Warren. That's too much, gentlemen. We need some real answers and as of now we don't even have an open case."

Johnson and Mead glared at the DA but didn't contradict her.

"Anything else?" Warren asked.

"One thing," Mead said. "The temporary restraining order keeping Lance Beck out of Rena Lynd's room is about to expire. He's been in the office every week demanding that we let him visit his parishioner."

"I don't see that we have any just cause to extend the restraining order. We haven't been hearing much from him lately," Warren said.

"Oh, he's been active as ever but less direct about it," Mead said. "His church is a seething cauldron of hatred focused on anyone who believes differently than they do. He's started publishing a series of pamphlets that show up all over town on the evils of the seven Families, the Devil incarnate, and even a call to clear-cut the Forest, blaming it for a host of evils. He told us he hadn't counseled a child or teen since summer. They'd closed the camp when the cook retired. He claimed the children he worked with had been housed in his home according to the lease agreement with SSG and they never had more than one or two at a time."

"Lying piece of shit," Johnson growled. "Sorry, your honor."

"Nonetheless, I don't see that we have just cause to extend the restraining order. Let him know he can visit miss Lynd during visiting hours and that he must, per hospital policy, check in at the nurses' station before and after his visit," Warren said.

End of Life

"KAREN, IT'S LEAH."

"Goodness, Leah. It's five o'clock in the morning. What are you doing up?" Karen said into the phone, still trying the squeeze the sleep from her eyes. Gee stirred beside her. Since Thanksgiving, it seemed Karen and Gee had been trapped in an endless loop, repeating themselves daily. They cherished every moment they could stay in bed.

"It's Dad," Leah said simply. "Irma called in the middle of the night. Dr. Mueller is with him now but he's unresponsive. They want to take him to the hospital but his living will specifically states that he's not to be removed from his home. It's about over. I don't expect he'll last the day."

"We'll be there shortly," Karen said. "I'm so sorry, Leah."

"We knew this was coming; just not when. Get your coffee before you come. No one is in the kitchen."

"I don't want to delay."

"Karen, you're his heir. There's no special prize given for being here when he passes. I think you have time."

LEVI WAS THE last to arrive. "How was the trip down?" Karen asked as she led him to Ben's sitting room where the rest of the family had gathered.

"Aside from the snow, it was no problem. Five inches of new snow adds one or two hours to the drive time. Fortunately, Mother called just as I was getting off my shift. I need to be back in forty-eight hours. They frown on students interrupting the schedule for family matters."

Rabbi Schlesinger was also present and sat by Ben's head as he quietly read a passage from the Torah. He and Ben's nurse, Irma, were the only non-family members present. Gee and Laura had both been accepted as Family. Dr. Mueller, Ben's physician for nearly fifty years, was sleeping in a guest room until he was needed. Celia and Jo Ransom sat to the side, barely in the room.

Levi went to the bed and took his grandfather's hand. "We're all here now, Grandfather. I'm sorry I made you wait so long. Thank you again for giving me your blessing. It's precious to me."

The rabbi took up reading again and Levi gave his mother and brothers a hug. If anyone had expected the old man to immediately release his spirit now that everyone was gathered, they were mistaken. Gee accompanied Laura to the kitchen a little after noon. Jo soon followed.

"There is always something ready to eat in the refrigerator," Laura said. "Leah said to just find something that people can nosh on and not try to set a table."

"Anything special for Hanukkah?" Jo asked.

"No. It doesn't start until sundown. There are no dietary restrictions but a lot of fried foods and sweets. A lot like Christmas, I guess."

"I see cold cuts and bread," Gee said, sniffing at the package of meat. "Pastrami."

"Get that and the spreads out," Jo suggested. "I see fresh vegetables. Do we want cheese?"

"Jo," Laura giggled. "You really aren't much of a Jew, are you? Never mix meat and cheese."

"Oh. I have so much to learn! I was raised Methodist."

"I was raised Lutheran," Laura confirmed. "How about you, Gee?"

"I... uh... have read a lot of Bible verses, I think. I don't know anything about the Torah."

"Well, only Jude tries to stay Kosher, though Ben stayed pretty close to it," Laura said. "We should be able to feed people without breaking too many taboos."

"Are there any pickles?" Levi asked from the door. "Grandfather always had the best pickles." Laura bent to the refrigerator again. "Hi. I don't think we've met," Levi said to Jo. "I'm Levi."

"I'm Jo. I guess we are some number cousins some times removed or something. I didn't know about any of this until this fall."

"I never did get the whole story. I spent the summer in Europe and only stopped here at Thanksgiving because mother wanted me to make nice with Karen."

"And?"

"It was no problem for me. In fact, a big relief. I was staying out of town because I was afraid Grandfather would try to make me his heir. Too much Family business for me," Levi said.

"It's like that in every Family," Laura said. "Between Jonathan and me, we're intermarrying with two other Families. My father, David, sees that as both a blessing and a threat."

"I've heard the same from the others I've talked to," Gee said. "Even Jo is being courted by another Family."

"Really?" Laura asked.

"Um... Thanks for outing me, Gee. I've been going out with Wayne Savage for a few weeks," Jo said, rolling her eyes at Gee. "It's not like we're engaged or anything. We're both Family outsiders and find it easy to talk about what we've observed since coming to Rosebud Falls."

"Oh," Levi said. He'd positioned himself nearer to Jo as he was making sandwiches. "I'm pretty out of touch with what goes on here, too." He crunched some more of his pickle as he glanced toward Jo.

GEE WENT TO visit the children in the afternoon at Karen's insistence.

"I'll call you if anything happens here, Love," she said. "I think Ben would approve of you going to be with them."

"I hope so," Laura said from nearby. "It will only be my fourth night with them and I don't intend to be late for their dinner, whether Ben is alive or not." She'd begun Monday as the children's night nanny and bracketed her time with them from dinner to breakfast.

Gee pulled on his coat. "Well, I may cross paths with you when I leave the hospital. My day just isn't complete until I get a hug from them."

The children were excited to show him the blocks Devon had brought them. They still weren't talking but their interactions seemed almost normal. When Gee returned to the house, he lay down on a sofa and slept for half an hour.

"IT'S TIME," KAREN whispered to Gee, waking him from his nap.

"How do you know?" he asked.

"Something just whispered to me," she said. "I don't know. Maybe it was a hallucination." The others stirred and gathered around Ben's bed. His eyes opened to look around but there was little sign of recognition in them.

Ben's lips began to move and everyone leaned in to try to catch what he was saying. All Gee heard was *"…halelu 'eth-shêmAdonay."* Ben took a shuddering breath and his muscles went slack. Rabbi Schlesinger reached over to close the old man's eyes.

"What was that?" Gee whispered. "What did it mean?"

"It was the beginning of Psalm 113," Jude responded. "It's past sundown. Hanukkah has begun."

Juggling Priorities

BEN'S BURIAL, OF course, had to be completed before sundown the next day. There was nothing Gee could do to help with that. Leah and her sons took care of most of the details but Karen was asked to accompany them. Gee took the opportunity to stop by the foresters' office before he went to visit the children.

"We found—or were directed to—two access points to the Wild Woods that no one knew about," Jonathan said. "Sheriff Johnson and Detective Oliver recognized the farm where the Alexanders died backed up to the Wild Woods on the southeast corner. They took us out there as part of their investigation. We found a re-tied break in the chain link fence on that side and two trails. One led to the lab and the other to one of the cleaned-out cabins. They were well-concealed but once we started looking for them, we spotted them quickly enough. We want to do a full inspection of the fence but there are problems."

"Like what?" Gee asked.

"Technically, we only have access from inside the woods," Jessie said. "Undergrowth and even trees grow right up to the fence. Some of the farmers on the other side have started demanding the trees hanging over the fence be removed so they don't get nuts falling on their property any longer."

"Why now? Haven't they always had nuts on their property?" Gee asked.

"Apparently, SSG paid them to clean up the nuts that fell in their fields. With the annexation, the farmers see the foresters as the most likely source of continued income. They're demanding cutting, knowing we'd rather pay them than lose a tree," Jessie sighed. "It's just greed."

"So, inspecting the fence?" Gee prompted.

"Since the other side of the fence is private property, we need permission to cross the farmers' land to inspect it. They seem to think if they play hardball, we'll cave in to the demands for compensation or removal of the trees," Jonathan said. "Plus, now that snow is falling, the fence is a natural drift line. We've got six inches of snow, officially, but the drifts are over three feet deep at the fence."

"Doesn't this south edge border a street?" Gee asked.

"Same but different," Jessie said. "The street is the new City Limits but all the property on this side is developed. So, this time instead of six obstinate farmers, we have forty city lot owners. We'll be able to do something eventually because they are in the City and we have the right to inspect our fences but we'll have to go into each yard and that will require permission."

"It looks like we have no option but to work our way along the fence inside the woods," Gee ventured. "The snow isn't as bad under the canopy, so I think I can take a crew in safely. "I'll have kids out here to volunteer tomorrow."

WHEN GEE GOT to the hospital to visit the children, Laura had already left. Dr. Salinger, however, was waiting. Penny Tomczyk, the children's librarian, had also been by to bring new books based on Gee's and Dr. Salinger's recommendations. An older woman stood quietly beside Dr. Salinger, observing the children.

"This is my mother," Dr. Salinger said. "I invited her up to see if she might be interested in becoming one of our nannies."

"I think Laura is doing well," Gee said, perhaps a little defensively.

"Yes. We've talked. I understand she had some emotional difficulties relating to the death of her fiancé several years ago and might understand the children as well as you."

"Possibly better," Gee answered. "I spoke with her at length a couple of months ago. When her first fiancé was killed, she was pregnant. A botched abortion has left her unable to conceive. She will be married in just a few weeks and I know she and Jude regret that she can't have children. It's been one of the factors in their extremely long engagement."

Gee went in to read to the children for a while before he had to leave for Ben's funeral.

One Eye on Main

TROY WAS NEARLY finished with the Friday morning broadcast, which included the news of Ben's death and the funeral that afternoon. Not that anyone would care. He certainly wasn't going to the old man's funeral. Nonetheless, he'd read the obituary, kindly provided by *The Elmont Mirror*.

He hadn't felt well in three weeks. The lackluster broadcasts were ample evidence of that. Troy thrived on popularity and attention but it all seemed hollow here. He was simply a vain, easily manipulated pawn in the Family games. *It's time to find a job in a bigger city. Maybe Palmyra or New York or Boston. I don't belong here.*

A young woman pushing a stroller paused outside his window—his 'One Eye on Main Street'—to read the program schedule and information on the sandwich board. She glanced up and Troy waved like he always did when people passed. She smiled and waved back. *Beautiful!* He jumped up from the console and removed his headset as Leslie Lake took over the seat for the afternoon show. Troy stepped out the door, pulling on his coat, and looked for the young woman he'd seen through the window. She was not far along and he hurried to catch up.

"I'm glad they keep the sidewalks clear," he said by way of greeting. "I'd hate to imagine you trying to push your baby in deep snow."

"I should get one of those jogger things that have big wheels," she laughed. "It would make it easier slogging through this."

"I'm Troy Cavanaugh. That's my day job," he said, pointing with his thumb at the window. "Other than that, I'm pretty much a bum."

"Hmm. I don't usually hang out with bums. This is new. I'm Taryn Taft. I just rented a place on the other side of the railroad and my landlord told me there was a nice sweetshop over here on Main," she said. "I thought we'd go exploring." Troy fell in step with her as they walked south.

"I stop by Jitterz nearly every day after I get off work. Please let me show you." Troy turned on all his charm, thinking a little time spent with Taryn might be what he needed to change his attitude. "What brings you to Rosebud Falls?"

"A friend down in Georgia recommended it," Taryn said. "A single mom starting over needs a new place." Troy stuttered in his walk, feigning slipping on ice. The thought of Georgia brought bile to his throat. He held the door for her as she maneuvered the stroller into Jitterz.

"Single? That's a tough life when you have a little one," he managed. Taryn seemed all too happy to share life's most intimate details.

"Richard and I divorced just before he shipped out overseas from Fort Benning. It had been rocky for a while and I got tired of all the other soldiers thinking it was their duty to comfort me. I had to move out of base housing anyway, so when Jolene, my friend, suggested here, I just packed up Ricky and headed north. And here we are."

"A delightful addition to our town you are," Troy smiled. "Birdie has the best coffee known in the area."

"Oh, I don't drink coffee," she said. "Never acquired the taste. I hope she has tea. And look at these pastries!"

"If Birdie is here, she'll probably want to read your tealeaves. Let me order for you while you get settled with Ricky." Troy approached the counter and ordered coffee for himself and tea for Taryn along with a chocolate croissant. Violet took his money in cool silence with a small shake of her head. "It's not like that," Troy whispered. "She's new in town." Violet made a little shrug and handed him his order. Troy regretted ever having taken her out.

But this was different. This Taryn. Few women had such an instant effect on him. And he was owed a good woman. He'd been told to be patient and she would come to him. He didn't expect such mystic gobbledygook from Deacon Stewart. But here was a charming young woman who had waited outside his window.

When Troy sat at the little table opposite Taryn, she was lifting the child from the stroller. "Come up here, Ricky," she cooed at the child. "Come and meet Mr. Cavanaugh. That's a big boy. Sit right up here." She turned the child toward Troy.

His heart stopped as he took in the features of the child and then looked into Taryn's blue eyes as she smiled at him. He tried to ignore the child's flat round face and tight slanted eyes as he focused on Taryn and tried to put his thoughts in order.

"They have all kinds of politically correct terms, like slow learner and differently abled," Taryn scoffed. "Ricky has Down syndrome. But he's the sweetest little boy you'll ever meet."

Troy nodded mutely.

Accompanying the Journey

BEN'S FUNERAL WAS at two o'clock. It seemed as if the rest of the world took a break as Gee and Karen sat in the chapel. Leah decided to hold the service in the funeral home rather than the synagogue to avoid confusion about where people should sit as most gathered were not Jewish.

Few people attended the service. Ben had not been to the synagogue in several years and was not personally known to the congregation. Most of his friends had died years ago. Family representatives seated themselves as Leah and her sons were ushered in to sit in the front row. Each wore a black ribbon. They were the official mourners and approached the simple wooden casket at the start of the service. The four tore the ribbons they wore.

"We are physical beings on this earth," Rabbi Schlesinger said. "The tearing of clothing is an ancient ritual showing an outward and physical sign of deep internal sorrow. It is a symbol of the rending of the fabric of the family. Prior to this moment the mourners have had the responsibility of preparing the body and themselves for this parting. Now the responsibility shifts to the community to take care of them. *Baruch atah Adonai, Dayan Ha-Emet*—Blessed are You, Adonai, Truthful Judge."

Leah and her sons returned to their seats as those few who understood the ritual and language responded to the rabbi, "*Adonai natan, Adonai lakach, yehi shem Adonai m'vorach*—God has given, God has taken away, blessed be the name of God."

The cantor from the synagogue sang a Psalm and Rabbi Schlesinger returned to the lectern for the eulogy. It was simple and to the point. It cited Ben's care and support for both the synagogue and the Roth Family. Then Levi was asked to join the rabbi and say a few words.

"Grandfather summoned me just two weeks ago when I was home for Thanksgiving. He gave me his blessing on the path I have chosen. But it was not simply to me that he wished to express his words. He asked me to convey his blessing on my mother and father and brothers, on the new head of the Family, Karen Weisman, on the new members of our Family, Jo and Celia Ransom, and on our spouses and loved ones. Yes, Judith, he even expressed his blessing on you and his sorrow at having been harsh with you. Grandfather had utmost respect for Karen's fiancé, Gee, and the difficult path he has followed since arriving in Rosebud

Falls. He gave his blessing in advance to the coming marriage of Laura and Jude and his sorrow that he would not be here to celebrate with them. But most of all, Grandfather expressed his love for Rosebud Falls, the Forest, and the Families that have guided her and protected her for the past centuries. He gives you his blessing as we move forward and care for our community. Thank you for being here with us today as we celebrate his life and part with his spirit."

The cantor sang another prayer. Leah and her sons were escorted from the room by Don, Judith, and Laura. The four men assigned to carry the casket were flanked by the seven Family heads and their heirs as it was moved to the waiting hearse. Gee joined the exodus and was shown to a car where Karen awaited him.

"What now?" he asked.

"We call this part the *Levayah*," Karen said. "The accompanying of the deceased to his burial so he does not make the trip alone. There will be a short graveside service and we will all cast a handful of dirt on the casket."

"In this weather?" Gee asked. "Will they even be able to dig the grave?"

"They're equipped," Karen laughed. Jo and Celia joined them in the car that trailed the two with the closest family members.

Shiva

As DESIGNATED HEIR and official new resident of the Roth Estate, Karen hosted the *shiva* in the mansion. Unlike the service itself, many more people attended the gathering after and since most were not Jewish, it went long after sundown. Gee felt many had come not to comfort the mourners, but simply to see the inside of the ancestral home. Ben had left the house rarely in the past five years and only had occasional guests. Many people the Family didn't even know came by just to get a glimpse of how the Families lived.

Karen had arranged to have a light buffet catered at the mansion and people circulated through the lower level rooms, many gravitating toward the veranda with its view over the river. On the bluffs opposite, the Cavanaugh estate commanded an equally impressive view. Gee stayed with Karen and tried hard not to be drawn into inevitable discussions about the children and the Wild Woods.

"Lynda, I didn't realize you knew my great uncle," Karen said when the waitress Gee knew as Raven from the Pub & Grub paused to greet her. Next to her was a lanky young man Gee recognized as Karen's long-time friend, Timmy. Lynda chuckled softly.

"Oh, the secrets," she said. "Not that they were intentional. Twenty-eight years, Karen. The first five of those I spent in the apartment above the garage. This room is where Timmy took his first steps."

"I had no idea," Karen said. "You were…?"

"When I was a pregnant teenager and had been thrown out of my parents' home, Ben took me in. There was a soft side to him that I don't think many people saw. I've worked as a part time housekeeper for him," Lynda said.

"Really? Would you like to stay on? I'm already overwhelmed with the thought of cleaning this place—even with Gee's help."

"If you are sure. I don't mean to talk business at a wake. But I *would* miss the extra income. I usually come in on Monday when the pub is closed."

"That is such a relief. You might think it's business, but you've just been a huge comfort to me."

"How are you doing at the grocery store, Timmy?" Gee asked.

"Good. Mr. Panza is nice. I can move the soup all by myself."

"That's great. He really depends on you." The young man grinned.

"Well, we'd better get to work. Even in this weather, Friday night at the bar will be busy and Sherry gets impatient if we aren't there before the crowd," Raven said. "I'll really miss Ben." She and her son left.

———————◁◆▷———————

"When do you plan to move?" Leah asked.

"Do I have to?" Karen whined. Leah rolled her eyes. "I know. What am I complaining about? I'm thinking after the first of the year. I know you'll want to clear out some of his things. I'll leave that to you."

"Just a few personal items," Leah said. "The mansion belongs to the Family. The head resides here. I do hope you'll move all your great-grandmother's papers back here, though. Aaron was very sneaky giving Ben the house but removing all the Family history."

"We may never understand the politics of that generation or why Aaron refused to acknowledge Celia. I think it's time, though. Even if we decide not to 'reveal' everything, I think we should stop concealing it. I'll move all the papers over here into the library and you can have access any time you want," Karen agreed.

"Thank you. I've hired Jo to learn the business aspects of the Family, by the way," Leah said. She sipped from her glass of wine and leaned her head back against the doorframe. "I'm sixty-seven. I expect I'll be around for a while but you need an advisor and business manager who can last as long as you do. Jo's a smart girl."

"I'm glad you think so. And Leah, I'm truly sad about Ben's passing and your loss. Even though we weren't close, he's been head of the Family my entire life. I don't think we even realize yet how much we've lost."

6

RUNAWAY

Footprint

GEE WENT TO THE WOODS Saturday morning seeking both the camaraderie of his team and the peace of the Forest. The long day Thursday, waiting for Ben to die, followed by the long day Friday, dealing with the funeral and family, had been mentally and emotionally draining.

The weather was crisp but the sky was clear. He thought it might make it above freezing by mid-afternoon.

"We only have two crews today, Gee," Jessie said. "Jonathan is sick in bed. That means I'll probably be sick in bed tomorrow since we share *everything*. We'll split his crew between us and try to get as much done today as possible."

"What should we work on?" Gee asked.

"I think we should go back out and trace the paths from the fence Jonathan and I found. We should widen them and look for any sign of side trails."

"Sounds good. Gear up, team. We're off to the woods."

Drake Oliver had become a permanent part of Gee's crew, joining Alyson, Shannon, Jeanie, and JD. The boy's brawn was a significant help in cutting and hauling brush. Gee cautioned his team to proceed more slowly since they were specifically looking for signs of another trail. It was backward from the way they had worked in the past. The girls and

JD moved in front, searching for trails, with Drake and Gee and two boys from Jonathan's team following behind to widen the path and remove the brush. This trail seemed to naturally pass near some of the larger trees so they could force their way off the path to measure and chart them.

They'd worked most of the morning and were planning to head back to the cabin to warm up and eat lunch when Shannon stopped everyone.

"Gee, we need you up here," she said. The others pressed back so Gee could join the smallest member of their team. She had moved to the left off the path toward another tree that looked to be about eighteen inches in diameter. Gee moved to where Shannon had stopped. She pointed. In the clear space around the base of the tree, snow had sifted into an even layer an inch or two deep. Unmarked, except for one small footprint. Gee pushed Shannon back toward the others on the path and pulled out his cellphone. He didn't press farther toward the tree but snapped photos of the print and the area around, even up the side of the tree to the lowest branches, about six feet above the ground.

"Let's move back," Gee told the team. "I want to consult with others before we decide what this means."

"It means someone is out here," JD said firmly. "Another lost child. We should be searching everywhere." He stomped on the trail as they made their way back to the cabin, showing his anger with every step.

"JD, look," Gee said softly, leading him to an open area near the cabin. "Do you see the snow cover here?"

"Yeah." He was still scowling, but focused on what Gee was saying. Gee broke a bit of icicle from the eaves of the cabin and threw it into the branches of a tree. A shower of snow from the branches fell in clumps on the snowfield below. The others gathered near him as he pointed to the various indents in the snow.

"Look. That dent over there looks almost like the one we just found," Gee said. "We jumped to the conclusion that it was a footprint. It could have been a print made by a falling clump of snow. That's why I want other trained eyes on it before we start tromping around out there."

"I see," JD said glumly. "Who do we call?"

"Sheriff first and then Jessie."

———————⊰◆⊱———————

Work slowed and people got cold. They went into the cabin and started the propane heater while the sheriff, Jessie, and Gee returned to the print. Jessie's team joined the kids and they talked about the recent discoveries.

"I don't know," Ryan said. He'd been working with Jessie and she'd held as tight a discipline on her team as Gee had. "As much as I want to discover something and think we're being of use, I don't want to discover that there's someone out here. A child like the little ones Gee is helping in the hospital. I mean, if they're here I want to find them but I don't want them to be here."

"I got really mad at Gee," JD confessed. "It seemed so obvious that we should search for whoever it was and help the poor kid. I don't think it was a falling clump of snow."

"You have to admit, though, that it was strange to see just one footprint," Shannon said. "How did someone get there to leave it? Fly?"

"We were being really careful looking for signs of a path but we could have missed other footprints," Alyson said. "We might have buried them because that wasn't what we were looking for."

"That'll change from now on," Jeanie said. "I'm just beginning to realize how big a job we volunteered for, you know?"

"It makes me sick," Viktor said. "If Jessie will have me, I plan to be out here every day during winter break. It's two weeks away and already I feel like it's too late."

"Let's not really make ourselves sick," Rebecca said. "I'd like to stay and help, but I'm a boarder at Flor. Even though they don't want me around most of the year, my parents require my presence during Christmas." Jeanie hugged her classmate.

"At least you have parents," she sighed.

"I didn't mean to sound ungrateful," Rebecca said. "There's no place I'd rather be than here with you all."

"Let's make a pact," Shannon said. "If there is a child in the woods, we *will* find and rescue him or her. We won't quit until we know they're all safe."

"Yeah."

"I'm down with that."

"Count me in," Gee said from the door of the cabin. The kids spun to look at him. "For now, let's turn the heat off and pack out. We're done for today."

"What was the decision?" JD asked as they hiked out of the woods. Gee hadn't said much.

"Inconclusive," he finally answered. "We didn't find any more prints. There was no sign of life."

"What do *you* think, Gee?" JD asked quietly.

"I'm with you, son. I think someone is hiding out there."

Fired

WHAT THEY HAD and hadn't found weighed heavily on Gee as he made his way to the hospital to visit the children. He was greeted with hugs and smiles now. As he played and told stories, he heard their laughter. It refreshed his soul.

Promptly at five-thirty, the door opened and a plump woman with gray hair and an apron rolled in the tray of food. She was jovial and Gee could only think she was like Mrs. Claus.

"Oh, Mr. Gee," she said. "We weren't expecting you for dinner tonight. I'll call for another meal to be brought up."

"That's not necessary," Gee said. "I just stopped to see the children and give them a hug. I met you once before, didn't I?"

"Oh, I'm just Grandma Sue," the woman said. "I'm Dr. Salinger's mother. I'm here for dinner and bedtime with the children on the nights that sweet Laura Lazorack is off. After dinner and baths, we'll have story time and some music. Then I'll tuck them in and sleep on the bed over there."

"I'm so glad the children have a Grandma," Gee said. "It's a comforting thought."

"I practically had to beg my daughter to let me help." She bustled around getting the dishes on the table. Gee got a hug from each of the children before he left. He paused at the observation window and watched as they sat at the table and bowed their heads for a prayer.

THE CREW SEEMED more dedicated than usual Sunday. Jessie, true to her own prediction, was sick in bed.

"You know what this means," Gee said. "We're working without a forester today. What's that mean, JD?" The boy blushed at being singled out after his confrontation yesterday.

"It means proceed with caution. Be watchful for any sign of a path or habitation. Don't disturb anything that might be a clue. Anything might be a clue," he answered.

"Take the lead of Team 1, JD. Viktor, take Team 2."

"Gee, with all due respect, Rebecca is a better choice for that than me. I'm a little reckless at times and she's more observant," Viktor said. Gee looked at a blushing Rebecca.

"Rebecca? It seems that Team 2 is yours. Same paths we were working on yesterday. Gear up."

It was a long six hours working in the woods, even with the half hour they took at noon to warm up and eat in one of the cabins. They were disappointed that nothing had been discovered when they hiked out at the end of the day.

MONDAY, GEE AND Karen began the long task of preparing to move. They decided to tackle the big task first and took boxes into the study to pack her ancestors' notebooks and library and Karen's notebooks and research. Hers was neatly ordered in three metal filing cabinets. Her great-grandmother's and great-great-grandfather's notes were in boxes, desk drawers, shelves, and stacks in the cluttered room. It would be a major task to unpack and organize them in the mansion library.

"Will we have to move into Ben's bedroom?" Gee asked.

"Hmm. I guess that depends on what you mean. If you are referring to the room he died in, no. The suite downstairs was all remodeled for handicapped access and Ben moved into it years ago when it became hard for him to make it upstairs. The real master suite is upstairs. I don't think we'll have any difficulty moving into that. No ghosts from at least the last three generations live there."

"I'll leave it to you, then," Gee laughed. "I just didn't want his ghost leaning over our shoulders while we're making love."

————⊰◆⊱————

THE REST OF the week found Gee cold and alone as he worked in the woods. On Friday, he had lunch with the children and then spent the afternoon hauling a sled down the paths and collecting cut brush to haul back out to the chipper. Saturday, he would have a full crew again and they'd start working down the fence line to clear a path and check for evidence that the other farms had accessed the Wild Woods. He found the simple drudgery of loading and dragging the sled to be a kind of meditative activity that allowed him to consider all the pressing problems in his life.

The three most important on his mind were the children, the Wild Woods, and his upcoming marriage to Karen with all its attendant complications. She was the new leader of the Roth Family. Leah and Don immediately raised issues of property ownership and a prenuptial agreement. They were surprised to find the extent to which Gee and Karen had gone to create their partnership before Harvest began. Now they were insisting that the partnership be voided and property equitably split before a new prenuptial agreement was signed and in force. Karen, of course, was angry about it and at the moment there was a stalemate. The LaCoes were being consulted. Opinions were pending.

The children were doing well—better than expected. Dr. Salinger was now observing just once a week and had high words of praise for the work of all three primary caregivers—Gee, Laura, and Grandma Sue. All agreed, however, that they needed to expand the children's socialization. Gee planned an outing with all the children the following Wednesday to the library for reading time. Both Colleen Zimmer and Wayne had agreed to spend a few hours with the children over the weekend to help engage them in some typical school activities for their age group. They had agreed that both coloring and puzzles were good activities, but there was a need to assess the children more thoroughly to see what they were capable of as opposed to what they were willing to do.

With all that on his mind, Gee hung his equipment at the foresters' office and headed home to make Friday night dinner for Karen. It brought a smile to his face.

————⊰◆⊱————

KAREN, ON THE other hand, faced Cameron LaCoe over the desk in Axel's office Friday evening. The staff had just been informed that the newspaper was hiring and would be moving to daily publication instead of Tuesday through Saturday. The new schedule would go into effect the first full week of January, meaning their first Monday edition would be released on January seventh.

That was not the news Cameron was giving Karen, though.

"You know it's for the best, Karen," he said. "Neither of us want this but we have to go with it."

"It's not a bad thing," Karen said. "Just hurts a little, you know? I'll miss writing and editing but I've also found I have a lot more responsibility I wasn't expecting now that Ben's gone. I was thinking about resigning anyway."

"I know what you mean," Cameron said. "Grandfather laid down the law to me, as well. He said that if I wanted to be the Family heir, I had to back out of the role of publisher and hire someone to take it over. My responsibility, now that I did Axel's job and fired you, is to simply hold the ownership in trust, not to publish the paper."

"I think Family heads and heirs in high profile jobs in the City is a thing of the past. For now, at least. We've had too much publicity in the past months. I think I'll consider writing that book we discussed a while back."

"And I'm going to be a productive member of my parents' law firm and start learning the broader management of our Family businesses," Cameron added. "For a while, at least. I'm thinking of taking the quartet on a tour. Elaine really blossoms when she can sing. I'll tell you this, Axel is relieved to have me out of his thinning hair." They laughed.

"You have to admit we all gained a much higher profile during the campaign for annexation than any of us intended."

"If the Families recede into the background, they have you to thank for it," Cameron chuckled. "The article you wrote for Election Day was a pretty heavy indictment regarding the secrecy and dealings of our local power structure."

"I don't have a problem with that. If *they* do, they should take it to the City Champion," Karen laughed, just as her cellphone chimed the distinctive notes of Gee calling. "Yes, Darling. I'm… What?— No. Just stay with her. I'll make the calls. I'll be there in ten minutes." Karen thumbed her phone and flipped through her contacts. "Sorry, Cameron. Family emergency. I've got to run. Good luck."

She dashed out the door with the phone to her ear.

Waif at the Door

GEE STOMPED THE snow off his boots before removing them and hopping in his stocking feet through the open door. The effort was vain as a gust of wind blew snow in behind him. He slammed the door against the frigid blast.

Once he'd changed clothes and had dry socks and slippers on, he headed to the kitchen. Karen would still be a couple of hours and he could get stew started. He made a short detour by the sitting room to start a fire and then happily started cooking.

The blanket of heavy wet snow they'd received made any outdoor activity difficult and Gee considered canceling his crew in the morning and just staying home. His contemplation of the tasks remaining continued during dinner preparations. Hearty root vegetables were placed in the cooker with browned beef cubes and sautéed onions. The welcoming aroma of the stew soon filled the kitchen.

Gee boiled water for a cup of tea and had just poured it when he heard the front doorbell ring. He wiped his hands and went to answer it.

A girl—or perhaps a young woman—stood on the lower step looking up at the house. When Gee opened the door, she took a step back as if preparing to flee.

"Hi. What can I do for you?" Gee asked lightly. She looked half frozen in tennis shoes and a windbreaker. She was not dressed for the weather at all.

"Is this where Karen Weisman lives?"

"Yes, it is. Are you here to see her? You look cold. Come inside."

The girl took another step back and looked around as if weighing her options. "Will you let me leave?"

"Of course! But you look half frozen. There's a fire burning in the sitting room and I was just making tea. Or would you prefer hot chocolate? Come in. Come in."

The girl visibly shivered and stepped inside only far enough for Gee to close the door.

"I'm Nina. Miss Weisman said… She said if I could get to Rosebud Falls… She said I could stay with her."

The effort of coming inside, the sudden warmth of the room, and exhaustion all seemed to catch up with the girl at once. Gee caught her as she collapsed and carried her to the sofa, feeling her cold sodden clothes. He quickly pulled a blanket over her and grabbed his cellphone.

"JULIA, IT'S KAREN," she said as she hurried up the street toward home. "One of the runaways I interviewed in the city has just shown up on our doorstep. Gee says she's wet, cold, and passed out. I need help to get her into something dry and warm. I don't want her to think Gee is helping get her undressed."

"I can grab Ellie before she leaves. Her shift just ended. As soon as I can get free, I'll be there. I'll tell Adam."

"That's as far as it should go until we know more. It's possible she's being followed. If she's sick instead of just exhausted, we'll get her to the hospital right away."

"YOU NEED TO report her," Adam said. "I don't see anything physically wrong with her other than exhaustion and exposure. She has a mild fever but that's to be expected. When she wakes up, feed her and keep her warm. She knows you, Karen. You should be close when she wakes up if possible. Otherwise, I'd like to run a full physical on her next week to make sure there's nothing else."

"So why do we need to report her?" Karen said. "She looks to be over eighteen and she's been alone and living on the streets for at least six months. She came here to be safe."

"Is she really eighteen? We can't know anything for sure. She may be a missing person. The law is pretty specific about what a doctor has to report," Adam said.

"There's no reason we need to do anything before Monday," Karen said. "I met her in the city and invited her to visit. She came. All we have at the moment is a houseguest who wasn't feeling well. Right?" Adam nodded his head reluctantly.

"Just call if she gets sicker. I don't think there'll be a problem but don't waste time if it looks like there is. Call me." He and Julia said their goodbyes and headed back to the hospital. Ellie lagged behind.

"Do you need any help, Karen?" the nurse asked. "I don't have anything pressing."

"Really, Ellie? I heard you had a boyfriend."

"Oh, God! Having Julia around is faster than a telephone," Ellie sighed. "I'm dating a guy, okay? But we don't usually go out in the evenings. It's unusual for me to have a Friday night off but he never does."

"Well, stay and have dinner with us then," Gee suggested. "I've been suffering from smelling it all evening."

"It does smell appetizing. If you're sure it's okay," Ellie responded.

The three sat at the kitchen table with bowls of stew and crusty bread from the market's bakery. Karen and Gee teased the story from Ellie. Gee recognized the man, Evert Krumb, the bouncer/bartender at the Pub & Grub. No wonder he wasn't available for dates on a weekend night. Their conversation was interrupted by a sniffle from the kitchen door.

"Nina!" Karen exclaimed. "Are you feeling strong enough to be up? Come have a seat and let's get you some food."

They shifted around the table to make room for the waif next to Ellie. Gee brought her stew and a glass of milk. She ate rapidly, a tear escaping from one eye as if she had not eaten in a long time.

Flight of Terror

"I SAW HIM on the street, looking for me," Nina said when Karen asked her why she had run away from her during their interview in September. "I can't go back there. They'll kill me."

"Really?"

"I heard Sir on the phone. He said I was too old for his market and if he couldn't find a buyer, he was sending me to the kennel for sale or snuff."

A shudder ran through all the adults.

"It's been three months," Karen said. "How have you survived? I was afraid you'd even lost the card I gave you."

"I went back to Janie. When I explained what happened, she hid me for a couple of weeks and taught me how to make money. She said everyone pays their way and my body was my bank account. She was very nice."

"That bitch!" Karen breathed. "She told me she was helping girls she found on the street. Helping them be better prostitutes!"

"Oh, God," Ellie moaned. She put a hand on Nina's.

"I can earn my way here, too," Nina said. "I know how."

"No!" Gee said immediately. Nina shrank into a little ball and Ellie put an arm around her, scowling at Gee. He calmed quickly. "Nina," he said softly, "there will never be a reason for you to pay your way with sex as long as you are with us. We—Karen and I—will provide anything you need and will help you learn other ways to make a living. You will never, ever be forced to sell you body for sex while you are with us. Never!" His voice was quiet but forceful. Nina looked up at him, fear still showing in her eyes as she glanced at Karen.

"That's right, Nina. Gee didn't mean to frighten you, nor did I. What you were forced to do with your sir and madam or with Janie is no longer necessary," Karen said. "Gee and I are about to move to a big house across the street and there will be a room just for you with your own bathroom and no one can go in it without your permission. We'll get you clothes and find a teacher for you. You will never be hungry."

"Bigger than this?" Nina said as she looked around.

"That was my reaction, too," Gee laughed.

"I'm so glad you followed the directions on the card and came to us," Karen said.

"I couldn't," Nina said. Gee looked at her thinking she was turning down their offer but Nina plugged on. "I don't know how to read. I showed your card to Janie and she explained what it said. When I left, I had to ask people to read the directions to me."

"I wish Janie had just called me. I would have come to get you," Karen sighed.

"She tried and said your phone didn't work. She said she knew someone else who would take me in and protect me on the street. I slipped out that night and ran away again," Nina said. Karen pulled her phone out of her bag.

"I'll call Janie and…" Gee placed a hand on hers and she caught his eye. "Maybe not. I should cool down."

"The time when your phone was crushed in the woods," Gee said quietly. "I didn't get you a new phone for several days and it had a new number. We got the old number forwarded to it."

"Oh, dear. How long have you been on the road since you left Janie's?" Karen asked.

"A long time. I get confused with days. They're all the same. I fell asleep in a truck that gave me a ride. He made me stay there for three days to pay him. When he let me out, I was in a big city… bigger than where Janie lives. It took me a long time to find which direction to go next."

"You poor child," Ellie said. "You're safe now. You're safe."

"I'm very sleepy now. As soon as I wash the dishes, may I go to bed?"

"Honey, you don't have to wash dishes. Let's find you a toothbrush and get you to bed," Karen said.

GEE WAS PREPARING coffee to take to Karen in the morning when he heard steps behind him. He turned to find Nina a few feet away. Her eyes were cast down with her head slightly bowed. Her hair was still wet from a shower and she was dressed in the track suit Karen had given her the night before. Nina was five or six inches shorter than Karen, so the hem of the trousers dragged on the floor around her feet. Karen had promised a shopping trip this morning.

"Do you want me this morning, sir?" Nina asked.

"Good morning, Nina. Of course we want you this morning. Nothing has changed," Gee answered. Nina unzipped the sweatshirt and knelt on the floor.

"How would you like me, sir?" she asked, tugging at her sleeves.

"Wait, wait, wait, Nina!" Gee said. Catching the shirt and pulling it back around her shoulders and closed. "Please zip your shirt. We told you last night you would never have to earn your way with sex again."

"Not even with you and Miss Weisman?" Nina asked. "I thought you must mean no one else. Don't you like me?"

"Yes, we like you," Gee said. "When we said you needn't earn your way with sex, we meant at all. You don't have to pay to be with us. We'll be like parents or guardians or, if you prefer, a big brother and sister. Do any of those sound good to you?"

"I don't know. I don't understand the world," she whispered.

"How about a cup of coffee? Would you like that?"

"May I, sir?"

"My name is Gee and if I offer, I mean it. Have a seat at the table. We'll talk a bit. Do you take anything in your coffee?"

"May I have milk?"

"Here you are. In a few minutes I'll make some eggs and cheese. Would you like that for breakfast?"

"Thank you, sir… Gee."

Gee was struck by how much she reminded him of an older version of the children. That thought started him thinking of what the children would have become had they not been rescued. Assuming they lived.

"What is your last name, Nina?"

"Last name, Gee?"

"Yes. My full name is George Edward Evars but everyone calls me Gee."

"Um… My full name is Nina. Everyone calls me Nina."

"Oh, my," Karen whispered from the doorway. "This is going to be difficult." This startled Nina and she scrambled away from the table to kneel in front of Karen. Gee gently took her arm and lifted her to her feet.

"Remember what I said, Nina? We're Gee and Karen. We don't own you. You aren't our servant. You needn't pay us with sex."

"I… just… can't believe…"

Karen wrapped her arms around the girl and led her back to the table. Gee brought Karen coffee and then heated a pan for eggs. He dropped bread in the toaster as Karen continued the discussion with Nina.

"You don't remember having any other name than Nina?" Karen asked softly.

"When I woke up, they said I was Nina. That's all I've ever known."

"Woke up?"

"Um... It's the first thing I remember... when I started to be me. I was told what to do and when to do it. I obeyed. I was never bad but sometimes I was punished anyway. It pleased Sir and Madam."

"How long ago was that?" Gee asked.

"A long time. I was little."

"I need to take Nina out to get clothes and essentials and someone is sure to ask her name. Shall we say she's a relative of yours?" Karen asked Gee.

"Mead would be here in a flash if he heard I have a known relative. And your family is well known. How about the daughter of a colleague you met in the city? Trouble at home and needed a place to stay a while."

"That's good. Nina, should anyone ask your name today, we'll tell them it is Nina... O'Hara. Your hair is reddish, so it should work to make you Irish. I don't believe there are any O'Haras in town who would ask about being related. We'll say your mother and I worked together in New York. She's quite ill and asked if you could visit me for a while."

"People will ask my name? Of me?"

"It is possible. Have you never met new people before, Nina?"

"Only other sirs and madams. They don't ask questions. Sometimes people I had sex with on the street asked my name but Janie told me to tell them it was none of their business."

"I'm afraid Janie and Sir and Madam gave you some bad ideas of what the world is like," Karen said. "How old are you?"

"I don't know. I was about this big when I woke up." She held her palm toward the floor a few inches above her knee. I can count. I was with Sir and Madam for six Christmases before my monthly blood started. Then they gave me to a new Sir and Madam. I was with them eight Christmases until I grew tall. Now no one wants me because I'm too big."

"Karen, we are going to find these people," Gee growled.

"Yes, we are," Karen answered coldly. "Right now, we need to take care of Nina and you need to go meet your crew in the Woods."

"I'll stop to see the children on my way home tonight," he said as he kissed Karen. "Grandma Sue should be with them for the weekend. If you get a chance to stop by today, maybe the children would like to meet Nina."

The Crew

GEE'S CREW SATURDAY morning was almost double the size of his normal workforce.

"What's up, guys? I don't usually see so many of you."

"Uh… Gee," Ryan Moffat said as he stepped to the front. "Most of the crews aren't working during the winter but we heard you're going to clear the fencerow and thought that was a job we could all help with. We've been working out here since Election Day and we want…"

"We want to find anyone still in the woods," JD broke in. There were nods and noises of agreement. Gee thought of Nina's arrival last night and nodded.

"I think we can use everyone but the work isn't going to be easy. The snow is drifted on both sides of the fence. We'll have to use the wagons we've converted to sleds but it will be muscle power that moves them. You push and pull. I don't have any problem with you working with your girlfriends or boyfriends as long as you can stay focused on what we're doing. Good?"

"Yes, sir," they responded.

"Okay, sort out who is on what tasks. We'll need a couple of people with shovels to clear snow, a measurement team for the trees we can reach, an extra cutter or two, and at least two sled teams. And I want a scout at the front looking for any sign of people. Divide yourselves up and get your gear."

Gee got his own gear and checked to see that everyone had hard hats and understood the reason. With the heavy snowfall, many overhead branches were creaking in the wind. They headed to the woods.

"Gee, how do we tell if a sapling is hickory with no leaves?" one of the guys asked.

"Let's look at the bark," Gee replied. "Even young hickory trees have a deeply recessed and scaly bark. Look at this one. The bark is smooth—almost slippery. And see how the twigs are dark red in color? That's a dogwood. You can tell the holly, of course, because it still has waxy green leaves on it. We're not cutting dogwood and holly just because they are here—only if they are in the way of the trail and sleds. In the spring, we'll come out and choose some of those to be transplanted elsewhere and probably keep a few thickets to help replenish the soil when we take out the nuisance plants like the firethorn."

"I feel like I should have known all that after two months working out here."

"Most of it I've only learned in the past few weeks," Gee laughed. "I'm sure Gabe is tired of answering my questions by now."

The kids chatted as they worked, encouraged by Gee not to exhaust themselves by rushing in the cold. The goal was to clear a six-foot break along the fence, except where that clearing involved taking out a hickory. As the clearing crew drew farther ahead of the sled crew, Gee pulled them back a bit.

"Let's see if we can get more of these trimmings out of here," he said. "James, could you hike back to the office and see if there's another sled available? Drake and Viktor, you've run the chipper before, haven't you?"

"Yes, sir," Drake answered.

"You're both over eighteen. Can you follow all the safety rules? We must be building up quite a pile of brush up there that needs to be chipped."

"No problem, Gee," Viktor said. "Gabe gave us a full instruction course, which included wearing ear protection and always working as a team."

"Go to it then, guys."

Unemployed

GEE GOT HOME in time to eat dinner with Karen and Nina. He'd stopped by the hospital to play with the children for an hour but left when Grandma Sue arrived to have dinner with them. As he walked home, he wondered idly whether Nina might open some doors to understanding how the children responded to adults. He greeted Karen with a kiss at the door but didn't move toward Nina—just smiled at her.

"How was your day?" he asked.

"I think we had a very good day," Karen said. "What do you think, Nina?"

"I have new clothes," the girl said shyly. "I've never had clothes that were brand new before."

"I'm glad you chose that sweater," Gee said. "It looks lovely on you."

"Thank you, sir… Gee."

"We had lunch with Marian and Devon," Karen continued.

"Oh, weren't they at the hospital today?"

"Yes." Gee smiled and turned to Nina.

"Did you meet the children, Nina?"

"Yes." Gee saw a tear start in her eye that she blinked back furiously. "They won't be like me, will they?" she whimpered.

"No!" Gee and Karen both responded, causing the girl to shrink back from the table.

"I'm sorry, Nina," Gee said. "I didn't mean to yell. I'm not angry with you."

"We just get upset about what was done to them and to you," Karen added.

"It was evil," Gee continued. "We are trying to help them heal from what was done. Like you are. I don't know what it was and won't ask you to tell me until you want to, but I know it was painful. We will be here if you ever want to talk about it. We want to help you and the children become all you can be… all you want to become."

"How can I know what I want? I don't even know what 'want' means," she cried. Karen held her as Nina leaned into her to sob.

"Nina, we'll explore together. We'll learn together. You're not alone."

"Will I have to go to the hospital like Brother, Sister, and Littlest?" she asked.

"No, Honey. They are there because it's the only place we can care for them right now. You may visit them any time you want, but you have a place to live with us," Gee said softly.

"You are so smart and kind."

"I'm not much of anything," Gee snorted. "Nina, back during the summer, I lost my memory. Five months ago. Whatever I am has been what I discovered since then."

"You are… like us?" Nina asked, puzzled.

"In a way, I am. I don't think anyone tried to use me and make me something I'm not, but I don't remember who I was before I woke up here in Rosebud Falls. I don't know what is best for everyone. I just try to do the right thing. And that means giving you a home, helping you learn about life, teaching you to read, and helping you learn to smile."

"MISS WEISMAN... UH... Karen?" Nina asked after dinner.

"What is it, Nina?"

"I don't know where a clock is. I am supposed to be in bed by nine o'clock but I don't know what time it is."

"Oh. Let's handle one thing at a time. You want to know where a clock is. There's one here in the kitchen. Do you know how to read that kind of clock?" The old analog clock that hung above the pantry had kept good time since Gee cleaned it and changed the batteries.

"Yes, ma'am. I learned my numbers and to read all kinds of clocks so I could always be where I was supposed to be at the right time."

"Okay. There is a digital clock next to your bed and a clock on the mantle of the fireplace. We have clocks on our phones and when we get you a phone, you'll have that, too."

"A phone? Me?"

"We want you to be able to call us if you need something and I'm sure you'll make friends you want to talk to, too."

"It's almost nine o'clock," Nina said. "I need to hurry to bed."

"You are old enough to set your own bedtime but you probably don't have the experience to understand how. Do you go right to sleep when you go to bed?"

"Um... mostly. If I don't, I pretend. My lights must be dark and I must lie in my bed with my eyes closed."

"Let's try this, Nina," Gee said. "If it feels right to you, you may go to bed at nine o'clock. But... you should never pretend to be something you aren't. If you want your eyes open, open them. If you want your light on, leave it on. If you want to read... well, I'll find books that you can learn from."

"We have this rule," Karen said. "When you close your door, no one will open it without your permission. If you leave your door open, we'll probably look in to see if you are okay but we won't come into your room without your permission unless there is an emergency."

"Um… Do I have to close it?" Nina asked.

"Whatever you want, Nina," Gee said.

"And I have something else for you," Karen said. "This little guy sat on my bed for twenty years and cuddled me many nights." She handed Nina a stuffed panda bear. "If you want to hold him, he is there. If you want to talk to him, he listens. If you want to throw him across the room, he bounces. If you want to take him to bed… well, he doesn't snore." She cast a glance toward Gee and he feigned innocence.

Nina looked at the threadbare stuffed animal in her hands and hugged it to her. She smiled through tears and thanked Karen before heading to bed.

Gee and Karen sighed in unison, poured glasses of wine, and went to their own bed.

―――――◁◆▷―――――

"WE CAN'T FIX them," Karen said. "Any of them. That's what Dr. Salinger told us about the children. It's just as true of Nina. If we tell her what to do, we reinforce the command structure. If we don't tell her, she's lost. They have to heal themselves and we need to provide an environment where it can happen. Where they are loved."

"We first saw it happening with the children when Littlest got the older kids to take her to the bathroom."

"By comparison, Nina is years ahead of them. She ran from her owners." Gee snapped around to look at Karen. "Yes, owners. Under the best spin you could possibly give it, Nina was no more than a pet."

"A pet they used for sex," Gee growled.

"Yes, but look at the independent action she took. She understood what it meant to be sent to the kennels and found a way to escape. She's been surviving mostly on her own for three months. Janie taught her that her body was the currency that bought her food, shelter, transportation. But when it sounded like Janie was arranging another master for her, she ran away again," Karen said. "She's shy because she doesn't know how to interact with people in any other way. But she's a strong girl. She'll make it."

"What are we going to do Monday when you go to work and I'm trying to help the children?" Gee asked.

"Oh!" Karen giggled. "With all the excitement last night, I forgot to tell you. I've been fired. I'm unemployed and we'll have to live off your income from now on."

"Oh, no! Karen that's terrible. My sweet darling, I'm so sorry." Gee hugged Karen to him and peppered her face with little kisses while he expressed his sympathy.

"Thank you for the sympathy and cuddles but I'm not hurt or stressed about it. It's not like I was working in order to put bread on the table. I can sympathize better with people who are in that situation, though. It was a shock to be told I was no longer needed," she said.

"Why?"

"Because I'm head of the Roth Family," Karen said.

"I had the impression the Families got along okay," Gee said.

"Not that. During the election campaign, my byline was influential. Too influential. When I became one of the seven Family heads, the perception of my being an unbiased champion of the people, changed. I'm no longer a reporter, I'm a mouthpiece for the Families," Karen said.

"I guess I understand. But you loved reporting. What will you do now?"

"First off, I'm going to devote more time to my husband-to-be and our new family. I'll write. I've been researching that book for years. It's time to start writing. And I'll try to keep the Roths from killing each other over trivia. I'll sit with the other Family heads and discuss nut production and Forest management and allocations of the Wild Woods. I'll help with the children and try to be a role model for Nina. And I will love my husband and make sure he knows it every day."

A Match Made in Heaven

IF IT WEREN'T for the child, Troy would have thought it was perfect. He'd known Taryn for less than two weeks and was besotted. When he'd agreed to handle the problem with Dr. Jones, he expected to be saddled with the girl and the child he'd fathered. But Taryn was more than he ever expected.

She was young and beautiful but not so young that he'd be considered a pervert. He reflected that she was older than Violet and no one had raised an eye when he dated the Meagher heir. But Violet didn't need him. Taryn did. She wanted him. It was a new feeling to Troy. He'd always chosen his conquests based on what they would do for his standing. Someone richer, more powerful. A Family merger. And that attitude had left him single in his thirties. He didn't need Taryn, especially with the anchor of a kid with Down syndrome. But she needed him.

Troy fantasized about what life would be like if he took Taryn and moved to Palmyra. Or even to New York. Of course, he'd be just one more voice in a crowd of radio announcers and not the One Eye on Main. That wouldn't be so bad. He'd rebuild his popularity. The award he'd won at the Radio Television Digital News Association Conference would go a long way toward getting him a job in the city.

He imagined them in a three-bedroom apartment where there would be room for children. Well, at least one more. That kid kept rearing his ugly head in Troy's fantasies. Was she worth it? Everything else seemed so perfect. They hadn't had sex yet but she'd hinted that she was interested. Hinted without throwing herself at him. So unlike the others. She looked up to him and did not reject any of his advances. It was he who had slowed things down, wanting to be sure this was what he wanted. There was that kid.

<hr />

"TARYN, WOULD YOU and Ricky like to join my family's Christmas celebration with me? There's a family dinner with just my parents, brother and his son, and me. And you and Ricky. Then on Christmas Day the whole clan shows up for a feast," Troy said as he sat opposite Taryn in the restaurant. Ricky played quietly with some beads in his stroller.

"Troy? You'd really take me to meet your family?" This was what her psychiatrist had told her would happen. It was just more than she'd hoped for. The therapist had used some drug on her that helped hypnotize her. But it was just to help her overcome her reluctance. She'd undergone drug therapy before. It was no big deal.

As an unhappy teen, she'd been rescued from an attempted suicide and brought back to a position of self-worth. There were drugs involved then, too, but the psychiatrist explained what each was for and she was so desperate for help that she'd agreed. She emerged from therapy a happy and well-adjusted teen.

She thought life with Richard Taft was idyllic. It was what she was made for. But his reaction to the handicapped child drove her back to the brink of suicide. She'd sought out the same psychiatrist who had helped her before. The doctor had suggested that she move to Rosebud Falls. The positive reinforcement of the drug and hypnotism made her ready to find the love of her life. And here he had just invited her to meet his family. Taryn was certain they would move in together soon and she would become Mrs. Troy Cavanaugh. Her fantasies would come true.

She need only accept what her psychiatrist had planned for her.

Finding Friends

GEE WAS SURPRISED Wednesday morning when Ruth Ann and Sally Ann Metzger arrived at the hospital instead of Marian and Devon. It was the first day of the school's winter break and Sally Ann was excited to help.

"Sally Ann's teacher, Ms. Zimmer, told her class about the children found in the woods and how isolated they were in the hospital," Ruth Ann said when Gee greeted her. "That put Sally Ann in campaign mode." Gee was beginning to worry about the children's long-term care. They had been in the hospital for a month now and he planned to take them to the library this evening for reading time as he had last week. They'd clutched his arms frantically until Devon and Marian showed up and helped. They needed a home and he once again started wondering if he and Karen could care for them now that they had Nina, too.

"Thank you for donating your time," Gee said. He turned to his young fan. "Sally Ann, you understand that the children are not stupid. They just haven't had the opportunity to learn important things like you have. Can you be patient with them?" The little girl looked pleadingly at Gee.

"Gee, can they have friends?" she asked.

"I think that's one of the things they need most," he answered, lifting the youngster in his arms. "If you can be a friend, that would mean more than anything." She gave him a hug and he let her down. Sally Ann took her mother's hand and together, they opened the door to children's world.

His crew was already hard at work when Gee got to the woods. Gabe had checked their equipment and gone over the assignments before leaning back in his chair in the office and waving them on. Gee observed the work and helped at each of the jobs for a bit as the teens made slow but steady progress down the fencerow.

"Gee, this section of fence is all new," Ryan said. "I went back and checked the fence at the border of the Forest. It's in no better condition than the one we tore down between the Forest and the Wild Woods. But the entire fence along the Wild Woods that we've been clearing is shiny and new."

"Good observation, Ryan. I'll ask over at SSG to see if they authorized replacement or if it was done by the farmers. This isn't exactly the type of fence farmers would normally erect," Gee said. The crew was ready to break for lunch and headed to one of the cabins. Working kept them warm but it didn't take long to get cold when they stopped for a break. They lit the propane heater and gathered around with their lunches.

"Tell us about the new girl," Alyson said. Gee looked at the tall girl with surprise written on his face.

"Uh... New girl?" he stammered.

"Mom said she met her up at the hospital with Karen Saturday," Alyson continued. "A friend of Karen's who came to live with you?"

"Well, she's eighteen but very shy," Gee said hesitantly. He was having to make this up as he went, not having expected the teens to be so up-to-date with their information. "She was... sick for a long time and is behind on basic things like reading and writing. Her mother's been ill and the stress was too much at home. Karen has become her guardian for a while. We're just trying to help her adjust to her recovery and to learn what has happened in the world while she was sick."

The kids looked at each other and it seemed they had more on their minds. Finally, JD broke the silence.

"She's like the children rescued from the woods, isn't she? Was she drugged and brainwashed?"

"Uh… JD, that is a lot to assume."

"Not really," Jeanie said. "We just want to know if she was found out here in *our* woods and if we can help."

"We don't know exactly where she came from," Gee sighed. "Let me just say that the life she has lived for the past ten or fifteen years is nothing at all like what any of you have experienced. We'd like to not make a big deal out of things just now. She just needs to adjust to a more normal life."

"Nothing's more normal than having friends," Alyson said.

"You would never turn a child away, Gee," Jeanie said. "Neither will we. It's not like we come out here to the woods and work our asses off for exercise. We believe we're here because children have been harmed here. Even if we never find another one out here, we'll make sure the woods and everyone in it is safe."

"You kids are something special, you know that?" Gee said. "I'll talk to Karen and Nina. When I got to Rosebud Falls with no memory of who I am, I felt like a stranger everywhere. Then, one-by-one, I made friends. Karen, Mead, Ellie, Marian and Nathan. You were all part of that, too. When you came to my house on Halloween, when you marched to take down the fence, when you volunteered to help in the woods. I'm proud to call each of you my friend."

7

CELEBRATION

Deck the Halls

"THEY WOULDN'T THINK I'm… uh… a bad person?" Nina asked when Gee told her and Karen about the kids' suggestion.

"No, they understand you've been through a lot but thought maybe you could just use a friend your age to have fun with," Gee said.

"I don't know what to do!"

"Maybe that's something a friend could help with," Karen said. "I've worked in the woods with all those kids and if they say they want to be your friend, that's exactly what they mean."

"Okay."

"Maybe we could invite one over this weekend to help decorate for Christmas," Karen said. Nina's eyes lit up.

"Christmas!"

"You like Christmas?" Gee asked.

"Yes. I like candy and cookies," Nina said. "And no one gets punished on Christmas or um… used."

"Do you celebrate Christmas, Karen?" Gee asked.

"I celebrate anything. It's winter and there is snow and decorations and a roaring fire and a tree. I like it all. What do you like best about the holiday, Gee?"

"I like the… uh… I remember… smells. Pine. Cinnamon. Turkey. I don't remember anything specific but I remember the smells. Isn't that funny?"

"It is," she said, reaching for the little notebook she always had near. "I'm going to write it down as a new memory emerging. Maybe we should introduce a whole bunch of new smells to you and see what they remind you of."

"An interesting concept," Gee agreed.

"Um… Gee? Karen? Can we invite Sister, Brother, and Littlest to have Christmas cookies with us?" Nina asked in a small voice.

"What a wonderful idea!" Gee said. "Let's make arrangements."

"I'll talk to Jude and Laura," Karen said.

"Jude and Laura?"

"Gee, they've fallen in love with the children. The only thing stopping them from asking for custody is the upcoming wedding."

"Do they have room for children in their home?"

"We have to move across the street soon. They can have this house," Karen said happily.

"WHO'S FIRST?" GEE asked his crew on Thursday. "Nina would like to meet someone." Jeanie raised her hand. Gee nodded.

"We all thought it might be easiest if the first person she meets was also an orphan," she said.

"You've all been giving this a lot of thought, haven't you?" There were nods all around.

"Then let's plan on Sunday. You can join Nina and Karen while I try to control this unruly crowd in the woods," Gee laughed.

"Hey!" they objected. And then pelted Gee with snowballs.

"WHAT'S YOUR FAVORITE thing about Christmas, Nina?" Jeanie asked. Karen had the two girls in the kitchen mixing flour and eggs for cookies.

"Um… Sweet things. Candy and cookies. Sir and Madam let me sit at the table and eat whatever I wanted on Christmas," Nina said. It seemed to be the only happy memory she had.

Karen started to reach for her but Jeanie already had an arm around her new friend. Karen kept the conversation going while the two girls comforted each other.

"Were there guests as well as Sir and Madam?" she asked. "Like we are having the children and Jude and Laura?"

"Yes. Not with the sir and madam I ran away from. But the others. And sometimes there were visitors who brought pets with them, like me… Girls and boys… It was…"

"You don't have to talk about it if it's painful," Jeanie said softly. "We can whisper about it later if you want."

"What is your favorite part about Christmas, Jeanie?" Karen asked.

"Mmm. Gravy! I've been at Flor for five years and it's not like they don't feed us. I know some kids at Rosebud High who don't eat as well as we do. But the gravy they make at Christmas is the best! They cook a lot of turkeys to feed two hundred kids and the drippings laced with butter makes the best gravy. They use real cream and flour to thicken it. It's so yummy my mouth is watering already." The girls laughed as Jeanie made a slurping noise.

"Maybe you could come help us celebrate this week, too. You could show me how to make that gravy."

"I… Really? You'd invite me, too?" Jeanie squeaked.

"Well, Jude and Laura will be here, so Gee and I have an older couple to talk to. The children have each other. There's no reason Nina couldn't have a friend with her, too. If you want to invite Jeanie to come to Christmas dinner, Nina, it's fine to do so," Karen said.

"Me? Invite?"

"This is your home, Nina. You are free to invite your friend."

"Jeanie! Would you come to Christmas dinner with us?" she said excitedly.

The girls bounced up and down as Jeanie screamed, "That would be so cool!"

Sharing Traditions

Gee's crew worked hard Sunday morning but were all too excited about being out of school for the holiday and about Jeanie visiting Nina to stay focused into the afternoon.

"What do you do for Christmas over at Flor, JD?" Leslie asked. She was the youngest of the crew working Sunday but had been the first one to suggest transplanting trees from the Wild Woods to expand the Forest. JD seemed more relaxed and flirtatious around the girls without Jeanie around. He put on a very sad face and looked at the girl from Rosebud High.

"We have an old dead branch one of the kids dug out of the dump last year," he started the tale. "It still had a little tinsel on it. It had a popcorn strand on it, too, but the rats got that. We've kept it hidden all year so the headmaster doesn't find it. Late Christmas Eve, when the adults are drunk into a stupor, we'll get the tree out and gather round to sing 'Silent Night.' Then we'll hide it again for next year and hope we live to see it again. Christmas Day, the staff is nice to us. The cook might give us an extra portion of gruel and if we're very lucky it will be hot."

"You are so full of shit!" Rebecca said. She threw a snowball at JD and for the next ten minutes, snow was flying all over as the kids lost track of what they were supposed to be doing. Gee laughed at them just before he was pelted with a dozen snowballs.

"I think we've accomplished all we're going to out here," he said, wiping snow from his hard hat. "Let's gather up the tools and get back to the office. We won't be back out until Wednesday. We have Christmas Eve and Christmas before then." The kids cheered.

"Why don't you all come over and see," JD said. "A lot of kids have left for the holiday. You know we're not all orphans. It's a boarding school."

"I'm taking off for home tomorrow morning," Rebecca said. "I'm taking my roommate with me."

"Come on, Gee," JD said. "The invitation includes you."

"If you're sure the administration won't mind you bringing guests," Gee answered.

"It's our home," Trevor said. "We follow the rules, but we live there and can invite friends over. If we have a guest for dinner, the cooks want to know in advance so they can have enough food. Otherwise we're pretty normal. We've been known to raid the fridge in the middle of the night like any other teens."

"Of course, there's only cold gruel in the fridge," JD mourned.

GEE HAD BEEN to the school when he made his plea for volunteers and had been given a brief tour of the complex of dormitories, classrooms, and facilities. The whole place was now decorated for the holiday and a large tree stood in the cafeteria. There was hot cider on the counter and several kids took advantage of the hot chocolate machine. Other kids filtered in when they heard the chatter of the crew, talking about Christmas traditions.

"I did a report on traditions at Flor del Día," Rebecca said. "I think everyone does some kind of report about the school during their stay here. It started as a soldiers' and sailors' orphanage after the Civil War. Some time around World War II, things started to change here and the school was opened for other boarding. We each get an allowance so we can go into town for ice cream or to the movies. We have a football team but not basketball. Everybody wakes up again in the spring for track and baseball, though."

"Good afternoon! It's nice to see some visitors," Evan Nygard said as he strode up to the table. The headmaster seemed full of holiday spirit as he wore a Santa hat, oblivious to the way JD had described him as a modern Bill Sikes. "Gee, it is always a pleasure to have you visit. Do I see friends from Rosebud High?"

"Yes, Mr. Nygard. I have a good mix of Flor and RHS students on my volunteer forestry crew. We decided to knock off early today and share Christmas traditions," Gee said, shaking the man's hand.

"Well, one of our traditions here at Flor del Día is that from Solstice to New Year's there are always fresh cookies at three o'clock. Enjoy!"

Right on cue, kitchen staff began putting trays of Christmas cookies on the serving tables and more students started wandering in.

"Wow! Every day at three?" Leslie said.

"Yeah, it's pretty cool," Rebecca said. "We can't just wander into the kitchen any time for a cookie and milk. The poor cooks would never get meals prepared. But this is like our time for a snack. Maybe it's a little less spontaneous than you're used to, but we still get cookies."

Devil Incarnate

GEE TOOK HIS leave as the kids enjoyed cookies and made new friends. He headed for the hospital to visit his kids. *His kids.* He knew he would never be able to adopt the children but he felt a special connection with them that filled his heart. It was the same with the teens on his crew, the same with the children in the library during reading time, the same with Nina. They were his kids and he was their champion.

"Gee!" Sally Ann called as he entered the room. She bounced out of the beanbag chair leaving a book and the three startled children behind as she hugged Gee. She turned to the other three and waved them closer as Gee knelt so he could hug all of them. When he stood, Littlest clung to his neck and he carried her.

"What have you been reading today?" Gee asked.

"We're reading about Paddington Bear," Sally said. "We read part of the story and then act out the parts with our animals."

"What a clever idea," he said glancing up at Ruth Ann. She shrugged.

"I'm not really needed," she said. "I just let the children figure it out. And kiss a booboo or hug a child. I guess that's important, too."

"It is. I didn't expect to see you so late this afternoon."

"Oh, the kids have been having such a good time that I couldn't see stopping. I have a book as well and have been reading." Gee glanced at the book she held. *Positive Parenting for Autism.* He smiled. "The psychologist said it would give a good basic grounding. There was a copy here. I think Laura has been reading it, too."

"I just thought I'd stop and say hi to the children before dinner," Gee said. He got down on the floor and began running a toy truck through a mass of building blocks.

"We should put things away that we aren't playing with," Sally Ann told the others. "I have to go home now." The children joined her and soon the books and toys were all put away except the stuffed animal each child held.

"We'll be back," Ruth Ann said. "Merry Christmas!"

"We're taking the children for the holiday tomorrow," Gee said. "They'll be back Wednesday afternoon."

"Oh, that's good," Ruth Ann said. "They need to get out of this room more." After hugging each of the children, Ruth Ann and Sally Ann left.

"And we should get ready for dinner," Gee said to the children. They immediately began setting their little table, spreading the cloth and putting a small vase of flowers in the center. All without a word. Gee had, however, heard some giggles as the children were playing.

A few minutes later, Grandma Sue arrived with dinner and Gee said goodnight.

———————⋖◆⋗———————

GEE WALKED DOWN the hall of the long-term care unit trying to figure out how he could get the children released to a good home. As he glanced in the rooms he passed, he saw people sleeping, watching television, and reading. One very old man looked up from a vacant-eyed stupor and his eyes focused on Gee.

"George," rasped the old man. "George." Gee went into the room and paused by the bed.

"Most folks call me Gee. Do I know you sir?"

"George, we shouldn't play in the quarry anymore. It's too dangerous," he said. "What they're hiding is none of our business." He seemed not to really see Gee and was talking to someone else who stood in his stead.

"What is hidden in the quarry?" Gee asked.

"Things they don't want us to know about. We have to stay away." The old man shifted his position slightly and said, "I won't challenge you for the Family leadership, George. It's yours. You needn't eat the nut. Don't eat it, George. Don't eat it."

Gee puzzled over this. He'd twice eaten the nut. He didn't think that was what the old man was talking about. Family leadership? Gee stopped at the door to look at the nametag. 'August Poltanys.'

"George!" the old man barked once more. Gee turned and this time he was clearly the focus of August's eyes. "Take care of Jan, George. He wasn't ready." He then closed his eyes and soon snored.

August Poltanys. Gee recalled being told that Jan's father, nearly as old as Ben Roth, had been in care for Alzheimer's Disease for fifteen years. Gee hadn't realized the care was here in the hospital.

He was near the end of the hall when he heard sobs from one of the rooms and stopped to look in. The sight was both touching and repulsive. Lying in the bed was a figure Gee recognized. Rena Lynd, the flirtatious checker at the Market who had been addicted to Lustre and then was pushed into the quarry when Karen was kidnapped. She lay silently in her comatose sleep with machines monitoring her vitals.

Next to her, a man held her hand, kissing it repeatedly and crying. "I love you, Rena. I will never deny you. Come back to me. You are the only one who can save me." Gee started to turn away when the man looked up and he recognized Pastor Lance Beck of Calvary Tabernacle. They held each other's eyes for a moment before the preacher dropped Rena's hand and moved toward the door.

"You!" he spat at Gee. "Begone, Lucifer. You cannot have her."

"How is Rena?" Gee asked softly, trying to avert the preacher's hatred.

"She wanted only to be loved. To be loved and cherished. You spurned her. Drove her to drugs and into fantasies. And so, she lies here, unable to hear me calling her. Go! You have done all the damage you can."

"I don't want to hurt Rena," Gee explained.

"She is surrounded by my love now. I have confessed it. My love is enough to combat all the minions of hell you send against her. I will not let her die unloved. Begone!"

Gee glanced once more at Rena's still form and backed away, not wanting a further confrontation with Beck. His last glance back showed the preacher kneeling by Rena's side, his head bowed over her hand in prayer.

Silent Night

GEE SAW THE van pull under the *porte cochère* and stepped outside into the brisk chill to help Jude and Laura with the children.

"You have a perfect car for transporting little ones," Gee said as he gave Laura a hug and turned to shake Jude's hand.

"We bought it last week, hoping for a chance like this. We even had car seats professionally installed," Laura said.

"I'm afraid the kids don't like it," Jude said as he opened the side door. "They haven't moved since I buckled them in." Gee looked at the children and saw vacant looks scarcely masking their terror. He started into the van and then backed out.

"You buckled them in. You need to let them out so they know you are taking care of them," Gee said. "Otherwise they might think I'm rescuing them."

"Oh, no!" Laura breathed.

"It probably has to do with them being confined. They don't understand it's to keep them safe," Gee went on as Jude lifted Brother out and handed him to Laura. Laura immediately cuddled him and cooed over him. He hugged her neck, a slight tremble in his hands. Next, Littlest was handed out to Gee.

"Littlest!" Gee said, hugging her. "You've come to visit me on Christmas Eve. You are such a wonderful present." Littlest gave a slight sob and pointed back at Sister. Jude had the oldest child unbuckled from the car seat and lifted her out. She was not as quick to be comforted by him as the other children.

"It's okay, Naomi. No one is going to hurt you," Jude soothed her. "We just wanted you safe as we drove the car. Now we are at Gee and Karen's house and having a nice adventure. There's nothing to be afraid of. I would never let anyone hurt you, Sister. You are precious and I will always take care of you." The girl began to relax in Jude's arms as he comforted her. They moved into the house, where Karen was waiting at the door.

"Merry Christmas!" she announced as she kissed each of the children.

"You can't imagine how strange that sounds," Jude said. "We just need to get used to being multi-cultural."

"Go on," Laura said. "You've been Merry Christmased by my family for years. There's no sense pretending you're unaccustomed."

"Yes, but... Karen!" Jude laughed as he helped the children out of their coats.

"Jeanie!" Nina yelled as she pelted down the hall and out the front door to greet her friend. Jeanie had a backpack and heavy coat on as she approached.

"Nina! You don't have shoes on! You'll catch pneumonia!" Jeanie yelled as she scooped her new friend up off her feet and carried her to the door.

"Oh! Cold!" Nina giggled as she was set down in the entry. Karen handed her a towel and Nina dried her feet.

"That's why you have boots for playing in the snow, silly," Karen laughed. "Hello, Jeanie. Merry Christmas."

"Thank you, Karen. Merry Christmas to you. Are these the children?" Jeanie asked as they moved to join the others in the sitting room. A huge fire was burning in the fireplace and the three children were mesmerized by it.

"Yes. Brother, Sister, and Littlest," Gee called their attention. They turned toward him. "This is Jeanie. She is Nina's friend. You remember Nina when she and Karen visited, don't you?" Jeanie and Nina got down on their knees, a sign the children now recognized as an invitation to hug.

"They're like little sisters and a little brother for you, Nina," Jeanie said. "Wow! Look at all the decorations! Did you see the Christmas tree, Littlest?" Jeanie took the little girl's hand and led her to the tree she'd helped decorate the day before. She began pointing out different decorations and Nina brought Brother and Sister to join them.

"Jeanie is a natural with the children," Karen commented as the adults sat watching the them play Candyland.

"I wonder if she'd be interested in becoming a kind of au pair when she's out of school," Laura suggested.

"Are you thinking you might become a full-time nanny and need an assistant?" Karen teased.

"Uh… Karen, as head of the family, maybe you could help us," Jude said. "We'd… We've been talking. We have all the papers ready to file to request custody. Would you and Gee support our request?"

"Of course we will," Karen said. "What do you need?"

"We talked to Judge Warren and he said we'd need to be married before he could rule on a custody hearing, but that's just a week away. And there will have to be inspections of our home and a background check on our criminal records. As if everyone in town wouldn't know if we'd ever had so much as a speeding ticket," Jude laughed.

"We don't have a very big house, but with the record of the children and their care in the hospital, we should only need the two extra rooms. CPS will require a separate room for the boy and the girls, even if they never use it," Laura said. We could have custody right after we're married if you support it." Laura looked at Gee.

"I'll support it," Gee answered. "Now tell me about Naomi." Jude blushed.

"That was a slip. It's another thing Judge Warren said. The children need names. We've tried a couple out and they seem to like them. We call Sister, Naomi, Brother, David, and Littlest, Esther."

"Those are lovely names," Karen said.

"Then we should adopt them," Gee said. "The names, I mean. Everyone should address them by their given names. What did the judge have to say about a last name?"

"There was some talk about giving them yours," Laura said. "Naomi, David, and Esther Evars. But we didn't want confusion to arise, either in the minds of the children or the public. We did a lot of thinking and if you approve, we'd like them to have the last name of Woods. Naomi, David, and Esther Woods. Sort of a tribute to where they were found and lived."

"At least it's not Quarry," Gee chuckled. "I agree. Karen?"

"If it is our choice, I think Woods is an appropriate last name. You didn't want to name them Roth or Lazorack?" Karen asked.

"I don't think we need to carry on Family names," Jude said. "In fact… well, Laura and I asked the judge if we could both change our last names to Woods when we're married."

"Oh! That's wonderful!" Karen squealed, getting a look from the children. As soon as they saw she was happy, they returned to their game. The four adults had a little toast and settled back down. "Now, about your living arrangement," Karen continued the conversation. "As cozy as your house is, don't you think it would be a little small for a family of five? Especially a family of five who wants a live-in au pair?" Jude and Laura nodded and sighed.

"We figure our biggest task after the first of the year will be finding a new place to live. We'd like to stay north of the river, but property prices are a lot cheaper down south. We haven't found anything just right yet, but we've been looking around," Laura said.

"Come with us," Karen said as she stood. "Nina and Jeanie, we're touring the house a little. Can you keep an eye on Naomi, David, and Esther? Just call out if you need anything."

"Okay."

"I've never seen your home, you know?" Jude said. "Your grand-mother and great-grandmother were never very friendly to Mom."

"We're breaking down all kinds of barriers," Karen said. "It's about time, too. If we're a Family, we'll all be a family. I just wanted to show you how the bedrooms are laid out. We're only using two of the rooms. This one is Nina's. You can look through the door, but we don't go in unless she invites us. It's the room I gave Gee when he moved in but... Well, we don't need it for the two of us anymore. These two smaller bedrooms share a bath and as long as I can remember have never been used. On the other side is our bedroom. It's a full suite with a sitting room, fire-place, bedroom and bath. If you can believe it, there's even a dumbwaiter from the kitchen. But it's nothing compared to the master suite. Great-grandmother moved into it the day her father died, I was told. Prior to that, she'd been in my room. I've scarcely opened the door since she passed away, though I know Gee has been in to clean."

The master suite was nearly twice the size of Karen and Gee's suite. It included a bedroom, bath, sitting room, and a study with a deck that overlooked the garden in back. Large closets next to the bath still held some of her ancestor's clothing.

"Good Lord!" Laura said. "It's bigger than our whole house!"

"This is nothing compared to the mansion across the street," Karen said. "This house has five bedrooms plus a small maid's apartment on the first floor off the kitchen. Do you think this would be big enough to raise a family in?" The stunned couple looked at their cousin.

"Karen? Are you saying...?"

"Family custom says Gee and I have to occupy the monstrosity across the street. That means the cottage here will be empty unless I find a nice young family to rent it. Cheap," Karen said.

"I thought you'd give this to Jo," Jude said.

"Jo is still rattling around in a two-bedroom apartment. She doesn't know what to do with all the room. This place would overwhelm her. Would you two be interested in moving in here with the children and maybe an au pair?"

Laura crushed Karen in a hug.

"THEY'RE SO PRECIOUS," Laura sighed. The four adults stood at the open door of the children's room watching the three nestled together asleep.

"Are you sure it's okay for us to use the master suite?" Jude asked. "We'll be so far away."

"Gee and I are right across the hall and we'll have both doors open," Karen said. "This will be a good test to see how well they do in their own room without an adult hovering."

After another fond look at the children, Jude and Laura said goodnight and went to the master suite. Gee and Karen edged down the hall to Nina's room. Karen pushed at the partially open door to check on the girls. Both seemed fast asleep. Once she nodded that they were decent, Gee looked over her shoulder. He wrapped his arms around Karen and squeezed her to him.

"Our own babies," he whispered. "Merry Christmas, Darling."

Holiday Memories

IT WAS POSSIBLE that the old house had not seen so much excitement and activity on Christmas morning since old Aaron had built it for his daughter after the war. Gee went to the kitchen while Laura and Jude got the children dressed. He found Nina and Jeanie sitting in their pajamas with cookies and cups of hot chocolate in front of them. Nina had a momentary start when she saw Gee.

"Is it… okay… sir?" she asked hesitantly. Gee stopped short and turned to the table. He knelt beside it and reached to softy touch Nina's hair.

"This is you home, Nina. I'm not sir. I'm just Gee and you do not need permission to eat or to share with your friend." She nodded slowly.

"Told ya so," Jeanie said, patting her friend's hand.

"This cookie looks good, though," Gee said. He broke a corner off one of Nina's cookies and popped it in his mouth, much to her surprise. "Mmm. I hope you saved one for me. Is yours just as good, Jeanie?" He reached for a corner of her cookie and she snatched the plate away, giggling at him.

"You're a cookie thief! She squealed. Then she broke off a piece of sugar cookie and pushed it into Gee's mouth. "We baked lots of cookies Sunday," she laughed. "Nina made this batch herself."

"What brilliant teens. Now, where was I? I think I was getting coffee ready for the old folks." He returned to his task and listened to the two girls talk. Karen came into the kitchen unnoticed by the girls and wrapped her arms around Gee's waist.

"I just remember always liking Christmas," Jeanie said. "There was excitement and presents and food. Then after the accident, I got passed around to a bunch of foster homes. Some were nice and some were just a bed in a room where you slept and tried to stay out of everyone's way. No one wanted to adopt a troubled kid like me. But when I was eleven, someone came to the agency and said Flor had room for me. The staff and other students at Flor del Día make a big deal out of all holidays. And birthdays. The first fall I was here, I found out about Harvest and fell in love with the Forest. The thing is, the longer I've been here and the more time that's passed since I lost my parents—it's been ten years now—the harder it is to remember them. I have pictures, so I know what they looked like, but mostly I just remember things like being happy at Christmas. I can't remember an actual conversation, though sometimes I'll start to do something and remember Mommy said not to or Daddy said brushing my teeth would prevent cavities. I guess you not remembering a mother and father makes us a lot alike in some ways."

"I remember Sir and Madam," Nina whispered. "As long as I obeyed right away, they didn't hurt me. If I was slow, I was slapped or spanked. The only time I ever said 'no', I was strapped down and beaten with a belt. I drank something they made and learned to behave properly. It wasn't the only time I was beaten but the only time for being disobedient. But on Christmas, there were no punishments. I could eat all the sweets I wanted. And no one would come to my room at night. There were six Christmases before I was given to the next sir and madam. Eight until I was given to the next. And then I ran away when they said I would be sent to the kennel."

"God, Nina! That's terrible. Fourteen years? I'm so glad you found Gee and Karen!"

———— ⋖✦⋗ ————

"OH, THIS GRAVY is very good!" Jude said at the table. "Did you make this, Karen?"

"No. I barely survive in the kitchen. Gee did most of the cooking, assisted by the two young women here," Karen laughed as they brought more food to the table. "They kept me out of the way by giving me coffee and cookies."

"Jeanie was responsible for the gravy," Gee said.

"It was Sarah, really," Jeanie said. "She's one of the cooks and is house mom for the older girls' dormitory. I begged her to give me the recipe Sunday night and instead she took me to the kitchen and got out all the ingredients. Then she had me help make the gravy and packaged it in a plastic container to bring with me."

"I know it's made with turkey drippings. How did she manage that before the holiday?" Karen asked.

"Oh, we have turkey a lot," Jeanie said. "There are two hundred of us to feed at Flor, so we have turkey and chicken often. Sometimes we have ham or pork and about once a week we have beef. It's not like we sit around and eat steak all the time. They don't skimp on making sure we have protein but it isn't luxury cuts."

"Well, make sure to eat plenty of roast, then," Gee said. "I don't know why I decided to do both turkey and roast beef, but I just knew I should stay away from ham."

"I'm sure I could have found something to eat," Jude said. "I know Karen is not Kosher and Laura only eats what I do to keep things simple." He scooted the children up to the table. Lacking high chairs and booster seats, Jude had brought the car seats in and strapped them to chairs so the children were at the right height to eat. They were cautious about being seated at the table but Laura tucked the safety belts out of the way and they relaxed.

"I learned about being a picky eater growing up," Laura said. "When I got to high school, I decided to become a vegetarian. That lasted for almost two years. I learned that I could choose *not* to eat whatever I wanted but the family wouldn't be limited by my choices. And if I wanted something Mother wasn't serving, I had to make it myself. I can't begin to tell you how miserable I made myself by eating a veggie burger when the rest of the family were getting big juicy hamburgers off the grill!"

"Littlest… um… Esther, do you need help cutting your turkey?" Gee asked.

Gee helped little Esther with her meat and she grinned at him. Before she tucked into the food, she folded her hands and bowed her head, then gave Gee a hug.

"Barukh ata Adonai Eloheinu melekh ha'olam shehakol niyah bid-varo," Jude said.

"And thank you to the hands that prepared this meal," Laura added.

"Thank you for the new friend I made this week," Jeanie said, getting into the spirit.

"And for the love we share around this table," Karen said.

"Thank you for new memories," Gee said as he leaned over to kiss Karen on the forehead.

"Uh… Thank you," Nina said. She looked at the little children who seemed to be fixed on her, waiting. "Thank you for giving us a home." The children nodded and everyone ate.

"It's not like we didn't celebrate the holidays," Jude said as they all sat near the fire watching the children play. "We did all the rituals and prayers for Hanukkah. We lit our candles and ate chocolate gelt and spun the dreidel. But then Dad would take us into Palmyra to the big department store and we'd sit on Santa's lap and tell him what we wanted for Christmas." They all laughed at the strange mix of traditions.

"I think we need to do the same thing with the children," Laura said. "Winter holidays are to celebrate, no matter what religious background they might have. You know, Jessie and Jonathan profess to celebrate solstice but they are just as happy to sit in front of the tree and open presents as everyone else. I think they tell everyone it's a solstice celebration so they have an excuse to pitch a tent in the Forest and… well, you know."

"How about you, Gee?" What's your favorite Christmas memory?" Jeanie asked as she sat on the floor with Nina helping the children build a Jenga tower.

"Well, this is kind of the first Christmas I remember," Gee said. The two girls turned toward him. "I think it will be the first Christmas Naomi, David, and Esther will remember, too. We'll have that in common."

"You don't remember anything, Gee?" Jeanie asked.

"Karen and I were talking the other day. Your senses have a memory that isn't connected to your brain or something. I smell the tree or cookies baking and I automatically think, 'Christmas.' I find myself humming along with carols I hear in the store and think, 'I like this one.' I knew exactly how to season and bake the turkey. I think the decision to have a roast with it had some sensory memory associated with it. And even sitting around telling stories seems like the right holiday thing to do. But I can't recall a face or remember a name."

"That's so sad," Jeanie said.

"Oh, not really," Gee said. "I am making new memories right now. From this point on, when I think of Christmas, I will think of you and Nina opening presents with the little ones. I'll think of holding Karen's hand and sharing stories with Laura and Jude. I'll think of rocking Esther in my arms until she falls asleep. You will all become my memories of Christmas and they will be happy ones."

The Slippery Slope

NINA ACCOMPANIED GEE and Karen to the Forest Wednesday. Gee thought he was going to work. The kids thought differently. They met thirty or so kids from Flor and RHS toting sleds and inner tubes, accompanied by several adults, including the headmaster from Flor. Jonathan and Jessie met them with their own customized toboggan and together, they all trudged up to the cemetery.

"This is the best sledding place in town," Alyson said. "With all the snow we got on Christmas, we have to take time to play!" Gee thought fleetingly about the work they needed to do in the woods but all children needed to play. For hours, sleds and inner tubes glided down the open area from the cemetery to the lumbermill.

Gee kept an eye on Nina as Jeanie introduced her to the other teens. Nina didn't say much but smiled each time Jeanie told her something about a friend. The kids from Flor del Día were used to welcoming other orphans among them and treated her as one of their own. By mid-afternoon, everyone had marched back to Flor for cookies and chocolate.

"Do you think she'd be better off here?" Karen asked Gee as they watched the kids talking.

"That's so hard to say," Gee responded. "I don't think she's ready to just be cut loose without an anchor. It's obvious she's ready for more friends, though. We should facilitate that. If we can."

"I'm glad to hear you say that."

"Me, too," said Mr. Nygard, joining them. "We will welcome Nina here when she can be here. There will be special events that she's invited to and might even be invited to spend the night with her friend in the dorm. With your permission, of course. But we don't have the facility for the kind of special education she needs. Jeanie's told me a lot about her and I'm glad for both girls that they've become friends. But RHS is more likely to be able to meet her educational needs."

"We have contacts there," Gee said. "I'll talk to Principal O'Reilly and Susan Parris, the counselor there. It has been too chaotic to do before the holiday."

"Speaking of which, I haven't had time since you started working with some of our kids to ask you to be a guest speaker for our senior forum," Mr. Nygard said.

"Senior forum?"

"Well, a bit of a misnomer as it's not based on grade level as much as subject matter interest. Each week we have a junior forum and a senior forum. The kids can choose for themselves which one they'd like to attend. It mostly breaks out by age, but also by topic. The senior forum has a wide variety of guests, most recommended by the students themselves. You are currently the most frequently requested guest speaker.

"I don't know what I'd talk to them about. I don't have either a philosophical stand or a technical expertise."

"The students seem to believe that you could share something about what it means to be a good person. Conversations you've had with some of the kids working on your crews have filtered into the rest of the school. This is a typical age for kids to start weighing their beliefs and values.

"I..."

"Do it, Gee," Karen said. "I think you might help them more than you think."

"Well, I guess, I'll try."

Remembered Terror

HAVING HAD SUCH a fun day sledding with the other teens on Wednesday, Nina promised to meet them the next day to help clear the fence path. At the foresters' office, a more organized crew awaited them. Jeanie and JD took charge of getting Nina properly equipped for her first day with the crew, which mostly meant a hard hat, gloves, and vest. She giggled when she saw herself in the mirror.

"I'll work with you today," Jeanie said. "Helping load the sleds is the simplest of the jobs but it can be pretty exhausting, too. We'll take a lot of breaks."

"Okay," Nina said as they stepped out into the Forest. The paths through the Forest were snow-packed and showed a lot of traffic. People in town loved to walk in the Forest in the winter as much as in the summer. At the edge of the Wild Woods, though, signs had been erected, saying, "Caution: Hard hat area." As the branches began to close in overhead, Nina tried to stay as close to the fence and open field as possible. She helped load the sled as quickly as she could and pulled hard to get it out of the woods to the chipping pile.

"Hey! Easy there, girl," Jeanie said. "Have a drink of water. We work steadily to accomplish things but we don't try to kill ourselves doing it. Rushing like you were, we won't last all morning. Are you okay?"

"It… My heart… I couldn't catch my breath in there," Nina gasped.

"Oh. I think I understand. The woods can be pretty spooky but we're safe with the crew. At least working along the fencerow, we can see a field and open sky. When we were working on the little trails that lead to the Patriarch tree, you couldn't see more than ten feet in any direction and the sky was completely blocked. It can be a little frightening and claustrophobic. Don't worry, girlfriend. I'll stay right beside you. Just grab on if you feel panicky."

"I'll try to do better," Nina said. "I'm glad you're with me."

"If it gets to be too much, we'll call it quits and go get hot chocolate or something. Ready to try again?"

The two girls got back to the Wild Woods and began working their way to the cutting team that was a good quarter of a mile into the woods now. Nina focused on picking up branches and loading them on their sled, studiously not looking around at the threatening woodland.

When they got to where they could see the rest of the team, Jeanie pointed.

"Look. They've found something. We've been trying to locate other trails into the woods. Maybe that's what's there. Come on. Let's go see." Nina followed Jeanie, still trying to keep her focus on the open trail and not on the dense woods.

When they reached the rest of the team, they saw Gee and Drake headed down a barely-recognizable side trail. They weren't cutting the trail wider, just pushing through to see where it led.

"I bet it's this one," JD said as he held the geocache handset for others to see. "It has to be. We mapped it about three weeks ago."

"Whose farm are we next to?" Viktor asked, pointing toward the fence.

"That information is not available on this device," JD answered in a pseudo-mechanical tone. A couple of the nearer kids laughed at his clowning but most were intent on the trail. Nina was drawn to the front of the group as if mesmerized. Gee and Drake were scarcely visible.

Her heart began to race. Her breath came in gasps. Her eyes dilated as she stared down the path. And when Gee and Drake pushed some blocking shrubs aside, she screamed.

Her shriek took everyone so by surprise that they fell away when she pushed back the way they'd come. Karen tried to reach her but was on the wrong side of the group of kids. Nina fled up the path and Jeanie went rushing after.

"Nina! Stop! I'm here! I'll help you. Please!"

Nina was blind in her panic, pushing into the brush instead of staying on the path that would lead her out of the woods. She flailed at branches. Her face was ripped by thorns. She spun with no sense of direction, hitting another path and following it blindly before she lost herself in the thickets again.

———◁◆▷———

WHEN GEE HEARD the scream, he forgot all about the cabin they'd just sighted and turned to run back down the path. Karen was still struggling to get through the narrow space between the teens so she could follow.

"Gee! That way," she cried pointing up the path. "She panicked!"

"Watch out!" Gee yelled. Two kids fell on their butts as he pushed past them. "Alyson! Take charge. Clean up and get out of the woods. Now!" Gee ran down the path in the direction Nina had disappeared. In just a few minutes, he caught up with Jeanie, who had been following Nina as closely as she could.

"In there!" Jeanie yelled. "I don't know how she got through but she went that way." Gee ducked his head to take the bulk of the scratches across his hard hat and plunged into the thicket.

Nina's trail was easy to follow but no less difficult to navigate. Gee found tears in his eyes as he thought about the punishment the girl must be taking to fight her way through this tangle and disappear. When he emerged onto another path, he examined the trail to determine which way she had gone. He turned right and fifty yards on, saw where she had plunged into the thicket again.

"Nina!" he called. "Stop, Nina. I'll help you." No response came as he followed into the next thicket.

Gee broke into a clearing and got his bearings. A hundred yards ahead he could see the yellow vest as she ran. He realized where he was and put on all the speed he could manage to overtake the frightened girl.

Steps from the edge of the quarry, Gee dove at Nina and brought her to the ground.

"Don't make me! Don't make me go back!" she screamed. "I'll kill myself. I won't go back!"

She beat on Gee as he struggled to get her into his arms.

"Shh. Nina. It's Gee. I won't make you go back. I won't let anyone hurt you. Shh, baby. You're safe. We won't let anyone take you away."

She continued to struggle for a few moments and then collapsed against him, sobbing. Gee managed to get his cellphone out and thumbed Karen's number.

"By the quarry. Bring a sled," he gasped, still unable to catch his own breath as he held the panicked girl.

He heard a tractor coming down one of the trails through the Wild Woods to the quarry. As it came into view, he recognized Gabe driving and pulling one of the larger sleds behind.

"How did you manage? So fast?" Gee asked as Gabe dismounted and examined the girl in Gee's arms. "Karen called the office. The girl's passed out. Let's get her to the Forest. An ambulance is on its way." They lifted Nina to the trailer and Gee climbed on, steadying her as he held onto the sled bouncing them around. At the edge of the Forest on a service road, an ambulance awaited. Nina opened her eyes as they transferred her to a stretcher.

"Gee?" she rasped, clutching his hand. "Please don't send me back."

"You're safe now, Nina. We're going to the hospital to make sure you aren't injured. I'll be right here with you."

NINA DID NOT want to let go of Gee's hand as she was wheeled into the examining room, especially when she was introduced to Doctor Poltanys. She had nearly the same response as the children when she heard the word 'doctor.' If she had not been held down, she might have rolled to her knees. She was comforted, however, as Ellie came to her side.

"Adam won't hurt you," Ellie said, responding immediately to the situation. Adam stood back a moment and let Ellie take over. "He's not really a doctor. He just plays one in the hospital." Adam snorted off to one side. "Now, we need to look you over and see if you've been injured. You have some nasty scratches on your face and your hands are all skinned up. Does anything else hurt, Nina?"

Ellie had visited Nina at the house several times and the girl knew her. The panic receded from her eyes under the nurse's gentle ministrations. Eventually, Adam got close enough to examine the girl and put stitches in one arm where a hawthorn had torn through her jacket and shirt. The other cuts and scrapes were shallow but were cleaned and antiseptic applied. From somewhere, Ellie produced Mickey Mouse Band-Aids to apply to a couple of Nina's cuts.

While this was going on, Karen arrived and was shown into the room. She was in tears and clasped Nina in an embrace.

"Oh, Nina! I was so scared for you. So afraid you'd be hurt. Run toward me when you are scared, Sweetie. Run toward me and not away. We will always protect you." After a moment's hesitation, Nina returned the embrace and everyone began to relax.

MEAD OLIVER SAT near the fire as he jotted down notes in Karen's sitting room. The children's toys had been cleaned up but the tree still stood proudly with its colored lights blinking. He'd been served cookies that Nina had baked along with a cup of Birdie's coffee.

"It was where I woke up. He told me I was Nina and I would go to Sir and Madam that day. He said Sir and Madam would take care of me if I did what they said like he taught me."

"How long ago was that?" Mead asked. Nina looked to Gee and Karen as her fingers fidgeted.

"Nina hasn't learned to add yet but she can count," Karen said. "From what we pieced together this week, she woke up fourteen Christmases ago." Mead shook his head sadly as he wrote it in his notebook.

"Do you remember what else happened that day?" he asked. "Did this sir and madam come to the cabin to pick you up?"

"No. After Doctor made me suck him until he squirted in my mouth, he put a bag over my head and carried me outside the cabin."

"He made you...! You couldn't have been more than five!" Mead exploded. Nina shrank back. "I'm going to dig the bastard up and kill him again!"

"Mead," Karen said softly. "Don't frighten Nina." She turned to the girl held protectively beneath her arm on the sofa. "Do you understand what that meant, Nina?" She shook her head. "What Detective Oliver said means that the doctor who did all this to you is dead. He can never hurt you again. Never." The sudden relaxation of Nina's body caught Karen off-guard. She thought her charge had fainted. Nina nodded her head.

"Sir's dog is dead, too. I stabbed him with the scissors before I ran away. He can't bite me or... anything anymore." Nina spoke the words without emotion. She was lost in memories and Karen feared it was too much for her.

"This gets worse and worse," Mead sighed.

"Nina, honey, what happened after Doctor put the bag over your head?"

"It had a funny smell and I went to sleep. When I woke up, I was still in a dark place, wrapped in a blanket. There were bounces and bumps for a long time and it hurt but I knew better than to make a sound. I did not want to be punished. I went to sleep again until someone lifted me and carried me to a car. When the bag was finally taken off my head, I was in a house. Sir and Madam led me to a bedroom. It was very nice. Not as nice as the one Karen gave me. It was all pink and frilly and had a bed with lace around the edges and a lot of toys on the bed. 'This is where a good girl will sleep. Are you a good girl, Nina?' Madam asked. I nodded. I knew not to use my voice unless told to. 'We'll see,' she said. Then she led me to a tiny room with a blanket on the floor. 'Until you show us how good a girl you can be, you'll sleep here. Now, use the bathroom there and clean yourself thoroughly. Then return here at once to sleep.' I did what I was told. I was a very good girl."

"And this sir and madam… they did the things the doctor did to you, too?" Mead croaked. Nina nodded her head. "Unless there is something else you want to say, I think we'll take a break for now." He stood and left the room.

He could be heard retching in the hall bathroom.

8

TROUBLED WATERS

Punishment

"SICK. IT'S JUST SICK," Mead muttered as Nina left the room. At a few minutes before nine o'clock, she stood and asked if she could go to bed. The poor girl looked like she was still in shock but had answered all Mead's questions. "Not only the people who bought her but that she was… erased… made… created… here. The cabins. The children. The doctor. It's all too much. That our town has been a hub of child trafficking." Mead shook his head and stood to leave. Karen and Gee walked to the door with him.

"We've known something was wrong," Karen said. "We just didn't know how bad it was."

"If we find any evidence that leads to her sir and madam, we'll end up going public with all of this, Karen. There won't be any way to avoid it. It will be national news and the FBI will be involved. You might as well warn the Families."

"The Families want this ended," Karen said. "Yes, there are some who simply want us to say the doctor was the end of the trail and the problem is solved. We know that's not true. Pàl is ready to disassemble his company brick by brick to find anyone who was involved. A researcher in a lab may have created the drug but he didn't come up with the concept and network for capturing children and distributing sex slaves. He didn't go out in the woods and build the cabins—even

172

with the help of a shift supervisor. Someone coordinated this and set up the network."

"And that someone is still in Rosebud Falls," Gee said.

"I'm going to find him," Mead vowed. "My son is Nina's age. My daughter is younger. None of our children are safe if we let this go. None of them."

"Let us know what help you need," Karen said. "Loren and Heinz are frightened old men who want everything silenced, but their heirs, Jessie and Cameron, aren't going to sit around doing nothing. David and Jonathan are offering everything they can to help. Jan has started sending staff at the hospital through specialized training for dealing with any other children we might encounter. We have people and money, Mead. We'll get whatever is needed."

"Thank you, Karen. I… need to go now." He looked toward the stairs where Nina had disappeared. "Take care of her. I need to go hug my daughter." Mead left and Karen fell into Gee's arms to be held.

"Let's go check on our baby," Karen said. "She's had a rough day."

They went up the stairs and paused at Nina's door. Karen knocked softly and peeked through the opening to make sure Nina was dressed before letting Gee look at the figure sleeping in bed.

But no figure was in the bed.

"Nina? Are you okay, Sweetie?" she asked, pushing into the room. There was a rustle at her feet and she snapped the light on full.

Nina knelt in a pile of blankets by the door, naked, with her head bowed. Gee snatched her robe from behind the door and pulled it over her shoulders as Karen knelt beside the distraught girl.

"Nina, honey. Why are you here like this instead of asleep in your bed?"

"I don't deserve a bed. I was bad," she sniffed.

"You weren't bad," Gee said, kneeling with Karen.

"I tore my new coat and shirt. I had to go to the hospital. I made you miss work. You had to call the police. I'm bad."

"No, no, no," Karen cried. "You were frightened. That isn't bad. I was frightened, too. So was Gee. Frightened isn't bad."

"You won't punish me?" she whispered.

"No one is ever going to punish you like this again, Nina," Gee said. "You will never have your bed taken away from you. You will never have to do things to other people." Nina collapsed forward into Karen's arms, sobbing. Gee held them both.

"It just takes time, Precious. Time to get over your fears. Time to heal. Time to believe," Karen said. "Let me help you get to bed now. We love you, Nina."

They stood and as Karen and Nina headed to the bathroom, Gee slipped out the door and closed it softly behind him.

KAREN FOUND HIM sitting at the top of the stairs with his head in his hands, shoulders shaking. She joined him and put her arms around him.

"She'll sleep now," she said. "She relived a bad part of her life, not only in the woods but in telling it all to Mead. She forgot she was with us and not with Sir and Madam. It was like she rediscovered her room after I got her face washed."

"She couldn't tell us any of that before the shock today," Gee said. "We knew she'd been mistreated and sexually abused but seeing the cabin triggered all the memories she was suppressing."

"I should have thought of it. I was shaken by that glimpse through the trees. I haven't been near a cabin during the few times I've been out helping. My first thought was 'that is where he tried to kill me.' I felt my heart speed up and nearly fled myself."

"I was afraid she'd stumble and fall into the quarry. I don't know how I caught her in time. I need to talk to Pàl tomorrow. The fence around that pit needs to be repaired and we need to determine what to do with it. With the border fence between the Wild Woods and the Forest down and paths cut, people can just walk through to get to it. It's dangerous. Having a sign that declares it a hard hat area isn't adequate."

"It should be filled in."

"More than that. It needs to be emptied first."

"Emptied? How do you empty a lake without filling it in?"

"There must be a way. I need to talk to Jan tomorrow, too. Something his father said."

"His father? How did you meet August? He's got Alzheimer's and is in terminal care."

"He's in the same long-term care wing as the children," Gee said. "I was passing the other day and he called to me by name. Not Gee, but George."

"He must have thought you were someone else. Alzheimer's is like that."

"Yes. Someone from his youth. A memory of playing hide and seek in the quarry and they shouldn't go back because of what was hidden there," Gee said. "More mysteries."

"I can't deal with more mysteries tonight, Love. I'm drained. I need to be held by my lover."

Raging Hormones

"Gee, need to speak with you," David said when Gee got to the office Friday morning. The weather was looking threatening and Gee wasn't sure if his crew would actually get anything done today. The wind was whipping snow horizontally out of the open fields east of the fence line.

"Sure. What's up?" Gee poured a cup of coffee and settled into a chair near David. The two men were the only ones in the office this early.

"You're going to have to talk to your kids about going into the woods for... personal reasons," David said.

"What do you mean?"

"I had one of the guys do a routine check on the cabins yesterday afternoon to make sure there was propane for the heaters. In addition to your fencerow crew, I've had people out assessing the thinner area of the woods up close to SSG," David explained. "They need a place to get warm. But Lee found a backpack in one of the cabins with a sleeping bag."

"Do you think we've got a squatter?"

"No. I think we have some hormonal teens who have found a place to be alone."

"Oh, no," Gee sighed. "You're sure?"

"There was an ID tag on the backpack. Lee left it out there until we decide what to do. It's your call, but something like that could reduce your volunteer crew to zero and start a hullaballoo about access to the woods," David said. "I'd go read them the riot act and probably ban a few from working, but that's me. You've got a different relationship with them and this is your baby."

"Thanks a lot."

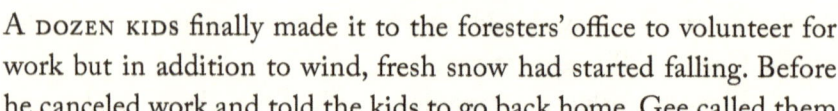

A DOZEN KIDS finally made it to the foresters' office to volunteer for work but in addition to wind, fresh snow had started falling. Before he canceled work and told the kids to go back home, Gee called them together.

"How's Nina, Gee?" Jeanie asked.

"She's doing okay. We found out, though, that fifteen years ago she was held in one of those cabins to be programmed for a life of servitude. Seeing the cabin yesterday was a real shock and sent her into a panic. You're all an important part of her healing and I want to thank you for that," Gee said. There were nods and Gee took a deep breath before plunging on.

"You're all an important part of the Wild Woods, too, and that brings me to an issue that only you can deal with. Guys, the cabins have been cleaned and heaters installed so we can work during the winter. They aren't set aside as a personal recreation area. I need you all to promise you won't go out there except as part of a work crew. I thought that was understood but it seems I need to make it explicit."

"Has someone gone out to party?" Leslie asked. "None of you guys drink or do dope, do you?" There was shaking of heads. Leslie was the youngest and perhaps most naïve. Gee was sure some of the older kids had experimented a little.

"It was me," Ryan said. "I went out to camp in one of the cabins."

"Us," Shannon said. "Ryan, you can't confess without me. Gee, we went out there to… because there isn't any place we can be alone. We just wanted to be together, you know?"

"I do know," Gee said. "And I know it's hard to make the right decision when there's an opportunity in front of you. Please understand, though, that if word of this reached your parents, you wouldn't be allowed to come back. I'm sure of that. We're going to have to lock the cabins. So, your actions affect more than just the two of you. Has anybody else had the idea of using the cabins as a private meeting place?" There were a few nods.

"We didn't even do anything," Ryan said. "I mean, we kissed and stuff but we got to talking and ended up leaving before anything else happened."

"And left your pack," Gee said.

"That was different," Shannon interjected. "That wasn't for us."

"What?"

"One of the things Shan and I talked about when we were out there and trying to get warm in front of the heater was the footprint she found. It wasn't far from that cabin. I mean, we were bundled up in our winter coats and had the heater going and we were still cold. If there's kids out there, they must be freezing. We left our snack food, drinks, and sleeping bag in case some kid stumbled on it and needed to get warm," Ryan said. Gee snapped his head toward David, who had been quietly observing. His brow was creased. Gabe, in his usual corner, brought all four feet of his chair to the floor.

"Please don't lock the cabins, Mr. Lazorack," Shannon said. "It might be the only shelter they have."

"We need to consider this, David," Gabe said. "What's our purpose been out there? If there are kids hiding, they might be too scared of the cabins to go in, but we shouldn't lock them out."

"Aside from you kids using the place as a private love nest, I have to agree," David said. "I was focused on the possibility of finding them, not of them surviving if we don't. Gee?"

"Yes. Okay. You kids have done it again. I'm proud of you. How can we put together a couple of bundles for each cabin? If you believe in this, I'm going to depend on you to figure it out. Go up to the school and sit down with a pad of paper and decide what needs to be in each survival kit and how much it will cost to put them together. I'll try to shake loose some money to buy the supplies."

"I'll fund it," David said. "Provided you all promise not to make unauthorized visits. I appreciate you wanting a place to go. I'm not that old. But you have to respect the vulnerability of our volunteer program and protect it."

"We will, sir," Ryan said. "I'm sorry we acted without thinking."

Trading Spaces

BY THE TIME Saturday morning dawned, a near white-out blizzard had descended on Rosebud Falls. "Worst storm in a generation," Troy announced on the radio. "Where's global warming when you need it, eh? I might end up spending the weekend here in the studio. Please shovel me out before New Year's Eve. I've got a hot date. So, for today, stay in, cuddle up, and stay safe. Here's a little jingle to get you started." His voice faded into the recognizable intro for 'Winter Wonderland' and Karen clicked off the bedside radio.

"I'm really tired of being woken up by Troy's voice in the morning," Karen said. "We need to find a different radio station."

"He's changed over the past few weeks. Have you noticed?" Gee asked.

"Yes. I'm betting the hot date he has on New Year's Eve is to his farewell party."

"You think he's being pushed out?"

"Yes. You should be prepared to find Wayne is unemployed, too."

"Judge Warren?"

"He has two more years to serve. If he's careful, he won't be asked to step down. District Attorney Mazzenga has an exploratory committee raising funds for a run at the position. Judge Warren won't be able to work miracles like giving people ID or arranging custody, though," she chuckled.

"Speaking of which…"

"Nina's ID is already in the works, as are birth certificates for the children."

"How is our teen treasure this morning? She seemed back to her normal self yesterday afternoon."

"I checked on her when I got up to use the bathroom. She was awake and bounced out of bed to hug me. She asked if she could make breakfast this morning and I agreed. I expect she'll be up in a few minutes to announce it's ready, so don't get too frisky there, mister." They both laughed and held each other in a deep kiss.

"Well, there won't be work in the woods again today. What shall we do?" Gee asked.

"Pack," Karen said. "If the snow lets up a little, we can walk over to the mansion and survey what we want to occupy and where we want things moved. We won't be moving a lot of furniture but I want to keep our bed. It's too comfortable to give up. Besides, the memory foam has memories of making love to you."

"We've made a big deal about telling Nina this is her home," Gee said. "We need to make sure she understands we aren't talking about the building but our family."

———— ⊲◆⊳ ————

NINA AND KAREN had a long conversation about things she owned now. They went through the bedroom and Karen pointed out her clothes, the few stuffed animals and books, and her bathroom supplies were all hers. The furniture could be moved to her new room or left behind if she found a room in the new house already furnished that she liked.

"Can Jeanie have this furniture?" Nina asked. "She really liked this bed and doesn't have one as nice. I would like her to have nice things because she is my friend."

"That's very thoughtful of you, sweetheart," Karen said. "Jeanie might not have space for this bed in her room at school. You know she shares her room with a dorm sister? But… I have a secret. You know that Jude and Laura and the children are going to move into this house?" Nina nodded. "They will need some help with the children. I think they are going to ask Jeanie if she would like to live with them and help take care of Esther, David, and Naomi."

"Jeanie likes them," Nina said. "I do, too. I could help."

"I think that's a wonderful idea. I know Laura would be happy to have your help. But if Jeanie moves here, guess where she'd be sleeping." Nina's eyes got big with wonder.

"Here? Here in my room?"

"Wouldn't that be wonderful? And your friend would be right across the street from you so you could see her whenever you both want to," Karen said. Nina grinned.

"Can we go see my new room now?"

————————◁◆▷————————

THE MANSION WAS as overwhelming to Gee as it was to Nina. It had been built and added onto to accommodate generations of extended family living together and had functioned that way until the great schism between Ben and his sister, Karen's great-grandmother, and their father's refusal to recognize Celia Eberhardt as part of the Family. Ben had further split the family when Leah married a gentile. Ben threw a fit and as long as Karen had been alive, had lived alone in the massive building.

Karen and Gee would occupy the master suite on the second floor. It had two bedrooms, a large bath, sitting room, study, and a breakfast room that overlooked the river and led to a covered deck set with a table and chairs. Money had never been an issue for the Roths. Both Aaron and Ben had spent freely to modernize the 150-year-old mansion.

"Are we supposed to have separate bedrooms?" Gee asked as he looked into the rooms.

"We'd better not!" Karen announced. "But we might need a nursery room handy one day." She waggled her eyebrows at him and he grinned.

"Any time soon?"

"Not until after we're married." They decided to make their intentions known immediately and have the beds moved out of both rooms. Karen's king-size bed from across the street would be moved into their bedroom. They would begin decorating the second bedroom as a nursery.

Nina chose a remarkably small bedroom—smaller than the one at the 'cottage.' Karen and Gee could see at once why she chose that room. It was decorated in a soft palette with curtains in front of a balcony overlooking the river. From her balcony, she could see the deck stretched across Gee and Karen's suite.

The closet was roomy but not so big that Nina's few accumulated clothes would look sparse. The bed was not as large as the bed in her former room but was very high. Two steps led up to the mattress of the old four-poster. From the bed, she could see out the doors to the balcony. It was cozy and comfortable and just a door down from the master suite.

Karen decided to move her great-great-grandfather's desk back into the library downstairs along with the papers and books they had been packing so carefully. Other family members needed access to those materials. The study in the master suite would be used for more personal pursuits like writing her book and Gee's coordination of volunteers.

"I'm going to invite Raven back to live here," Karen sighed. "I think she'd be interested in cutting some of her hours at the bar in exchange for more time and money to take care of the house here. Um... That means Timmy would move here, too."

"Nathan says he is doing well at work and is adjusting to the routine with no problem."

"That's part of what I was thinking. Right now, they live in a two-bedroom apartment. That's not a comfortable place for a single adult woman and her twenty-eight-year-old son. There's a rather nice maid's apartment behind the kitchen. It's smaller than what she's in now, but Timmy could have the carriage house apartment. It's where he lived the first few years of his life, so it should feel familiar. And it would give him some semblance of freedom without being too far away for Raven to help."

Gee looked at his fiancée and smiled. "You're going to fill the mansion with people in need, aren't you?" She bit her lip.

"Maybe not all of it," she said hopefully. "But Ben *did* say to fill the space with children. They don't *all* have to be ours."

THE REMAINDER OF the weekend was filled with the bustle of packing. Karen decided to move her entire bedroom furniture suite to the mansion and Laura agreed to accept the replaced furniture. Once she could get through the snow, Jeanie came to help Nina pack. Then the two girls enthusiastically helped Karen and Laura repaint the children's two rooms and decorate them. Everyone knew the children would use only one of the bedrooms—at least for now—but Monday, the furniture store delivered a double bed for one room and bunkbeds for the other.

"Are you even ready for your wedding?" Karen asked Laura Monday morning, New Year's Eve.

"It's on autopilot. Jude and I have lived together for six years, telling people we were getting married. The wedding itself is kind of a shrug to our parents. Rabbi Schlesinger will conduct the service, but it will be at Mom and Dad's. Just the families—which includes you, don't forget."

"We wouldn't miss it. What else would we be doing tomorrow?"

A small truck arrived to remove what Gee, Karen, and Nina had packed and take it to the mansion. An hour and a half later, it returned with the bedroom furniture for Laura and Jude's guest room. Then the truck went to their modest home and loaded out everything to move to the Weisman house. In all, the move took the full day and Karen tipped the workers double for having moved everyone on New Year's Eve.

Rather than spend the night in their new home, Laura and Jude went to the hospital and spent the night with their children.

Fire Sale

"THEY WANT TO buy our land," John Daniels said. Five men stood with cups of punch in a corner of the church basement after the 'Watch Night' service. It wasn't as big a turn-out as in previous years and the men on the board of trustees were doubtful about the future of the church. But the news that the foresters wanted to buy land adjoining the Wild Woods was disturbing. "I've seen them moving along the inside of the fence, clearing it and checking for breaks."

"We replaced that section in September, right after the monk died."

"The trail is still there."

"Maybe you should go ahead and sell," Deacon said. "Retire down south where it's warm. Florida is sounding better all the time."

"Like Simon retired?" Darren Cole barked. "Do you plan to kill us all off?"

Deacon looked around at the five board members of the church.

"Did any of you see bodies?" he asked in a low voice. "The timing seemed too convenient to me. I think they disappeared and if they had the help of a witness protection program, we're all in danger. I'm out of here with the spring thaw."

"They'd find too much if they investigated my barn," Daniels said. "We did too much staging from there."

"Burn it."

"What?"

"If you lose your barn, your equipment, and your livestock in a big fire, then you'd have a reason to be discouraged, sell out, and leave town. Probably even get a sympathy offer. We've been good here since our fathers started this. There isn't going to be another generation to pass it on to. Savage is investigating the books and has already called the church lease into question. It's been scrubbed clean, so we can just walk away from it."

"What about Beck?"

"He'll do whatever we say. We have enough on him to put him away for life. If the videos of his conversion therapy ever surfaced, he'd be locked up forever. And prisons being what they are, forever wouldn't be a very long time."

"Too bad about it all," Daniels said. "Such a loss."

"Might as well enjoy the profits," Cole said.

"No forwarding addresses," Deacon said. "And have your women scrub everything down."

Mazel Tov!

THE WEDDING, AT noon on New Year's Day, was held at the Lazorack home. It was a simple ceremony. Jude's brother Levi stood with him and Laura's sister-in-law, Jessie attended her. There was no canopy or breaking of a glass, however the rabbi gave seven blessings and pronounced them husband and wife. Rebecca Lazorack served a buffet reception for the twenty or so guests of the Roth and Lazorack Families.

"So where are you honeymooning?" Jessie asked Laura.

"In our new home. Don't expect us to come out until Friday when we go pick up the children," Laura laughed. "Except you know we'll be up there every day until we can bring them home."

"You're stacking up a lot of the major stressors all at one time. New marriage, new home, new children…" David said.

"At least I don't have to take over as a Family head," Jude laughed at his father-in-law. "David, we have a piece of paper now but you know Laura and I have been married in our hearts a long time."

"I'm not trying to be negative, son," David said. "I just want you to know if you need anything, you have family here to help."

"I'll always appreciate that," Jude said.

"And so will I, Daddy," Laura added. "But you have to come over and meet your grandchildren soon. You know we named our son after you."

"If you say that too loudly, your mothers will want to know why the girls aren't named Rebecca and Leah," David laughed.

"Grandchildren!" Rebecca said. "I'm too young to be a grandma!"

"All the better to enjoy the children," Karen said. David tugged at Gee's sleeve and led him aside.

"How are the children, really, Gee?" he asked.

"They're improving daily. Jude and Laura have already made a big difference in their lives. I've never seen the children expressing so much social interaction as on Christmas when the whole family stayed with us. It was good for Nina, too," Gee said.

"So, she's recovering okay?" David took another sip from his glass of champagne. "It sounded pretty traumatic."

"It was… terrible, David. I was afraid we'd lost her. And then when she told us about her life, I thought we'd lost her again. You can't imagine, David. You just can't imagine. We have to keep searching for children. We sat with Mead Oliver and ran numbers. Our estimate is that as many as three hundred children could have been trafficked through our woods in the past fifteen years."

"I'm not letting the Families sweep this under the carpet," David growled. "They've been known to do that. They want everything resolved and don't want to look any further. It happened with my father's death. The minute Gaston said, 'Accidental death,' they wanted nothing more than to get him buried and out of sight. It was the same with Meagher's great-niece. The van was found down near Palmyra, wiped clean and then burned. The case was handed over to the state and the Families washed their hands of it. None of us are immune. Karen revealing the truth about Celia Eberhardt made them want to hide their heads in the sand again."

"You're a Family head," Gee reminded him.

"I wish I wasn't but I won't abdicate to Jonathan yet. It wouldn't be fair to him and Jessie. Especially now that you've opened the Wild

Woods to us. It's not fair to you or Karen or Wayne, either," David said. "Dealing with Family politics should be left to toothless old men. I just hope you'll improve things."

"We'll do our best."

"By the way, the kids have started assembling survival kits to put in the cabins. Maybe your crew could take the first batch out tomorrow if the weather cooperates."

"We'll do it."

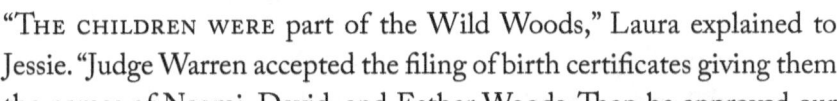

"THE CHILDREN WERE part of the Wild Woods," Laura explained to Jessie. "Judge Warren accepted the filing of birth certificates giving them the names of Naomi, David, and Esther Woods. Then he approved our name change as part of our marriage."

"So, you're not really fostering them," Jessie said. "You're really adopting them."

"Sort of. Their birth certificates will list us as the parents," Laura answered. "They're like Gee with no identity and no memory. DNA tests have come back with no missing person reports and otherwise show the obvious. Northern European heritage but so well mixed that they could have come from anywhere in America or Europe. And they aren't related within five generations. They might have come from anywhere in America or Europe. From overseas, from Canada, or stolen from anywhere in the United States. They're *our* children now."

"How long are we going to get away with things like that?" Jessie sighed. "I understand the necessity, but sometime it's going to backfire and blow up in our faces. There's an EPA inspector coming out to examine the woods and the Forest. He'll make rules about what has to be preserved and what has to be removed in order for us to keep control of it. We can expect the DEA to show up and demand to see the LaRue research on Lustre. If we can't show that we now account for every nut, they could order the Wild Woods clear-cut."

"That's too heavy a discussion for a wedding day," Jonathan broke in. "We're not going to let anyone cut our trees. So, let's have another glass of champagne and toast my sister and her husband."

Fair Play

GEE'S CREW LOADED a sled full of survival kits. They had rejected the idea of sleeping bags because of the cost and opted instead for large microfiber blankets that could be made into compact rolls. They included ponchos and socks in the kits with school sweatshirts. Finally, they included energy bars in plastic containers as the only food they dared leave in the cabins and not risk invasion by small animals.

It was the first time the crew had made the circuitous trip to all six cabins and they discovered there was no single path that led to all. Heavy snow sometimes fell from the high branches, resulting in a screech from one of the kids who got a batch down her neck.

"You should see it," Jeanie said as they trudged from one cabin to the next. "She has the cutest room ever. She doesn't want to come back out here, though. Finding that cabin really freaked her out." Jeanie had spent New Year's Eve with Nina and stayed with her on New Year's Day while Gee and Karen went to the wedding.

"Why doesn't she come live with us at Flor?" Annie, a tenth grader asked. "Are you adopting her, Gee?"

"Well, in a way. We're her guardians. But Nina has special education needs at the moment," Gee said. "Flor isn't equipped for that. We'll be going down to Rosebud High next week to see if we can work out a program. We might have to do a lot of tutoring. And she gets a little nervous around groups. She's making progress, though."

"So, what are you going to talk about when you come for senior forum next week?" Trevor asked.

"What's that?" Alyson broke in.

"We have a weekly forum for high school and invite speakers in. Then we have a chance to ask questions and discuss what was presented," Jeanie said. "Gee is going to speak next week."

"You all invited me. What do you *want* me to talk about?"

"The battle of good versus evil," JD volunteered. "I feel somehow like the Wild Woods is a battleground. We know the trees are good and the foresters are good but evil people made drugs and brainwashed children out here, too."

"That would be interesting," Shannon said. "I wish we had a program like that at RHS. But how do you even know what's good?"

"Yeah. It's hard to tell. Everyone thinks they've got a corner on 'good' and if you disagree then you're bad," Trevor admitted. "That preacher from Calvary Tabernacle spoke to us before Christmas. He had all the words about love and goodness but he sounded evil."

"That's because you challenged his quote of a Bible verse. The preacher got all wound up and told us we were all going to hell and needed to come to his church so he could 'teach us the ways of righteousness'," Jeanie said.

"He was creepy," JD said. Especially, the way he looked at the younger kids. Which I'm sometimes mistaken for. Like he'd already written off the high schoolers but wanted to get his hands on the twelve-year-olds."

"Talk about what makes a good person, Gee," Ryan suggested. "You've helped us. Not that we're all good persons, but we're trying."

"I'm not sure I know what makes a good person," Gee answered. "I'm just like you. Trying to live a good life and do what's right."

———————◁◆▷———————

Thursday, the crew was back on the fencerow. It was a more reserved group who focused on the task of clearing and finding more paths. They'd had a difficult discussion when they met in the morning.

"We should go check to see if anyone took supplies from the cabins," JD suggested. "Then we'd know for sure if someone was out there."

"What if that scared them away?" Leslie asked.

"Why would they be scared? We're kids just like they are."

"Really, JD? How dumb can you be? We might be kids but if they are hiding in the woods in this weather, we are nothing at all like they are," Jeanie said. "We go home to hot meals and warm beds. They hide."

"They're probably more like wild animals than people," Viktor surmised.

"Viktor, what a terrible thing to say," Alyson said, snatching her hand from his.

"I'm being practical, not critical. If they're out there, why haven't they just come out to see us? We're out there almost every day. But no one comes."

"Are you saying they aren't out there?"

"No. I'm saying they are afraid of people, just like the natural condition of a deer is to avoid places where humans are," Viktor defended himself. "If we keep trampling on areas where we leave things it will look more like we're trying to trap them than help them."

"I think there's an element of truth to that," Gee finally said. "We should do nothing more than what we usually do. We can use a cabin that is nearby to warm up and eat our lunch. If we're being watched, that's an expected behavior. It wouldn't frighten anyone and you can check supplies when we do that. Otherwise, we should stay away from the cabins and pray that those who need help find it there."

The crew had been convinced but weren't happy about it as they returned to clearing the fencerow. Eventually, things smoothed out and normal chit-chat returned to the group.

———◁◆▷———

"I DON'T KNOW," Barrett said as he clipped out a particularly tough batch of thorns and ducked his head back to keep from being scratched. "Those guys are mean on the court. And the refs give up and stop calling them on the fouls. I hate having to play them in the first game after we get back to school."

"What are we going to do?" Jim asked. He was another of the basketball players who had joined the crew.

"I say we give it right back to them," Lonnie said. "I'm tired of getting kicked around the court by them."

"I agree," Barrett said. "I'm not going to put up with it. They play nasty, we play nastier."

"I've never seen you play 'nasty' in our pickup games," Gee said. "I haven't been to a game at the school yet. It doesn't seem to attract as much attention as football. Do you usually play a nasty game?"

"It's a football town but we've got a good roundball team," Lonnie said.

"And we play clean ball," Barrett defended himself. "But when you've got an opponent who plays dirty, what are you going to do?"

"Why would that affect how *you* play? I mean, you play clean ball. Why would you start playing dirty?" Gee asked.

"Well, because they do it," Jim answered quickly. Barrett seemed to be thinking.

"I understand the other team doesn't play the way you do. Call it playing dirty. Call it cheating. Whatever. Why would you start playing the way they do?"

"How else are we going to win?" Barrett asked.

"Is winning what's important?" Gee asked. "I don't know if I can explain it. How are you going to feel after the game? I've taken a few psychological profile tests since I got to Rosebud Falls to see if I'm a danger to anyone since I don't have a memory of everything. It's like one of the impossible questions they ask on them. Would you rather lose to a team that cheats or win by cheating?"

"Oh." All three boys were lost in thought as they bent to clear more brush.

Icy Waters

FRIDAY, THE TEMPERATURE dropped steadily all morning as they worked on the trail. Instead of snow falling from trees, a fine mist of icy particles hit and clung to the branches. A crust of ice formed on the deeper snow drifts and footing became treacherous. A rifle-like crack rang out and they looked up to see a thick limb break away from one of the trees and crash to the ground, partly on the fence ahead of them. Gee called a halt and headed the kids out of the woods. They were met halfway by Jonathan coming to get them.

"We're calling the foresters in from everywhere. When we get this much ice on the trees, nowhere is safe," he said as he helped pull the loaded sled.

"Is it like this every winter?" Gee asked.

"Hasn't been this bad in a long time. And this won't help." Stinging bits of ice fell from the sky in increasing sheets of sleet. "This keeps up and you kids won't start back to school Monday," he laughed. "Let's get tools in the shed and get inside where it's warm."

The office was too crowded for everyone and the foresters offered to use the tractors to pull sleds loaded with kids back to Flor del Día and down into town. David held Gee back and the two men grabbed a cup of coffee to sit and talk.

"We'll be having a guest next week. Roy Waters from the EPA will be up from Washington for an environmental assessment. He's keen to know if there is an environmental impact from our work in the Wild Woods."

"Isn't it private property?" Gee said. "Does the Environmental Protection Agency have any say over that?"

"Well, yes and no. They can't tell us specifically how to manage the Forest or the Wild Woods but they can list rules we have to abide by. For example, he could find some hibernating red squirrel and decide we are endangering its natural habitat. Then he could tell us we have to preserve all the dogwood we can for them to live in. We'd have to show we were abiding by the ruling until we could get a court to hear the case and get the injunction lifted. Other things, he might just suggest."

"Like we should rake the woods to prevent wild fires," Gabe snorted from his usual corner of the room. David chuckled.

"Roy is one of the few left in that department that has a lick of common sense," David said. "We've worked with him before. He'll probably say things we already know, like the trees need to be thinned by thirty percent. But he won't tell us we have to cut or how to manage the process. He'll be more concerned about how reducing the understory will affect water runoff and if nuts washed into the water supply are a potential contaminant"

Gee rubbed the worry stone in his pocket, finding the engraved ridges comforting. He wanted to get home where it was warm and dry soon. He imagined an evening of watching movies with Karen and Nina while they munched popcorn. It would be their first opportunity to try out the TV room in the mansion.

"I appreciate the update, but why are you telling me about this?" he asked.

"Because you're in charge of the Wild Woods. You'll have to guide him and answer questions," David said.

"I will? I am?"

"Gee, haven't you noticed that other than an occasional helper, there hasn't been a forester leading a team in the Wild Woods in three weeks. Your student volunteer teams have tripled in size and you're sending them out in independent student-led teams that you supervise. Haven't you been the one directing where we were cutting? What paths were important and when to change emphasis to the fencerow? What paths need to be cut toward the Patriarch? I think all that qualifies you as managing the Wild Woods."

"But I don't know…"

"We're short-handed, Gee. It was okay to assign foresters to the Wild Woods in the beginning. If I assigned Jonathan to manage the Wild Woods instead of you, he'd still get student volunteers, but only about half as many. He gets out there to answer questions, to teach, and to give advice when he can, but you are the lead. You overruled him about harvesting the saplings near the Patriarch and finding a way to transplant instead. It's your baby. Run with it."

Gee let David's words wash over him, trying desperately to find an answer to the nagging question of why he was so invested in the Wild Woods. Karen had been rescued. The children had been found. Nina had told about the cabin usage that went back fifteen years. He'd found the Patriarch. Why was he still driven to care for the Wild Woods?

"I'll do my best," he said softly.

"I know you will. Now, let's talk a little about your strategy for dealing with Waters.

BETWEEN THE EARLY sunset and dense cloud cover, night fell rapidly. Gee carefully navigated the icy paths toward town, once sliding on his butt for nearly ten feet before he regained his footing. The ice storm had let up but the temperature had dropped further and wind whipped particles of ice through the trees and across the fields.

He stepped onto the Tenth Avenue bridge, grabbing for the railing as his feet started to slide. After he caught his balance, he spent a moment looking downstream at the water that had been his introduction to Rosebud Falls. Even today, he could not believe the foolishness of diving from the bridge to save Devon. But now the boy was more precious to him than ever and he knew he would do the same again if necessary. The water rushed down a center channel with ice growing out from the banks. Only the rapid current kept the center channel open. Half a mile upstream on the West Branch where the canal connected above the dam, the water was frozen solid. Kids had been out ice skating on the canal.

He saw headlights approaching along Riverside Drive from the south and thought the driver was going too fast for the icy conditions. He decided not to move from the slight protection of the bridge walkway until the car had passed.

His theory proved true. Turning from Riverside onto Tenth, the car fishtailed, spun, and then drifted toward the bridge. It wasn't really going that fast, he thought, but there was no traction beneath the locked wheels at all. The front bumper hit the concrete bridge rail opposite Gee and the car spun to the side and down the embankment.

Gee was on the move before he heard the crunch and splash of the car hitting the river rocks below. He had his cellphone in hand before he reached the other side of the bridge to look over at the car. It took a moment for him to identify the black car in the dark waters.

"9-1-1. State the nature of your emergency," the operator said.

"This is Gee Evars at the Tenth Avenue Bridge in Rosebud Falls. A car has missed the turn and crashed down the embankment into the water. Number of people is unknown. It's dark so I can't tell how deep it is but the headlights are definitely under water. I don't see movement."

"Help has been dispatched. Please stay on the line. We may need further information." Gee held the phone as he carefully navigated the steep slope near the bridge abutment toward the submerged car. His feet slid out from under him and he stopped with a foot at the water's edge, held by one of the rocks. Crawling more than walking, Gee moved upstream toward the falls. At this distance, he could see the car better, though darkness hindered his assessment.

"The vehicle is in about four feet of water if my guess is right. It is leaning far to the left downstream and is wedged against a good-sized boulder."

"Rescue vehicles are approximately seven minutes away. Is there any sign of movement in the car? People?"

"Nothing. But... The driver's window is shattered. The car is definitely filling with water."

"Police should be with you shortly. Please stand by."

"There's no time," Gee said. He pulled off his coat as he moved farther upstream from the car, now being hit by the freezing mist from the falls. He tossed the coat and his hat on the ground with the cellphone and started into the water.

Thin ice near the shore broke under him as he pushed toward the car and caught the rear bumper, keeping from being swept along in the current. Pulling himself along the passenger side of the car to the wheel well, he got another handhold and fought his way to the backdoor handle. It offered little purchase but the current pushed him against the car and let his feet touch the rocky riverbed in chest-deep water. He made his way carefully along the side of the car, reaching the passenger door window without having his feet swept from under him. Using the edge of the windshield as an uncertain grip he pulled out of the water and plastered his face against the window. He searched the interior for signs of life.

The airbag had deployed and was floating on water above the steering wheel. He could see the pale hand of the driver and no one else. Gee pulled at the handle of the passenger door but it did not move. *Locked.* He looked frantically about for something to smash it open but all he had was water.

The honeycomb pattern spreading from the left side of the windshield toward him showed the safety glass was held in place only by the tough plastic laminate between two layers of glass. It was the weakest point Gee could find and from this angle he could see the man's face, partially submerged. Gee raised a wet gloved hand and pounded down on the windshield. It took four blows with all the strength he could muster before he managed a hole. He tore at it with one hand while keeping himself anchored to the car with the other. His quickly numbing feet were wedged into the front wheel well.

Gee reached through and grabbed the man's hand, tugging toward him. Of course, the movement was minimal, stopped by the seatbelt, but the face turned away from the water as the head flopped closer to the shallow side. In that moment, Gee recognized the unfortunate driver.

Using both freezing hands now with one grasping the steering wheel, Gee squeezed himself through the broken windshield and into the front of the car. His sodden clothes threatened to drag him under the dash. A frozen eternity after losing his left glove, Gee managed to release the seatbelt and drag the man toward the passenger side of the car. A light swept the water and penetrated the rear window, then came to rest on the car. Gee continued to pull the man over the console and found the passenger door handle. The door was on the upper side of the car and Gee fought both the current and gravity, pushing with his feet against the gearshift to press the door open and push himself into the gap.

"Help!" he called toward the light. "I have a man who is still alive! Help!" His voice sounded feeble but Gee could see more lights in front of the flashing blue and red emergency vehicles being trained on his position. He closed his eyes against the brightness and held on.

9

RECRIMINATION

In Stitches

"AS YOUR DOCTOR, I'm ordering you to stop jumping in the river, Gee," Adam said as he stitched the cut on Gee's leg. Ellie held a tight pad against the jagged cut on his arm but Adam had decided the leg injury was worse. Gee could feel a slow trickle of blood on his face as well. He sighed.

"The first thing I remember is the sign for the Pub & Grub," Gee said.

"Yeah, get your smartass comments out before your future wife gets here," Ellie said. "She won't be amused."

"How is Beck?" Gee asked, wondering why he was being treated before the injured man.

"Gaston's with him. We split up the task."

"The coroner?"

"He's also a damn fine doctor on the staff here," Adam said. "Though it would have made everyone happier if he was conducting an autopsy. Why would you risk your life for... that man?"

"He was hurt," Gee said. Adam and Ellie both sighed. Adam moved to the cut on Gee's arm. Ellie used a damp cloth to wipe the trickle of blood from above Gee's eye. Gee winced at the shot of local anesthetic Adam gave him before cleaning the wound and beginning to stitch it closed.

"Gee!" Karen cried when she saw him on the table, tattered clothing in a pile on the floor.

"Mask, Karen!" Ellie said. "He has open wounds and we don't want them infected."

"My God! You're bleeding!" Karen said. "Do something!"

"Karen you'll have to go back to the waiting room if you can't calm down," Adam said. Karen caught her breath and regained her composure.

"I'm sorry. Gee, I love you. I had to see that you were alive. I need to go back out and wait. Nina is out there and she's scared to death."

"Take her to the children's room," Gee suggested. "I'll be okay until Adam decides on a bigger needle. Nothing's broken. I'm just a little scratched up. I love you."

"We *think* nothing's broken," Ellie said. "When Adam's done with the worst of the cuts, we're getting Gee into x-ray."

"Okay. I love you, Gee. We're here for you."

"Make sure Nina knows I love her, too, Karen."

------------◄◆►------------

MEAD OLIVER HAD no better opinion of Gee's good deed than Adam had. Gee was wheeled into a room after x-rays had shown no fractures, even though he was bruised from the battering of the current and rocks.

"You couldn't have waited for the rescue vehicles?" Mead demanded.

"He would have died."

"Maybe. No great loss."

"Mead…"

"Gee, you rescued your greatest enemy. Do you think that will change things? Lance Beck is still going to blast you from the pulpit. He's still going to invite parents to send him their children for conversion therapy. He's still going to poison the minds of the community. But you dragged him out of a wrecked car, kept him breathing, and held him above water while you risked drowning."

"I had to do it."

"I know. And I respect you for it." Mead sat heavily in a chair and took out a notebook to scratch in as they talked. "Finding Nina. Her panic in the woods. We know he has something to do with it all."

"Nina's time in the Woods was before Beck came to town, Mead. We can't blame him for that."

"We're all edgy," Mead sighed. "We lost one of our ambulances on the way to help. Slid off Fairview Avenue and nearly ended up in the river itself. We only have two tow trucks in this town and we need both to pull the car out of the river. But one is pulling the ambulance back up to the street while the other is anchoring the car so it doesn't dislodge and crash downstream. If we have an emergency right now, we have one ambulance that could respond. No one should be out driving on this ice."

"I wasn't driving, Mead."

"I wasn't blaming you. Just, like always, you're in the middle of it," Mead said in frustration. "Okay. We got to the point where you were smashing out the windshield and getting lacerations on your right arm," he continued. "Tell me more."

"Things got confusing. It was… really cold. I lost track of which way was up. I know I lost a glove trying to unfasten the seatbelt. I remember dragging him across the seat and wedging the door open with my shoulder. And calling for help. He started to wake up and I struggled to keep him calm. But I don't remember much else until they fastened a harness around me and dragged me through the water to shore. Then it was the ambulance."

"Had to hold Beck in the ambulance to wait for you because the other one was off the road," Mead said. "Gave the fire and rescue boys a real workout. Finally stretched a ladder across to the car to make a bridge to reach you. And you weighed about twice as much with your waterlogged clothes. I brought your coat, hat and cellphone in for you, by the way. I don't think you have any clothes left."

"They aren't letting me go home tonight. Karen will bring me clothes in the morning."

"She's a bit of a wreck comforting Nina," Mead said. "Should be back soon, though. Laura is up with the kids and they're all hugging Nina."

"She'll be fine," Karen said as she walked into the room. "I could have been back sooner but they told me you were in x-ray."

"Just bruised, not broken," Gee said.

"Just lucky," Karen responded.

"I have everything I need for now," Mead said. "Let me know if you remember something we should check out. It looks pretty clear at this stage."

"Thanks, Mead." The detective left the room. Free from doctors, nurses, and police for the first time, Gee held out his arms and Karen flung herself into them.

"I'm sorry, Love," Gee said as he tried to calm her tears. "I didn't mean to frighten you and Nina."

"I know," she sniffed. "Nina was… Oh, Gee! She thought she was to blame. She just kept saying she was sorry and please not to send her away. What could I do? I had to stay and tell her what happened and that it wasn't her fault. She's still so afraid we'll send her back to her former masters." Gee held her and petted her hair, though his arm was stiff and he had trouble reaching her. "She's okay with Laura and the children now. I'll bring her down to see you and then take her home."

"Karen, about Beck…"

"You never have to explain something like that to me," she said, cutting him off. "I don't like him. I want to believe he's responsible for all the bad we've found… the kidnapping, Rena, the children… I want him to be struck by a bolt of lightning as he stands distorting the Word of God in his pulpit. But God is silent. Maybe the accident was God finally taking action and coming up against you, the Champion of the City, thwarting god's best move. Or maybe the accident was simply another test to show how pure you are. No matter, I'm not the judge. I am your lover and your supporter and your helper and your partner."

"I love you, Karen. You are my refuge as well."

———— ⋞◆⋟ ————

"I WAS SCARED," Nina said as she sat on the edge of Gee's hospital bed so he could give her a hug. She'd come in to say goodnight before they went home.

"What were you scared of, Nina?" Gee asked. "Do you know?"

"I thought it was because you were nice to me. I knew it was my fault and you'd punish me because you were hurt." Karen edged up on the bed behind her and stroked her hair.

"Honey, why would you be punished because Gee was hurt. You didn't have anything to do with it. You didn't cause the accident or make Gee foolishly jump in the water. Who would ever punish you for that?"

"Sir and Madam. Sometimes they watched television and punished me for what they saw. Sometimes they came home late at night and took me from my kennel to punish me for what they saw or did when they were gone. It's all my fault. I get punished."

"Kick the dog," Gee whispered. Karen jotted down notes. Everything relating to Gee's or Nina's past was important. "Nina, I will never…" he glanced at Karen and she nodded. "We will never punish you like that. We will not blame you for things you do not control. And even if you do something wrong, we will never, ever hit you or abuse you. We want you to be safe with us, not frightened."

"Even though you got hurt?" she squeaked.

"Trust me. I've been told by people who know, how foolish I was tonight and how I deserved the injuries I got."

Nina hugged him again and stood up so Karen could kiss Gee.

"They're keeping you overnight, but I need to take our girl home and get her to bed. We all have a big day tomorrow helping the children move to their new home."

"I wouldn't be much company tonight," Gee yawned. "They brought me another blanket and I'm finally getting warm. I love you."

Karen and Nina left to walk the half dozen blocks home.

Homecoming

GEE WAS RELEASED in time to help the children pack.

"My! Where did you get so many clothes?" he laughed as each child brought shirts, pants, and underwear for him to see before putting them in the little suitcases. Laura and Jude had been buying things for the children and now it all had to be boxed and taken to the house where the new family would be living.

Esther stood watching Jude carry the box of books to the car with her lip trembling. She looked uncertainly at Gee and he held his arms out. She launched herself into them and he carried her around the room assuring her. The children had lived here for seven weeks. It was the only home they'd known since being found on the truck. Seeing the familiar things disappearing from the room and the room gradually transforming back into a sterile hospital room instead of their home was obviously stressing them.

"Once upon a time, there were three children who went on a great adventure," Gee began. The children had heard Gee tell stories enough times that their focus snapped to him and he sat on the edge of their bed, Littlest still in his arms. Gee continued his story. "'What do we need for an adventure?' the big girl asked. 'A bear,' said the boy. 'A book,' said the girl. 'I need Brother and Sister,' said the little one. She took the hands of her brother and sister and with bear and book they went on a hunt for adventure." Gee paused in the story as Laura brought winter coats for the children.

"It's cold outside," she said. "The children need to bundle up warmly so they can go on their big adventure. Naomi, can you help Esther with her coat, please?" Now that they were engaged in the process of actually leaving, the children became more active and walked to Jude's car. The main roads were deemed safe for travel but the children were still nervous about being fastened into the car seats. Gee and Jude gently reassured them and showed them that Laura and Jude also fastened seatbelts.

Three vehicles made their cautious way from the hospital to Laura and Jude's home, formerly Karen's. Grandma Sue had agreed to a temporary position as live-in nanny for the children and would begin training Jeanie when she was available. Her car was filled with boxes of the children's toys.

Jeanie was waiting at the door with Nina to welcome the children to their new home. The children understood quickly which rooms were theirs and put their toys and books in the room with bunkbeds with their clothes and bedtime things in the room with a double bed. Grandma Sue moved into what had been Karen's bedroom suite and the children visited her as they explored their new home.

<hr>

NINA AND JEANIE helped the children into different sized booster seats at the dining table when pizza was delivered. Prayer before meals had morphed into a simple bowing of heads as one of the adults said, "Thank you for this food." It was a compromise among Jude's Jewish prayer, Laura's Lutheran prayer, and Grandma Sue's Baptist prayer. The adults agreed to keep it simple.

Pizza was a new experience for the children and they were soon decorated with tomato sauce from ear to ear. The laughter of the teens was infectious and the children were soon giggling as well.

"Come to Mommy, Esther. Let's get your face cleaned up." The child immediately went to Laura to have her face washed and give her a hug. Naomi and David lined up next and then scampered off to their playroom.

"That was quick," Karen said, as Laura watched the children head upstairs. Gee reached to take Karen's hand. Laura turned and blushed as Jude wrapped her in his arms.

"Well… It's just… We're parents!" she burst out.

"It's a dream," Jude said. "We have children of our own."

"I'm so happy for you," Karen said. "It's wonderful that the children are responding to you so well. You really are a Mommy and Daddy."

Jeanie had a quick whispered conversation with Laura and Jude as they cleared the table. She nodded at Nina. Nina tugged at Karen's sleeve to get her attention.

"Mommy, may I spend the night here with Jeanie?" she asked. Karen's mouth dropped open. Nina waited expectantly.

"Um… uh… Is it okay with Laura and Jude?" she choked out.

"We told Jeanie she could invite her. Jeanie's headed back to Flor tomorrow afternoon but this bedroom will be hers when she is with us," Laura said.

"Then yes, Sweetie. Do you need to run home and get your night things?"

"Yes. Thank you." She and Jeanie left for the quick trip across the street to pack Nina's overnight bag.

"Wow," Karen sighed. "Wow."

"It sounded like you are parents, too," Grandma Sue said softly.

"Wow," Karen repeated.

Making a Family

"I'M SO SORRY you were fired, Troy," Taryn said as she sat beside him on the little sofa in her apartment. It was late Sunday evening and she'd just gotten Ricky settled in bed. Monday would be the first morning Troy did not need to get up early and head for his window on Main Street as people started moving in Rosebud Falls.

"I knew it was happening before Christmas," he said. "It's a backlash against the Families." He pulled Taryn into his arms to kiss her. Their relationship had moved quickly after Christmas with Troy's family. Even his mother had taken to Ricky as if he were her grandchild. Christmas Eve, Troy and Taryn had slept together for the first time. She melted into his arms, compliant to his every wish.

"What will you do?"

"I have a pretty good following and this isn't the only station that reaches Rosebud Falls. But I'm thinking a fresh start somewhere would be good. Anyone with a Family name around here is going to have a hard time being in the media or politics," he said.

"The Families are funny. Everyone looks to you for help and then pushes you away from the places you could do good," she said. "I've never seen a place like this. Of course, I haven't really traveled that much. What are they going to do with your morning show?"

"Oh, they were very clever. We've had a kid as an intern doing weekend slots for several months. He managed a mid-year graduation from high school and they are moving him straight into the Eye on Main. He's nice enough but he's about to come face-to-face with the hard reality of having a full-time job in the public eye. You don't sit in that window and pick your nose."

"Troy, you talk bravely, but I know deep down you're hurting. You've been in that job since you left broadcast school," Taryn said. Troy was amazed again at how gentle and empathetic she was. She was simply perfect. "I just want you to know… I'm very comfortable with you, Troy. If you want me, I'll be whatever you need me to be. You can talk to me. You can cry with me. You can make love to me. Whatever you want, Troy." He looked at woman curled in his arms. Ten years younger and so willing to please him. Wanting to take care of him. What was he waiting for?

He spared only a flicker of a thought for the mentally challenged child in the next room.

"Is that true, Taryn? You'll be whatever I want?"

"Yes."

"Will you be my wife?"

"Troy! Do you mean that? Yes! Of course I'll marry you."

"We'll probably have to move away from Rosebud Falls," he said. "I've sent out queries to some bigger cities. We'll need to move."

"I only just got to Rosebud Falls a couple of months ago. I'm not that attached."

"Then let's find a justice of the peace and seal the deal tomorrow."

"Tonight, let's make love," she responded. She led Troy to her bedroom and into her bed.

SATED AND CONTENT, the couple fell asleep in each other's arms. He was roused from sleep when Ricky fussed in the next room and Taryn went to attend him.

What had he done? If he married Taryn, the mongoloid child came with the deal.

Oh well. Kids like that often died young, didn't they?

School Day

STILL STIFF FROM his escapade in the water, Gee sat at the table with a cup in his hand. Nina was busy at the stove as she chattered about her weekend with Jeanie and the children. Laura taught the two girls how to make pancakes and Nina insisted she wanted to fix breakfast for Karen and Gee.

"The children are like me," she said as she chatted away. Karen came into the kitchen and Gee poured her a cup of coffee as Nina mixed the batter. "Except, I talk now. I didn't before, though. I wasn't allowed to say anything when I was with Sir and Madam. You are so nice to me! You ask me things and let me answer. I think Naomi will begin talking soon. I thought I heard her whisper something to David Saturday night."

"That would be wonderful, Sweetie. Soon they'll be ready to start school, like you will," Karen said.

"Will I really go to school? I've learned my ABCs and counting up really high. I want to read books like Gee reads to us."

"We don't know what kind of classes they will recommend for you," Gee said. "Ms. Parris will talk to you and ask you a lot of questions this morning. Just remember that all you have to do is answer the best you can. This isn't like a test you have to pass. It's so we'll know how to help you learn."

"Will… um… Ms. Parris want me… to do things?"

"Things?" Karen asked. Nina hung her head. Karen jumped up to hug the girl and Gee moved over to flip the pancake on the griddle. "*No one* will ask you to do things like that again. And if they do, you can say no. If anyone tries to make you have sex with them, tell us and they will never try again. Do you understand me, Honey? No one will abuse you like that ever again!"

"WELL, WHAT DO we have?" Principal O'Reilly asked as Nina and Susan Parris joined them in the conference room. Gee and Karen had spent most of the hour while Nina was being tested chatting with the principal. "Was it difficult, Nina?"

"I don't know things Ms. Parris asked," she said.

"Not everything, but you know some of the very important things."

"Tell us all about it," the principal suggested. A well-disciplined child counselor, Ms. Parris began by addressing her remarks directly to Nina.

"You are a very intelligent young woman. Very smart. Talking to you has convinced me we should talk to the younger children Gee rescued."

"I didn't really do any rescuing of the children or of Nina."

"I understand and won't argue the point," Susan said. "Often, when there is long-term drug and physical abuse—even prescription drugs for ADHD and other common treatments—we find the child is damaged intellectually. Nina, you have been deprived of an education but you are in no way intellectually challenged."

"Is that good?" Nina asked.

"Yes! It means you want to learn and you're capable of learning. So, we want to help you learn as quickly as you can." Susan finally turned to Gee and Karen. "Which is our problem. Nina needs the fundamentals of an elementary school education, though she will probably advance through them rapidly. I don't think she should be placed in a class of six-year-olds and forced to progress at their pace. Socially, she as at the level of a new high school student. She's new in the adult world and is learning to make friends but she is still a little shy as she feels her way. Sexually… Nina has experience that I hope no other high school student in Rosebud Falls has suffered. This has given her a distorted view of sexual maturity that relates strongly to reward and punishment. And finally, we have the issue of age. Nina is eighteen. Technically, that means she is an adult and the school system does not have an adult education program. I don't think we can help her here at the school."

"That might be," the principal said, "but let's focus on what Nina needs and wants before we decide how to provide for her." The discussion went on for an hour before any conclusions were reached.

"So, what we have in the near-term is a homeschooling program that would be guided by and supplemented by an elementary school teacher. If the testing shows good potential, the Woods children should also be included even though they might not progress as rapidly as Nina. Nina is highly motivated to learn. She could potentially join some appropriate high school classes next year," O'Reilly said.

"Nina, how much you learn and how fast is up to you. Your schooling right now will focus on reading and math, two things that you'll need all through your life. Without them, it is hard to live independently. That doesn't mean you have to leave Gee and Karen one day. It means being able to find a job, go on a date, drive a car, shop in a store, use a bank. You might decide you want to go to college one day. Right now, we want you to feel safe and confident whether you are at home, walking down a street, or in school with your friends," Susan concluded.

"Thank you," Nina said.

"Yes. Thank you very much," Karen added. "We will do whatever we can to help Nina be a healthy and happy member of our family."

"THAT WAS MORE exhausting than I prepared for," Principal O'Reilly said as he sat opposite Susan in his office.

"I should learn, but I never seem to," she sighed.

"So, what is your concern."

"It's only moderate. We have a lot of students who interact with Gee on a regular basis. He takes them to the woods and talks to them. Today, I saw two girls and a boy all give him a hug when he was in the hall."

"Do you think he's behaving inappropriately?"

"No. I have no reason to suspect that. I'm more bothered by Nina."

"How so?"

"During our evaluation, I questioned her about her sexual experience. I was shocked beyond anything I let show in our meeting. Thankfully, she's spoken to the police and they are trying to find her 'sir and madam.' In my book she was saying 'owners.' She was abused for years in every way you can imagine. When I asked if she had been sexually active with Gee and Karen, she firmly said no. But when I asked if she would have sex with either of them if they asked, she just as firmly said yes. It's not that I don't trust her guardians, but with her desire to please and her level of compliance, they could easily slip into the same kind of abusive relationship."

"I see. Your recommendation?"

"Wait and see. We just need to hope they are of as high character as they seem to be.

Waters in the Woods

"ROY, I'D LIKE you to meet Gee Evars. Gee, this is Roy Waters, Environmental Protection Agency, General Harassment Division," David said at the forester's office on Wednesday. The two men had known each other for many years and had an easy relationship. "We asked for another snowstorm but Mother Nature could only delay his visit briefly." Gabe handed Gee a cup of coffee and returned to his usual seat in the corner.

"Don't let your boss fool you, Gee. This is a *pre*-harassment investigation. I need to make up some facts before I start harassing," Roy said.

"That sounds fair," Gee said. "I'd hate to think you harass people without making up facts first."

"What's the real issue today, Roy?" David said. "It looks like you came dressed to do actual work."

"I've been a supporter of your Forest Management Program since I joined the agency in '88. You have a good program," Roy said. "But not long ago, reports started filtering in about accidents, poisonings, and even drug manufacturing. I took it upon myself to come out and check the condition of the new land you've acquired and hopefully write an innocuous report that pulls attention away from you. That doesn't mean we won't have some issues to address regarding the air, water, or quality of life in the Rose River watershed but, with luck, it might divert the attention of OSHA, DEA, CDC, FBI, or any other alphabet soup you care to name.

"I've asked Gee to lead you out into the Wild Woods that we acquired to show you what we're doing and how we plan to manage things this spring," David said. "Gee's on limited duty this week because he got banged up in a non-work-related incident this weekend. He can walk okay, but we don't want him pulling at any of those stitches. It's been too cold and icy recently to do any real work in the Wild Woods, so wear your hard hats and goggles. Watch for falling ice."

"How CAN I help today, Mr. Waters?"

"Just Roy, Gee. I've looked across the fence at the Wild Woods on occasion but had no reason to go into it. Whenever I was on that side of the fence, it was to check the operation of SSG and condition of the quarry. I'd like to visit that while we're out here."

"We've cut some paths and this one leads from the Forest to the quarry."

"What is the purpose of the paths?"

"We're doing a mapping and survey of the hickory out here. I'm also cutting a path down the fencerow on the east to determine what kind of abatement we need to do for nuts falling off Forest-managed land," Gee responded. He avoided the search for missing children and the suspicion that some could be hiding in the woods.

"Sounds reasonable. You'll be clearing all the underbrush like was done in the Forest?"

"That's under investigation. The land out here has been neglected for a hundred years or more. We're assessing how much work and of what kind we need to do. I expect it will take us until next Harvest season to reach a solid conclusion."

"Pull up here a minute, would you?" Roy asked. Gee stopped the ATV and Roy carefully stepped onto the crusty snow. He examined a section of thorn thicket along the path. "I see you have some experience with Pyracantha."

"The thorn bushes? Yes. There are some places they're so thick we might have to bring in a brush hog to clear them."

"They're not common to this region."

"We don't know, but we suspect they may have been planted a generation or two ago."

"Why?" Gee thought about his answer carefully before responding.

"It's pure speculation on my part," he said. "This area grows the same kind of trees and has the same kind of nuts as those in the Forest. But it hasn't been managed or harvested. My guess is that the firethorns were planted to keep people out of the Wild Woods and control the nut traffic."

"I see. Be careful of those trees, by the way," Roy said pointing at a hawthorn. "The firethorn is nasty and tough, but the hawthorn can be deadly. Its thorns are small branches that can be sharp enough and long enough to go right through you." Gee thought of Nina's torn coat and shirt.

"We've had some experience with torn clothing. We're issuing heavy canvas coveralls when we get back out here in the spring."

"Good. Let's go." They got back on the ATV and Gee continued to point out areas of interest, showing the mapping of large trees on the geocaching software. Roy continued to give helpful pointers but seemed uninterested in collecting samples of soil of plants until they reached the quarry. Here he removed a rope and bucket, having Gee help him toss it into the quarry to collect water from fifteen feet below them. They had to weight the bucket with a large rock to break through the ice on the surface.

"This water has always had a high concentration of bromide sulfate in it," Roy said. "It's what gives the water it's pinkish cast. In running water, the solution bubbles out and when the river goes across the falls and rapids, it is essentially purified. My question is, will clearing the underbrush in the Wild Woods have an impact on water quality here at the quarry and downstream."

"I see. Is there anything else in the quarry besides the stone or the runoff from the woods that could contribute to the high concentration?" Gee asked.

"I suppose someone could have dumped a couple of truckloads of heart pills in the bottom. Gee, a few years ago we passed a quarry reclamation act. Most of the provisions are left up to the states to develop and enforce. This quarry hasn't been worked in over seventy years. Maybe a hundred. But it is grandfathered in as 'inactive' rather than 'abandoned.' I'd still like to see a full reclamation project out here but it's nearly a hundred feet deep in the center. If the water is safe, having it filled and used for recreation might be the best abatement we could hope for."

"We'll keep an eye on it."

"I'll be back in the spring to compare the levels after the melt. Now, I'm cold and I'd like a cup of Birdie's good coffee before I head back to DC."

Tutors

THE MANSION WAS bustling Saturday. Or at least the kitchen was. Gee and Karen were having their first dinner guests and were learning more about the kitchen and a few of its antiquated idiosyncrasies.

"That burner doesn't light automatically," Karen said. She produced a long-stem lighter and held it near the gas jet to light the back-left burner. "The ignition seems to work on all the others. I'll have to call a service person to fix it."

"This house needs an instruction manual," Gee replied. "Okay. As soon as the noodles are soft, I'm ready to assemble the lasagna. Do we need to worry about meat and cheese together?"

"The only person it matters to is Jude and I have a vegetable and cheese version for him." She took a moment to peck Gee on the cheek.

"I finished cleaning my room," Nina said as she came into the kitchen. "And I vacuumed all the floors upstairs. Except… I didn't go into your room, just the empty ones and the hall."

"You're such a big help. We'll work out a signal for our room just like we do for yours. If the door is closed all the way, we'd like privacy so please don't enter. If it is open, you may come in," Karen said.

"I was only allowed to be in my room or the kitchen when I lived with Sir and Madam, unless they had me on a leash," Nina sighed.

"Thank you for pitching in, Nina," Gee said.

"I talked to Laura and to Jeanie and to Grandma Sue," Nina said. "They've been explaining what it means to be part of a family. I don't think Jeanie knew some of it. I'm sad she doesn't have a family."

"I know, Sweetie," Karen said, hugging the teen.

"One of the things I learned when I came to Rosebud Falls is that having a family isn't just about a name you were born with," Gee said. "I think some people look at the seven Families and only see a family tree. But our family is the people we choose to love and have near us."

"We love you and I know Jeanie is discovering people who love her as well. Like you do."

"I… never had a friend before. At least the children have each other. I think I'd remember if I had a brother or sister," Nina sighed. "What can I help with next?"

"Well, it's early in the day yet. Do you remember where dishes and silverware get placed on the table?"

"Fork on the left of the plate. Spoon and knife on the right."

"Very good. And how many people will be at the table for dinner?" Karen asked. Nina started counting on her fingers.

"Ten!"

"Hmm. I think you forgot to count someone." Nina's face fell.

"Who?" She named off the guests.

"You, silly girl. You count, too."

"Oh! I forgot me," she giggled.

"And when you set the table, be sure you allow for the children to be next to adults and give them plastic plates and glasses."

"They don't get to use nice things. That's mean."

"No, honey, it's not to be mean. Their hands are little and things slide around. They would be very upset if they dropped a glass and it broke. We want them to enjoy the meal as much as everyone else does," Gee said. Nina thought about it for a moment.

"You aren't mean. I knew that. I just didn't understand. Jeanie and I will help them with their food so they enjoy the meal, too!" Nina scampered off to begin setting the table and to get booster seats on the chairs for Naomi, David, and Esther.

"Remember, no matter where she sets things, it will be perfect," Karen whispered in Gee's ear. He nodded and began layering the hot noodles in the casserole.

LAURA AND JUDE arrived with the three children and Jeanie promptly at six o'clock. Nina led the children to a room next to the parlor where she'd discovered a playroom. They happily went about discovering what was there.

Jo and Wayne arrived a few minutes later.

"Whoa! This place always sets me back a step when I see it," Jo said. "You must rattle around in here!"

"We're working on ways to fill it up," Karen laughed at her cousin. "We even have a nursery!"

"It will take me a few minutes to become accustomed to having adults around," Wayne said. "Spending my life with first graders sometimes leaves me craving grown-up conversation."

"Aren't you providing grown-up conversation, Jo?" Karen teased.

"Ka-ren! Be nice."

"Come all the way in, friends," Gee said, collecting coats and hanging them in the foyer closet. "I think there are plenty of adults for conversation this evening and we can enjoy the children, too."

"So, HOW'S THE book coming, Jude?" Jo asked. "Your mother said you've been working on it for two years."

"My mother's idea of philosophy is that you say whatever pops into your head and consider it profound. Nothing against Mother's view of the world but writing about the subject is a little more complex than that," Jude answered. "That being said, getting married, moving, and becoming parents has slowed down the writing a bit."

"And here I was hoping you'd be able to help me with *my* book," Karen said.

"You're working on a book?" Wayne asked. "I wondered what you'd be doing now that you're not at the newspaper."

"I've been researching and collecting material for a book about sex trafficking for ten years," Karen said. "I have reams of data, interviews, and more recently, personal experiences. It's tricky, though."

"We need that book," Jude said. "When I think about the future that was awaiting my children, I get so furious I can't contain it. I'm afraid some of that has bled into my own manuscript."

"The problem has many facets," Karen said. "I'm sure we could both write books from the same research and they'd be completely different. Not that we'd necessarily disagree with each other but we'd each see something unique. I could write an entire volume on the ill-advice and ineffectiveness of laws intended to stop trafficking. They're feel-good laws. People wipe their hands and say, 'There, we did something.' In reality, they often do more harm than good, villainizing the victims and disguising the perpetrators."

"Is there a law against Sir and Madam?" Nina asked, keenly following the adult conversation as she helped David cut up his lasagna.

"Yes, Nina, there are many laws against what they did," Gee said. "The biggest problem is we don't know who or where they are. And if we found them, we would have to prove they did the bad things to you. That is one of the problems Karen is referring to."

"We have small victories," Wayne said. "You got away, Nina. You should have been found when you were Esther's size and saved from everything you went through. When I think of how I first found these three huddled in a blanket and hidden in a shipping container... I'm just so thankful that Laura and Jude are here to love them and make them their family. That's what children deserve." Jo squeezed Wayne's hand as silence surrounded them. They all took a moment to just look at the children—all five when you included the teens.

"Nina, how's your math coming?" Jeanie asked, breaking the silence.

"I have cards that show all the numbers and the plusses. It's hard but I counted how many people would be here tonight so I could set the table." She started giggling as she looked at her friend over the top of David's head. "I forgot to count me!"

"Just think. Once you learn all the numbers and letters and the ways they can be combined, we'll be able to read Jude's and Karen's books," Jeanie laughed.

"Who's doing the teaching?" Wayne asked. Karen waggled her fingers.

"We've barely gotten started from the material the school provided. I'm totally lost doing it," she said.

"Me, too," Laura agreed. "The children are learning to count and can show me the right number when I ask for three blocks or something like that. But they're still non-verbal."

"Maybe I could help," Wayne said. "The school's already suggested— not too subtly—that I will probably want to join my grandfather in the business rather than teach school next year. A couple of parents have said they don't like their children being taught by a Savage. They associate the name with the Wild Woods and how the company fought the annexation. I'm afraid there are more stories out there about the horrors of the woods than you can imagine."

"Would you consider tutoring all four?" Karen asked. "We could find a way to match instructional time with your schedule."

"I'd like to but it would be difficult while I'm still teaching. I could consult with you each week to make sure you're on track and answer questions. But I have a day job dealing with thirty little angels in my classroom."

"Angels?" Jo laughed. "I thought you called them monsters the other day."

"Let us not forget that Lucifer was also an angel," Jude nodded.

"Mommy!"

The room fell silent and forks dropped as all eyes focused on little Esther. Her milk glass had slipped through her greasy fingers and dumped down her front. Big tears welled up in her eyes.

Laura moved so quickly that Jude scarcely caught her chair to keep it from crashing to the floor. She had the little girl in her arms and set the empty glass back on the table.

"It's okay, Littlest," she said, using the pet name Gee had first given her. "Mommy's here. It's just a little milk and we'll get it all cleaned up. Don't cry, Esther. Everything will be okay." She held and danced Esther toward the bathroom. "Mommy's here. Mommy loves you."

David and Naomi looked terrified. Jeanie and Nina were startled but wrapped an arm around the children. Gee reached across the table to take Naomi's hand.

"You're safe, Sister," he said softly. "No one is angry." The older girl swallowed and bit her lip, looking toward the bathroom where Laura had taken Esther to clean up.

"She'll be right back," Jude said. "Mommy is just making sure Esther is dry and clean. Do you need to use the bathroom, too?" Both children nodded. "Come my precious children," he said as he scooted their chairs back and helped them down from the booster seats. He held their hands as they followed where Laura and Esther had disappeared.

Nina and Jeanie looked at each other with open mouths.

"She spoke," Jeanie whispered.

The Trials of Job

"It is a difficult story to understand," Pastor Beck said from the pulpit. "How could God allow Satan to destroy all Job had built? Satan wiped out Job's herds, killed off his family, and afflicted him with disease. Job's so-called friends told him to curse God and die. But Job remained faithful."

Deacon looked out at the congregation from his seat near the lectern where he'd read this morning's scripture.

Then the LORD answered Job out of the whirlwind, and said, Who is this that darkeneth counsel by words without knowledge? Gird up now thy loins like a man; for I will demand of thee, and answer thou me.

The congregation was less than half the size it had been just a few months ago. Those who remained were not the nicest people. They came to fuel their anger without regard to its direction. No matter what passion the preacher put into his words, he would never attract new members again. It might be time to close the church. Permanently.

———◁◆▷———

"I LOOK AT this congregation and I see Satan's hand at work in the empty seats—seats that so recently were filled by weak Christians who could not suffer the tribulation set upon us. We have been vilified by the press, investigated by the police, harassed by the Families, and, yes! even attacked by the hand of Satan himself. What other explanation, I ask you, for the murder of Brother Reef at the hands of the police? What other reason for the comatose body of Rena Lynd? What other explanation for the deaths of Simon and Janet Alexander? How else do we explain the burning of John Daniels's barn and the loss of his livestock, leaving a destitute family? Yes, and even my near demise in the icy water of the river a week ago. And to add mockery to his machinations, the devil himself plucked me from a watery grave and said, 'See here! I have saved you. Worship me!'

"Why? Why, Lord God do you let Satan send the hordes of evil against your faithful? I weep in sackcloth and ashes."

Pastor Beck bowed his head over the pulpit and then lifted his eyes toward heaven.

"And then the story of Job came to me and I knew the mind of God. Where, he asked, was I when He laid the foundations of the world? And who am I to think that I can understand the mysteries of the universe when all Jesus has asked of me is that I believe on him and be saved?

Behold I am vile; what shall I answer thee? I will lay mine hand upon my mouth. Once have I spoken; but I will not answer: yea, twice; but I will proceed no further.

"Gentle brothers and sisters, we will continue to endure the hardships Satan in all his guises subjects us to. We will continue to repent of our sins and do the work of our Lord. We will stand fast against the tides of misfortune that Satan hurls at us. But we will not deny God!

"Believe on Him and ye shall be saved."

Senior Forum

"I LOOKED AT the questions you gave me this morning," Gee said to the gathered upper classmen at Flor del Día. There were nearly a hundred students in the multipurpose room where they would later eat lunch. Gee noted several students from RHS who worked on his crews were in the audience. He wondered if they had received special permission to attend or were simply cutting classes to join their friends.

"You asked two main questions. 'What does it mean to be a good person?' and 'How can I become a good person?' I think the questions are pretty similar because if we know what it means to be one, we should know what to do to be one. Right? A good person." He hesitated and looked around. It shouldn't make him so nervous to talk to the kids. He did it every day in the Forest. But they all looked at him like he knew a great secret. He barely knew his name.

"The problem is, I don't think I know.

"Is there supposed to be a rulebook that has a checklist in it? 'Answer yes to eight of these ten questions and you are a good person.' I have no idea what those ten questions would be. I don't know if I'd pass the test. Maybe if it were six out of ten. Is that good enough?" the kids laughed at his deprecatory humor.

"Seriously, why ask me? The Christians have a rulebook. The Jews have one. The Muslims have one. The Buddhists have one. There is no lack of rulebooks for life. You could probably follow the High School Athletic Association Football Rules and be a good person for all I know.

"Why don't you answer the question for me? What do you *think* makes a good person?"

Gee stepped down off the low platform stage and walked out among the students so they could respond. He pushed the mike toward a young woman near the aisle. "What do you think?" he asked.

"Um… Being kind, I guess." He nodded and turned to a young man on the other side and two rows back.

"Being honest?" the boy asked. Gee nodded. A boy farther down the row raised a hand and Gee handed the mike to him.

"Being brave. Like you are." Gee chuckled and shook his head.

"There's a fine line between being brave and being foolhardy, and it keeps moving," he said. He handed the mike to another girl.

"Helping the weak or helpless. Like you helped those children they found."

"Littlest spoke her first word out loud last weekend," Gee enthused at the mention of the children. "They are miracles of life. I'm so happy for them." He completely ignored the suggestion that he had helped in any way and the kids all got caught up in his joy as they clapped for the children. Then Gee saw Trevor stand up and hold out his hand. He handed his crew member the microphone, knowing that it was often left to Trevor in these forums to ask challenging questions. Gee wasn't prepared for the one that was asked.

"Why did you save that preacher?" Trevor asked. Gee blinked back his surprise.

"He was drowning." Trevor kept hold of the microphone.

"He's a bad man. He stood in this hall and told us all we were going to hell because I corrected his misquoting of a Bible verse. He looked at the young kids here at Flor like he wanted to eat them. He drugged his congregation and tortured kids into converting from being gay. He incited his congregation to throw nuts at you in the parade, lied about knowing that monk who tried to kill you, called you the devil. He stood up here and said you were Lucifer and the Forest was the Devil's Playground. How could you…? Why would you save his life when God put him in a river to drown?" Trevor handed back the microphone and sat down. His accusation hung in the air and the students were silent. Gee returned to the front while he thought about the question and waved the Headmaster back to his seat.

"I don't know, Trevor. From what you are saying, you believe— maybe all of you believe—the world would be a better place without Pastor Beck in it. I didn't know who was in the car until I smashed out the windshield and reached through it. But then I recognized him so I can't tell you I didn't know who I was helping. I could have let him drown. Maybe I could even have helped him drown and made sure of it. No one would ever know. And we believe the world would be a better place because there would be one less evil in it.

"But that wasn't the question you asked at the beginning of our time together. You asked what made a good person. So, I ask you, would *I* be a better person if I let him drown?"

Gee sat on the edge of the platform and looked at the students. They were quiet and he saw some nodding and some shaking their heads.

"I think, Trevor, that you might have unlocked an even bigger question. What makes a good world? And that comes right back to the original question. The answer can only be 'good people.' If something makes you a better person, by extension it makes the world a better world. If it makes you a lesser person, it makes the world a lesser place.

"When I was reading to the children in the library Wednesday night, Ms. Tomczyk handed me a book of Indian legends. Among them was a story credited to the Cherokee that said an old man counseled his grandson by saying,

> There is a terrible fight going on inside us. Two powerful wolves strive for dominance. One is evil. He is anger, arrogance, self-pity, envy, sorrow, regret, greed, guilt, resentment, inferiority, lies, pride, and ego.

"It was that last one that made me think this wasn't quite the way the story was told among the Cherokee. I'm not sure when ancient Indian legends acquired words like 'ego'," Gee laughed and then continued the story.

> The other wolf is good. He is peace, joy, contentment, love, hope, serenity, humility, kindness, benevolence, empathy, generosity, charity, truth, compassion, and faith. The same fight is going on inside every one of us.
> The grandchild asked, "Who wins?"
> "The one you feed," said the old man.

"It is a nice illustration, whether authentic or not. It might mean something different to each of us. I don't believe a little pride in your accomplishments is a bad thing, for example. Pride is a great motivator because it feels good and so we want to do things that make us feel that way.

"I am a baby among you. My memories of life go back only six months. Still, I have known since the day I arrived, all I want to do is feed the good wolf. And I hope that one day he will be strong enough within me to make me a good man."

10

436 PEACH STREET

Scars

"THIS HAS BEEN an exciting week from what I hear," Dr. Poltanys said as he clipped the stitches from Gee's leg.

"The children have finally begun to vocalize. Not all words but they are getting very good with 'Mommy' and 'Daddy'," Gee said. Whenever someone mentioned things being exciting, Gee thought of the children.

"I'll bet that thrills Laura and Jude," Adam chuckled.

"Yes. There was a little confusion when Devon called Marian 'Mommy' but it didn't take them too long to sort out the relationships. And then Nina…"

"How is she doing?"

"She started calling Karen and me Mommy and Daddy. It helped the kids but it really shocked Karen. We figure she's only ten years older than Nina."

"Age is irrelevant. She has twenty years more experience. How do you feel about it?"

"It threw me the first time. I didn't know what to say. We never push her for a display of affection but a few days ago, I commented about how well she was doing with her numbers. She gave me a hug and said, 'Thank you, Daddy.' I was blown away. Karen and I have a daughter and she's already almost out of her teens."

"Are you happy about that?"

"Very. Ow! I didn't expect pulling those stitches to hurt."

"I used a lot of small stitches to try to minimize scarring. You'll still have a couple of new scars, I'm afraid."

"How did your other patient from that night fare?" Gee asked.

"The preacher suffered more from hypothermia than physical damage. A few bruises and abrasions caused by the inflating airbags. Other than that, he suffers from an intolerant and abusive disposition aggravated by an attitude of religious superiority and homophobia. The condition is probably terminal."

"So I've heard."

"The kids at Flor didn't go easy on you yesterday, did they?"

"News travels fast."

"I saw Evan Nygard yesterday. He mentioned it."

"I'm just… Do you suppose that if I regained my memory, I would understand why I saved him?"

"You might find a list of circumstances that shaped your outlook on life and responses to emergencies. I'm not sure that equates with under-standing." Adam inspected the wounds again and told Gee to dress. "Gee, I see a lot of injuries. I remove tonsils and appendixes. I treat diseases. In short, I see broken people. Once I remove an appendix, the patient heals. They're missing an appendix but they're no longer broken. You're missing your memory but you aren't broken. When it comes to being judgmental and disdainful of the stupidity of human beings, I'm the one who's broken, not you. Just keep being who you are. You've taught me a lesson."

In the Blood

GEE WALKED OUT along the fencerow Saturday morning with a couple of his crew, but between snow, ice, and wind, they decided it would be at least the next weekend before they could get anything done. Instead they headed back to the foresters' office and went over the maps.

"If it wasn't so cold, we could do something," Gee said. "But until it gets above zero again, I'm not taking anyone out there."

"None of the foresters are out," Gabe said. "No reason a bunch of teenage volunteers should be. Go home and enjoy your family."

That was a good plan. Gee found the children and Jeanie visiting at the mansion. Laura and Jude were in a lively conversation with Karen about the purpose and intent of law. The two families spent much of their weekend together as Naomi, David, and Esther were watched over by Nina and Jeanie.

Monday morning, Karen, Gee, and Nina decided to start the day with a trip to Jitterz rather than make coffee at home. The sun came out and it looked like the day might warm up at last.

"Well, look who's graced our doors," Birdie said when they entered the coffee shop. "Are you thawing out?"

"I'm not betting on clear warm weather yet," Gee said. "Even on a sunny day, it's still too dangerous to go into the woods with ice falling off the trees."

"Birdie, I don't think you've met Nina yet. Nina, Birdie owns the coffee shop. What would you like, dear?" Karen asked.

"Hello, Birdie. I'm Nina. May I have coffee with lots of milk?" Nina asked. She was gaining confidence and poise the longer she was with them. Birdie smiled at her.

"You certainly may! Elaine, would you please make a special latte for this young woman?"

"Yes, Birdie," the singer/barista said.

"While you're waiting for your coffee, why don't you sip this tea?" Birdie said to Nina as she guided her to a chair. "I'll take the cup from you as soon as you're finished."

"Thank you, Birdie." Gee and Karen sat with her. "This is good. It warms my tummy!"

"That's a good thing on a cold day, isn't it?" Karen laughed. Nina focused on sipping the tea until Birdie approached with their other drinks and breakfast sandwiches.

"There's stuff in the bottom of the cup!" Nina said.

"Those are your tealeaves," Birdie said, trading cups with her. "Now, we'll look into your cup and find out who you are."

"You can tell who I am by looking at tealeaves?" Nina exclaimed. "Who am I? Where did I come from? Do I have parents? I mean other than Gee and Karen?"

"Easy, child," Birdie laughed. "What I see is who is inside you, not your identity. And what I see is a very bright and outgoing young woman.

All you need to be successful in life is a little education and opportunity. You've not allowed your past to misshape your spirit. You don't hold anger and resentment inside you. That is very good. You hold your new family and friends as precious. These are things that are important to your life." Birdie paused and looked at the leaves with a puzzled expression as a group of teens entered the coffee shop.

"Nina!" Jeanie cried. "You remember Barrett, don't you? And Alyson and Viktor? Come and join us." Nina waved at her friends and turned to Karen.

"May I, Mommy?"

"Of course you may, Sweetie. We'll be sitting here for a while. Take your sandwich." Nina carried her latte and sandwich to the table where Jeanie and Alyson were sitting while Barrett and Viktor ordered for them. Karen and Gee smiled after her and then turned seriously toward Birdie.

"What else is it?" Gee asked. "You saw something important."

"She belongs here," Birdie said. "Have you had a DNA test done?"

"The police sent it out to the missing children database. No matches," Karen said.

"You should try the services where you sent Gee's DNA," Birdie declared.

"Do you think she's related to me?" Gee asked.

"Maybe," Birdie said, puzzling over the tealeaves. "But I'm sure her parents or grandparents are from Rosebud Falls. The connection is in her blood." Birdie stood and called to the kitchen. "Violet, dear! What was the name of the DNA testing company you sent a sample to?"

"The one that said I was half Haitian instead of Jamaican like my mama told me?" Violet laughed. She came over to the table and wrote down the name of the lab.

"Yes. I should have told you long ago. Your father is Haitian. I'm full-blooded Irish myself." They all laughed as Violet returned to the kitchen.

"I recognize this one. I sent Gee's sample there but there were no matches," Karen said.

"I just have a feeling," Birdie sighed as she looked over at the teens.

⚬◆⚬

"I THOUGHT YOU would all be in school today," Nina said to her friends. "Gee said school was Monday through Friday."

"Yes, but it's a holiday," Alyson said. "We don't have school today so we decided to go outside and play."

"Want to join us?" Jeanie asked. "We're going sledding."

"In the woods?" Nina asked timidly.

"Not the Wild Woods," Barrett jumped in. "You remember where we went sledding after the first big snowfall? The track runs from the cemetery to the lumber mill."

"Oh, I remember! It was fun."

"And if you are with us, we promise not to let anything bad happen to you," Viktor said. Alyson squeezed his hand.

"I'll… um… ask Mommy," Nina said.

"WHAT DO YOU think of that?" Karen asked as they watched Nina leave with her friends. Gee sighed.

"It's what we want, isn't it?" he said. "We want her to have friends and to be independent."

"But…?"

"It's hard to let go and not worry about her."

"Yeah. We have to, though."

"I think I need to do some work at the foresters' office," Gee said.

"Where you can see the road up to the cemetery? Karen nudged him.

"I'm not going to spy on them. I just want to be… you know… close enough to respond in an emergency."

"I love you," Karen said. "Go off and do your work. And keep your eye out for our daughter. Just in case."

The Bookhouse

THE WEATHER THAT kept Gee and his crew out of the woods also allowed him more time for other activities. He especially enjoyed sitting in Karen's study while she worked on her book, and was often joined by

Nina as he helped her with reading or writing. Nina was progressing well and while the elementary reading material was below the level of her life experience, she discovered a joy in being able to sit with a book and puzzle out the words. Her math skills were progressing much more rapidly. She seemed to have an affinity for numbers.

Gee also spent time with the younger children at Jude and Laura's house, often with Nina accompanying him. All three children now used words and phrases, most starting with 'Mommy' or 'Daddy'. It was clear that living full-time with the newlyweds had created a familial bond far more quickly than was possible in the hospital. Marian and Devon were almost daily visitors to the children. Ruth Ann and Sally Ann visited at least one evening a week and on the weekend.

Through the chaos of the fall and winter with all his added responsibilities, Gee had still maintained his role as reader in the Wednesday evening Bookhouse program at the library. As soon as she'd discovered what he was doing and that the younger children went there as well, Nina joined him. She sat with the little ones Gee read to. Many assumed she was just another adult piece of furniture and climbed into her lap.

So, when Wednesday evening came, quite a parade of people left the Woods and Evars households and walked to the library together.

<hr>

"Go ahead," Sally Ann whispered. She was just loud enough that Gee could hear her talking to Naomi. The two girls were near the same age. "You can ask Gee to read a favorite book. I'll help you get it and you can take it to him." The two disappeared behind the shelf of children's books and soon emerged as Gee finished reading a story for the very little ones. Littlest—Esther, Gee reminded himself—sat cuddled on one side with Devon snuggled against her.

"Gee, please?" Naomi said as she approached him. Gee set aside the book he was about to read and looked at Sister.

"What book do you want, Naomi?"

"George monkey," the girl said. Her own stuffed monkey was tucked securely under her arm. Since introduced to her in the hospital, she'd seldom been seen without the toy.

"*Curious George in the Snow,*" Gee read from the cover. "Come look at the book Naomi has chosen." The rest of the children leaned forward as Gee held the book out for them to see. "Have you been outside to play in the snow? My favorite thing is to come inside and have hot chocolate after I've played. What do you think George's favorite thing will be?" Various suggestions were made by the children, including snowmen, angels, sleds, and ice. "Let's see what the story says."

Naomi claimed the seat opposite Esther and Brother David leaned against her. A handicapped child Gee had seen only recently crawled to Nina and held out his arms. She picked him up with a smile toward the child's concerned mother. There was a little more shifting around as children found seats on the laps of adults or snuggled up together on big pillows before Gee began to read.

Surveys

GEE WAS IN the foresters' office Thursday, poring over the printouts of geocache maps near the Patriarch when Gabe interrupted him.

"I think you have company," he said, pointing to the door. Gee turned, finding David, Wayne, and Pàl.

"Just who we were hoping to see," Wayne said as he shook Gee's hand. "How are the kids?"

"All excited about being outside in the snow. Yesterday they were all at our house playing in the big yard. The little ones have built a snowman and covered nearly every square inch of lawn with little angels. Nina was right down there helping."

"Gee, Pàl asked for assistance on a tour through the woods and down to the quarry," David said, circumventing greetings. "He'd like to meet the Patriarch, so I volunteered you."

"My pleasure," Gee said. "In fact, I was just considering stopping by your office this afternoon with a couple of questions."

"Shoot," Pàl said. "Anything I need to look up?"

"Maybe. Do you know if SSG maintains the fence along the boundary of the Wild Woods—what is now the new City Limit?" Gee asked. "A lot happening lately and I haven't had a chance to ask before this."

"It seems likely. I'll have to look through the records to find out for sure," Pàl said. "With the new arrangement between us and the City, that might be a subject for discussion this spring. Is it in bad repair?"

"You know we've been clearing the area next to the fence the past few weeks. That whole first section of nearly half a mile looks brand new. I was just wondering how new it is."

"If the company bought and installed that much six-foot chain link fencing, it should show up on the books," Pàl said. "Do you know how much that would cost, David?" David pulled out his phone and tapped the keys on the calculator.

"Rough estimates, twelve to fifteen thousand at the price we get. Depends on whether posts were needed and if you replaced the barbed wire on the extenders, too. Materials *could* run as much as twenty grand if everything was replaced. And more if it goes farther than the half-mile Gee has pointed out," David said.

"Wouldn't someone notice that big a project?" Wayne asked. "That must have required a pretty good crew to install."

"Who'd notice?" David asked. "One side of the fence is Wild Woods. The other is farmland, barely visible from the nearest road. Gabe? How about a ride out to inspect Gee's work on the fencerow? We could do that while Gee is guiding Pàl and Wayne."

"I could stand to stretch my legs a bit," the old forester said. All four feet of his chair made contact with the floor and he reached for his coat.

"Gee, there's a four-seat ATV fueled and ready. Why don't you take Pàl and Wayne in that? Gabe and I will take one of the smaller ones."

"This is the Patriarch?" Pàl said sadly. The trail was narrow but clear with the number of people who had come out through the snow to visit The Tree. "I wanted a chance to see this as much as to talk about the quarry. But it's not the tree I want to see."

"Why's that?" Gee asked.

"I thought it might be the Savage Family tree, but it isn't," Pàl said. "I was never introduced to it before my grandfather took me to Scotland. I don't know where our Family tree is."

"I bet we'll find it when we close that church and evict the preacher from the house," Wayne suggested.

"Unless they cut it down," Pàl suggested morosely. "I'm feeling chilled. Let's move on to the quarry."

Gee drove the two down a network of paths, pointing out two of the cabins they passed. They didn't stop to investigate them. When they reached the quarry, Gee drove carefully around the rutted road that circled it, sometimes having difficulty identifying the track through the snow.

"Why would our former management replace all the fence along the Wild Woods border and not this fence?" Wayne asked, looking at a rusted section of fence that had been torn back to give access to the rim. There were several places where the fence was collapsed or missing completely. "This is a real hazard."

"The kids believe it's haunted," Gee said. "Maybe 'believe' is too strong a word. It seems there is a 'secret' path from the lake to the quarry. In the summer, this is where older kids come to drink and go skinny-dipping at night. It's where Ryan and Shannon were headed the day they saw Karen kidnapped."

"Hmm. Hate to spoil their fun, but we have to do something about this. It's a miracle no one has fallen in and drowned."

"It could hide a world of secrets," Gee agreed.

"Roy Waters' report to me was a thinly veiled threat about needing to have a reclamation plan," Pàl said.

"What are our options?" Wayne finally asked.

"The general dimensions suggest we've taken between 800,000 and 1,000,000 cubic yards of stone from this hole. The deepest area is a hundred feet down. It's tiered, like an inverted wedding cake, with a spiral road around the edge. That's a lot of volume. A truck can transport ten or twelve cubic yards of gravel. Somewhere around 75,000 dump loads to fill the hole."

"My God!" Wayne breathed. What choices do we have?"

"We could add some safety features. Make the slope around the edge gentler. Put in a beach and call it a park," Pàl said. "Or we could just erect an extra strong security fence and hire a patrol twenty-four-seven to keep people out."

"Or a combination of the three," Gee said. "Fill the area on the low side and create a gentle slope. Fence off the most hazardous areas. Stock it with fish. If they'll live. Waters suggested the levels of some chemical were extra high. It might not be safe."

They mulled over the ideas as they walked along the lip of the quarry, currently frozen over.

"How long ago did you stop quarrying?" Gee asked.

"I haven't been investigating it with all the other shenanigans the former board was up to. It's been a hundred years since it was producing any quantity. There were occasional lifts up until World War II. That's when my grandfather took the company public and converted it to sand and gravel instead of limestone. Why?" Gee did some calculating in his head.

"I think something was going on down there during or right before the war," he said.

"Why do you say that?"

"Something Jan's father said when I visited him."

"You visited August Poltanys? I thought he was too far gone to communicate."

"It was an accident. I sort of stumbled into his room. His mind isn't in the present. He called me George but I don't think he knew me. He was desperately trying to convince George that they shouldn't come to the quarry again because of what they'd seen."

"You should talk to Jan about that and see if he can make sense of it," Pàl said. "I barely know my own Family, let alone his. Dee says August has had Alzheimer's for a long time. Amazing he's still alive."

"Well, for now, it looks like we have about thirty grand worth of fence replacement to deal with," Wayne said. "And then we'll have to plan for dump loads of gravel."

"WHAT DO YOU think, Loren?" David asked as he drove the head of the Cavanaugh Family along Fox Hill Road east of town. A sale sign had been erected in front of the Alexanders' property where the unfortunate couple had been poisoned.

"What do they want for it?"

"Their only daughter lives in Indiana and wants to get rid of it as quickly as possible. Says she has no pleasant memories of living here. She's asking three-fifty. The house could be subdivided off with a couple of acres and sold for at least half that. We'd get thirty-eight acres backed up to the Wild Woods for about one-seventy-five."

"What about the property next door? We've got a murder here and a fire there. Arson?"

"Not according to the sheriff. Fire investigators found a slow propane leak in an old connection. When the automatic heaters kicked on for the cattle, it sparked the propane which lit the hay. Damn shame about the animals and equipment but they were probably all dead before anyone even realized there was a fire. It was all the firefighters could do to keep it from spreading to the house. John Daniels' grandfather bought the place in 1938, so it's been in the family for eighty years. Not like the Alexanders who just bought their place after Simon went to work for SSG. So, we have eighty acres with a good farmstead even without the barn. John is pretty distraught over the loss but I'm guessing a million-dollar offer would change his outlook on life."

"And why are we interested in these two properties?" Loren insisted. David knew he was just trying to put the pieces together in a logical order so he could prepare a business case.

"They back up to the Wild Woods," David said. "They're a natural 120-acre extension of cleared land. We have hundreds of strong young first-generation trees that could be planted out here and have an orchard with the potential of matching the production of our most prolific area of the Forest. It's an investment in the future of the Forest."

"And easier to get productive than the Wild Woods itself," Loren said. "I'll put production estimates together. Put in a contingent offer and let's call the Family heads together."

Back to the Woods

BY SATURDAY MORNING, the sun had been out three days in a row and the ice had melted from the tree limbs. It was deemed safe for the crews to resume work and Gee was pleased with the number of volunteers who showed up. Jessie and Jonathan joined them at the foresters' office.

"Wonder if we could raid your crew for a couple of volunteers," Jessie said.

"What do you need?"

"A good caliper person and a cache recorder," Jessie answered. "We're planning to map the transplantable trees that surround the Patriarch. We designed a separate section of the cache because we'll be recording the smaller trees this time. We want to see what we can effectively remove to create the least stress on neighboring trees."

"Dad says we're going to get land to expand onto, so we'll be in full transplant mode when the sap stops running this fall," Jonathan said. "We just have too much prep work to do to get any transplanting done before they start sprouting this spring."

"Do we know where they'll go yet?" JD asked. "Oh! I volunteer to record the cache."

"Thanks, JD. If you can be spared, we'd like that. We have some ideas but part of planning a project is knowing what you have to work with," Jonathan said.

"Could I do the caliper things?" Leslie asked. "Alyson taught me how." She was the youngest of Gee's crew and the only freshman among them. Gee noticed she always stayed near geeky JD. He seemed oblivious.

"That rounds out all we need," Jonathan said. "Did we deplete your resources to much, Gee?"

"We have a good-sized crew today," Gee laughed. "Without Leslie, we'll have to figure out someone else to wiggle into the tight spaces but we'll manage." He turned to the rest of his crew. "Gear up and let's get started. Hot chocolate at our house at four o'clock if we can get a good day's work in before it gets too cold." There was a little cheer and his team headed for the fencerow.

⁃⊲◆⊳⁃

"He's not mad at you, Trevor," Viktor said as the two larger boys loaded cuttings and branches onto a sled. Despite a few bare patches on the path, the sled still moved more easily through the woods than the wagon.

"If he was mad at you, he'd have to be mad at all of us. We all wanted to ask that question. Talk to him."

Gee fell back from the trimming crew enough to help the two boys get their sled turned around and loaded again. Trevor took a deep breath.

"I hope you're not mad at me, Gee."

"I have no reason at all to be mad at you," Gee chuckled. "What's on your mind?"

"I was pretty snotty at the forum last week and I want to apologize for the way I came off. I guess it's not that uncommon for me. I'm sorry."

"Don't worry about it. You made me think."

"Us, too. Angela… er… Ms. Jamison, our social studies teacher, suggested we consider a bunch of ethics questions to see where we stood. Some of them were pretty brutal, like having five people on a sinking raft that would only hold four and having to decide which to throw overboard."

"Some questions just don't have a good answer," Gee affirmed.

"Even questions we thought we knew the answer to," Trevor continued. "Knowing everything we do today and given a time machine, would we go back in time and kill Adolf Hitler in his crib? We started out with everyone saying sure. That would save the lives of six million Jews. Then she asked if that would be enough, or would we have to track down other key people in the organization like Goebbels and Goehring and kill them? Was there any way we could eliminate the threat without killing just as many people—probably a lot of innocent people—or causing their death by creating a leadership vacuum?"

"From what I've read, that's always been an ethical question about time travel," Gee mused. "What if we did one little thing that caused a change in the timeline. But we don't often bring it into the present. What if we do one little thing today that causes the future to shift? Isn't that just as important?"

"How can we tell unless we know the future?" Trevor asked. "That's what you were getting at, isn't it? We concluded that even knowing one future didn't foretell what would happen if something was changed. When it comes down to it, the only scale we have is exactly what you said. Would going back and killing Hitler make me a better person? Or would it just make me a murderer? You really helped us learn something."

THE KIDS WERE excited to gather at the mansion for hot chocolate after a day in which they cleared over a hundred yards of fencerow. The hard work had been broken by both heavy discussions and by riotous singing as the kids started adapting some of the Harvest songs to the process of clearing the woods of debris.

Several kids were already in the house holding cups of cocoa before Gee got home. Jessie and Jonathan had arrived with JD and Leslie as well. It was the first time the house had not looked huge and empty to Gee.

"Daddy! Daddy!" Nina shouted as she rushed to him. Before he had his coat off, she'd wrapped her arms around him for a hug. "Guess what! Guess what!" she demanded but before Gee could venture a guess, she continued. "I went to the woods! And I didn't get scared… very much. And I saw the old Tree. And Mommy says you'll get married there and we'll really be a family!"

Gee was overwhelmed. He looked at Karen's benign smile.

"I'm so happy you went to meet the Patriarch," he said. The Tree is very special to me."

"I know," she whispered with awe in her voice. "He's as old as you are!"

The kids nearby laughed and there were comments about Gee being as old as the trees in the Forest. Soon pizza arrived and Gee's age was forgotten.

"You TOOK NINA to the Wild Woods?" Gee asked Karen when things had finally settled down.

"It wasn't completely spontaneous but I wasn't sure she'd go until we left," Karen explained. "We've been talking all week about what you do in the woods and how you are making it safe so we can get married there. Nina had interesting questions about marriage and whether she could be married, too. It's been tricky."

"I'll ask Penny Tomczyk to add some books about family life to our reading list," Gee suggested. "It would probably help all the children."

"As long as they don't paint too narrow a description," Karen said. "I don't want her to think there is only one kind of family. Anyway, I called Jessie and Jonathan yesterday about arranging a little excursion. They said they had work to do near the Patriarch and would get a couple of kids to accompany us so Nina wouldn't feel alone. I have to hand it to Jessie and Jonathan. JD and Leslie are about the least threatening kids you've got on your crew. They kept Nina engaged and talking all the way to The Tree."

"I'm just excited that she made that leap after her last time in the woods," Gee said.

"I think part of it was giving her permission to be frightened and assurance that we would be with her. You know, this being a parent is exhausting," Karen laughed.

"Yeah. But look at the kids. Our baby has friends and they consider themselves welcome in our home."

"A couple of those boys are definitely interested in more than friendship but they're being respectful. She looks like one of their contemporaries. But listening to her tell a funny story about being confused between the numbers six and nine helped them understand she's not yet at their level. She's like a little sister to nearly everyone here, even though she's the oldest among them," Karen said.

"So how was she when she finally saw the tree?"

"She climbed it."

"What???"

"Not high but just up to the first branch. She sat on it like she'd been born there. We talked about what the wedding would be like and her part in it."

"Which is?"

"How could anyone else be my maid of honor?"

"That could be difficult," Gee sighed. Karen turned to him with concern written on her face.

"What is it, Gee?"

"I was going to ask her to be best man."

Reports

THE DAYS WERE clear but cold. With his crew back in school, Gee made little progress on the fencerow and focused, instead, on loading piles of brush from other cutting sites to take to the chipper. One or two loads was all he could manage before the cold drove him inside. He found other foresters in the office, as well. No one could stand the biting cold for long.

"Gee," David called to him. He was in a close conversation with one of the foresters. "You've worked with Darrell White before, right?" Gee shook hands with the forester. "I think we should keep this among the three of us but Darrell discovered something." Darrell shuffled around.

"Might be nothing," he said. "We got a call from a neighbor on the south side of the woods about a fallen limb across his fence this morning. You were already out so I took a four-wheeler around by the quarry and down to SSG in order to get to the guy's house. It was a pretty good-sized limb and it took an hour to get it cut into chunks and off the fence. I'll have to go back down tomorrow and fix the fence. By the time I got the wood cut, I was freezing. I decided to get myself warmed up and cut through the woods to cabin six. I didn't notice a thing disturbed in the cabin except that when I tried to light the heater, I discovered it was out of propane."

"How much have we been using the cabins as warming huts?" Gee asked.

"Not much," David said. "We equipped them all with heaters but we just haven't sent anyone out there for over a month unless they were working with you along the fence. I don't send foresters out in this kind of cold."

"I disconnected the tank and loaded it on my cart to bring in for a refill," Darrell continued. "But I got to thinking and went back inside. You know those survival kits the kids put in the cabins? I checked the one inside. I couldn't remember what all was supposed to be in the kit because I didn't help with them, but I was sure there was supposed to be food. There was none in this one. I think someone's been using that cabin."

Gee crumpled onto a seat next to David. He looked at the other two men.

"In this weather. We need to check all the heaters and replenish all the kits," he said. Whoever it is could freeze to death."

"I agree," David said. "Darrell, keep this under your hat. If we make the wrong move out there, we could scare someone away and make it worse for them. Gee, you and I should load the utility unit with a fresh tank for all six cabins and head out to change them."

"We should take food."

"We don't have supplies to restock and I think heat is more important."

"I agree. Let's get going."

David and Gee wrapped themselves as warmly as possible, loaded six propane cylinders on the utility ATV and headed back into the woods.

"WE NEED TO go out and help them," Karen exclaimed when Gee told her about their discovery as they lay in bed that night. She was ready to get dressed and go right then.

"We are helping him, her, or them," Gee said. "They are staying as hidden as they can from us. We didn't open any doors this afternoon when we replaced tanks. We found one other empty, but all had been used. David and I kept scanning for tracks, but whoever it is walks carefully, even where there's snow. Darrell said the survival kit he checked looked completely undisturbed but there was no food in it. Tomorrow, we'll start dropping energy bars off at each of the cabins. I just don't want to scare them away."

"Gee, it could be children," Karen wept. "Like Naomi and David and Esther. Or like Nina. What are we going to do?"

"We're going to hold our arms open and hope they'll trust us enough to come into them," Gee sighed. "It's all we can do."

WAYNE SPENT AN hour Thursday after school stopping by both the Woods house and the Roth mansion. Before he went home, he sat with Gee and Karen with a cup of tea and plate of cookies Lynda Raven had baked that morning.

"Nina is progressing well," Wayne said. "I left her with the younger children so I could talk to you. They are all excited to be learning."

"Anything we need to be aware of?" Karen asked. "I'm following the plan you laid out as well as I can."

"The biggest difficulty they're having is comprehending things that are beyond their experience. Usually, by the time a child reaches Esther's age, for example, she's absorbed a huge amount of information about life from her environment. She knows what a family is, what colors are, how to build with blocks, the sounds that all the animals make. Nina is better at that than the little ones but even she has limited experience. It's hard to get the concept of a horse galloping across the plains, for example, if the only horse you've ever seen is a stuffed unicorn."

"Oh, wow. What can we do to help things along?"

"More field trips, for one," Wayne said. "Broaden their horizons. Nina's socialization with friends is helping her immensely. Cooking has been good for all four. Work with Laura and Jude to find anything of interest for them. I know the weather has made it more difficult, but take them shopping. Look at antiques. Artwork. Eat in different restaurants. Visit a farm so they can see animals. Safe animals."

"What do you mean by that?"

"The little children love *Good Dog Carl*. Naomi read it to her sibs this afternoon while I was there."

"There are no words. Just pictures."

"How do you read the book in the library?"

"I just talk about what is happening in the pictures," Gee said.

"Exactly. You should listen to Naomi tell the story. You might get a different feeling for it. Nina, on the other hand, is terrified of *Good Dog Carl*. I'm sure she's had a bad experience with dogs—possibly with Rottweilers specifically. Books are teaching aids, broadening experience and helping with critical thinking. But books also build on common assumptions of experience. The children don't have that foundation. The more experiences the children have, the faster they will progress."

"I assume Laura and Jude are on board?" Karen said.

"Yes. I think you might have a four-footed neighbor before long. Jude suggested a puppy."

"Oh, my! Do you think we should do the same for Nina?" Karen asked.

"Nina can help you decide on that. She's smart, just inexperienced. She might prefer something less intimidating to her, like a rabbit or a potbellied pig." Wayne laughed at their open-mouthed expressions. "I know Nina has visited the school and the children," Wayne continued. "Why don't you make a field trip to our house this weekend. Jo and I would like to experiment with entertaining guests to see if we get along in the kitchen. Sunday night?"

"That sounds like fun!" Karen said.

"I haven't been down your way in quite a while," Gee said, noticing that Wayne had said 'our house,' not 'my house.'"Let's plan on it."

Family Matters

"You want us to put up two million dollars to buy and transform 120 acres into an extension of the Wild Woods," Heinz said. The Family heads had gathered at the Roth mansion out of habit from the years that Ben could not or would not travel.

"In general, yes," Loren said. "This isn't just blind speculation, though. The proposal you have in front of you shows that within five years this 120 acres will have greater productivity than any equal-sized patch in the Forest. Less than half the budget you see is for land purchase. The remainder is to add foresters and staff to do the transplanting. The trees in the shade of the Patriarch are the straightest and most beautiful I've ever seen."

"What does Gee think?" Heinz asked, looking at Karen.

"Uh… I've not discussed it with him," she answered.

"I think he should be at this table," Jan said firmly.

"He's not Family," Loren responded. Jan shook his head.

"No. He's not Family. He's Forest. Not even David and Jonathan have a greater affinity for the Forest and Wild Woods. It's the nut."

"I don't like to admit it," David growled. "But you're right. We shuffled the Wild Woods off to him because the foresters didn't have time to deal with teenage volunteers before winter. I'm sure not going to eat a nut like he has."

"Twice," Karen said. The men turned to stare at her. "Gee discovered the Patriarch on Thanksgiving. He was a little vague about exactly what happened. It was similar to what occurred with the grandfather tree before Harvest but this time he didn't fall into a coma. He slept for an hour and came home. But when he told me the story, it was the same as the first time. The tree gave him a nut and he ate it."

"I've looked all around the Patriarch and have seen no sign that it's bearing," David said. "No nuts on the ground, no shells, nothing. But one nut dropped in Gee's lap? I have to agree. He needs a seat at the table."

"Can we get him here now?" Pàl asked.

"No. Nina asked to go to the library again to get more books, so Gee took her," Karen said. "And we need to have Collin present, too. If Collin wants to appoint a representative instead of coming to meetings himself, that's fine. But the Meaghers have been absent too long."

"He's a little disruptive," Heinz chuckled. "But I agree. It's time all the Families and the Forest were at the table."

"We need to act soon or the properties will go on the open market. I put a contingent offer in on the Alexander place and planned to meet with John Daniels tomorrow."

"I think we can proceed," Karen said. "We know the financial condition of both Gee and Collin. Money for the purchase will come from those seated here. I'll guarantee Gee's portion."

"I think the six of us should guarantee both Gee's and Collin's portion," Pàl said. "It's the right thing to do." There were nods of assent around the table.

"I'll make the offer and remove contingencies," Loren said. "When Gee and Collin can be represented, we can agree on a strategy for the expansion."

LOREN'S HEADACHES WERE far from over. He found his sons waiting for him at home. The news that Troy was moving wasn't completely unexpected but the tensions were still high.

"Boston is a long way from home, son," Loren said as he faced Troy.

"Not so far. Three hundred miles. If you miss my voice you can probably still get the station here. It's a good station and they like my style. I'll miss the Window on Main but I really won't miss Rosebud Falls that much."

"So, when do you leave?" Clark asked.

"Anxious to get rid of me, brother?" Troy's relationship with his older brother had always been strained. "I start Monday. Taryn and I will be back next weekend to move our apartments."

"Taryn Taft?" Loren said. "The girl you brought home for the holidays? I thought you'd be through with her by now." Troy turned on his father, seething with anger.

"It's Taryn Cavanaugh now," Troy snarled. "We were married in Boston last week."

"Married?" Clark barked. "The great playboy, Troy Cavanaugh, married a woman with a retarded kid? She can't be *that* good a fuck!" Troy connected a solid right to Clark's stomach that doubled him up.

"Says the man who lives in a separate house from his wife," Troy snarled. "She couldn't stand to live with you any more that the rest of us can."

"All right! Cut it out, you two. You're grown men, not school boys," Loren shouted. Clark straightened up, holding his stomach.

"Always the spoiled little twit," Clark spat. "Daddy just kept you from getting your ass whipped again."

"I said, shut up!" Loren said. "There's no end to my disappointment in both of you. Troy, there are supposed to be agreements. Prenuptials. Did you get anything signed?"

"Just write me out of your will, old man. I'm through with this Family and I'm through with Rosebud Falls." Troy stormed out of the house.

Funny Number

"ALL MOVED IN, Raven?" Gee asked when he saw the former waitress/new housekeeper in the kitchen cleaning the oven. She started, bumping her head on the stove.

"Oh! Sorry, um… Mr. Evars. I was getting an early start…"

"I'm still Gee, Raven. Please don't start treating us like royalty. I still stop at the Pub & Grub occasionally for a beer, you know."

"At the Pub & Grub you're just another guy occupying one of my tables. But here, you're my employer. It changes things."

"I'm sorry to hear that," Gee said. He understood somewhat, though when he worked at the Market with Nathan, he didn't remember treating him any differently than at home. "Still, your employers prefer to be called Gee and Karen. Could you manage that?"

"Sure. I just need to get comfortable with the work. And everything."

"How's Timmy adjusting?"

"He loves his new apartment," Raven laughed. "But it made him so nervous! He had to recite the route to work several times and asked me at least a dozen times when he should leave so he would be there on time. He'll adjust but he needs to get his routine set. Once he's driven to work a few times, it will become second nature. He knows his limitations and does his best to compensate for them."

"It's only two miles and a straight shot," Gee said. "I'm sure he'll be fine."

"Mr… Gee, you don't really understand. Timmy does fine if his routine isn't disrupted. Mr. Panza at the Market has been really good with him. He has a list of the things he needs to do each day and he does them. Efficiently, I'm told. But if he pulled out of the driveway and turned right instead of left because he was distracted by something, he might be in Syracuse before he realized he should have been to work by then. We just need time to make it routine."

"I hope this arrangement is an improvement for him and not a setback," Gee said. "Nathan is very pleased with how hard he works. Karen thought this would be a benefit for both of you."

"Oh, it is! Please don't think we're ungrateful. I'll still put in some hours at the pub and Timmy will, too. But it's nice to think that I don't have to pull fifty hours a week to make ends meet," Raven said.

"Hello, Miss Raven," Nina said brightly as she bounced into the kitchen. She paused long enough to give Gee a quick hug and then went to prepare her morning cup of coffee.

"Good morning, Miss Nina," Raven answered. "You look bright and lively this morning."

"I get to help Gee and my friends in the woods today," she said. "I promise not to get scared of the cabins again, Daddy."

"Don't worry about that, sweetheart. If you get scared, come straight to me and I'll help you," Gee said.

"You don't have coffee yet!" Nina said. "I'll pour it."

"Will you pour me a cup, too, please?" Karen asked sleepily.

"Here, Mommy," Nina said, stopping to hug Karen before handing her the coffee. "Are you coming to the woods with us?"

"No, honey. I just reached a very important part of what I'm writing and want to keep working on it this morning."

"You were so involved last night, I don't think you knew I kissed you goodnight! I have no idea when you came to bed," Gee said, giving Karen a kiss. "Are you sure you got enough sleep to keep writing?"

"If I get too tired, I can take a nap."

"I thought you didn't work at the newspaper any longer," Raven said.

"I don't," Karen answered. "I'm working on a book that shows the intents and actual results of sex trafficking legislation in the country. Many laws have no effect at all while even more make the problem worse by punishing the victims instead of the perpetrators or by being applied to completely unrelated activities."

"I had no idea," Raven said, glancing at Nina. "I'll stay out of your area while you're working today but if you need anything, let me know."

LATE SUNDAY AFTERNOON, Gee, Karen, and Nina parked near Wayne's home in the Orchard Project. Just a few months ago, Gee had helped his friend glaze windows and paint the house. He noted that with the beginning of school, Harvest, Friday night football, and the chaos of settling his grandfather at Savage Sand and Gravel, many of the tasks Wayne had planned had been delayed. The rusted swing set, for example, still sat in the front yard, surrounded by snow.

Karen took a deep breath and closed her eyes. Gee understood. It might be a different color than she remembered, but the house held the memory of a nightmare that had driven Karen for fifteen years. Gee knocked on the door. Nina stood next to him, singularly fascinated with the brass house numbers.

"Funny number," she said repeatedly as she tapped on the last digit of Wayne's address. Gee didn't pay much attention to her as Wayne opened the door to greet them but a slight ping as a brad hit the porch caught his attention. Nina was playing with the loosened six, turning it upside down and right side up.

"Funny number," she repeated. Karen stood looking at her with her mouth open.

"I'll need to replace the doorframe in the spring," Wayne laughed. "The wood is so punky the nails keep falling out."

"Funny number," Nina chanted. "Six. Nine. Six. Nine." She twirled the number all the way around and then spun on the porch as if she'd just become aware of her surroundings. "Rocko! Rocko! Come! Swing!" She dashed off the porch and sat on the one remaining, rusted swing seat, kicking her feet up and giggling.

Karen slumped against Gee and he caught her as she fainted.

11

EMERGENCE

A Child Returned

GEE PICKED KAREN UP and carried her to the sofa in Wayne's living room.

"What on earth happened?" Jo asked, coming in from the kitchen.

"Gee, let us take care of Karen so you can tend to Nina. She'll trust you more than me." Wayne directed. Gee reluctantly gave care of his lover over to Wayne and Jo as he ran outside to see Nina now swinging quietly on the rusty chains. Gee approached her slowly.

"Nina? Are you okay, honey?" She looked up at him with eyes gradually focusing.

"Gee? I had another mommy and daddy once upon a time. I don't remember them. Isn't that strange? I just remember the funny number and swinging." She swung back and forth one more time then hopped up. "My bottom's cold now! Can I have a swing at home, Daddy?"

"Yes, of course you can," Gee said. "We might have to wait until spring to get it in the yard, but you can swing all you want. Who is Rocko?"

"I don't know. Rocko is what you yell when you go swing."

"We'll find out. You'll remember whatever you want to. Let's go see how Karen is doing." Gee took Nina's hand and they walked to the door. She giggled and spun the funny number one more time before they entered. When she saw Karen, Nina rushed to her.

"Did you fall? Are you okay, Mommy?"

"Oh, sweetheart! Is it really you?" Karen cried. She held Nina in a close embrace. "I swore I'd never stop looking for you. I promised I would find you one day. Is it really you?"

"Mommy, it's me, Nina!"

"Yes, of course it is. I love you, Sweetie."

"I'm not sure I understand what just happened," Jo said as she brought water for Karen. Gee pulled her and Wayne aside, giving Karen time to just hold Nina.

"Your house has a history, Wayne," Gee said. "Fifteen years ago, a child was kidnapped from the swing set out front. She was three or four years old and never heard from again. Karen had been babysitting."

"Oh, my God!" Jo breathed. "Nina?"

"I don't know. Maybe. The street number and swing set triggered a memory."

"Then she must be the little girl," Wayne concluded.

"Back when Karen was kidnapped and force-fed nuts… You know her phone was destroyed and lost. I expect it's one of many secrets we'd find in the quarry if it were drained. I got her a new phone and set it up to have her old number forwarded to it. She'd no more than turned it on when she got a message. It was a picture of your front door and the text, 'We aren't through with you yet, little girl.' We've always suspected Karen's kidnapper was connected with the event fifteen years ago."

"Karen and Nina could be in danger," Wayne said. "All of you. We need to be alert all the time."

"We'll have the DNA test results back soon. That will confirm things."

"Why would that help? Do you have DNA from the parents?"

"In a way. The little girl who was kidnapped from here was Collin Meagher's great niece. The DNA test would show that Nina and Violet Lanahan have a common grandparent or great-grandparent."

"I don't care," Karen said as she sat up straighter and pulled Nina with her. "It doesn't matter what the DNA says. It doesn't matter what the history is or if her memories come back. What matters is that I have Nina here and now. She is no different than the sweet girl Gee and I adopted into our home and our lives in the first place. If she is Collin's great niece, it still doesn't matter. She is Nina and is our daughter."

"I agree," Gee said as he stood beside Karen and wrapped his arms around both women. "We are a family. We came from different directions and adopted each other." Everyone breathed a sigh of relief as tension drained from the room.

"Well, family," Jo said. "Why don't we gather at the table. Dinner is ready."

———————⋖◆⋗———————

THE DINNER OF spaghetti squash with tomato and meat sauce was a delight. Nina wanted to know all about the strange squash and asked if Karen would help her shop for one and cook it at home.

Nina's use of the word 'home' did more to relax Gee and Karen than anything else. She had asked if she could have a swing 'at home.' She wanted to cook 'at home.' She told Jo about her room 'at home.' To Nina, the mansion was home and Gee and Karen were her family.

They had not progressed far into the meal when someone knocked at Wayne's door. The knocking was persistent and sounded almost desperate. Gee moved to stand opposite Wayne as he answered the door. Events of the evening had been too bizarre to take chances on an unexpected visitor.

An old man stumbled forward when Wayne opened the door. He had a scarf wrapped around his face and a long coat. Wispy gray hair fluttered around his head. His hands were bare and as Gee caught him, stopping a headlong tumble into the house, he noticed the man was dressed in pajamas and wore slippers.

"Here," Gee said, holding the man up. "Take it easy. We've got you."

"Come in and get warm," Wayne said. "You aren't dressed for cold and snow. Who are you?" There was a muffled sound as Gee helped the man unwind his scarf.

"Collin?" Gee said. "Are you well, Mr. Meagher? Should we call an ambulance."

"No," rasped the old man. "I had to come here. I haven't been in this house in fifteen years but I had to come."

Jo and Karen shuffled dishes at the table and pulled up another chair. Jo set an additional place and poured hot coffee for the man. He was seated in his pajamas and bathrobe and gratefully sipped the hot liquid.

"Your feet must be freezing," Wayne said. He ran up the stairs and was back a minute later with a pair of wool socks, a towel, and a heating pad. "Let's get your wet slippers off and dry your feet. When Granda stays over, he often gets cold and has a heating pad in bed with him."

Collin was still shivering and Karen grabbed the quilt she'd leaned against on the sofa to wrap around Collin's shoulders. The whole time he was being fussed over, Collin did not cease staring at Nina. He finally heaved a big sigh and focused on the others at the table.

"Thank you," he whispered. "I had to come here. He didn't give me time to dress."

"He?" Gee asked.

"The tree. The nut. I don't know who talks to me anymore. Maybe I am the nut and I've fallen from the tree. I just had to come here and see. My little Renee is home."

"Eat some dinner with us," Wayne suggested. "We're all trying to work things through. Please, relax and get warm and fed. We'll work out what happened.

Nina looked curious as the old man was settled at the table but showed no sign of recognition. No one had said she should stop eating, so she continued to lift a fork full of the squash and sauce to her mouth. Jo placed a helping on Collin's plate and he finally took note of it, his quaking hand eventually calming.

<hr>

"COMPULSIONS," COLLIN SAID. "Heinz always maintained he felt nothing when he ate the nut. But his cousin died. You know. You've eaten the nut," he said pointing at Gee and then Karen. They'd moved into the living room after dinner and Jo prepared hot chocolate for all of them. There was inadequate seating in the sparsely furnished room, so Wayne brought a dining chair to sit on.

"It's like having hallucinations," Karen said. "Sometimes I look at something familiar and it is suddenly something entirely different. It takes a while to straighten out which is real."

"They're both real," Collin said. He looked toward Gee.

"I don't know," Gee said. "The first time I heard a voice in my head and carried on a long conversation. The second time... at the Patriarch...

I felt that I'd just made a huge commitment to the woods. The only message I heard, if you will, was 'I'm bringing my children home.' We'd already found the children and then Nina showed up."

"Thank you for your hospitality, Savage," Collin said to Wayne. "Thank you for preparing the place for her to awaken."

"Why don't you spend the night, Mr. Meagher?" Jo suggested. "Wayne has a room fixed for his grandfather's visits. In the morning—in the daylight—we can get you back home and not worry about you freezing." Gee smiled at how familiar and at home Jo was in Wayne's house. All evening, she'd acted like she lived there. Perhaps she did now.

"So kind of you. So kind," Collin said. "You wouldn't have a drop of whisky, would you?"

"Can you stand scotch instead of Irish?" Wayne chuckled.

"Nothing wrong with my neighbor's whisky," Collin said. "I'll continue to have Violet as my heir," he continued after Wayne handed him a glass and he took a sip. "She is prepared for it and she visits me every day. Fine young woman. And it would be unfair to saddle Renee with that after so long isolated from us. Violet will take care of her."

"We'll take care of her, Collin," Karen said.

"Yes, you will. You swore to never stop looking for her. I thought it was just the raving of a distraught twelve-year-old girl, but you never stopped. You fulfilled your promise. Renee could not have a better home."

"Can Renee come to live with us?" Nina asked. "We have a big house and I would be her friend."

"Renee is a... nickname Uncle Collin remembers calling you," Karen explained. "It was a long time ago and he forgets you are Nina sometimes."

"Oh, that's okay. I forget lots of things," Nina said. "But we do have lots of bedrooms, ya know."

Talking to the Tree

AFTER THE BUSY weekend, Gee took Monday off and went shopping with Karen and Nina. It was an educational excursion and the three went into every store on Main Street between the river and Jitterz. In addition to clothing, antiques, jewelry, art, and cellphones, Karen took them into the offices of *The Elmont Mirror* where she was greeted warmly as a former colleague. Seeing her with her family, even Axel seemed less caustic and said they missed her.

After lunch at Jitterz, they continued south to the Rexall Pharmacy and across the river to Grimm's Market and the Farm Fleet Store. It seemed like a much longer walk going home than it had been going south.

"GEE, I'D LIKE you to take a walk up to the Gem Estates," David said Tuesday morning. "The seven Families weren't the only residents of this area who filed claims to land. And not all were interested in the Forest. The original owner of that plot of land didn't get along with the Families at all. We're talking ancient history here, back before the Civil War. When the City was platted, that piece of land was included and there was a lot of pressure to include his land in the Forest. Instead of succumbing to the pressure, the bastard went out and cut every tree on his land. Every single one. The trees were hauled out and used for firewood from what I've heard. Eventually, the land was acquired by a developer who wanted to build big country estates to rival the homes of the Families."

"I've seen it from across the lake," Gee said. "It didn't register that it was even a part of the City."

"Well, the development was a disaster. They're big, cheaply-built houses, that are in less than great repair now," David said. "But as part of the City, there's quite a bit of public land that was never developed. The developer defaulted on his loans and the City bought out about half the area—all undeveloped. Now that we've started talking about transplanting trees and are acquiring the farms next to the Wild Woods, we're thinking about planting on that undeveloped land. Of course, none of the land along the lake is available or along the creek that borders the south edge. But that leaves about fifty acres up there that we could plant on. There are survey stakes that should be sticking up from the ground high enough to be above the snow."

"What do you want me to do?" Gee asked. David sighed.

"I try not to get mystical about the Forest," he said at last. "But the trees grow best where they want to be. Just go out and look it over and tell me if you get any strong feelings one way or the other. We've decided you represent the Forest. Not its management, but the trees themselves. Tell me what you think and whether some of the transplanted trees from the Wild Woods would like to make that their home."

Gee thought it was a strange request, but he grabbed his walking stick and set off to explore.

THE DEVELOPMENT WAS depressing. The surveyed land was kept mowed in the summer so it wasn't overgrown like the Wild Woods. It stretched out in front of Gee as a smooth white sheet of snow. The dense wood of the Rose Hickory staff in his hand was comforting and, despite the cold, Gee stripped off his glove so he could feel the wood as he walked. Cut from the wedding tree, the staff had been given to him for his part in the ceremony—falling out of the tree. But it gave him a link to the Forest that he carried with him always. He could feel energy flowing from around him into the staff.

It seemed that even the staff was depressed when he walked across the bare field.

He was impatient to get back into the Forest where the air seemed to change his outlook on life. The Forest was alive and lovingly cared for.

At the south edge of the Forest, he crossed into the Wild Woods and the vibrations from his staff changed again. They were untamed and even a little dangerous. Gee walked all the way to the south edge of the Wild Woods where he could see the offices and piles of sand and gravel at SSG.

He decided to visit the cabins on his return to the foresters' office. The day had warmed considerably and he was confident no one would be at the cabins. He would just check the supplies he and David had left there a week ago.

The first cabin he came to seemed untouched. He saw no tracks nearby and checked the gauge on the propane tank to verify that it was full. This had been the cabin Darrell had first discovered was out of fuel. There was no sign anyone had been back to it. He continued working his way north through the woods until he reached cabin four, the one they had labeled the lab. Here the situation was different. The propane cylinder registered at half-full. Inside, foodstuffs were missing as was a tarp and poncho. There was no guarantee this was used by children. Any homeless refugee might have made it to the cabin along the new paths that had been cut. Yet Gee could feel the presence of children who had been held there against their will. Over the years there may have been hundreds. And they had rescued only four. He needed to find the others. As many as possible.

Gee looked out along the path that led toward the Patriarch and started walking. In the clearing beneath The Tree, Gee found a hollow of a root and sat down. Looking up, he smiled at the thought of Nina sitting on the lower branch, swinging her feet as she talked to Karen about the upcoming wedding.

Secure in his niche of the tree, Gee lay his staff across his lap and thrust his ungloved hand in his pocket to warm it up. After a few minutes, he took it out again and looked at the oblong white stone he held. It was so much a part of him and he held it so often that he seldom thought of it. He looked at the pattern etched in the stone. A single vertical line, crossed by five lines, not quite perpendicular to the vertical. Or perhaps it was the other way around and was a horizontal line crossed by five nearly vertical lines.

He held the stone against his staff and positioned it in various ways. He wanted to sketch it there but all he had was his pocket knife. With the point of the sharpest blade, he slowly etched the design into the wood of the walking stick. Looking at last at his work, he nodded his head and put away the stone and the knife.

He leaned back against the tree with the staff still across his lap and went to sleep.

An hour later, he woke from a peaceful if chilly nap. He needed to come out here more often, he thought. He needed to just walk in the woods and talk to the trees. He needed to be here when The Tree called his children home.

Tension on the Council

"So, YOU BELIEVE she's your niece's daughter?" Jan asked Collin. Eight people sat around the table now. Violet Lanahan, a bit confused over what she was seeing, sat behind her Uncle Collin. Family Roth, Karen Weisman. Family Poltanys, Jan Poltanys. Family Nussbaum, Heinz Nussbaum. Family Cavanaugh, Loren Cavanaugh. Family Lazorack, David Lazorack. Family Savage, Pàl Savage. Family Meagher, Collin Meagher. And Gee Evars of the Wild Woods. It was the first time all the Family heads had been together at the table in many years.

"She is," Collin said. "As much my niece as Violet is."

"And your heir?"

"My choice stands. Violet is my heir."

"And you don't want any more proof than her response to a house number? We required more than that of Celia and Jo Ransom."

"The DNA test results should arrive in the next day or two," Karen said. "They should show the connection between Nina and Violet."

"Have you ever heard from your niece, Collin? I mean Renee's mother, Dora Lisle?" Loren asked.

"She went downhill faster than I did when Dirk committed suicide. Always drunk and finally just wandered off. She might still be living or she might be dead," Collin stated flatly.

"We could request an exhumation of Dirk's body and get a DNA match from that. It would be the closest," Heinz said.

"Why do you care?" Collin exploded at the gathered Family heads. "Fifteen years ago, when there was a fresh trail, none of you would help me find her. None of you would use your resources to track her down. You know who took her! You've always known. I was the one who stood up and resisted SSG's move to clear-cut the Wild Woods. I was the one who organized the proxy battle. And I was the one they came back at to get revenge. They took my little Renee and you did nothing!"

"We were under *sàmhach*," Heinz said. "You know we were banned from investigating independently."

"And who imposed *sàmhach*?" Collin demanded. "You let a mis-used notion of Family honor prevent us from taking action when we could. Delayed just long enough to lose all trace of her. Who declared *sàmhach*?"

"Ross Lerner," Jan replied. "The old police chief. Dad was upset about it. He was already beginning to lose his bearings. He raved about the secrets of the quarry all the time."

"He told me about that a few days ago," Gee said. "I don't know that we'll ever find out what those secrets were."

"You talked to August? He hasn't said a word in five years," Jan said.

"He called me George. Said we couldn't go back to the quarry again. Asked me not to eat the nut."

"George was his cousin. Dad wasn't going to challenge him for Family leadership. He wanted to be a doctor. George insisted that the only way he'd truly be head of the Family was to eat the nut. He did and died," Jan said. "Some of the Family accused Dad of goading him on but grandfather made him his heir anyway."

"It didn't move him enough to help in the investigation," Collin said, determined not to let the conversation stray. "None of you. None of your Families would help. Now Renee is back."

"And nothing else matters," Karen said vehemently. "Nothing changes from the way it was a few days ago. Nina is Gee's and my ward. She calls us Mommy and Daddy and I will protect her like my own flesh and blood. It means nothing more to you than to a brood of old hens. Let's get on with what the meeting is about." The older men at the table scowled at her but none said anything.

"Well, then," Loren finally broke the silence. "I move we approve the expansion of the Forest through acquiring the two suggested farms, and others if we can, and transplanting trees from the Wild Woods."

"Is there any further discussion needed?" David asked. "Gee and Collin, you weren't here for the previous discussion. Anything to add?"

"I yield the floor to my esteemed colleague, the City Champion," Collin intoned, reverting to the slightly crazy persona he usually appeared as. Gee raised an eyebrow.

"I spend a lot of time in the Wild Woods. I know it's too dense but I'm committed to saving every sapling," Gee said. "Those that can be transplanted with a reasonable expectation of survival should be. If the larger ones near the Patriarch can't be moved safely, they should be left where they are. They've stood in the shadow of the Patriarch for this long and have grown straight and true. They are his children and he has called them home."

"It's not good for productivity to have too many of them too close together, Gee," David said. He'd heard the argument before, so Gee assumed he wanted the other Family heads to hear as well. "You might need to consent to thinning some of them."

"I'm not concerned about productivity," Gee responded. "The Wild Woods should stay wild."

"It's a danger to have it like it is, Gee," Loren said. "A wildfire could destroy more than the Wild Woods itself."

"I understand the concern, Loren. I need to do some maintenance that we've already started. Clearing the fencerow has been an important part of the process. Mapping the trees should continue, as well as cutting more trails. Certain invasive species should be removed and controlled, especially the firethorn. But the Wild Woods has a different ecosystem than the Forest. There's wildlife, for example. Clearing the dogwood, holly, hawthorn, and ferns would upset the natural order of it. It could even have a harmful effect on the water table. It isn't another nut orchard. It's wild."

There were sighs around the table as the heads realized their commitment to the Wild Woods was in Gee's hands. He was passionate, not only for the trees themselves, but for finding any additional lost children. Since Thanksgiving, nearly all the work in the Wild Woods had been done by Gee and his high school volunteers.

"Agreed," Pàl said.

"Agreed," Karen joined. At last all seven Family heads had agreed to Gee's conditions.

———◁◆▷———

"I'M TOO OLD and feeble-minded to sit at this table," Collin said. "Newspapers are better company. I'm assigning Violet as my permanent proxy. She'll tell me anything I need to know."

"There's precedent for that," Karen said. "Ben assigned the same role to Leah until he made me his heir."

"I'd like Jessie involved," Loren said. "My sons are worthless regarding the Family. Clark's a competent business manager but he only sees

the business. He can't see the Forest for the trees, as they say. And Troy…
He's gone. I don't expect him to ever be back."

"I won't push Jonathan into the role," David said. "But I'll let him
take as much as he wants. If Jessie gets more involved, he will as well."

"Wayne won't return to teaching next year," Pàl said. "He's agreed to
start an orderly transition into the company. I'm sad his heart isn't in it.
I'll stay active as long as possible."

"Fine boy," Collin said. "Gave me a nice bed to sleep in one night.
Fine boy."

"I don't think the council is ready for Cameron," Heinz said. "Or
that he's ready for the council. We'll work together for a while. As long
as my health holds."

"That's how I'm handling it with Zach," Jan said. "He's got a
good head and is handling some of our business. He just needs more
experience."

"And Gee is Gee," Karen laughed at her fiancé. "And on March sixteenth, we'll go to work trying to make sure there are suitable heirs for
the Roths and the Forest."

"Are you announcing something to us, Karen?" Pàl asked.

"Yes. I hope you will all join us at the Patriarch to witness our wedding vows on Saturday the sixteenth. You are at the top of our guest list."

"We'll work on making sure the path is easy to follow, with your
permission, Gee," David affirmed. "I think the Patriarch will become a
place of pilgrimage when people learn about it this summer."

Cutting Losses

THINGS WERE EASIER when the monk was around. He could tell the
recluse to do something and it would get done. If he had a dependable
lieutenant now, Deacon might have stayed and milked the business for
everything he could get out of it. SSG had been profitable enough to
give him a steady flow of income but strategically, it had been a good
cover for his other interests.

He didn't own enough shares to need to file his intent to sell so had
started dumping his stock right after the damned Scotsman had shown

up. As Nixon said, "Once you've sat at the head of the table, there isn't any other seat of interest." Great man. Opened China. All those lovely women and willing workers wanting to get out. That was a profitable time.

He knew who was buying his shares, of course. The damned Families all had buy orders under various covers. But at the inflated price Deacon was selling his shares for, they were funding his retirement from the trafficking industry. They'd crap if they knew.

The other rats were abandoning ship as fast as they could scurry. Or dying aboard. Dr. Jones was no longer a threat. Simon Alexander and his wife were always nervous and threatening to go to the police. Deacon had been there that Friday night to deliver cash to them. The smug smiles of self-satisfaction died on their faces as the light went out of their eyes. The Daniels had left before the ink was dry on the sale of their farm. He'd handled many of the product transfers from his barn.

Deacon hated getting involved directly.

Getting Troy to do the job on Jones was easy. He had no conscience at all. And he could never open his mouth without admitting to murder. That got rid of the failed experiment as well. Jones had been so certain that he could alter a child before birth under the influence of the drug that Deacon personally endorsed it. All he succeeded in was creating a retarded ghoul. It took months of careful reprogramming to get Taryn back to a usable condition. She was a nearly perfect little Stepford Wife and would never stray from devotion to her husband and son.

That left the preacher. Lance Beck's obsession with the girl in the hospital, Rena Lynd, was dangerous. That was Deacon's failing. He didn't realize how they had bonded and when Beck sent her to the cabin 'for safety', Deacon had allowed Jones to treat her like any other reprogramming candidate. Deacon used the girl to summon that damned reporter and then got rid of her. Or so he thought. Who knew some snot-nosed kid hero would dive into the quarry to save her? The quarry hid a lot of secrets. She could have been one more. She had to go. And so did Beck. It remained only to determine how.

And then Deacon Stewart could quietly retire with no one the wiser.

Floodwaters

AN EASTERN SEABOARD weather front pushed days of torrential rain inland. It melted the snow but the ground remained frozen. The runoff from the north flooded the canals and the Rose River overflowed its banks.

"Haven't had floods like this in fifty years," Gabe said from his corner chair in the foresters' office. Gee, Jonathan, and Jessie sat with him, monitoring the situation. All other foresters had been called out of the Forest to volunteer in town and around the area with emergency services.

"According to the last report, the water is almost up to Riverside Drive. The Fairgrounds are flooded and there's a report of coal being washed into the West Branch at the Exchange," Jonathan said as he marked areas of the map.

Gee's phone rang and he listened intently.

"Nathan says Silver Creek has backed up at the confluence with the river. There's water across Main Street just south of the Market. He's been in touch with other merchants and all the way south to Walmart, they have crews moving merchandise off lower shelves because water is coming through the doors from the parking lot. Nathan's doing the same thing at the Market."

"Does he need anything?" Jessie asked.

"He's staying open as long as possible. There's a line of people stocking up on supplies. It will probably take a week to restock after this is over," Gee answered. The office phone rang and Jonathan snatched it up as he marked the map with the new information.

"Darrell's with the volunteers at the hospital," Jonathan said when he hung up. "They just went on emergency power and it looks like most of North Main is dark."

"That means your place is probably dark, too, Gee," Jessie said. "You should be home with your family. Why are you even here?"

"I ask myself that question a lot," Gee chuckled. Then he got serious. "I... I need to go check on the Wild Woods. The Patriarch."

"In this?" Jessie exclaimed. "The Patriarch has surely stood more than this in its life."

"Do you think it's too dangerous to go?" Gee asked. They looked over at Gabe to get an answer. He rocked his chair onto all four legs and stood to shuffle the City map off the map of the Forest and Wild Woods.

"Stay away from the gully," he said. "If Silver Creek is backed up, the gully will be flooded as well. Water will be washing into the quarry. The safest area is probably the path you've cut along the fence. The land rises to the east. Be watchful for unexpected new creeks or gullies created by the runoff. If you cut from here to Cabin Three, you could pick up the finger path to the Patriarch over here. I don't think it's too dangerous but that doesn't mean it makes sense. What do you think you'll find?"

"I don't know," Gee said. "The trees are calling. I need to be there."

"Take an ATV. You can navigate the paths at least as far as the cabin with it," Jonathan said, pointing out the features on the map. "Take a four-wheeler, not a three. The path Gabe mentioned is the shortest, but this one is wider. It's where Jessie and I have been working."

"Thank you," Gee said. "I'd better call Karen first."

———◁◆▷———

"THE LOWER GROUNDS are underwater but the mansion was built above the floodplain," Karen said. "We're all safe. Jude, Laura, Grandma Sue, and the children are all here with us. Raven's been on the phone every half hour to make sure Timmy stays at the Market and helps, even though his shift is over. Nathan is keeping him working. It's safer for him than driving back here."

"How is Nina doing? And the children?"

"Uncomfortable. Jeanie plans to come join us this afternoon if the bridge is clear. It's built high so that shouldn't be a problem," Karen said. "I don't know what else to say, Gee. None of the kids have done anything strange but they are almost as quiet as when they used to go into their waiting state. They keep looking up at the windows like they expect something."

"Is there anything you need before I head into the woods?"

"Emergency power? I can't believe a place this size doesn't have its own generator. We have candles and Raven found a stock of electric lanterns and batteries. We have food. Just come back safely to us. Soon."

"I will, Love. I don't know why I feel…"

"Do what you need to do, Gee. We're safe."

GEE STARTED THE four-wheeler, letting the engine settle into a smooth purr before putting it in gear and easing out of the foresters' equipment shed. He stopped to close the door, wishing he had a canopy on the open vehicle instead of just his poncho. Keeping to the higher ground on the east edge of the forest, he entered the Wild Woods on the fencerow path his crew had worked on through the winter.

He recognized the side path they'd cut from the fence to Cabin Three, the spot where Nina had panicked and run. The place was still spooky. He looked through the door of the windowless cabin and flashed his light around the interior, hoping to see someone sheltering there. He thought the survival kit had been opened and a poncho was gone.

The canopy as he moved deeper into the Wild Woods was denser than the Forest. Even without leaves, the thick branches above diverted the water stream so it was less torrential as he eased the ATV down the wider path.

At the end of the trail, Gee jockeyed the ATV around until it was facing back the way he had come. Taking his bearings, he started pushing his way through the low scrub and ferns toward the center of the ring of saplings. When he reached the shelter of the Patriarch, he breathed deeply—perhaps a sigh of relief. He was home. A leaky, drafty home, but home nonetheless. He leaned against The Tree with his staff in hand and breathed in the energy of the Patriarch.

Are the trees here sentient? Does he really speak to me? Or am I simply accessing some primitive part of my brain that draws me to him?

Gee closed his eyes and let the calm wash over him. He slowed his breathing and let the sound of the rain fade from his consciousness. He could hear his own heart, his own breathing, and the breathing of others.

His eyes snapped open. He could still hear the soft breath nearby. Moving as slowly as he could, Gee turned to face the tree and look up. Up into the eyes of a child. Then Gee saw a second child, arms protectively wrapped around the first, sharing a single poncho. A dull blanket stuck out from under the poncho, perhaps providing some warmth. The army surplus camouflaged poncho almost disappeared into the tree's protective shelter. Gee's hand moved slowly to the pocket of his emergency pack. He found the energy bar he searched for and unwrapped it, trying not to create any sudden movements that might panic the frozen children. He brought the bar to his mouth to take a tiny bite and reached out to offer the bar to them.

"Food," he whispered. "I will not hurt you."

Hunger overruled fear and one of the children reached out for the bar, offering a bite first to the other before taking a bite himself. Him. A boy and a girl about the same age. Perhaps just adolescent.

"I can help you get warm and dry," Gee said softly. He leaned his walking stick against the tree and the girl tracked it. She reached out her hand but couldn't touch it. "Do you want to touch the stick?" he asked. Still worried about frightening the children, Gee exercised all his self-discipline to move slowly and lift the stick toward the children as if offering his hand to a small animal. The girl touched it, her eyes drifting closed. The boy also reached out and gripped the staff, his eyes closing. The three, connected by the staff, Gee heard a whisper deep inside himself that said simply, "My children."

ONCE THEY HAD established contact through the sharing of food and the touching of the rose hickory walking stick, the children became docile, losing the frightened look he had first observed. When he lifted his arms to them to help them down from the tree, they glanced at each other. The boy slipped down beside Gee. He lifted his arms to the girl.

Gee was certain the boy could not be strong enough to catch the weight of his companion and stood ready to catch the girl and support her helper. But she did not attempt to get down. Instead, the poncho shifted as she lowered a tiny bundle to the boy. Then she let Gee lift her down from the tree. He reached into his pack again for an emergency 'space blanket' and put it around the boy to keep him somewhat dry and hold in his body heat.

The children were compliant and held each other under the dual protection of the blankets and poncho. Gee started the ATV and headed out of the woods. He thumbed his cellphone as soon as he had a signal.

"Karen, please notify the hospital that I am on my way there with children from the Wild Woods," Gee said calmly.

"Children! Gee, do you need an ambulance? How many?" Karen shouted.

"I think I can get to the hospital in the ATV more quickly and safely than an ambulance could get here. The rain has let up a little and I have the children sheltered. I have a boy and a girl, post-pubescent. Perhaps twelve or thirteen years old. And a baby."

Genesis

KAREN MET GEE at the hospital, doctor and nurses at the ready. Gee asked them to proceed quietly like they had with Nina and the children. Instead of being led to an emergency room, they were taken to the room the children had occupied when they came to the hospital. They walked calmly, occasionally reaching up to touch Gee's walking stick as he walked beside them.

"Clean up and dry clothes first," Adam said softly. "They seem steady but underfed. We need a natal check on the baby as soon as we can. And soft clothes. I don't want them stripped and left in hospital gowns."

They removed the poncho and dirty blankets as Ellie prepared a tub for the teens. Gee took the baby from the girl and she watched as he looked at her child. A natal nurse arrived with a scale and baby bath and set up to do her assessment. She noted Ellie gently stripping the teens out of their clothes and helping them into the tub.

"Together?" she asked, alarmed. "It's a boy and a girl!"

"I don't think they have any secrets from each other," Gee said softly, handing the nurse the baby, now revealed to be a little girl.

"You mean… she's theirs? I thought she was a little sister," the nurse sighed. "I guess I'm not quite as liberal-minded as I try to convince myself."

"How is our baby girl's health?" Karen asked as she replaced Gee in the crowded bathroom.

"Seventeen inches," Nurse Edmonds responded. "Are you the grandmother? Eight pounds, two ounces. She's undernourished but if that tiny thing in the bathtub has been nursing her, it's a wonder she hasn't starved. They're all so quiet."

"How old do you estimate the baby is?" Karen asked.

"You don't know?" the nurse asked. "Can't the little girl tell you?"

"Please guess," Karen prodded her.

"We deliver many babies who weigh more at birth than this little one. I would guess two weeks under normal development but the little girl needs a maternal exam. She looks to be well-healed if this is her child. I'd guess more like a month."

Karen stifled a sob and looked at Ellie. "In the coldest part of winter. Alone in the Wild Woods."

"The Wild Woods?" Nurse Edmonds asked. "Are you saying these are children rescued from that dark place? God have mercy on us!"

"You weren't briefed?" Karen asked. "Of course you weren't. We just requested a post-natal checkup. How would you have known?"

"But I thought the three children rescued were younger," the nurse said.

"These were just found today," Karen said. "Which means there could still be more out there."

"One hears such strange stories," the nurse mused. "I'm not superstitious but the idea of children living wild just a mile from town is hard to grasp."

"We'd appreciate you keeping this quiet until we've had a chance to make an announcement," Karen said. "I'm going to contact the police and newspaper now."

"Of course. I'll... um... wait until the news is official before I say anything." She swaddled the baby and handed her to Karen, then gathered her equipment and the vial of blood she'd extracted. She handed Karen a bottle of infant formula. "Feed her. Often," she said. Adam took the vial of blood where he was preparing to examine the teens. Karen sat on the commode where the teens could see her feed the baby while Ellie worked efficiently to wash their hair. The kids seemed to enjoy the attention, grooming each other as Ellie washed them.

After the bath, they were dried with big towels and wrapped in fluffy white robes. The girl went immediately to Karen and held out her arms for the baby. Karen smiled as she handed the baby over.

"What's your name, Sweetie?" she asked the girl. The young mother just shrugged. Gee turned to the boy.

"Can you tell us your names?" he asked. The children seemed to have no difficulty understanding what they were asked but shook their heads. "Well, for right now, why don't we call you John and Jane," he smiled as he led them to the bed where Adam was preparing to examine them.

"If you call that sweet baby girl 'Boy' we are going to have words," Karen admonished. Gee smiled at her.

"No, I think Grandma should think of what to call the baby," he grinned at her. Karen opened her mouth and closed it again. "Now, John, the caregivers here want to check to make sure you are healthy. They want you to grow big and strong so you will be able to care for Jane and your baby. Can you hop up on the bed and show Jane how you can help Caregiver Adam do your examination?" Gee carefully avoided using the word 'doctor' around the children, based on the reaction the younger children had just three months ago. Nina had also been nervous when they mentioned the doctor.

Adam nodded his approval and gave the boy a thorough examination, finishing by taking blood. That was the only part the boy didn't like, but he put up with it. Ellie gave him a sweat suit to wear and he pulled the fluffy robe over it.

Jane handed the baby back to Karen and got up on the bed. She shed her robe, showing a developing body and a bit of milk leaking from her nipples. She was obedient to every request of the doctor, even during the pelvic exam that would have freaked out most teenagers. She disliked the prick of the needle as much as John had. She donned the new sweat pants but just pulled the robe over her shoulders. She took the baby and held her to her breast.

"We'll need to watch that carefully to see that the baby is getting enough nourishment," Adam said. "I'll know better when we get blood tests back from the lab. All three children seem to be in reasonable health, though a little stunted in their growth due to a subsistence diet. I'll order food and it should be here shortly. It looks like you've just been elected to more hospital duty. I'll get more helpers in who were involved last time but this will be different than working with the little children. You won't have Laura to spend the nights, either. The kids must have had some kind of shelter to be able to survive a birth in the coldest weather of the century."

"How will we ever know?" Karen asked. The baby stopped sucking and Karen held out her arms. Jane gave up the child but kept her eyes on Karen as the baby was bounced and patted until she had a big burp.

"So," Adam continued, "names so we don't get things mixed up in the lab. John, Jane, and…?"

"Gen," Karen responded.

"Jen as in Jennifer?" Adam said.

"No, Gen as in Genesis. A new creation has come to the Wild Woods."

THOUGH VERY QUIET, John and Jane did not seem unable to make themselves talk, unlike the little children a few weeks ago. But their whispers to each other were so soft, they went undetected for several hours. Gee left Karen with the children as he went home to collect Nina and bring her to visit. Jeanie accompanied the Woods family to their home.

Nina had been helpful immediately, hearing the whispers first. She joined the whispered conversation. These children were more on a par with where Nina had been when she arrived than with the younger children.

Following old patterns, Gee settled into the beanbag chair in the evening and read aloud. The little family joined him on one side with Nina and Karen cuddled on the other.

"You need to write stories, Gee," Karen suggested.

"What would I write?"

"Stories of the Wild Woods, where our children were found."

"Our children?"

"I believe we are about to have more residents at Roth House."

The Nest

"THE QUESTION IS, 'Are there more?' We've been scouring the woods all weekend. We've replenished all the propane tanks and survival packs. I don't know what to say. There are a thousand places they could hide if they had the skills," David said to the gathered group of foresters on Monday morning. "The flood waters are receding but there are still treacherous places, especially around the creek, gully, and quarry. We can send more foresters out there but what are we looking for?" Everyone turned to look at Gee, expecting him to have an answer since he had found the little family. It was apparent that David was frustrated with the search. No one knew if there was anyone still out there.

"Nests," Gee whispered suddenly. Then more loudly. "We've been looking on the ground. The children were in the branches of the Patriarch. I'm betting they had a nest, possibly moving to lower branches during the worst part of the storm. There are no more cabins. We should be looking up."

"And you're all too noisy," Gabe admonished. "When a human goes thrashing through the woods, the animals take shelter and are still."

"They aren't animals," Gee protested.

"Don't get your undies in a bunch. They don't deal with people. They're there to survive. You said it yourself. When you found them, they stayed still as if willing themselves invisible. For self-preservation, they'd do the same in their nests when they hear ATVs and noisy people. They won't come out until they sense the intruders are gone.

"Which is probably how they stayed hidden from the doctor. He would never have climbed a tree to look for a runaway. And if anyone is still out there, they don't know Jones is dead," David said. "They could believe we are all his minions."

"I'm going back to the Patriarch," Gee said, picking up his walking stick. "No ATVs making noise. Just have them at the edge of the Woods where we can call for them if needed. Jonathan and Jessie, are you in?"

"Definitely," they answered.

"Start at Cabin One and look for access up into the trees. Maybe from the roof. If you find it, settle down and wait. You'll have to see if you can outwait a rabbit." They nodded.

"Why go back where you were if you already found the children who were there?" David asked. "Shouldn't you move to one of the other likely access points?"

"I need to climb The Tree," Gee replied.

GEE WAS SILENT as he approached the Patriarch. He found it easy to move through the Wild Woods without making noise, even with the boots he wore. The massive tree seemed unusually quiet. No breeze rocked its branches causing squeaks and cracks. No birds or animals scurried about. Ten feet overhead, branches became so tangled, Gee wondered if he could make his way through them.

He looked at his equipment, inspected by David before he left the office. Pulling himself to the first limb, he sat where Nina had a few days previously. It didn't seem right to attack The Tree with all this gear as if it were a mountain to be conquered. It was a friend who had sheltered the children. One item at a time, he removed gloves, goggles, hard hat, and boots, dropping them to the ground next to his walking stick. Finally, he dropped the safety harness and his coat. The temperature was above freezing but it would not take long for the cold to hamper him.

He stood on the limb, his toes feeling the rough texture of the bark, and began to climb. Whispers of encouragement in his mind guided his feet and hands as he rose higher above the ground. At thirty feet, he could barely see glimpses of the ground below. He used his cellphone to capture pictures of the new world he had entered. And then he continued to climb.

Above, branches thinned and he could see the sky but no sign of a nest. He wedged himself into a fork of the tree to rest, looking around and then down. Ten feet below him, he could see it. The nest was so well concealed that he had missed it while looking up. He snapped a picture from above and climbed back down to where the children had lived. Perhaps for months. Only the incongruous presence of dried ferns laid over the top of the canvas had exposed the nest to Gee from above. Still, the nest was wet from the recent rains.

It was large enough for the children to cuddle in. One of the microfiber blankets from a survival kit lined the bottom. A pile of dried mushrooms was covered over by more fern leaves. And next to it, Gee found a stash of hickory nuts.

12

ON THE RUN

Awakening

"ADAM!" GEE PANTED when he found the doctor. Adam looked up from a cup of coffee in the hospital cafeteria. Julia and Mead sat with him.

"Are you hurt, Gee?" Adam asked as he started to stand.

"No. Winded. Ran from the Woods."

"That's… about three miles," Mead offered. "Why are you running?"

"No driver's license. The children, Adam. They've been eating nuts in the woods."

"What? That's not possible. Their blood tests showed markers for RDH in their system but they'd get that from long-term use of Lustre."

Gee put the dirty blanket on the table, causing those seated to pull their cups and dishes out of his way.

"This is what was in the children's nest in the Patriarch. A blanket. A few ragged clothes. A plastic cup. Mushrooms and nuts. There were plenty of broken shells to indicate they'd been eating them," Gee explained.

"And a butter knife?" Mead said, spotting the flash of silver in the pile.

"That and the cup are the only domestic things I could find. And here. The remains of their shoes. I don't know how far they walked to get here, but they are completely worn out."

"We need to get a nut tested," Adam said. "Maybe these don't have the concentration of RDH in them that the nuts in the Forest have."

"Or we could be dealing with addicts who have developed an immunity to the poison," Mead speculated.

"You know, I ate a nut from the Patriarch the first time I found him." Gee said.

"You did? When?"

"Thanksgiving. It didn't seem to have the same effect that the first nut had. And remember, Karen ingested seven of them when she was kidnapped. I assume they were from the Wild Woods," Gee said.

"We should run another sample of your blood and Karen's to see how the markers compare to the children," Adam said. "I don't see any signs of withdrawal in the children. In fact, I was going to suggest you can take them home now."

"We can... What?"

"They aren't sick. When the little children were here, we were feeling our way. They were unresponsive and we tried to figure out what was wrong. Nina was never admitted because, aside from her damaged memory, she wasn't sick. These kids are like her. They need a healthy diet and people who will take care of them. That's what a family does," Adam said. "I plan to release Jane, John, and Genesis Evars into the care of their family."

"Pending the judge's approval," Mead added.

"You're saying Karen and I are their family?"

"Convince me otherwise, Gee."

"WHAT DO YOU think, Karen?" Gee asked. Mead gave him a lift home after their meeting at the hospital. "It's... So much of the work falls on you now. I don't want you to feel like I've gone out and created a burden for you."

Karen grabbed Gee's head and turned it toward her before kissing him passionately. Tears streamed down her face. She pulled away to look at him and then kissed him again.

"Do you think the only child that mattered to me was Renee? We found her. Nina is here. But if we could adopt every child who has been taken and abused, I would."

"We'll need more help."

"I've already asked Raven if she would be interested in helping with the children. I'll put her on full time instead of as a part-time house-keeper. What were Ben's last words to us? 'Fill this house with children.' You don't think he meant I should become a baby factory, do you?" Karen laughed through her tears. Gee hugged her to him.

They heard a sniff and turned to see Nina standing in front of the sofa.

"Nina, honey, are you upset?"

She shook her head and Karen shifted so Nina could sit between them.

"You... won't send me away, will you?"

"Absolutely not!" Gee said. "Nina, this is your home. We would never send you away. Aren't you the one who reminded us that we have a lot of bedrooms?" She released a shuddering breath.

"I... knew that. I was afraid. When Sir and Madam got a new girl, they sold me."

"Honey, we don't own you. We love you. When we bring more children into our home, we'll love more. We don't need to take away from you to give to Jane and John and Gen," Karen said. Nina considered a moment and began to smile.

"It's like Jeanie! I don't have to stop being friends with her to be friends with Leslie. And that means I can love Mommy and Daddy and still have room for John and Jane and Gen."

"You are growing up to be such a loving and kind daughter," Karen said, hugging her.

———— ◁◆▷ ————

"Do you want to come and live with us?" Gee asked the children as they sat together in the hospital room. Karen cuddled baby Gen and Nina had chosen to sit close beside Jane.

"Will we be together, sir?" John asked. He hugged Jane possessively. They still spoke softly but seemed to have as much language skill as Nina. They had lived rough for nearly a year but had poor experiences living in a house with their owners.

"First, I am not 'sir'. I'm just Gee. John, we don't own you. No one is ever going to own you again. We will give you a home and a safe place and invite you to be part of our family. You and Jane and Gen will live with us as long as you like and we will help you learn and become independent as your own family. Is that what you want?"

"Yes, sir. I mean yes, Gee."

Jane had not spoken more than a few whispers to John. Karen looked to her.

"Jane, this is your choice as well. Do you want to live with John and Gen in our home as a family?" Jane looked at John and visibly relaxed. Her smile was radiant when she looked at Karen.

"Yes, ma… Miss…"

"Just Karen, dear."

"Yes, Karen. You won't take us away from each other?"

"No, sweetheart. Not at all."

"Then yes." She clung to John.

"Judge Warren needs to ask you some of the same questions so we can go home," Gee said. "Just answer him honestly, even if it is different than what you told Karen and me. We'll wait outside."

A HAPPY PARADE left the children's room. Adam and Julia followed the family of six and chatted with Mead Oliver and Judge Warren. All four had witnessed the agreement between the children and Gee, Karen, and Nina, verifying they all wanted to live together. It would take time and proper paperwork to make it a permanent arrangement but the Judge had signed temporary custody over. There had been one stipulation the Judge required and talked it over carefully with Jane, John, and Adam. After the exchange, Jane had received a birth control implant. She sighed when the bandage had been applied to the insertion point.

"Someday I might want another baby," she said. "I love Gen. But it was very hard and hurt a lot. Caregiver Adam said it was because my hips haven't grown up yet. When I grow up all the way, then John and I can have another baby."

"That's very mature of you, Jane," Karen said. She held baby Gen again and smiled at the gurgling infant. "You have a good Mommy, Gen. And Grandma will be right here to help."

John stopped in the hall so abruptly he was almost run over. Jane followed his eyes into the room they were passing. John reached for Gee's hickory walking stick and asked for it with his eyes. Gee found the children all liked to reach out and touch the stick but was puzzled by John's request. He nodded and let John take the stick. They followed the boy into the room where Rena Lynd lay silently in bed, Pastor Lance Beck sitting beside her.

"What is the meaning of this?" Beck asked. "Are you here to rejoice in my suffering. Dr. Gaston has already told me she won't last much longer. Let her go in peace."

Without hesitating, John and Jane approached the bed opposite where Beck sat and laid the hickory staff next to Rena. They carefully moved her hand and wrapped it around the smooth wood. Both children held her hand against the staff.

The room was silent, Beck shocked to stillness by the children. Rena gasped, her eyes flashing open as a long moan escaped her lips. For a moment, Gee thought it was her death rattle. Lance reached for her hand and she turned her head toward him. A piercing scream issued from her throat.

Mead was in action and pulled Beck's hands behind his back, snapping handcuffs on him. Never one to wait on formalities, Mead immediately started asking questions.

"Is this the man who attacked you, Rena?"

She shook her head and looked at Beck, tears forming in her eyes.

"I loved you," she whispered. "You didn't have to send me to them. I would have done anything for you."

Judge Warren held up a hand, silencing Mead. Adam and Julia efficiently began checking Rena's vitals. She never let go of the staff.

"Welcome back to the land of the living," Judge Warren said softly as he looked at Rena over the children's heads. "Rena, do you know who did this to you? Who you were sent to and who pushed you into the quarry?" Rena nodded slowly.

"Dr. Jones," she said. "And Deacon Stewart."

PASTOR LANCE BECK was freed, protesting that he knew nothing about her treatment and believing he had sent her to a place where she would be safe. Rena, however, made it clear that she did not want him to come near her again. Ever. He left in tears.

She was so exhausted from the sudden awakening and dramatic outburst, she could hardly keep her eyes open. Julia stayed with her as she fell asleep, having given Mead and Warren enough information to generate an arrest warrant for Deacon Stewart. The story was one of drugs and rape. Before she drifted back to sleep, she looked up at the children and smiled at them.

"Thank you," she whispered, "for bringing the Forest to me." She released the staff and dropped off to sleep.

"She's very weak," Adam said once they were in the hall. "Even now, I don't know if she will make it. We'll do everything we can."

"I'll start the warrant," Mead said to the Judge. "I'll need Sheriff Johnson. Stewart lives about ten miles south of town."

"Have him meet us at my office," the judge said. "And get lots of backup. State police if you need them. This is the end of the road for him."

"How DID YOU know she needed the staff?" Karen asked the children during dinner at the mansion that evening.

They had been happy but not overly impressed by the little suite of rooms that Karen showed them to—just a bedroom and bath. Raven had prepared a big meal, having already told Sherry at the Pub & Grub that she could no longer work there. Timmy sat at the table with the rest of the family and Gee realized they had adopted the young man with a mind as damaged as the others. He stood as soon as he had finished eating and announced that he needed to wash dishes at the pub. He left.

"When Gee found us, we were afraid. We stayed away from the evil men," John said. "We hid in the trees. But then we touched his stick and everything was okay. We knew we could trust him. He belonged to The Tree and so did we."

"When we saw the girl in the room, we recognized her," Jane added. "We saw her come to the cabin. The evil men visited her every day. Then she left and never came back. We... felt... she belonged to The Tree. So, we took the stick to comfort her."

"Will she be all right?" Nina asked.

"We don't know yet," Karen said. "The caregivers will do all they can for her."

Jane asked for her baby, being held by Raven. As soon as she had her, she gave the infant a tiny breast to suckle.

"We will help to give Gen more food from a bottle so she can grow strong like the two of you," Karen said. "You scarcely have enough energy for yourself, Jane. Always eat as much as you want so you can grow."

The girl smiled and whispered, "Thank you."

Fire

DECEIVED. HE HAD been deceived. Could his own deacon have been the one who tried to kill Rena? Lance Beck went straight from the hospital to the church. There, he knelt at the altar to pray.

How could it be possible for the church of God, his flock, to sink so low? Had he, on a mission to save children from the evil influence of homosexuality and disobedience, been used for some unrighteousness by his Deacon? He had taken the sins of those children on himself. Done unspeakable things to show them the way to salvation. With the assistance of the drug created by Dr. Jones, he had carefully wiped away their evil natures and made them obedient to every word of their parents. They'd been brought to him one at a time over the past ten or more years for instruction that he gladly gave.

Yes, the unwashed sinners of the town would likely not approve. Some would even condemn him as a child abuser. But those people were the first to condemn the youth of today for not having respect or the discipline that their parents, themselves, had failed to instill in them. They didn't dare even spank a disobedient child for fear of accusations. Yet in his years in the ministry, Lance Beck had turned many a child from the depth of depravity and raised them up whole—a pleasing sacrifice unto God.

What witchcraft had that Satan worked with those children to animate Rena and cause her to make such accusations? The Champion's magic wand laid across her hands while she rejected her love. It was preposterous and the people of Rosebud Falls let themselves be bewitched by his spells. He had come to town to sow discord. Even within this church.

Preaching had not been enough. It was time for Lance Beck to take action. If the community refused to recognize the evil of the Forest and the enchantment they were under, then he had to destroy the Forest. Like Elijah, he would call down the fire of God and destroy the priests of Baal and their heathen shrine. He was called. He would begin with the cabins, ready tinder in the Wild Woods. From there he would attack the very bastions of evil in the Forest. The foresters' office, the lumbermill, and that sick breeding ground of insolent and parentless adolescents, Flor del Día.

Lance Beck rose from the altar, a new and recharged crusader. He needed fuel for his fires.

That was when the preacher recognized the scent of gasoline. He sniffed at himself wondering if he had spilled some when refueling his new car. A noise below him drew his attention and he used the chancel stairs to go to the basement. A single light, left always on so they could find the switches for the lights in the basement, scarcely illuminated the bottom of the stairs. He stepped around the corner to see Deacon Stewart emptying a five-gallon gas can on piles of literature, tables, and the paneled walls. Another can sat nearby.

"You!" Beck cried out, surprising the older man. "What are you doing? It's true! How can you abide the House of the Lord, murderer!"

"What? Ah! She's dead then. One less stop I need to make tonight," Deacon sneered, noting the preacher standing on the gas-soaked wooden stairs. "Your services are no longer required by this church, Pastor."

Beck charged across the wet floor at Deacon and was met with the can, thrown at him. He slipped to one knee and Deacon snatched up the other can to throw at him as well. Beck fell back to the floor, gasoline soaking his clothes. "This is your resignation!" Deacon yelled. He stepped back to the foyer stairs and flicked a lighter at the thin trail of gas he had left there before escaping up the stairs.

"No!" Beck cried. He scrambled back toward the stairs he had descended, the flash of fire engulfing him before he had made the second step. In agony, Beck climbed toward escape, spreading the fire to drapes and carpet. Overcome by pain and fumes, Beck stumbled to the chancel where he fell across the altar.

"Father, forgive them for they know not what they do," he whispered as the flames consumed him.

MEAD AND JOHNSON were speeding out of the city when the call came through for all emergency vehicles to immediately proceed to Calvary Tabernacle where a fire threatened nearby houses and the surrounding woods.

Johnson looked at his counterpart and shook his head. He turned into a drive about five miles south of town and backed out to return. Four other units copied his move, turning on their emergency lights and sirens.

Family

"THE HOUSE WE lived in was like this," John said. "Mother and Father were very rich."

"Mother and Father?" Gee asked.

"That's what they told us we had to call them. Mother and Father. The only words we were allowed speak were, 'Yes, Mother,' and 'Yes, Father.' They came to play with us each evening. We ate dinner, cleaned our rooms, played dress-up, or school. Sometimes we were rewarded for doing a job well. Some rewards were pieces of candy. Others were being petted. They liked to pet us all over. Usually, they found something wrong with what we did and punished us. They liked to spank us and then pet us."

"John, do you know who these people are?"

"Mother and Father. We never saw anyone else. The first time we'd ever been outside was when we ran away. We didn't know there was so much outdoors or how big the house was until we saw it. We took our clothes and the cups and plates we ate from. This is the only one left. We took a knife, afraid that if we took too much, they would look harder for us. We knew about money and took what was in our play store. We found out later the money wasn't real," John said.

"We weren't dressed like other people," Jane added. "The clothes we had were like the ones on Esther's little doll. People stared at us so we hid and ran and hid some more. We found places where people dumped food and ate there. We took clothing we found in houses we snuck into and left our play money in exchange for it. Mostly, we just kept walking until we found the woods."

"It's almost too much to comprehend. I'm glad you ran away, but why? Did they hurt you?" Karen asked.

"Jane started to bleed. They were mad. They said they didn't want teenagers, they wanted children. They were going to get rid of us and get new ones. We knew what it meant when people threw things away. I didn't want Jane to be thrown away," John said.

"We were alone in our rooms most of the time and learned how to open the locks on our doors so we could be together after playtime," Jane said. "And petting each other was much better than having Mother and Father pet us. I understand that is how we got Gen."

"Why did you come here? I mean to the woods?" Gee asked.

"We didn't know where we were going. We ran and we hid and one day we recognized where we were. The woods is where we woke up when Mother and Father got us."

"Again, waking up. Just like Nina said she woke up at the cabin," Gee said.

"The cabins were scary," Jane said. "We thought we'd be safe there but then we saw the evil men with the children who were there. We hid in the trees."

"How did you survive? Eat? Stay warm?" Karen asked. Jane and John looked at each other and were silent as they thought about the question. "It's okay. You were desperate children. We won't blame you for anything you did." Finally, Jane nodded and John continued.

"The women."

"What women?"

"Women came to the cabins to take care of children, clean, and cook. When we first arrived, we didn't know what to do and a woman saw us. She looked around and held a finger to her lips. The next morning, there were blankets and some food near the cabin. For a few weeks clothes and food were hidden near the cabins where the evil men couldn't see them.

We tried to live on the ground, hidden in the bushes and thorns but then the children left and the women cleaned the cabins and left," John said.

"We were going to move into a cabin but we saw the woman in the hospital brought to one of them so we knew they weren't just abandoned. The evil men came every day. When we saw what happened to her, we moved deeper into the woods and found the big tree. We built our nest."

"I brought you everything I found in the nest. We've washed the other blanket and clothes and gave you the knife and cup. The only thing we didn't give you were the mushrooms and nuts. We can feed you much better and we are worried they might not be healthy for you," Gee said. "There were no other clothes or blankets. Did you lose them when you made the nest in the tree?" The children shared a look with each other. Again, a slight nod.

"The Tree said to trust you," John said warily. "You won't hurt them, will you?"

"The trees? No. We are trying to save and protect the woods."

"The other children."

Gee and Karen paled.

Raid

"POLICE! OPEN UP!" Sheriff Johnson yelled as he pounded on Deacon Stewart's door. Silence answered. He pounded again and prepared to have a deputy break down the door. Just before the deputy swung his heavy metal ram, the door cracked open and eyes looked out from below Johnson's chest level. "Open the door," the sheriff demanded. "I have a search warrant for these premises and an arrest warrant for Carl Stewart, alias Deacon. Let us in."

The small person scuttled back from the door, leaving it ajar. Johnson pushed it open and entered. Mead and two deputies followed closely, hands on their sidearms.

The room was immaculate though not ornate. The officers sniffed fresh wood polish. A tiny Asian woman crouched on her knees near the fireplace, a child huddled next to her. Mead called in a woman trooper standing by to assist. She moved immediately to the huddled woman. Officers spread throughout the house.

"Where is Deacon Stewart?" Johnson asked the woman. The trooper hushed his voice and repeated the question softly to the frightened woman.

"He leave. Say come back for Li when house clean. Li work very hard."

"I'm sure you do, Li," the trooper said. "Your house is very clean." She seemed to know how to put the woman at ease as she beamed in pride. "Did Deacon go alone?" The woman shook her head.

"He take boy. Girl stay to help clean."

"That makes things messy," Mead grumbled. He thumbed his cell phone. "Put an APB on Deacon Carl Stewart," he said into the phone. Turning to the woman he asked, "When did he leave?"

"Early. Three o'clock?" the woman answered. Mead returned to the phone.

"Currently presumed to be within four hours of Rosebud Falls, direction unknown. Look up his vehicle registration and add it to the notice. Warning: He is wanted for murder, assault, and kidnapping, and is believed to have a male child with him. Consider him armed and dangerous. Get it out now, Mary," he barked into the phone.

Johnson nodded.

"Get the woman and girl to the hospital and then a safe house," he suggested to the trooper. "We need to search this place and it's going to take a while. We've been up all night. Damn fire."

The trooper agreed and moved the two outside to a waiting ambulance. The woman was afraid because she had not finished cleaning and Deacon would be back for her. It took a few minutes for the trooper to convince her that she would be safe and they would make sure Deacon knew she had done a good job of cleaning.

"You stink," Mead said, looking at Johnson. He sniffed at himself. "Me, too. If it weren't for that damned fire, we'd have been here at midnight—before he ran. That church is just more trouble than it's worth."

"I bet he didn't get here to pack until the church was burning."

"You think?"

"I think you can add arson to the list of crimes he's wanted for. That fire was definitely deliberate and went up much faster than even a wooden church should. The fire chief was sure an accelerant was used. Any word on the preacher?"

"No. We didn't find him home during the fire. We put out a missing person notice. He could be traveling with Deacon," Mead said. "Where do we start?"

"Deputies!" Johnson yelled. Two sheriff's deputies and two policemen moved into the living room, already wearing latex gloves. State troopers were searching the grounds and outbuildings.

"We're looking for any information that will help us locate and convict Deacon Carl Stewart. That includes drugs, papers, bills, journals, canceled checks, maps, and hidden passages where children might have been concealed. There could be children in hiding the housekeeper didn't know about. Box and carry everything. Itemize it. Chain of custody. We don't want any tainted evidence when we put this bastard away for life." The deputies and officers nodded and went about their work. "Mead, you should call Savage and search Stewart's office."

"I have the warrant. I'll head there now. At least we have a friendly CEO over there," Mead said. "I'll talk to you later."

Mobilizing the Search

"THERE COULD BE how many more out there?" David shouted at Gee. Sunday was not going to be a day of rest for anyone.

"John said there had been eight of them in the Patriarch nest when it started to snow. When the worst weather hit and the temperatures dropped, they moved into one of the cabins but the children don't like it there. That was probably the cabin Darrell discovered was out of propane. We were out of the woods completely for three weeks and when I got volunteers back in there, we focused on the fencerow," Gee said. "Jane gave birth in one of the cabins but as soon as she could climb, they moved back to the nest in the Patriarch. The kids divided up the supplies they had and scattered. They've seen others in the past month but have not talked to them."

"We'll need every forester in the Wild Woods," David said. "Jonathan, start calling them up. We need to search as if lives depended on it. They do."

"We also need to be calm and non-threatening," Gee said. "Don't send them in all at once and send them from different directions. These children have been abused and fled. They are very good at hiding."

"How long have they been out there?" David asked. "How long have we had frightened children living in the wild within a mile of our Forest?"

"Jane says they got here before the nuts started falling off the trees. That was about September, I'd guess. Just before Harvest," Gee said.

"Six months! And traffickers moving kids through before that. How could we have missed this for so long?" David moaned.

"David, these children are different than the first three little ones we found. They're more like Nina. Older adolescents whose training or brainwashing failed at some point and they ran away from their owners. They will hide," Gee said. "Our best bet is to spread out, find likely places where they might travel—like to water—but don't try to invade them. The same things Jessie and Jonathan have been doing the past couple of weeks. Let's set out more survival kits and increase the amount of food in them." David nodded agreement.

"I see what you're saying. If we try to ferret them out, they'll dig deeper. We need to lure them. Tame them," he said. "Let's start getting survival kits together. Do you want to call in your volunteers?"

"I'm torn," Gee said. "They have a lot of enthusiasm but sometimes lack restraint. I'll figure out who to talk to."

DNA

A WEEK AFTER the three children had been released to the custody of Gee and Karen, Judge Warren sat in the conference room he often used for less formal meetings. Nothing in this room went on anyone's official record.

"The good news is that we located a list of contacts," Mead said. "We don't yet know the relationships, so we're proceeding slowly."

"What kind of contacts?" Judge Warren asked.

"We have his cellphone log and have identified most of the parties he called. There were the expected contacts that could be part of the trafficking or might just be from church and office. Jones, Alexander, Daniels, Darren Cole, Beck, and the attorney, Matt Hogue. But the other numbers look like he was running for national office or something. Reclusive, rich, foreign, in government. Our suspicion is they may have been customers. We also found a map with locations of various warehouses and dates next to them. We suspect these may have been the drop points for loads of stone that concealed children. Larry Syre has become very cooperative in identifying places he dropped and picked up loads."

"So, what's the bad news?"

"It's no longer our case. Or maybe that is good news—I don't know. We were definitely in over our heads."

"It's gone federal?"

"Yes, sir. The longer Deacon is on the loose, the more likely he is to have crossed state lines. His Asian housekeeper has been cooperative with the state patrol and spoke through a Chinese interpreter. She first begged not to be sent back to China. She's illegal, smuggled into the US in the trunk of a car shipped by container. Her contact on this end got her the job with Deacon two years ago. She has not been allowed out of his house in that time. And no, the two children are not hers. They were brought to the house in November—about the same time we found the kids in the truckload of stone. The boy Deacon took with him is about seven, she thinks. The sum is, FBI involvement. They thanked us for the evidence and took over the case. What they haven't done yet is ask for access to any of the recovered children. We gave them a full report and they said that part was up to us. They were interested in criminals."

"Just as well. If they recovered a kidnapped child, they'd turn him over to CPS and the kid would be in worse shape than before. Good news?" Judge Warren asked.

"It's been a busy week. I've asked Gee and Karen to join us, if you don't mind, your honor."

"I find that encouraging. Call them in."

Gee and Karen were accompanied by their attorneys, Jack and Gretchen LaCoe. After they were greeted and everyone settled, Judge Warren turned the floor over to Mead.

"We have a DNA match for one of the children from the missing persons data base," Mead began.

"Which?" "That's wonderful!" Gee and Karen both exclaimed.

"Take it easy. You might not be as excited once I tell you. We have a match for the little mother you call Jane Evars. She was reported missing eight years ago, at age five. Her real name is Susan White. Initially, her father was suspected of kidnapping her out of spite for his ex-wife. He was exonerated when he was convicted of an armed convenience store robbery with his image on video surveillance at the time of the kidnapping. That was in Washington State and as a third felony he was sentenced to life on their three strikes law," Mead said. "A real winner."

"But her mother. As much as I love Jane and want to keep her with us, her mother needs to be contacted," Karen said. Tears were in her eyes. They all realized the implication of the thirteen-year-old girl being given into the custody of her natural mother.

"Can't," Mead said. "She committed suicide by needle on the fifth anniversary of the kidnapping—three years ago."

"Suicide by needle?" Gee questioned.

"Fentanyl overdose. It wasn't her first attempt."

Karen was openly weeping now, held by Gee and comforted by Gretchen.

"What is that?" Gee asked.

"Synthetic heroin," Mead explained. "Last year it caused more deaths than HIV, car crashes, or gun violence. It was a major contributor last year to the reduction by five months in life expectancy of an infant born in the United States. First time life expectancy has dropped since the end of World War II."

"Judge, what does that imply regarding Karen and Gee's custody of the child?" Jack asked.

"Nothing immediate," Warren answered. "An effort should be made to discover any other close relatives. Custody laws always favor a near relative over anyone else. Further removed than grandparents, siblings, and parents' siblings and there is an equal chance that Gee and Karen would retain custody. And, of course, the same would be true if the relative was found unable, unwilling, or unfit to take custody," Warren said. "I'll accept suggestions, but I don't see any reason to adjust custody at this time."

"I believe, your honor, the child's true name should be registered and changed on the custody papers," Jack said. "That would keep things completely transparent."

"And we need to tell her what her real name is," Karen said. "It isn't right to go on calling her Jane when her name is Susan."

"She may prefer it," Gee said. "She has no memory of what her name was before she was brainwashed. It's the same as Nina not remembering her name was Renee. She prefers to remain Nina."

"And the DNA report on Nina?" Warren asked.

"Confirms she and Violet share lineage from Collin's father. It's as close to positive as we'll get unless we manage to locate her mother," Karen said.

"Well, Collin is satisfied, so I suppose that's what's important. Yes, Gretchen?"

"Your honor there is the matter of registering the baby's birth certificate. The children are vague about the age but based on ancillary data—like weather—we've fixed the date of birth as approximately January fifteenth. We would like to suggest a birth certificate be issued listing Susan White, aka Jane Evars, as mother with father tentatively identified as John Evars, pending the possibility of a future DNA test revealing his true identity. Dr. Poltanys has confirmed by paternity test what we already knew. John is the father and Jane is the mother. We would also like the court to request an official birth certificate for Jane so her identity can be legitimized. We all know how difficult having no confirmable identity can be." She glanced over at Gee and he nodded.

"Agreed," Warren said. "Any other business we need to cover at this time? Adjourned."

Salome

"A WEEK AND still no children," David said as he met with the team Saturday afternoon. "Gee, are you sure they're still out there?"

"No. That's the problem," Gee sighed. "They could have scattered after the cold weather broke. I just feel they are there somewhere."

"We know at least someone is out there," Jonathan said. "Two of the survival kits were raided. They left everything but the food, which tells us where their priorities are right now."

"Not only out there, but starving," David said.

"It also shows they are waiting until night to collect," Gabe offered. "Each survival kit and cabin has been watched during the day, from a safe and non-threatening distance."

Gee puzzled over this bit of information. The foresters replenished the broken kits and left, hopeful that at least the food would help the hidden ones. Gee went home to talk to Karen.

A SMALL PARTY was in progress when he got home. Jude and Laura and the younger children were there. He could hear their squeals from the playroom with Jeanie and Nina's voices joining in. Gee assumed John and Jane were with them but the voices of the two were still so soft even he had to strain to hear them at times. Raven and Timmy carried trays of cocoa and cookies toward the playroom. Karen quickly got up to greet her fiancé.

"Having fun this afternoon?" Gee asked.

"You wouldn't believe…"

"Gee!" A patter of little feet preceded a tight grip on Gee's leg as Esther clung to him. Karen moved back a step so Gee could scoop the little girl up into his arms.

"My little Esther! Oh, I'm so happy to see you! Are you excited about something?" Gee asked. Esther started to speak and stopped as if trying to get the words she wanted, her lips finally puckering up.

"Puppy!" she burst out. She pointed to the playroom and Gee carried her there looking down at the little ball of fur running in circles from child to child. Esther squirmed and he set her down.

"Is this going to start a trend?" he asked as he wrapped an arm around Karen.

"Our fault!" Jude announced proudly.

"We found him online and picked him up this morning," Laura said. "The poor thing is going to sleep soundly soon."

"I think John and Jane are as awed by the little thing as they are by their daughter," Karen suggested. "We are going to have to consider a pet soon. Look at Nina." The teen giggled as she held the puppy in front of her face while he licked at her.

"Kids, there's hot cocoa and cookies," Raven announced from behind them.

"Can puppy have a cookie?" little David asked.

"We have special cookies just for puppy," Laura said as she went to her purse and retrieved a puppy biscuit. "Why not put puppy in his bed now so he can eat his cookie? We should pick a name for him."

The children scrambled to get their cocoa and watch the new addition as he lay on the cushion and chewed at his treat. He hadn't finished it before he fell asleep.

"Karen, let's go into the kitchen for a minute," Gee whispered as Laura talked to the children about names. It was a good exercise since each of the children could remember being named.

"What is it, Love?"

"I'm going back to the woods tonight," he began.

"Alone?"

"Yes."

"I hate to think of you alone out there. Do you want me to come, too? Raven could watch the children."

"I think it will be best if I just sit there quietly. At least one child is coming out at night to get food from the survival kits. I think I'll fix a thermos of hot soup and some sandwiches and sit under the Patriarch to invite them for a picnic," Gee said.

"You don't think they're dangerous, do you?" Karen asked.

"No. but even if they are, they don't deserve to be treated like animals. I don't know if any will show up just because I'm camped there. I just need to try."

"Come home to me in the morning? Please?"

"I will, Love. And I will probably be in bad need of a shower and some real sleep. I haven't camped out in… I don't know how long."

"I'll keep the bed warm."

GEE TUCKED HIMSELF into a sleeping bag, propped against the Patriarch with a survival kit beside him. Before going to sleep, he poured himself a little soup, which he drank with a sandwich. He laid the thermos on the kit with another sandwich and settled down to sleep as well as he could.

When he woke in the morning, the sandwich and thermos were still there, untouched. *It was only a possibility.* After having another cup of soup, he packed his gear, leaving the survival kit behind. This kit, however, had no food in it.

GEE WANDERED INTO Jitterz just as it opened Sunday morning. Elaine handed him his coffee and a sweet roll.

"You don't usually come in before you shave in the morning," she giggled. "Are you growing a beard?" Gee felt his rough cheek and grimaced.

"Elaine, are you poking fun at the customers?" Birdie said as she came out of the kitchen. When she saw Gee, she started laughing, too. She reached out and plucked a bit of bark from his hair. "Slept rough last night?"

"In the woods. Birdie, there are more children out there. I can feel it." Gee was near desperation. At any moment a child could be beyond help.

"You're going to have a big family before you even get married," the fortuneteller said. "Don't give up. They need you as much as you need to find them."

"You can feel it, too, can't you?" She nodded. "Do you know what they have endured? The cold spell, the snow, the rain. I'm so afraid I will look up into a tree and see a dead child. Please tell me I won't, Birdie." He couldn't remember feeling so helpless. Hopeless. The Haitian held Gee's eyes.

"I see only love and care in your eyes, Gee. I see no lurking tragedy."

Gee slept much of the day, repeating his vigil Sunday night with no better results. Monday, he stayed home with his family, being sure to hold each of the teens and the baby for a while. The energy he received from them revived his spirits and his determination.

"TONIGHT? IN THIS?" Karen asked as he prepared to camp again on Thursday night. It would be the fourth time he stayed out, sleeping at home every other night. Rain and wind had been threatening all day and the first drops were beginning to fall with the night.

"What better time?" he asked. "I'll spread a tarp and have a dry space. I can only hope." He heated the soup for his thermos and filled it.

"Oh, sweetheart, I hope, too. When you are out there, I find myself sitting up late, supposedly working on my book but not getting any writing done. The children… They're aware. I've seen Nina standing with John and Jane on the veranda, looking out southeast toward the woods. They're tense. I pray that you will be successful and we can help the children of the woods."

"I love you, Karen. We share a mission."

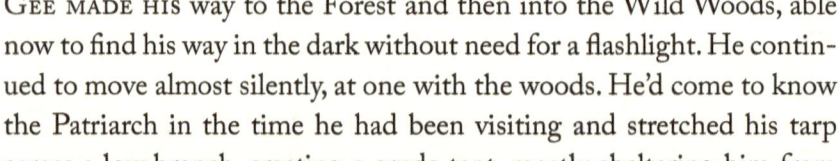

GEE MADE HIS way to the Forest and then into the Wild Woods, able now to find his way in the dark without need for a flashlight. He continued to move almost silently, at one with the woods. He'd come to know the Patriarch in the time he had been visiting and stretched his tarp across a low branch, creating a crude tent, mostly sheltering him from the rain. He anchored the edges of the tarp and crawled under, leaning his walking stick against the tree at his head.

Opening the survival kit, he removed the ground cloth and spread it beneath his shelter, laying his sleeping bag on top. The rain increased and Gee read a book on his cellphone. He drank a bit of soup, more to release the aroma in the makeshift tent than to assuage his appetite. He arranged the blanket from the survival kit next to him and placed the thermos and a sandwich on it along with a cookie Raven had baked that morning. He crawled into his sleeping bag and rested until sleep claimed him.

HE SENSED THE presence more than he felt movement. A silent hand stretched above his head to the walking stick. Gee calmed his breathing, letting the stick be moved. The child—it had to be a child—was still. He could hear breathing and knew he or she had not left. Eventually there was a sigh and Gee felt the child wrap up in the blanket and lie down beside him, the stick between them.

—————◁◆▷—————

GEE OPENED HIS eyes, gray half-light barely a threat to the darkness. Beside him he saw a dark head of hair. By the height, he estimated it was an older teen. He could not tell anything else except that the sandwich was gone and his walking stick was clutched tightly by the youth.

Gee crept out of his sleeping bag and slipped his boots on without disturbing his visitor. He stepped into the edge of the surrounding trees to relieve himself and then returned as quietly as possible. The chill air made him shiver and water still dripped from the branches overhead.

Inside his makeshift shelter, he saw eyes wide open, watching him approach. He sat at the end of his sleeping bag, not crowding the teen— he thought now it was a girl—as he reached for the thermos. He poured soup into the cup and took a sip. Then he held it out to her. She pulled herself upright, another blanket wrapped around her shoulders, and accepted the cup. She took a sip and started to hand it back.

"Go ahead. It's for you." She looked relieved and savored the soup as she drank it. He poured more into the cup and offered her another sandwich, which she accepted. When she had finished eating, she pointed up into the tree.

"Where?" she whispered.

"The boy and girl and baby?" Gee asked. She nodded. "They are together, safe and warm and well-fed." The girl sighed heavily. "Would you like to be safe and warm and well-fed?" Gee asked. Tears sparkled in the teen's eyes and broke down her cheek as she nodded. "I'm Gee. What's your name?"

"Salome. That's the name I was given before I went to my first master."

"You've had more than one master?" She nodded. "Do you know how long since you awoke?" She thought a moment and then nodded again.

"About five years. My parents sent me here to summer camp because I liked a boy. I felt funny the whole time I was here and forgot everything about the boy. And lots more. Men showed all about how bad boys were and said I should always be obedient. A preacher saved my soul and said Salome was a good biblical name for a girl like me. I went home but didn't recognize people. They gave me to my master. He kept my mind all muddy so I wouldn't fight having sex with him. I only remember it hurt but I had to obey. Then I was sent to another."

"When did you leave to come here?" Gee asked. The girl sighed deeply.

"Before Christmas. It took a long time because people who helped me wanted to keep me for themselves and I had to keep running away. I don't know why I came back here. This is where the camp was. I thought maybe I would remember more. But I knew my master would kill me soon. Especially when he found…" She lowered her head, tears still streaming and cupped her stomach.

"You're pregnant?" She nodded. "Will you walk with me to where you will be safe and warm?" he asked. She looked at her feet in ragged socks. Gee searched in his backpack for a clean pair of socks and handed them to her. She held them against her cheek. After she put them on, Gee handed her a pair of moccasins. They were a little big for her but would protect her feet as they walked. He unfolded a space blanket to put under the wool blanket on her shoulders and led her outside.

"I will serve you," she said. "Please keep me warm and don't kill me."

"Salome, you never need to serve anyone like that again," Gee sighed. "You'll be safe and warm and fed. No one will hurt you." She looked ready to cry but hugged the walking stick tightly while Gee worked quickly to take down the shelter and fold the tarp neatly on top of the remains of the survival kit. He put two energy bars in the kit and packed everything else in his backpack.

They both held the walking stick as he led her out of the woods.

Custody

"THIS IS A different level of trafficking," Warren said.

"It ties the youth reclamation camp, the church, and Lance Beck directly to the child sex ring and abuse," Gee said. "And the parents. They sent her here and then sold her. Their daughter!"

"We can't bring Lance Beck to justice now," Mead said. "The forensic report confirmed the charred remains in the church were the preacher. You risked your life to save him from drowning so he could burn."

"Perhaps. I still had to do it."

"So, everything comes down to Carl Stewart and he's gone to ground somewhere," Judge Warren said.

"And he's on the FBI's most wanted list now," Mead said. "They'll find him."

"There are still the women John and Jane talked about," Gee said. "Were they all illegals like the Asian woman found at Deacon's?"

"Circumstantial evidence links Mrs. Alexander with cleaning the cabins. Li cleaned Deacon's house with the same cleansers. Paul identified them as one of those pyramid sales products where everyone becomes a dealer and sells to ten dealers below them," Mead said. "We suggested the FBI get sales information from the company."

"I'd bet on the members of the church," Warren said. "Put your mind to it, Mead. You'll come up with a way to identify them."

"What about Salome?" Gee asked. "That's what I actually came to ask about."

"According to Dr. Poltanys, she was treated more roughly than either Nina or the new Evars family," Warren said. "Scars from beatings and bondage. Tears of sensitive tissues. And pregnant, of course. In some ways, she is still in better condition than the other children."

"How so?" Mead asked.

"She remembers. Not everything. Adam speculates that part of the purpose of the drug was to cloud the memories and preferably to wipe them out completely. She doesn't remember her name or where she lived, but she remembers being a child, learning to read and write, going to school, and having friends. You'll have a rough time with her, Gee. She wants to keep the baby when it's born. Are you sure you and Karen can handle another?" Warren asked.

"Karen is with her now. They've already bonded," Gee said. "Leah came over yesterday to review accounts with Karen. She said we could afford to adopt all of Flor del Día if we wanted to. We just want to help the children we can."

"Noble," Mead said. "You're still getting married, aren't you?"

"Ten days. You've got your invitation."

"Very well," Warren said. "The girl wants to retain the name Salome?"

"It's an interesting phenomenon," Gee said. "Like Nina, it is the name she was given when she woke up. John and Jane don't remember a name. They were always called 'baby', 'brother', 'little girl'. That sort of thing. But Nina and Salome identify with the name they were given when they awoke. She wants to keep it."

"If I get my hands on those bastards…"

"Mead, don't make idle threats," Warren reprimanded him. "I'm extending the temporary custody of the seventeen-year-old girl identified as Salome to you and Karen, Gee. We'll have a quarterly custody review for all your wards. Dr. Salinger may request a visit at any time to review the children's progress and health. Thank you for stepping up, Gee. We should begin recruiting potential foster parents in case more children are found in the woods. You said John and Jane mentioned as many as eight at one time. I'm confident you'll find more."

13

TO HAVE AND TO HOLD

Continuing the Search

GEE SAT IN THE ROCKING CHAIR holding baby Genesis and giving her a bottle. The baby sucked hungrily while staring at him. He sang little nonsense songs to her as they rocked. Nearby, Nina, Salome, John, and Jane played a card game, laughing at the play. Karen brought Gee a glass of wine and set it on the side table.

"I guess you can have wine since you aren't actually nursing her," Karen giggled as she kissed his head.

"I think our girl has had enough," Gee said. Gen spit the nipple out.

"Oh, good. Give her to me for the after-dinner burp." Karen spread a cloth over her shoulder and took the baby, patting her gently on the back and cooing to her. Gee looked up to see Salome standing next to his chair.

"Will you feed my baby when it's born?" she asked softly.

"Yes, of course," Karen said.

"And you don't want sex? I will do that if you want. You feed me."

"No, Salome. What you have experienced in your life is not what real life is supposed to be. We'll love you and care for you, feed you, give you a place to sleep that is warm and dry. We'll treat you like our daughter and it is not the role of parents to have sex with their children. Nor to order them to blind obedience. It might take a while for you to understand your limits and we'll protect you while you grow into the young woman we know you will become. But no one is going to force you, ever again," Gee said firmly.

"I wish you had been my master," she sighed.

"Oh no, dear," Karen said. "It is not about having a better master. It is about learning to master yourself. Don't worry. You'll learn."

GEE'S TIME IN the woods was more limited as his wedding approached. He now had five children living under his roof with Karen. Six if you counted Timmy, who often joined the others for games in the evening. He returned to the Patriarch Sunday night but did not hear so much as a rustle of wind in the branches. Still he was comforted by the presence of The Tree. Monday morning, he stopped by the foresters' office before heading home.

"We know there are others," Jonathan said. "Jessie and I spent the night at a drop point near one of the cabins Friday night. Nothing. But when we toured the survival kits Saturday morning, two had been torn open. Food, socks, and the moccasins were gone."

"The moccasins were a great idea, Gee," Jessie said. "We're putting moccasins and socks in every survival kit."

"So far, every child we've found in the woods has been barefoot," Gee said. "They walked a long way to get here."

"Why?" David asked. "Why are the children coming to the Wild Woods? You'd think the place they were abused and brainwashed would be the last place they'd want to return to. And how do they find it? How do they even survive to get here?" David scrubbed at his graying hair with both fists, looking as frustrated as all of them felt.

Gee looked at the head of the Lazorack Family and thought back to his first meeting with the gruff man near the mill. In just eight months, David had aged. Grayer. Wrinkles created deep-set lines around his eyes. The burden of the Forest his father had left him had been doubled by the burden of the Wild Woods and the acts revealed there.

"Does the Forest speak to you, David?" Gee asked softly.

"I… don't know what you mean. Do I hear voices? No. Do I stand around talking to the trees? No. Is there a constant tugging at my heart to be here, to protect the Forest and never leave? Yes."

"I think that's what the children feel as well. A constant tugging at their hearts to be here and never leave," Gee sighed and sat back. Over in his corner with a book and ever-present cup of coffee, Gabe just nodded. "They don't remember the specifics of how they were abused before they awoke. There are triggers. None of them like the cabins. They're afraid of the evil men. But they think of the trees as their protectors and the Wild Woods as their birthplace."

"Evil men," David sighed.

"It's the term the children used to describe what they saw. And then they saw us. We tore down the fence. We crashed through the woods, cutting paths and making noise. We invaded the space they came to be safe in. How could they tell if we were good or evil?" Gee asked.

"And what changed?" Jonathan asked. "John, Jane, and now Salome have all come out of the woods with you. How did they know you were one of the good guys?"

Gee pondered the question for a minute, stroking up and down the walking stick, the cool smooth wood a comfort to his hand. He looked at the spot where he'd carved the rune from his worry stone.

"I wish I knew what it means," he said softly. "Well. I guess we just keep waiting and watching. Be present. Bring food. What else can we do?"

"Your crew was here Saturday," Jessie said. "We had them work on preparing the path to the Patriarch for the wedding. They're good kids and want to do more. I wish we could use them to stay in the woods at night."

"I'd agree but I don't want to be responsible for teens sleeping out in the Wild Woods. I should talk to them and explain what's going on," Gee said.

"They've responded well to your previous conversations," David said. "They'll surprise you."

"I'd better go home and make sure the bride knows I'm still alive," Gee laughed. "She worries about that sometimes."

Painting the Future

"Gee, I know you're busy with the children and preparing for your wedding, but could you spare some time to come up to the hospital and visit a lonely and broken-hearted person?" Adam asked over the phone Wednesday morning.

"Of course. Who do you want me to visit?"

"Rena Lynd."

"Ah."

"There was a flurry of activity after she woke up. First Mead and Sheriff Johnson wanted her to positively identify Deacon as her assailant. Then the feds came in to verify the information. She drew pictures of him and that solidified the case. Then the excitement trailed off. It's been three weeks of sitting alone deciding if she would live or die. And then she asked to see Pastor Beck."

"Oh, no. She didn't know."

"No. She wailed when she was told he was dead. Blames herself, of course. Gee, she was getting stronger but now I'm afraid she's lost the will to live."

"I'll go see her today." Gee disconnected the call and sat to think. He'd first met the cashier at the Market when he started working there. A bold, flirtatious young woman with pink hair and a determination to embarrass Gee. He could tell she was taking some kind of drugs. It was only after she had overdosed and gone out of control in the stock room that Gee found she was using the fantasy enhancing drug, Lustre Plus.

While Rena was in rehab, she'd shown her talent as an artist, doing police sketches. When she was released and disappeared, nothing was heard from her until Karen got a call the day she was kidnapped and Rena was pushed into the quarry.

Gee wondered how he could help her. She'd fallen in love with the pastor of her church, been betrayed by him and sent to the woods, and then sent him away when she awoke from her coma. How could Gee help mend this broken person?

Karen had gone shopping for school supplies this week and Gee thought she had gone a little overboard. He was thankful, however, when he finally found what he was looking for in one of the bags. He pulled on his coat, shouldered his small pack, and gripped his walking stick as he headed to the hospital.

———————◁◆▷———————

"Good morning, Rena."

"Gee?" She turned her head away from him as he entered her room.

"How are you doing this morning?"

"Fine." It was obvious the conversation was going to be difficult. Gee took a deep breath.

"I want to apologize for the part I've played in your misery," he said. "I tried to do the right thing but that doesn't always seem to work out the way we planned. I'm sorry."

"What? That's stupid!" Rena nearly shouted. "You tried to save me when I overdosed. You tried to find me when I was in the woods. You saved Lance when he crashed in the river. You and your stick and your children… woke me up. What do you have to apologize for? You can't help being the Antichrist."

The statement was so incongruous Gee snorted trying not to laugh. Rena was so startled she looked at him and then allowed a small laugh as well.

"I'm sorry, Gee. I don't know what to think any longer. I'm confused and alone and I just want to die."

"Rena, life is not always fair. Many people were deceived. How can we get you strong and healthy?" Gee asked.

"How can I ever get what they did to me out of my head?" she sighed.

"There are others struggling, too. John and Jane were treated by Dr. Jones and Pastor Beck. So was Salome. The three little children were boxed up under a load of stone to be sent to Georgia. You're not alone."

"What should I do?" she whispered.

"I wonder if you would consider helping me with a project. I'm writing a book of children's stories set in the Wild Woods."

"Why would you set stories for children in that awful place?" she asked. "They drugged me and raped me. I never want to think of it again!"

"Yet, the children are returning there. After all they underwent, this is where they awoke and where they have returned to reclaim hope. All I'm asking is that you take a look at the story and think about pictures you could draw," Gee said.

"I don't have…" Gee handed her a sketchbook and box of colored pencils from his backpack, along with his manuscript. "I guess I do have materials. I'll look, but won't promise. I don't have anything else to do and nowhere to go. Why are you trying to help me, Gee? I made life miserable for you. I accused you. I injured you. I believed all the stories Lance told about you. Why are you still nice to me?" she asked.

"Your life is precious. How could I try to save the children of the Wild Woods and not you?"

"Kind of a turn the other cheek thing, huh? You won't fight back," she sighed.

"I don't think that's quite true," Gee said. "I believe I would defend myself if attacked physically. But words only have the power we give them."

"Give me the manuscript and leave," she commanded. "I want to draw something."

Here's to Your Journey

THURSDAY AND FRIDAY were barely contained chaos in the Evars/ Weisman household. The children had become intensely interested in the wedding. Nina, having received a birth certificate showing her date of birth and the name Renee Lisle, petitioned Judge Warren to have her name legally changed to Nina Evars. Jane, John, and Salome were happy to have the last name of Evars and as far as they were concerned, the wedding would make them all officially a family.

Raven took charge of coordinating the reception, which would be held in the mansion. The guests in the Wild Woods would be limited to family, Family, and immediate circle of friends. But after the formalities, much of the town would stop by the reception, just for the chance to see inside one of the Family mansions and catch a glimpse of the mysterious children of the woods.

Gee's crew, wanting to be involved, had worked after school cleaning the main path to the Patriarch so it was wide enough to use the ATVs to transport guests from the foresters' office. The older youth would shuttle guests to the Patriarch and return them after the ceremony.

When the final RSVPs had been tallied, thirty-one people would attempt to gather under the canopy of the Patriarch as Judge Warren performed the wedding.

MEAD WAS ABOUT to leave the office and lock up when his phone rang. Glancing at his watch, he answered, irritated. Sheriff Johnson greeted him.

"What is it, Brad? I'm about to leave for the wedding," Mead snapped.

"I know but I thought you should carry some good news with you as a wedding gift."

"Good news?"

"FBI has arrested Deacon Carl Stewart. A major sting is now underway."

"Fantastic. Who knew they could move so fast?"

"I'm told they captured Stewart days ago. He's not the kind of friend you want to have. He decided if he was going down, everyone was. We should also expect an influx of homeless children within the next month as they are processed through Child Services."

"Holy shit. Any idea how big the Roth Mansion is?" Mead chuckled. "Thanks for the news, Brad. I'll get it to them as quickly as I can." He disconnected and pulled his coat and hat off the rack. He scrubbed at a spot on the lapel, spitting on a corner of his handkerchief to use as a sponge. Satisfied it was as good as it would get, he turned to the office door and ran into a woman raising a hand to knock.

"Excuse me," she laughed. "There was no one out front."

Mead looked at the woman. About five-seven, long black hair plaited into a braid, deep brown eyes. She looked almost Native American, an impression accented by a beige leather coat that hung to her thighs. She wore sensible flat shoes and Mead increased his height estimate by an inch or two.

"Sorry there was no one out there," Mead said, trying to justify the emptiness of the police station. "I was about to close the office. Saturdays, the sheriff's office next door handles the traffic. How can I help you?"

"I hope you can help me find someone. I'm looking for George Evars. He is likely going by the name Gee."

"Uh… Yes… I know Gee. Just on my way… I'm sorry, I didn't get your name," Mead stumbled.

"Of course!" She held out a gloved hand for Mead to shake. "I'm Rebecca Annette Evars. Just call me Rae. Everyone does.

FOR A MOMENT, Detective Mead Oliver was tempted to tell the woman he didn't know who she was talking about and suggest she try Palmyra. But he'd just said he knew Gee. And if Rebecca Evars was Gee's wife, he could be about to commit a felony. He looked at the time again and sighed.

"His wedding is scheduled to begin in twenty minutes. I was just on my way. You can ride with me."

"Ah," Rae said quietly. "I made it in time."

Mead was uncharacteristically quiet on the short drive. The barrage of questions he was known to shout at once suddenly dried up in his throat. The implications overwhelmed him. The 'Rae' who had inscribed Gee's book was somehow related. The great mystery of the man's identity was about to be revealed and Mead found he did *not* want to hear it.

He didn't know what to do and could think of no alternative but to take Rae to the wedding tree and call Gee aside before the ceremony started. He pulled up to the foresters' office and stepped out of the car.

"Drake, keep it where I can get out. I'll take a two-seater and drive myself. In case I'm needed for an emergency." The boy looked at him, puzzled as the keys landed in his hand.

"Yes, sir. Viktor has a two-seater by the front door. Um… You know there's spotty cell service out there, right?"

"I have my radio. If the sheriff needs me, he can reach me." Mead conducted Rae to a small ATV and Viktor stepped aside, having seen the interaction between the detective and his friend.

"Here's a map, sir," Viktor said. "It's the only trail that's fully clear and packed down."

"The kids seem to have a lot of respect for you, Detective," Rae said. "It's nice to see them cooperating with the police."

"Mmm. Drake's my son. I know most of them pretty well." He maneuvered the ATV along the path, glancing at his phone for the time. When he pulled up at the end of the trail, he pointed. "That's the path to the tree where the ceremony will be," he said, pointing to the obviously trampled trail through the saplings. "I need to turn the buggy around."

"Certainly. Thank you." Rae moved to the path as Mead watched her beige coat disappear. He thumbed his radio.

"Sheriff, standby for possible fireworks at the wedding. Please have the kids at the office ready to run transport earlier than expected."

"Problems?"

"I don't know yet. As soon as I do, you'll be the first to know."

"I'm headed to the Forest now."

Mead moved along the path through the trees as the first tones of Pàl's bagpipe could be heard.

"Gee!" Rae called as she rushed into the clearing beneath The Tree's canopy and hugged him, placing a kiss on his cheek. She touched his cheek with her fingers. "Baby smooth as always," she laughed.

"Um... Excuse me... Who...?"

"It's me. Rae!"

"Rae? From the book?" Gee tried desperately to find an association with the face in front of him. Vague flickers of happiness crossed his mind but nothing specific other than the inscription in his copy of Homer's *Odyssey*.

"Rebecca Annette Evars. Gee, what's wrong?" Gee paled, stumbling back into Wayne.

"You're... Are you... Are we... married?"

"Gee? You don't remember? I didn't know." She looked into his eyes as if willing him to recognize her. "We're not married. I'm your sister. I'm here to celebrate your wedding with you."

"How did you know? You know who I am?"

"Yes, I know who you are. I saw a copy of your local newspaper and your wedding announcement was in it. I was afraid I would miss it. You are my brother and I am so happy you've found the love I always hoped you would."

"My sister. I have a sister." He leaned heavily on his staff as he absorbed the news. "I didn't know." Rae's attention was caught by the walking stick and she pointed at the carving Gee had made in it. She touched it and Gee felt her through the staff. It was a soft comforting touch accompanied by a whisper in his mind.

My child.

"You remembered this," she said.

"I have a…" Gee fumbled in his pocket for a moment and pulled out his worry stone with the engraving of a vertical line and five horizontal lines crossing it.

"Yes," Rae said. She reached in her own pocket and pulled out a stone, almost identical. She matched the two stones together and they seemed to make a single whole. "Our family symbol."

"Gee? Is everything okay?" a worried Karen asked as she hurried across the clearing. This was not how she imagined her wedding march.

"I… I have a sister," he said, still a little dazed. She did seem familiar in a way. "She's come to our wedding."

"I didn't know he wouldn't recognize me. I'm so sorry I interrupted. I was just excited to finally find him. You must be Karen. Your name was in the newspaper, too."

"Do we need to… postpone things?" Karen asked. A bit of moisture escaped from her right eye and she hurriedly wiped it with the back of her hand.

"No!" Rae said. "There's no reason to postpone because of me."

"Excuse me," Judge Warren said. "Can you affirm that this is indeed George Edward Evars, also called Gee, and that he is known to you?"

"Yes. I've known him since the day he was born."

"I think that will set many minds at ease in our town. Gee and Karen? Do you want to proceed?"

"Yes!" Gee said, turning from Rae and embracing his fiancée. "Karen, will you still marry me?"

"Yes, I will! Let's get this part done so we can all go back and get to know each other."

Uninvited Guests

Pàl resumed his wedding march on the bagpipe. Karen decided not to retrace her steps but called Nina to her side, handing her the simple bouquet of flowers she held. She took Gee's offered hand and they faced the Judge.

The ceremony was simple with traditional civil vows. They placed rings on each other's fingers and kissed. Judge Warren declared them husband and wife. Then there was moderate chaos as the guests approached to congratulate the couple and to meet Rae.

"We both left several months ago on a quest to find the Children of the Red Tree," Rae said. "I didn't know it was a literal tree." She reached out and touched the Patriarch, letting her eyes drift closed. "He's calling his children home," she sighed.

"Gee," whispered John as he tugged at his sleeve. Gee turned to the boy and gave him his full attention. John's voice could barely be heard at the best of times. The young father pointed to Gee's walking stick. "Please?" It was not the first time he had taken the stick from Gee and it was easily given over. Gee watched as John quickly disappeared into the surrounding saplings, Jane and the baby watching from the edge.

"You found the children," Rae said excitedly.

"We've found eight," Gee said. "Is that what I was supposed to do here?"

"There is so much to talk about. I can't believe that you don't remember anything. It must have been the nut."

"I ate the nut in September. I lost my memory at least two months before I ate the nut in the Forest," Gee said, shaking his head.

"You ate a nut in September?"

"Yes. And another on Thanksgiving. Why?"

"The wise woman gave you the nut to eat in June and sent you on your quest."

"Another...?"

There was a sudden hush beneath the Patriarch as John led three ragged children through the trees, all with a hand extended to touch Gee's walking stick. Karen rushed to Gee's side from where she was talking to Jo. Everyone else fell back away from the children, deferring to Gee's experience.

"I see," Rae whispered. "You don't find them. They come to you."

"Welcome, children," Gee said, kneeling on the damp ground. "Would you like to come with us and be safe and warm and fed, like John and Jane and Salome?" They seemed to have difficulty associating the names with the children but after looking closely at the other children, they each nodded. They all wore moccasins that had been left in the survival kits. They each carried a small bundle and had a blanket around their shoulders.

"We'll walk out of the woods together," Gee said. "And then you can come home to eat. We'll tell stories of how you came to be here."

They heard the ATV start up and noted Mead and Ellie had gone ahead. The others at the wedding parted to let the little family pass first. Adam and Julia followed behind the children assessing their condition as they walked. Underfed and dirty, but Adam saw no signs of other disease or injury.

THE SMALLEST OF the new children, a little girl about nine, latched onto Rae's hand as they walked from the Wild Woods into the Forest. The girl seemed to be equal parts fear of continuing and fear of going back. Rae wondered how she had been chosen to cling to for comfort.

"Those moccasins are a bit too big for you, aren't they, little girl? Would it be easier if I carried you?" Tears streamed from the little girl's eyes as she nodded and Rae picked her up to follow the procession. She noticed Gee had lifted the little boy, maybe a year older than the girl. The third child apparently in her mid-teens, was supported between Karen and Salome. The other four children—all Gee's and Karen's wards, Rae was told—followed close behind. John continued to carry Gee's walking stick.

Arresting Developments

"SENATOR HARLAND GRAVES, Mrs. Roxanne Graves. FBI. We have warrants for your arrest and a search warrant for your real estate and personal property. Please come with us quietly," the agent said when the senator opened the door.

"What's the meaning of this?" the senator blustered. "Arrest for what?'

"Unlawful imprisonment, kidnapping, child trafficking, rape, child abuse, sex with a minor, and slavery." The senator and his wife blanched, her fingernails digging into his arm. "We are searching for two children delivered to this address three months ago. Also, for any sign or indication of their present or former residence, communications with other known traffickers, and any other evidence of foul play. Please come with us."

"I demand to see my lawyer!"

"You may call your lawyer from the FBI holding area. I must inform you that you have the right to remain silent and refuse to answer questions. Anything you say may be used against you in a court of law. You have the right to consult an attorney before speaking to the police and to have an attorney present during questioning now or in the future. If you cannot afford an attorney, one will be appointed for you before any questioning if you wish. If you decide to answer questions now without an attorney present, you will still have the right to stop answering at any time until you talk to an attorney. Knowing and understanding your rights as I have explained them to you, are you willing to answer my questions without an attorney present?"

"No!" the senator barked at the same time his wife whispered, "Yes."

The agents immediately separated the two, leading the senator directly to a secure vehicle and his wife back inside the house.

"Where are the children?" a female agent asked Mrs. Graves.

"The kennel," she whispered. "A passage under the kitchen. Once part of the Underground Railroad."

Agents swiftly moved to uncover the entrance from inside while others moved outside the house to locate a building that would qualify as a kennel. Mrs. Graves led the agent to an office where she produced telephone logs and pointed out six numbers of other traffickers. The agent quickly verified that one of the numbers was Deacon Stewart's.

"It's time to go," the agent said. "I'm sure there will be more questions at the office."

The meek senator's wife moved with surprising speed as she grabbed for the agent's sidearm, raised it to her chin, and fired.

"Fuck!" screamed the agent as two others rushed into the office. "Get an ambulance. Fuck, fuck, fuck. Why did she have to do that?" Blood was spattered across the agent's face and clothes. Another agent led her out of the room to a bathroom where she threw up long and hard.

———◄◆►———

DEACON'S JOURNAL HAD names and phone numbers of contacts along with details of transactions. There had been no sense trying to protest his innocence. In a move typical of his life, he determined to take as many others down with him as possible. He gave details to agents about 'product deliveries,' distributors, and clients. By the time he was finished, he'd implicated thirty people and organizations. Then he was led away to solitary confinement for safety.

Among those listed were politicians, known criminals, religious figures, corporate executives, and foreign nationals. Nearly a dozen upstanding families protested that they had worked with an adoption agency and despite the steep price the agency had provided exactly the type of child they were looking for. Those would be surprised and horrified to find they had adopted a kidnapped child or a baby abandoned by parents at a hospital or 'safe zone.'

The business had been going for fifty or more years but became more closely allied to training slaves with the development of Dr. Jones' drugs. Deacon's father had started 'placing refugees' soon after World War II but didn't have the stomach for it that Deacon had.

Still, through all of the collapse of Deacon's empire, there was nothing to implicate Troy Cavanaugh in either the death of Dr. Jones nor the rape of a fifteen-year-old a few years earlier. Cavanaugh married Taryn Taft and moved to Boston. He was unlikely to ever return to Rosebud Falls. He only knew and only cared about his own problems having been taken care of. He would never incriminate himself by volunteering information. The perfect woman had shown up on his doorstep, fallen in love, and married him. Troy was a happy man and closed the sight of Jones suffocating in the plastic laundry bag held over his face out of his consciousness.

And Deacon knew his daughter and her handicapped son had a safe place to live their lives. That's how these things were supposed to work out.

The Disconsolate and the Displaced

AN AMBULANCE WAITING at the foresters' office transported Karen, Rae, Gee, and the three children to the hospital with Dr. Adams riding in front.

"We're just going to the hospital for a little while," Gee explained to the boy sitting in his lap and the girl sitting opposite next to Karen.

"Caretaker Adam is going to check to make sure you aren't injured or sick. Once we're sure all you need is food, we'll go home where there are clean clothes, soft beds, and lots of food for you."

"Thank you," whispered the oldest girl. It was a relief that at least one of them could and would communicate.

"Did you live together in the woods?" Karen asked. The girl shook her head.

"Near. We came to see The Tree. He said it was important. Then the boy showed us the stick and we trusted him." She looked from Karen to Rae to Gee and asked, "Will you send us back to our owners?"

"No," Gee said firmly. "We will take care of you and you will be safe." The girl sighed and sank against Karen. "I'm so tired of hiding. I'd even go back."

The boy Gee carried was now sound asleep.

"It looks like you might need more nannies," Rae said as she petted the little girl's head. "I don't want to increase your burden, but if I'm welcome, I'll stay and help."

"Our house has many bedrooms, Rae," Karen said. "We'd love to welcome you there. And the help is appreciated."

THE CHILDREN WERE examined, bathed, and given warm soft pajamas and robes. "We have more clothes for you at home," Karen explained. The children continued to touch their pajamas and rub their cheeks into the soft robes.

"Jude is out front with the van," Gee said. He pocketed his cellphone.

"I called Leah to ask her to run to Walmart and buy more clothes. Each child will probably have a full wardrobe by the time we reach home," Karen said.

"It must be large," Rae commented as they settled into the van for the short ride to the mansion.

"It's the Roth Family ancestral home," Karen explained. "They just kept building onto it whenever there was another child who got married or a new generation born."

"If I counted correctly, you now have eight wards, a sister-in-law, a live-in housekeeper and her son, and you plan to bring the young woman I met who draws pictures home soon. On the reservation, that would almost fill one of our huts."

"Oh, my," Karen breathed. She looked at her husband and touched his hand. He shrugged. "And there may be more."

IN THE AFTERMATH of the interrupted wedding reception, many gathered quietly in the mansion's sitting room. It was unusual for Family heads to meet together where others were also present but they were all too overwhelmed by the day's events to object. Rae held baby Gen in the rocking chair with a bottle. John and Jane were asleep on pillows in the playroom. Nina, Salome, and Raven sat with the new children, talking softly and making sure they had plenty to eat.

"We're going to need more foster homes," Judge Warren sighed.

"We'll be okay," Karen said. "Rae is going to stay and help. That makes four adults and eight children."

"We'll help with support," Loren said. "Maybe we need to set up a fund to subsidize the Evars and Woods families."

"That's good as far as it goes," Warren said. "But there's more."

"More children in the woods?" David asked. "How did they survive? What can we do?"

"The trees took care of them. That's all any will say," Gee said.

"We're not just talking about the children in the woods," Warren said. "Mead? Better tell them." The detective had arrived at the house well after most of the guests had left.

"I was called back to the office right after the wedding," he said. "Sheriff Johnson and I had a conference with the FBI Agent in Charge. They are mopping up their operation with arrests of over fifty people believed to have been involved. There might be more."

"Jesus! Fifty?" Collin muttered. "Hang them all!" Violet, standing behind her uncle, gently rubbed his shoulders. The old man sighed.

"Some may be questioned and released," Mead continued. "It seems there were several who dealt with an adoption agency and believed they were legitimately adopting an orphaned child. The parents and children are all distressed over the separation. The children are in foster homes while the parents are questioned and will probably be reunited within a week."

"But they think the children who were adopted were actually trafficked?" Pàl asked.

"It seems there is a kind of underground capture system in place. Children who might have been at risk as either homeless or unwanted, or dropped off believing the agency was a safe haven," Mead said. "We won't have details for a while but the problem is with the other twenty children they've found so far."

"Twenty children?" Heinz said. "How old? What is their condition."

"The ages run from about five or six up to late teens, though few know their actual age. Most know nothing about their real parents and over half don't speak at all. Like the Woods children were," Mead said. "Since we—and I say that in most general terms, meaning Gee and Karen—are the only ones the FBI knows who have experience with children in this condition, they've asked us to function as temporary guardians."

"Twenty children," David whispered again. "And possibly more in the woods. You can't handle all that, Karen. No matter how much help you have."

"Why do they want to send them here, Mead?" Warren asked. "Aren't things like this usually handled by CPS in the local region?"

"I asked that," Mead said, the corner of his mouth pulling back reflexively as his left eye squinted. "Raids are still going on. The FBI can be as close-mouthed as the Families under *sàmhach*. They don't want any locals involved. Second, if the condition of these children was widely known, every do-gooder and religious nut in the country would come out of the woodwork wanting to convert them to their religion, political persuasion, moral code, or whatever. We've seen it in the aftermath of Waco, Ruby Ridge, Eldorado, Operation Cross Country and anywhere a major raid has been conducted. There's a line of people ready to save the poor dears by indoctrinating them into their own weird beliefs."

"They could keep them hidden," Warren suggested. "They don't have any trouble doing it with the refugee children."

"We have experience," Gee said. "That has to be driving it. They've latched onto the fact that we've already rescued children and figure we know what to do. Besides, it's our responsibility. They came from our woods."

"That's the other reason," Mead affirmed. "On the advice of Dr. Poltanys, the children have all had blood drawn and tested. Most have shown RDH markers in their bloodstream. We have the best aftercare for the drug in the country as no one else has devoted much attention to it." Silence greeted the news.

"The heirs," Heinz finally said. They turned and waited for him to continue. "This is a Family matter. We were supposed to protect the Forest and the city. We failed. But look at us. We're old. None of us save Karen and Gee could take on children young enough to be our grandchildren or great-grandchildren. Gerta and I are seventy-five years old. We couldn't care for them. But we have room. If I invited the Quartet to live with us, I think they would welcome the opportunity to redeem the Family by fostering children."

David looked at Loren and nodded his head.

"We have the larger estate home of our two households," Loren said. "If Jessie and Jonathan agree, we could do the same."

"We cut down the size of our estate when we built the retirement home," Jan said. "Zach has a nice place, though, and teenage daughters to help. I'll talk to him."

"Drake is a senior and can't wait to move out," Mead said. "Maybe seeing someone who doesn't have a home would be good for him. I'll talk to Rita."

"There are others like you," Gee said. "Many with children who have been begging to help in any way they can. Colleen and Luke Zimmer. Nathan and Marian Panza. Ruth Ann and Dale Metzger. We need to begin canvassing in the morning."

"I expect we may see the first children tomorrow afternoon or Monday at the latest," Mead said.

"I'll make sure there are temporary facilities for them in the hospital. We'll get them checked up and fed, at least," Jan said.

Honeymoon

KAREN SIGHED DEEPLY as she sank into bed next to Gee. There had been a little difficulty getting the children settled for bed, not the least of which was naming the newest rescues. The names they had brought with them were not decent to be spoken aloud. The little girl accepted the name 'Rose' when she was given a flower from Karen's bouquet. Rae suggested the boy, a year or so older than Rose, needed the name of a strong tree because he had been so strong in the woods. When she said, 'Ash,' the boy wrapped his arms around her waist and hugged her. The fifteen-year-old girl said simply, "Merida."

"Your name?" Gee asked. She shrugged her shoulders and nodded. No one was certain if she remembered her name or had already chosen one.

Rose was attached to Rae and Gee's sister was bemused by the attention. Rae took a room with two twin beds and gave Rose one of them.

"That's awfully cramped for an adult," Karen said. "If you are going to have children, Rae, we need to give you a suite."

"Me? Children?"

"Tomorrow, we'll take a look at the downstairs master suite. You might want to raise your family there," Gee chuckled.

"Um… You are as devious as when you were a child, Gee," Rae said. "This room is fine for tonight. It's as large as the house Gee and I grew up in." Karen grabbed her notebook and jotted that down.

Ash was happy to have the room next to Rae and Rose when he discovered they shared a bath and would not be far away. Salome and Merida were bonding and Salome invited the other fifteen-year-old to take the second bed in her room. Once all the children and guests were settled, Gee and Karen finally had time alone.

"Not exactly what we planned for a honeymoon," Gee sighed as he pulled Karen to him. "And no rest tomorrow."

"I don't know. I never imagined anything past the moment I would crawl into bed with my husband," Karen said. "My husband," she whispered again.

"Are you okay with having my sister move in?" Gee asked.

"It's a big house and she's family," Karen yawned. "We received four more people into our household the moment we said, 'I do.' That will require a little discussion. But I'm a newlywed. I just want my husband to make love to me now. Would that be okay?"

"I love you, Karen Evars," Gee whispered. "It is the only thing I have known for certain since the day I arrived in Rosebud Falls."

RAVEN HAD WORKED in a bar or restaurant for nearly thirty years. She knew all aspects of serving a lot of people. She calculated ten for breakfast and added herself and Timmy. Before anyone else was awake, she was in the kitchen with an egg and cheese casserole in the oven and three packages of cinnamon rolls ready to slide in when she saw a sign of life. She made coffee and turned to find Nina sitting at the table.

"Is there anything I can do to help, Raven?" Nina asked.

"I think everything is about ready," Raven smiled at the girl. It was not unusual for Nina to be the first one in the kitchen and Raven wondered briefly at her timing when Timmy walked in from his garage apartment. She kissed her son on the cheek and he went to the table, sitting opposite Nina. "I don't know how many will arrive for breakfast at once. Did you hear anyone else stirring upstairs, Nina?"

"It sounded like Rae was talking to little Rose when I passed their room. Ash's door was open and he was sitting on the floor just inside. I invited him to come with me but he pointed to Rae's room. I think he's waiting for them."

"Well, it's Sunday morning. I'll get the sweet rolls in the oven. Why don't we feed everyone from paper plates? Since we don't know when people will arrive, there is no sense setting the big table. We'll just let people fill and take their plates to the table when they arrive. What do you think about hot chocolate?"

"That would be very nice," Nina said.

"Can I have hot chocolate, Mom?" Timmy asked.

"Yes, you may. I'll get it started. Nina, can you find the paper plates and napkins, please?" Raven poured milk into a pan to heat and began mixing cocoa and sugar in a smaller bowl. She added a few drops of vanilla to the milk. Others would just mix a package of instant hot chocolate but Raven preferred to make the beverage from scratch. By the time Nina had the plates and napkins out and placed silverware on the table, Raven was stirring the cocoa mixture slowly into the milk.

"Are we too early?" Rae asked from the doorway. She held two small children by the hand. Both Rose and Ash were dressed in soft sweatpants and T-shirts.

"I've just removed the eggs from the oven and the cinnamon rolls will be out soon," Raven said. "Coffee? We can start the children with orange juice."

"Please," Rae said. Nina brought the jug of OJ to the table with plastic glasses, remembering when little Esther had first come to dinner and spilled her milk. Rae seated the children at the table and gave them glasses of juice. Soon eggs were on plates and they cautioned the children to eat slowly and be sure not to burn themselves on the hot food. It was a lesson, however, that had to be learned by experience. Rae squeezed her eyes shut, realizing the children had not had hot food in a very long time. The cinnamon rolls were wildly popular.

Over the next half hour, others slowly filtered in to breakfast, drawn by the smell of fresh cinnamon rolls. The last to arrive were Gee and Karen.

All the children stopped eating.

The newest children were unsure of what they were to do. Led by John, Jane, and Gen, however, they each got up to get a quick hug from the newlyweds and then return to their breakfasts. Gee stood, a bit bemused, as he found himself with Gen and a bottle still in his arms. Jane was busy eating her own breakfast.

AFTER BREAKFAST, THE clan began to get organized. Raven helped prepare the downstairs master suite. Ash looked a little bewildered when Rae led Rose into the suite and showed her a room of her own and where Rae would sleep.

"Rae, I think you have another," Raven whispered. Rae turned to look at Ash.

"Ash, would you like to live in this suite with Rose and me?" Rae finally asked. The silent boy nodded his head.

"There's nothing in this room but a desk," Raven said. "Ben had one put in but always used the library."

"Can we get another bed?"

"I think so." Raven went to find Karen. Gee had called Drake, Viktor, Ryan, and Trevor to ask them to help move furniture and soon the boys were hauling a bed and mattress to the former office and removing the desk. As soon as they had it arranged, they were called upstairs. Hearing what was happening in the mansion, several girls from Gee's team arrived to help as well. Alyssa and Shannon moved in to Rae's suite with bedding, clothes, and a few toys.

Upstairs, the boys worked in the mini suite near Gee and Karen's room. Gee had the sitting room cleared and brought in a drawing table, desk, and easel. Two of the boys began painting the room while the other two moved on to make sure the other four bedrooms had twin beds and dressers. Gee and Karen were unsure of how many children they might ultimately need to house. Jeanie, Leslie, and Rebecca, accompanied by Nina, Salome, and Merida, took charge of seeing that all the rooms were clean, made up, and welcoming for children of any age with stuffed toys, books, and art.

Everyone knew more children were coming.

14

EIGHTH FAMILY

In-Gathering

"THE FIRST CHILDREN HAVE ARRIVED," Adam said when Gee answered his phone Sunday afternoon. "We'll need volunteers soon."

"How many children?" Gee asked.

"So far, we have twin girls, about six years old. They have a little language skill but it has mostly been used to ask where Aunt Ann is. The feds compiled a dossier on the children from what they could locate and were kind enough to include a couple of toys from the girls' room. These two were being raised by a couple in Ohio as their nieces and have completed first grade requirements as homeschooled children."

"It sounds like they might not be in bad shape, then," Gee said.

"Don't count on it. They show other signs of having been… abused."

"Damn it!" Gee exclaimed. It was unusual for him to swear and Karen looked up, alarmed.

"Three more older kids have just arrived. It will take an hour to get checkups and clothes for them," Adam continued. "Leah got here first thing this morning with half a department store worth of children's clothes and shoes. The hard part may be keeping the children from being overwhelmed. Or overwhelming ourselves."

"Thank you, Adam. I'll be there in half an hour to help coordinate the volunteer nannies and meet the children. We'll figure out when

Karen comes over and I think Rae wants to visit as well. I'm not sure Rose and Ash will let her out of their sight, though," Gee said.

"It's not like I'm superstitious or believe in any metaphysical hoohaa about the Forest," Adam said, "—after all, I'm a doctor and scientist— but... I think you should bring your hickory staff with you. Just in case one of the children uh... recognizes it."

Beneath Still Waters

THE FBI STING operation expanded throughout Sunday and by the end of the day Monday, the hospital had taken in some thirty children, the last flown in from Seattle and driven from the airport to Rosebud Falls, weeping the entire way. At least they had not arrived all at once.

Gee was not happy to learn agents had questioned each child extensively before giving them even the smallest comforts. The children arrived sullen and uncooperative. As Gee looked through the files on each child, he discovered they had little information to give.

The teen flown in from Seattle had been used as a human shield when agents approached the home where she'd been held near the Canadian border in Idaho. A sniper had killed the man holding her and she'd been covered in his blood. Inside the house, agents found the dead bodies of a woman and three more children. When the teen arrived at the hospital, her clothes were crusted with blood and she had not stopped crying. Ellie took charge of her personally and bathed and comforted her.

Gee had been on the go the entire time, first, simply meeting the children and then reading to small groups. No matter the age, the children all seemed mesmerized by his voice when he read, enjoying equally the simplest picture books and chapter books provided by Ms. Tomczyk, the librarian. His walking stick was casually leaned against the wall behind his reading chair and a few children were brave enough to reach out and touch it. There were no miraculous healings or opened memories.

Nor was Gee alone in his efforts. Ruth Ann, Sally Ann, and Dale Metzger helped Sunday afternoon. Sally Ann immediately bonded with the little twins, insisting she needed to stay with them Sunday night in the hospital. The Panzas all participated in meeting and reading to the children. Even Marian's father, Rupert Grimm and his young wife Onyx, took a turn meeting the children and caring for them.

Monday, volunteers arrived almost a fast as the children. Colleen Zimmer took the week off school and her husband, Luke, joined in reading and talking to the children. The Nussbaum Quartet, Cameron, Elaine, Krystal, and Gail, sang in every child's room, often getting them to sing along. Mead and Rita Oliver stopped by, pledging to return as needed during the week.

TUESDAY AFTERNOON, GEE, Karen, and Rae went to the hospital to visit the children and then to complete the mission they had started on Sunday and been waylaid—they planned to formally invite Rena to live with them. John, Jane, and Gen joined the adults, leaving the other children in the care of Nina and Raven. The children were eager to meet the new rescues and moved easily from room to room, whispering to them. They spent a long time talking to an adolescent boy and a young girl. Then they joined the adults to visit Rena. Adam tagged along to confirm to Rena that she was ready to be released. Mead Oliver joined the group to sign off on Rena being independent and willing to join them.

Rena sat in a chair with a reading table pulled over the arms. She was intent on her paper and pencils and didn't look up until Dr. Poltanys spoke to her.

"Oh! I was busy. Gee! Look what I've drawn!" Gee moved over to the budding artist and leafed through her sketchbook. Not only had the girl made beautiful illustrations, she had included the story, neatly printed in blank areas of each drawing.

"Rena, these are beautiful," Gee whispered. "You have such great talent. We should test the story and pictures with some of the children. Would you like to do that?"

"Oh, yes. Gee, can we really publish the story?"

"I think so. Karen?"

"Definitely. This will make a beautiful children's book. The transformation of the woods from sinister to friendly is amazing. Would you like to come home with us?"

"Um… Visit?" Rena asked. "Can I do that, Doctor?"

"Not only to visit, Rena," Adam said. "I believe Gee and Karen are offering you a place to live. And I would bet a studio to continue your art."

"Really?" Rena asked. "After everything I've done and who my friends were, you'd still let me live in your home?"

"Absolutely, Rena. You just have to know that in addition to John and Jane and little Gen, there are five other children living with us, as well as Timmy Raven and my sister, Rae. It's a big house, but there are a lot of people."

"How soon can I be with you?" she asked. Dr. Poltanys had her discharge papers with him and signed off on them. Rena had very little to pack. Karen, Ellie, and Julia had brought her a few new clothes over the past few weeks and Karen helped her pack a small bag while Gee joined his sister, Adam, and Mead in the hall.

"George! George! Where are you?" an old voice called from a nearby room. Gee recognized it as August Poltanys. Adam sighed.

"He rouses himself to call out two or three times a day," Adam said. "I honestly don't know what's keeping him in this world. He's ninety-one years old as of yesterday but didn't recognize anyone in the family who came to visit." Gee drifted toward the door, drawn by the old man's plaintive voice. As soon as he could be seen through the door, August started calling.

"George! George! Come here. Don't eat the nut, George. We can't come here anymore. We have to stay away." His words were nonsense, but his eyes were fixed on Gee. Gee moved over near the bed to comfort the old man. As soon as he was near enough, August reached out and grabbed Gee's walking stick in a viselike grip.

"Ahh!" he sighed as he struggled to sit. Rae moved to the other side of the bed and helped Gee get the man upright. Adam took a hand and checked his grandfather's pulse. "A final moment of clarity before I pass," August said, his voice calm. "You've come for the children," he said looking from Gee to Rae and back. "They're not in the woods. They were buried in the quarry on the lowest level, just as the water was starting to fill it. Terrible disease in the Wild Woods. Everyone was banned and they built a fence. The few people who lived there either fled or died and the Savage gave them peaceful burial. No one knew what happened.

One day there were people living in the Wild Woods and the next there were none. We thought we'd lost you all. George wanted to tell everyone what happened but that was when we got the news that the seven heroes had all died in France—including my older brother. Everything was chaos and George decided to eat the nut to prove he was the rightful new heir. He died. I didn't want to be head of the Family. Never challenged him. Begged him not to eat it. And I'm sad I passed the Family to my son at such a young age." He looked up at Adam. "You're a good doctor. You look like my son. I hope we're related." With that the old man's grip on the staff loosened and he slumped back. Gee and Rae laid him gently on the bed and watched him sleep.

"It won't be long now," Adam said. "If you'll excuse me, I should call Dad and Zach. They'll want to be here." The doctor paused at the door and turned back. "Thank you, Gee."

———◁◆▷———

"COME HOME TO me, said The Tree. I will make you safe and warm. I will not let you be hurt again. And the children came home and found the fearsome dragon had been sent away. The Wild Woods was once again a place where they could be safe and play together. The end," Gee said as he showed them the last picture Rena had drawn of children sitting together in a huge tree. It was remarkably like the Patriarch, but the tree was red and Rena said she'd never seen the Patriarch. Nonetheless, the children wanted to see all the pictures again and the older kids all had a comment about what they saw.

Rae was quiet as the new family organized itself for bed. Rena was shown to her suite and spent an hour crying on Karen's shoulder, thankful for her new chance at life and remorseful for all the mistakes she had made. Ultimately, Jane settled Rena down through the simple expedient of placing the baby in her arms. Startled, Rena sat and rocked little Gen until both were nearly asleep. Perhaps it was because she was so young that Jane had almost no hesitation to hand her baby to any adult who was interested, including the older teens. Earlier in the day, Rae had fed the baby as her own shadow, Rose, looked on.

Rose and Ash were an inexplicable phenomenon to Rae. At forty, she had resigned herself to never having children. She'd never met a man she was that interested in. But Rose had adopted her and tagging along behind was Ash. Rae continued to read one last story to the children before she tucked them in. She suddenly had a three-bedroom apartment and two children. She returned to the sitting room to find Karen, Gee, and Raven having a glass of wine. Gee quickly poured Rae a glass and invited her to join them.

"Are your little ones asleep?" Karen asked.

"My little ones," Rae mused. "I never expected when Gee and I set out to find the children, what the quest would mean."

"Can you fill in some of the gaps? You know Gee has no memory of his life before he came to Rosebud Falls," Karen said.

"So you say. Yet the story you wrote and Rena illustrated could have come straight from our family legends," Rae said. "The memories are lurking inside. We are called the People of the Red Tree. Our people are not forgotten."

"We sent inquiries to all reservations when we discovered Gee's DNA had Native American markers," Karen said. "Why didn't they respond?"

"Two reasons, I suspect," Rae said. "By the way, had I heard of it, I would have come immediately but I was gone on my own version of the quest. First, our family has lived off the grid for at least seventy-five years. With few records, it is hard to know if it was our grandparents or great-grandparents who sought shelter as refugees. The woman we call Grandmother is likely not related to us at all. But the tribe sheltered and protected us when our people fled from the Wild Woods. The second reason is selfish but I can't blame them. They would not betray the source of their funding. Each year the tribe receives a substantial payment from a trust fund with the caveat that it continues to care for the People of the Red Tree. They might not have spent all the money on our people, but we never went without."

"Someone paid to keep us hidden?" Gee asked. "Why? Are we criminals?"

"No. And that is the quest we went on. There have never been many of us but now there are scarcely a dozen left. When our parents died, Grandmother continued to educate us. She told us the stories and sang them to us from the time we were little. We learned to read and write and do math. We had all the modern conveniences but we were never registered as part of the tribe. We were refugees."

Rae's voice took on the same story-telling tones that Gee used when he read to the children—a voice that kept them mesmerized.

THE PEOPLE OF the Red Tree lived in the Wild Woods much as they had for generations. The powerful Families of the nearby settlement kept their corner of the woods free while their European neighbors cultivated and groomed the fields and Forest nearby. There was plenty for both and they intermarried, some leaving the woods and some few Europeans staying with their native spouses in the simple dwellings they built there.

The men of stone asked the natives for a license to dig a hole and take the stone for buildings in the growing city. Their promise in return was to always take care of the People—to defend them from the greed of their neighbors. And with this agreement, the People continued to live a peaceful life.

But there rose men in the city who lusted for the woodland of the People. The only way they could have that land was if the People were gone. And so, they conspired to poison the People with disease and take their land. Many died. Those who lived, fled and became refugees in the lands of distant cousins.

The people of stone, however, kept their promise. They protected the Wild Woods from the greed of the city men and sent white man's money to care for the refugees at every turn of the seasons. Still the People lost their homeland. They lost their memory of where the homeland lay. And they mourned their failure to bury their dead and honor their ancestors.

When at last there were only a few of the People surviving, the wise woman sent a brother and sister on a quest. They must find the children of the People and be sure they had been buried and honored in their deaths. The brother and sister chose different paths in their search. The sister followed the trail of dollars that had sustained them over the years, journeying to the large city and finding the trust that provided for them.

The brother, however, took the fruits of The Red Tree, the heart of their people, and followed the path of vision quest. He went away into the mountains to seek the vision and was not heard from again.

—————————◁◆▷—————————

"You and Gee?" Karen whispered. Rae nodded. Gee looked on with a faraway gaze that said maybe some part of the story had opened a curtain on his life.

"I found the manager of the trust after weeks of searching. Everything is done automatically by computer now. The young woman who managed it did nothing more than balance the accounts and verify payments. But she listened to my story and suggested that her grandfather had once managed the trust and might be able to tell me more. I had to wait for the grandfather to return from traveling abroad. While waiting, I studied with the manager and learned how the trust was set up and administered."

"And you found us here?" Karen asked.

"When the grandfather returned at Christmas, he agreed to speak to me but didn't trust that I was from the People of the Red Tree until he had asked me many questions. He checked my answers against journals and diaries, many of which he had to retrieve from a storage room. Finally, we pieced together the location of the woods and the continued payments that the Savages made to provide for the People."

"The people of stone," Gee mused. "Pàl told me his grandfather incorporated the company, which had been privately held, and leased the quarry and Wild Woods from a blind trust. Payments are still made every quarter for the lease and a percentage of the profits from mineral rights. Even though the former board of directors bent provisions of the lease, the terms were ironclad and penalties for failure to pay would put an end to the company."

"And that, apparently, is why the fence was erected between the Forest and the Wild Woods," Karen said. "Savage or SSG has fought every attempt to annex the land for nearly a hundred years."

"According to the old man in the hospital, our dead were buried at the bottom of the quarry," Rae said. "We have found our lost family. But in searching for our own children of the woods, Gee has found other lost children. You found the treasure of the Wild Woods, my brother."

"And he was the one who cast the votes at SSG to favor annexation and replace the board. That opened the Wild Woods and let him find the lost children," Raven said, caught up in the romance and adventure of the story.

"Your name suggests you and your son might also be related to the People," Rae said. "Have you had your DNA tested to see if you are related to us?"

"No. How could…? You mean I might be related to you and Gee? That would be… I just… I hardly…" Lynda Raven seemed unable to complete a sentence. The idea that she might be part of this legend was overwhelming. But so had been the thought of raising a son by herself and she had done that. With determination in her voice she collected herself. "I'll test but it makes no difference. I have a good job here with Gee and Karen and a whole bunch of children to take care of. You have your mission. I have mine."

ON WEDNESDAY, GEE was surprised to see Wayne and Jo at the hospital.

"It turns out that I have a bigger home than I thought," Wayne said. "Once their investigation of Lance Beck was complete, the police released his mansion to its rightful owners. Granda recognized it as soon as he saw the windows overlooking the lake. So, Jo and I have decided to move in together and see about helping some children. Oh, by the way, Karen, we found the Family tree."

"That's wonderful, Wayne. Are you sure you are ready for this Jo?" Karen asked.

"Tell me you're ready, even now, Karen," Jo said. "I've figured one thing out and it's going to take me a long way. I've fallen in love with Wayne. And I believe he feels the same about me. I've known for sure since the night you brought Nina to our home. This is right for us."

IT WOULD STILL take the better part of a month to get the children out of the hospital and into approved foster care with Dr. Salinger interviewing each proposed household and each child.

The biggest surprise to all four adults was Nina. She took it upon herself to teach the other children, both at home and in the hospital. She shared bits of her own story with them. She taught them to count, though some did so silently, holding up the right number of fingers when she asked them to identify a number. And though her reading level was elementary, she selected books and read to her new brothers and sisters.

Over half the children had been moved to foster care before the month was out and most of the others were spoken for.

Carrying on the Work of the Lord

"I WANT YOU to know that Pastor Beck and I had our disagreements. No one is perfect. But we were brothers in Christ Jesus," Reverend Curt Probst said from the pulpit of the First Assembly Sunday morning. "It is tragic to see what the power of evil can do in our world. We are told that he abused children. We are told that he drugged his congregation. We are told that his deacon trafficked in children and drugs and burned his church. It is a stretch of the imagination to believe such things of the baptized believers in Christ Jesus."

"Amen!"

"I hear you. But God did not appoint me Pastor Beck's judge. That soul has gone before the great throne to show his innocence or be convicted of his guilt. I am not a man to exonerate what the courts of public opinion have decreed. I am here only to exhort, to uplift the people of God and hold a light on their path that they might not stumble in their march for truth."

"Praise God!"

"We, children of the beloved cross, must ever be watchful lest we fall to the devil's subtle temptations. And in this city we call our home on earth, we know those fine-sounding temptations are the work of the devil. Do they come from the great Families—the founders of this place? Sadly, many temptations do. Do they come from the unholy reverence our neighbors have for trees that bear poison fruit? I pray for their souls. Do they come from the doctors and lawyers and judges and police and bankers and politicians and rulers in corporate offices? Dear God! Save us from those who would lure us away from you."

"Amen. Praise the Lord. Halleluiah."

"We are told that children have been brought to our city, in need of the love and care of Christian parents. Yet they have been given over to the guardianship of the very people who brought this curse upon our town. Why have the people of God not been called upon? Why have the children been prevented from hearing the loving message of Christ? Or do these evil overlords of Rosebud Falls know in their hearts that once the truth is spoken, the children will turn against them?"

"Speak the truth, Reverend!"

"The truth is this. There is only one path. Only one light. Only one way to salvation. Jesus said, 'I am the Way, the Truth, and the Life. No man comes to the Father but by me.' We, as the children of God, must be ever mindful to shine God's light on the City of Rosebud Falls. We must be vigilant in correcting its errors. We must stand for truth when all around us is a lie. Dear brothers and sisters in Christ, the day may come when we—when you yourself—are the last bastion standing between our beloved city and eternal damnation. We may never—I dare say that we *will* never know the truth about what happened at Calvary Tabernacle. But we will fight. I say, fight!"

"Fight, Brother!"

"We will fight for the very lives and souls of the children who have been planted in this town against their wills, against their parents and guardians, and against the nature of God. We will stand in the streets. We will campaign at the polls. We will shout until the very Forest echoes our complaint. Render unto God what is God's. Let the little children come to me!"

———— ⟨✦⟩ ————

KENDRA MAZZENGA SAT in the back of the church. Few people knew she was the district attorney, nor that she was preparing a campaign for the judgeship in two years. If the election were this year, she'd be whipping the congregation up herself. But she had to walk a careful path. She needed a conservative movement that was not tied to the Families in order to run a successful campaign.

And she needed to be just liberal enough that even the people who were most appalled by the activities of Calvary Tabernacle were convinced she was a champion—the real champion—of the city and the people. Right now, she needed a local case she could try publicly and get a guilty verdict. All the people related to the trafficking were dead or moved to other jurisdictions. Someone in this town—preferably some-one related to the Families—needed to pay the penalty of guilt.

Then she could win an election. She only needed to keep a watchful eye on the disposition of the children, the behavior of their foster parents, and on the conservative congregations like this one who were so easily influenced. She needed a target and timing was everything.

Leaves of Wisdom

"Relax and drink your tea," Birdie said. "Your coffee will be ready soon." She looked from Gee to Rae to Karen. Rose and Ash sat on either side of Rae. Gee held baby Gen while the older children sat together in a corner of Jitterz with sweet rolls and cocoa. The family had decided on an outing this Saturday morning, giving Raven a chance to sweep through the house with her new helper, Rebecca, a senior at Flor del Día, who had been hired for weekend help. The older teens had been told explicitly that they had done a good job helping keep the house orderly during the week but that they deserved a day off, too.

"What is this?" Rae asked, sipping her cup of lukewarm tea. "It's very tasty."

"A blend I use to open the eyes." Rae was startled enough to push her cup away. "No, not your eyes. Mine," Birdie laughed. "There is nothing in the cup but tea." Gee sipped the last of his tea and set the cup in front of Birdie to show his sister. Birdie picked it up, swirled the leaves and looked into it. She sighed.

"What is it?" Gee asked.

"It's not over," Birdie said. "I see you have begun to remember bits of your past and will learn more. But what you learn will be stories told to you as if about a different person. Your past and future are bound up in the present. More children will seek you out. Some with their own pasts locked away. They find you a comfort and a guide on the path of life."

"More children?" Karen sighed as she set her cup down. Birdie picked it up, swirled the leaves and looked up at Karen with a smile.

"Three paths lead the children here. Some from the hospital. I fear we have not seen the last of this round-up the police are conducting.

Some from the Wild Woods as they make their own way back to where they awoke. And even some," Birdie smiled, "from your womb. Including the one growing there now."

"I've... What? I'm... pregnant?" Gee caught his wife of a month in his arms, almost crushing little Gen between them. He kissed her. "We're going to be parents!"

"We already are, Love," he whispered. "We'll welcome this one as well." Jane saw the embrace and retrieved Gen from Gee, holding her on her shoulder and bouncing until the baby burped. She settled with her new family and continued whatever conversation they had begun.

Birdie turned to Rae and Gee's sister handed over her teacup. Birdie looked, swirled the leaves again, and looked longer.

"Do you see anything in my cup?" Rae asked. Rose had finished her chocolate and Rae picked her up, dabbing at the corners of the girl's mouth with a napkin. She set Rose down. Ash took his little sister's hand and led her to join the older children, not at all interested in what Birdie had to say.

"The fulfillment of a dream. A family of your own," Birdie said. Rae sighed and looked after her children. It would take weeks for paperwork, investigations, and approvals, but they were her children already. "But I see a mission as well. When your brother came to the city, we made him our champion. We will make you our teacher. Yes, all these special children need to be taught and the schools will be hard-put to handle the problem. But it is not only the new children. The lore that has been passed down to you is needed by our people. Healing. Mind and body. You have stories we need to hear in order to get past the pain of previous generations. You have the guidance that we need. Gee, too. You are his memory."

Rae looked at her brother and smiled.

"I'd like to learn, too, Rae," he said. She simply nodded.

Uneasy Alliance

THE FAMILY HEADS were not united. They had met individually and as small groups but not all together as they attempted to sort out various

Family legends and partial histories. Gee and Karen and the younger heirs were intentionally left out of these meetings.

Pàl and Wayne had thoroughly explored the mansion on the lake where the preacher had lived the past ten years. Pastor Beck had no relatives or heirs they could find. The church trustees had scattered and many were arrested. Pàl canceled the leases. Surprisingly, they found the mansion largely unchanged from the fleeting memories Pàl had of it from childhood. There was an abundance of religious texts on the library shelves, but they did little to displace volumes that had been there for decades. Even the furnishings were much the same as Pàl remembered, though he had the altar and cross removed before Wayne had seen them. He sat at the desk and pored over the many volumes of diaries that had been on the shelves undisturbed for seventy-five years or more.

The same was occurring at Family estates throughout the city. What the heads were discovering was not pleasant.

--------⊲◆⊳--------

"Aaron had not yet become the head of the Family," Karen sighed as she looked at journals from the 1930s and 40s. Leah sat across from her, scouring estate records from a century ago. "He was raised by his uncle who had no sons. But Aaron called him a secretive man who did not share his wisdom."

"A trait Aaron either adopted or inherited," Leah said. "I am so glad you are opening the archives to the family."

"It might not be a happy revelation, any more than my discovery that Aaron had hidden Celia's relationship," Karen said. "Ah, well. Aaron's father and uncle had undergone the challenge and ate the nut. The uncle survived."

"Dad told us about that back in October at the Family meeting. His grandfather challenged his brother and lost. Aaron was adopted by the winner," Leah agreed.

"Yes. Aaron says that in 1938, just before the war, there was a severe flu epidemic that 'killed many people.' He says it was believed the source of the flu was in the Wild Woods and so it was fenced off."

"That would be not long before August saw the burial in the quarry,"

Leah said. "Both Dr. Poltanys and Detective Oliver agree on the basic content of August's last words."

"I'm not sure it speaks well of the Savages," Karen sighed. "But I've visited their Family tree and it is as strong as all the others."

"ACCORDING TO OUR records," David said, "there was a sudden die-off in the Wild Woods. The foresters were dispatched to render aid and were turned back by armed guards from the quarry. A few days later, Bryce Savage had a fence erected and presented the Families with a lease for the entire acreage that had once been the woodland and the quarry, all the way to his own property on the lake. The lease showed the registered owners to be a trust in New York City and all inquiries as to who bene-fited from the trust were ignored."

"It looks like a land-grab on the part of the Savages and now they have a so-called witness to the trust who just happens to be Gee Evar's previously unknown sister." Loren said.

"Just listen to yourselves," Heinz said, trying to settle the other heads. "There's no sense blaming people who are long dead. What are we saying changes? Anything?"

"We acknowledged Gee as an equal at the table of Families and still we left him out of this meeting and left the Roth out as well," Jan said. "That should paint as clear a picture of the Families as we can make. He's Champion of the City, the Forest, and now the Children. And what has he asked for in return? Does he want a new fence around the Wild Woods? He presented a plan for restoration of the woods to its native condition and that plan includes transplanting hundreds of trees onto newly acquired farmland and in the Gem Estates. It extends the culti-vated Forest by 150 acres. We all agreed to that. What does any of our research or any of our stories change in Gee's role? I don't see the point in even discussing this."

"It's a smirch on the character of the Families," Loren insisted.

"A well-deserved black mark, I'd say," Pàl stated flatly. "Heinz, you're holding something back." The Nussbaum scowled at the Savage.

"Our Family has journals, too," Heinz said. "They aren't flattering. Of the Nussbaums or any of the rest of us. I... The Nussbaum Family, among others…" He paused to look at each of the other Family heads. "…We owe the People of the Red Tree an apology and restitution."

"SSG continues to operate out of the leased land," Pàl said. "As always, we pay our lease fees and percentage of resource profits to the trust. As far as I can tell, that's the main source of income Gee and Rae have ever had. Paid blindly to support them. It hasn't made them rich as most of the revenue goes to the general well-being of their host tribe. Gee has the proxies of all the orphans' shares of SSG, which gives him say over what we approve at the company. And not once has he asked for anything other than the betterment of the city and the Forest. From my standpoint, nothing changes."

"If you don't like him, you can always challenge him," Collin Meagher chuckled. "All it takes is to walk out to your Family tree and take a nut. I did it. Long time ago. When you wouldn't help find my niece. And look who found her and whose last name she took as her own rather than her father's or her ancestors. Look at us. Soon the names of the Families will be blended and lost. Instead of Meagher, there is now Lanahan. Right Violet?"

"And you know I won't be eating any nuts, *Uncail*," Birdie's daughter said. "Don't we have a funeral to attend? I don't like these old man meetings where everyone isn't here. Don't call me back unless the table is full." The old men were shocked at the young woman's attitude but acknowledged her assertion that Gee and Karen should have been included.

She was also correct about the funeral. August Poltanys had never woken up again after his moment of lucidity with Gee but had clung to life for another month. He'd finally passed on Sunday.

FOUR MONTHS AFTER they had buried Ben at the Jewish cemetery, the Families accompanied August's body to Rose Park Memorial Garden, the cemetery overlooking the Forest. Just a few months ago, the teens had been sledding and inner tubing down the track toward the lumbermill. It was a quiet funeral; all August's friends were long-since gone. He had been in a home or the hospital for so long no one knew him.

"Thank you for participating," Zach said to Gee and Karen as they prepared to leave.

"I had a couple of conversations with your grandfather, Zach," Gee said. "Losing one, even one so old, is a loss to our community. I felt the same when Ben died."

"I know you have a big family for support, but if there's anything we can do to help, let us know, Zach," Karen said.

"Maybe you could give me pointers on dealing with two new children in our family," he laughed.

KAREN HEADED HOME to be with their family but Gee took a walk in the woods after the funeral. He had been so busy with the children that he hadn't been into the woods since his wedding. It was now April and small leaves put a green haze over all the canopy and softened the light filtering through.

Gee was happy to see that even though he hadn't been into the woods, his volunteer crews had. Trails other than the main one to the Patriarch had been trimmed and mowed. The crew had tackled the thorns that nearly filled the gully. It would be a long process, but they had made a dent. Three teens working after school in the longer daylight hours looked up to greet him.

"Hey, Gee," JD said. "I hope you don't mind us working without you."

"It looks like you've got your work cut out for you," Gee said. "I'm glad to see you tackling this."

"The floods loosened the roots. It's like this is all one big plant. When you start pulling up a root, you find it's connected to the next stalk as well. The foresters gave us these protective suits so we wouldn't get too ripped up."

"Who's with you?"

"Leslie and James. School gets out early on Wednesdays so we decided to take advantage of the daylight." The two other kids waved at Gee but continued their work. JD stepped up close to Gee and lowered his voice. "Gee, go quietly to Cabin Three. Trevor's found someone."

Gee moved out of the gully and quickly down the path toward the cabin. He fell into a rhythm that left his footfall almost silent. He entered the space near the cabin and moved quietly around it. On the far side, Trevor sat facing another teen on a tarp.

"It's a fresh orange," Trevor said, handing a slice to his companion. "I'm sad that you don't get this kind of food every day. I can only come out a couple of times a week. Won't you let me take you to Gee?"

"Gee has the stick in his hands. Does he beat you with it?" Gee heard the soft tones of a girl's voice, lowered to almost a whisper like John and Jane.

"Gee wouldn't do that. The stick is part of the woods. It would protect you like your tree does."

"My tree doesn't make me have sex."

"Lisa, if you come with us, no one will make you have sex again."

"I like sex sometimes. If you want, I'll have sex with you," she said. Trevor sighed.

"You're very pretty, Lisa. I'm attracted to you. But right now, you're vulnerable and I don't think it would be right for us to do that. It... wouldn't make me a better person to take advantage of you. Please come with me to meet Gee and Karen. They won't treat you meanly, either. We're young. We still need grownups to help us."

"I'll come with you Trevor," she said. "I know he's here. I can feel his eyes." Trevor looked up and saw Gee standing silently at the corner of the cabin.

"Then let me introduce you," he said.

Lisa was eighteen and had lived in the woods for less than two months. She'd seen the wedding but did not know the other children so stayed away. A week ago, she'd met Trevor. He gave her part of his food. He'd come out every other day since then to bring her food and talk to her.

The caregiver—Lisa knew they avoided calling him 'doctor' because of the bad doctor who had hurt them—examined her in the hospital. Ellie had helped her get a bath but didn't touch her or stare at her. Then she went with Gee to the mansion where Karen and the others waited.

The family had grown.

"Will I still be able to see Trevor sometimes?" she asked.

"You may see any of your friends you want to," Karen said. "Nina's best friend, Jeanie comes over often. Sometimes we invite all the volunteers in the woods over. I'll help you contact Trevor and invite him when you're ready."

"Nina?" Lisa said looking at the girl. "Nina! I remember you. I came to live with Sir and Madam and you were there. Then you left and I never saw you again."

"I remember now," Nina said. "Don't worry, Lisa. I'm not mad at you. Gee and Karen won't send me away because you are here. Not like Sir and Madam did." The girls began to slowly build a friendship, discovering they had overlapped owners for just two weeks but were in the same circle. Lisa had been blindfolded and taken to a place in the mountains where she was left. Her owners had simply driven away, leaving her with a small pack of food and warm clothes. There was a trail and she just kept walking until she'd reached the Wild Woods. It took a few weeks.

BY THE END of the sixth week after the children started arriving from the FBI sting, only three remained in the hospital. Thirty-seven had been placed in foster care, some with hopes of adopting. Five had been returned to parents from whom they had been kidnapped. And four others went back to the people they had lived with who were exonerated, believing they had legitimately adopted the children. The reunions were evidence enough that the children considered them their parents.

The three remaining in the hospital were fully withdrawn from their environment and did not respond to any stimulus. One seemed intent on counting and used fingers to keep track of his number. Gee had listened closely and heard the boy whisper, 'eight hundred thirty-two thousand four hundred ninety-nine.' The child continued.

A little girl grasped a crayon and colored on a sheet of paper until every spot of white had been covered. Then she started with a different crayon and covered the page again. When she was given a fresh sheet of paper, she repeated the process, methodically coloring in all the white with her crayon.

Finally, one young teen girl sat staring into space. A nurse moved the girl to a toilet once an hour but often had to clean up her messes. Feeding her was a mechanical process. She was so badly damaged that Adam thought the only hope would be to put her in a nursing home.

All three had been unresponsive to touching Gee's walking stick.

Restoration

"AGREED."

"Agreed."

"Agreed."

The Families had voted. They sat at the accustomed table in the Roth Mansion. Gee sat next to Karen with Rae seated behind him. Heinz, Jan, and Pàl sat with their heirs—Cameron, Zach, and Wayne—behind them. Loren, David, and Collin elected not to attend at all and sent Jessie, Jonathan, and Violet in their stead. It was the first time in anyone's memory that the majority of the votes cast were cast by people under forty.

"Then the Families are all agreed. We acknowledge Gee Evars as head of the Red Tree People, Rosebud Falls' eighth Family," Heinz stated. "Gee, if there are still others of the Red Tree People being sheltered or scattered where you and Rae can find them, we ask that you invite them to return to their home. We further acknowledge that you, as beneficiaries of the ownership trust, have full management control of the area known as the Wild Woods, including the portion occupied by Savage Sand and Gravel."

"Thank you for your faith," Gee said. His voice seemed softer than normal, influenced by the quiet children he and Karen had adopted. "I hope the Savages and the foresters as well as the other Families will help guide me in caring for this area."

"Are you going to drain the quarry to recover the bodies buried there?" Jonathan asked.

"No. Rae and I discussed this with the Savages and went over their journals. We have agreed the children of the Red Tree People were honorably buried. That fulfills our initial purpose of coming to Rosebud Falls. We do not wish to disturb their rest. We will work on a restoration plan for the quarry. It is a large hole full of water. We believe it might become a recreation area with the right abatements. It's going to take a while."

"And we'll be able to continue with plans to transplant trees?" Jessie asked.

"With your help and guidance, we've agreed moving trees is essential to the restoration of the habitat and health of the Wild Woods," Gee said to his friend.

"Gee, are there more children?" Wayne asked.

"Yes. I'm afraid so. And with spring warming things up, it will be more difficult to spot them. They will have less motivation to come out of the trees. Another child, Lisa, came out this week, thanks to the patient contact with one of the volunteers from Flor. She has been accepted into our home. The children who come by way of the Wild Woods have run away and are cautious about people. We plan to start taking our foster children on field trips to the woods this summer in hopes they will draw others out."

"If I may," Rae said, breaking in. Gee turned to her and nodded. "I believe Lisa is an example of what we might find this summer. The FBI raids rounded up eighty-four traffickers and rescued over forty children. No one believes that's everyone. We believe that other children, probably teens, will be dumped like Lisa was. Some might be shuffled off to pimps in the bigger cities and some could just be taken like an unwanted pet and dumped in the country. Their owners will scrub their homes of every trace they were ever there in hopes that an investigation will not reveal anything. Those are the lucky ones. Some children who have been brutally abused or who know too much may be more permanently disposed of."

There was silence in the room as the Families let what Rae predicted soak in. The city's work in rescuing the children of the Wild Woods was far from over.

"We've started a fund," Karen said. "Not simply for ourselves. We have asked two dozen families so far to accept foster children. They are not all wealthy. In fact, many have more love than money. Some of the children will stay with their foster parents until they are of age and can make their own way. Some, we hope, will be adopted. And some, sadly, will never be able to function independently. So, Gretchen and Jack LaCoe have organized a foundation for us to help support the families with foster children, providing food, education, and healthcare. The foundation will be administered jointly by First Rose Valley bank and by the Savage Credit Union."

"I'm in," Violet said. "I'm a single chick living with her parents and can't act as a foster parent myself. But we can use Meagher funds to help endow the foundation. Sadly, they are meagre Meagher funds but I'll direct the payments from the orphan's trust stock to the foundation." There were nods around the table.

"Is there anything else we need to discuss?" Heinz asked.

"Are we sure we've eliminated the drug trade through our nuts?" Jan asked.

"We believe so," Pàl said. "The inventor of the drug is dead and the process is now closely held by LaRue Labs. The apparent mastermind of both the drug distribution and child trafficking is in jail. And while not part of the Forest, the Wild Woods are now under management and will have their own volunteer patrol, especially as we approach Harvest. Our biggest risk regarding the drug Lustre is that someone manages to synthesize it. We've heard that synthetic drugs coming on the market are more lethal than their original counterparts."

"So, Gee, any new memories emerging?" Jan asked.

"The first thing I remember is the Pub & Grub," Gee began. They laughed at Gee's well-known line about his memory. "It's hard to say. So much of what Rae tells me sounds familiar and after I've heard it, I think, 'Sure, I should remember that.' But as far as dredging up memories on my own, I'm afraid they're no more than a tickle around the edge of my mind or an automatic response to a situation, like knowing how to start the lawn mower even though I don't remember ever using one."

"So, Gee remains our City and Forest Champion without a memory," Jonathan said. "We continue to support the rescued children and to look for more. We help in the management of the Wild Woods, including transplanting trees and restoring the quarry. We have eliminated the drug traffic and the human traffic through the Wild Woods and our community. Wow! What do Family heads do in their spare time?"

"Make sure there's an heir," Pàl said, looking sternly at his grandson.

"We're fostering a child to get practice," Wayne said. "Jo and I would like to be married beneath the wedding tree at Harvest." The others at the table applauded.

"And when is yours due, Karen?" Violet asked with a smirk.

"Thanks to your mother, that cat was out of the bag before *I* even knew it." She looked lovingly at Gee.

"Perhaps," he said, "we will be able to introduce her to the world at Christmas."

THE
END

www.ingramcontent.com/pod-product-compliance
Lightning Source LLC
Chambersburg PA
CBHW051330250626
47155CB00007B/2542